The Invisible SOLDIER

BERNARD WELLS

PAGE PUBLISHING, INC.
Conneaut Lake, PA

First originally published by Page Publishing 2021

ISBN 978-1-6624-4038-0 (pbk)
ISBN 978-1-6624-4039-7 (digital)

Printed in the United States of America

INTRODUCTION

The invisible soldier. What can I say about the invisible soldier that saved my life and the lives of many others? That soldier has not been seen for anyone to have thanked him, congratulated him, or thrown him a parade. That person, that man, is not just an urban legend; that soldier has the government's attention, making them wonder, "Who in the hell is he?"

I have never heard of such a soldier in my life, and I would've, as I have served in the MAF Service for well over thirty-five years. My crew and I could've used such a soldier as our guardian angel, to protect us. If the government has had such soldiers in their training all these years of wars, then they would've saved a lot of lives and grieving moms, dads, sisters, brothers, and friends, those hoping for their loved ones to not be placed in death and distress of having to go through loss. The government has all this power of technology with all those satellites in space, but they can't seem to find a man that they call the Invisible Soldier and bring him back to his family, placing him on a pedestal of bravery and honor for his service to his country and to his fellow citizens, men and women. As for my understanding about this invisible soldier, I cannot find one living soul in the government to tell the world who he is, what his background is, who his family is, if he has children, and why he does the things he does. Those questions truly need to be answered by someone, especially when it comes to a person of his caliber.

I cannot tell you, readers, where this soldier saved me, or from whom he saved me, but I will tell you this much for sure: this soldier acted as if he were many but was only one and removed me from a

3

hellfire of bullets that were being fired by twenty men with automatic weapons. I came out without a scratch or even a speck of dirt on my clothes, or even on my shoes. All I know is that I was very well protected by this man from head to feet, and when he said, "You're out now, General, you're safe, sir," and I was about to say, "Thank you, soldier," he was gone in that split a second. I blinked, he was gone, and all those shooters were lying dead side by side in an orderly fashion. Their weapons were lying among them as the detectives and police officers were all stunned. The detectives and police officers truly thought those twenty men were lying there, shooting at me, until I told them what I knew of what went down. I pointed at the five directions where the shots were coming from to the detectives and police officers, and all they did was smirk and laugh. And one of them replied to me, "Impossible, sir. There is no way for them to have been over there, shooting at you, and now lie down here in an orderly fashion as if they fired those shots from this position. Now, if they were in those directions, then who the hell placed them here neatly with their weapon? Now, tell us, what really happened, General?"

And I told them once again…

I came out of the restaurant and got into my car, and all I heard were gunshots being fired, all I saw were the flashes from their guns lighting up the areas where they were as if it were daylight. I was balled up like a newborn baby, with the hellfire of bullets being fired at me. The next thing I knew, I was being picked up by someone and carried to a safe haven. And let me remind you, I stand at six feet, eight inches and weigh at 295 pounds, and this individual picked me up in a hellfire of bullets and carried me off to safety, and as I got up, I saw exactly what you see now in front of you. I'm not sure what happened here tonight, and I'm sure as hell the rest of the years that I have to live here on earth will never give me the chance to explain and express how I was saved and who saved me from those twenty shooters firing over there, firing three to four thousand rounds of live ammo at me, trying to kill me. But I had a guardian angel watching over me and protecting me at that precise time.

I did not see him kill those men and lay them down neatly beside one another along with their weapons. You know, the most confusing part about this whole chaotic fiasco is, I did not see this person, this man who came to rescue me, when he sat me down once I was safe, and said, "General, you're okay. You're safe, sir." When he left me, hell, I did not see him line those twenty men and their weapons neatly in a row about twenty-one or twenty-two feet away from me. I can only say that I heard his voice. That's why I call him the Invisible Soldier, because only a true soldier can do what this man did, calling me a general when I did not have my uniform on. How did this guy know that I am a general, a retired general at that?

I know he knew that I was grateful toward him for saving my life. You know, I only heard of stories about this person, until this person came to my rescue at 11:05 p.m. on December 5, 2015, in Bangkok. I thanked him by saying, "Thank you, soldier!" I yelled it out loud in the night, on this scary night, to this soldier. And the next day, a soldier that stood at my door on their watch post passed me a note that read, "You're welcome once again, General." It was signed ___ . I did not know what this meant, so I reported this information and note to the authorities, but they could not find the person who wrote it, and the Bangkok authority could not recognize the signature of this person, this man, this soldier.

So I dedicate this story to this person, this soldier that I, General Benson "Shotgun" Thorp III, call the Invisible Soldier. This introduction is not the best part of this soldier. The research that I found on him is the best part. You will always ask yourself as you read about him the same thing that I ask myself: Who is he? Where did he come from? Who trained him? I don't know if he was made as Adam was made or if he was born as a child, grew into a young man, and became this soldier that nobody really knows of. Anybody or anyone can be found or, even with just a glare, be seen, but this guy cannot be seen, even if he carries you to safety. How is that possible? How can you be invisible and invincible from the hellfire of bullets coming at you, with not even one drop of blood on the scene?

No blood, no torn clothes, no pictures, no witnesses, no footprints, nothing of this person, just twenty dead bodies with their weapons, and my story of how it happened is all you can get out of anybody or anyone about this invisible person, or I should say, the Invisible Soldier.

If this soldier has immortality, then I understand him for being invisible. So whenever and wherever this soldier is, I want you to know that we, the people, owe you more than you can add up on an adding machine.

So now I shall tell the people of the research that I have made. I have followed his journey and of my finding the man that we call The Invisible Soldier.

This is my account of this journey, and I want you to enjoy it.

CHAPTER 1

Lieutenant General Robert "No Pity" Kristoff joined the Marines when he was only seventeen years old. He had two choices at the age of seventeen years old, and joining the Marines wasn't his idea, but he preferred it over going to prison. The judge that he was facing was a hang-'em-high type of judge. Every person that went in front of this judge later went either to prison or to a branch of the armed service. Robert Kristoff knew of people who went to prison and died by the hand of another person or on death row. This judge truly did not show any mercy or pity to anybody who came in front of him, and everybody called him the Honorable Judge Karl "Hang 'Em Highs" Whelm.

Robert Kristoff pleaded guilty to three counts of business burglaries and two counts of auto theft of joyriding, for all of which he was facing at least twelve years.

The deputy that was escorting him into the courtroom said, "Son, I know you're young and all, but you better get yourself together. You have messed up your life as of now. This will follow you for the rest of your life, son. You could've been a lot of things besides a criminal."

As they made it inside the courtroom, the judge asked, "Who's up next?"

The prosecutor replied, "A young man with case number 005K2129, Your Honor."

Judge Hang 'Em High said, "Step forward, son." Kristoff stepped forward, and the judge continued, "So you are the one who's been burglarizing my business and stealing my cars, huh?"

Kristoff was about to speak, but the judge cut him off, saying, "Hush your face, boy! Did I ask you to speak? I see that you want to be a fighter, huh? I have two places for a person like you. You really think you're a badass, huh? I should send you to prison, but I don't think that'll help you out as it should, so I'll do something else for you. Since your mommy and daddy can't make you out of that man that they know you can be and be proud of you at the same time, I'm going to help them out to help you. Major Steven Stevenson, will you please step forward, sir?"

Major Stevenson stood up and walked over next to the deputy and Kristoff and Kristoff's attorney, saying, "Yes, Your Honor."

Judge Whelm said, "Major, I don't want to send this young man to a prison. I prefer to send him on a journey toward the biggest part of his life. Can you help me, Bone Breaker?"

Major Stevenson replied, "Karl, you haven't called me that since we were in combat. Yes, I can help him. I got a place he'll enjoy. Believe that smile won't be there any longer once I'm finished with him."

Judge Whelm said, "Mr. Robert Kristoff, I'm placing you in the hands of the United States Marine Corps. If you ever come in my courtroom again, then you'll find out why they all call me Judge Hang 'Em High Whelm. I will not show you any mercy. There will be no mercy or pity. Remember, that'll be no pity for you, son, no pity at all. Your case is hereby dismissed upon your registration into the Marines. If you don't, then I'll be as maximum as I can, every count. Do you understand me?"

Kristoff replied, "Yes, sir."

Judge Whelm said, "Okay, Major Steven 'Bone Breaker' Stevenson, he's all yours. If he doesn't get on that bus and sign up, please let me know and I'll issue a warrant out on him, okay?"

Major Bone Breaker replied, "I'll do that, I'll just do that. Thank you."

As they walked out to the bus station, the major gave him his bus ticket, without a suitcase. Robert Kristoff got on the bus with only the clothes he had on; he was on his way to boot camp.

He was 143 pounds, stood five feet, seven inches, and had an I-don't-give-a-damn attitude and a temper to match. This made Private First Class Robert Kristoff a very dangerous young man. His drill instructor could not believe the punishment that he was laying upon this young soldier.

One time, early in the morning, at 0300, drill instructor Sergeant Charles "Ibdam" Patterson jumped on Private First Class Kristoff's back, wrapping a twisted-up pillowcase around his mouth, zip-tied his wrists, and placed a .45 auto up to his temper, whispering into his ear, "Breathe hard and you're dead, make a shuffling sound and you're dead, and if you ask any questions after I release you, you're dead. If you understand, raise your left eyebrow."

He raised his left eyebrow. Sergeant Ibdam said softly in his ear, "Good," as he took him off his bed without waking up the other soldiers.

Sergeant Ibdam placed him on the back of a trailer bed while the private was still in his underwear, T-shirt, and socks. It was thirty-six degrees and early in the morning as the drill instructor drove this jeep through icy water at forty-five miles per hour on this dirt road. Private First Class Kristoff was trying to keep himself from falling off the trailer. He brought his hands from behind his back by taking his legs through his arms and taking the pillowcase from his mouth, tying it around the knob of the trailer to keep himself from falling off.

The drill instructor drove forty-eight miles from the base and stopped the jeep so deep into the woods that they ran out of road. Sergeant Ibdam got out of the jeep and went to the trailer with his knife drawn, saying, "Hold out your hands."

Private First Class Kristoff held out his hands without saying a word. Sergeant Ibdam cut off the zip tie and gave the private his backpack, ordering him to put the backpack on. He did as he was told without any question. The drill instructor then took off his watch and put a timer on it with an extra ten minutes because that was how far he was from the road to the woods. The watch read 0400 hours as Sergeant Ibdam looked into Private First Class Kristoff's eyes and gave him two big buck knives. He said, "I know you're in your underwear, T-shirt, and socks. Now, with this backpack and these two buck knives, one in each hand, you'll have exactly one hour and fifteen minutes to return to the base in the same direction that I brought you to this spot. I'm giving you a direct order to return the same way, and I want you to leave a trace of yourself to prove to me that you did exactly as I commanded you. Do you understand? Raise your left eyebrow if you understand."

Private First Class Kristoff raised his left eyebrow. Sergeant Ibdam turned his back to Private First Class Kristoff and walked off, getting into the jeep, cranking it up, and he said, "You have one hour and ten minutes now to make it back to the base. If you're not there by then, then I'll be declaring you as AWOL. And if you do understand, raise your left eyebrow!" He said the last part in a very loud voice.

Kristoff raised his left eyebrow.

Sergeant Ibdam replied very loudly, his voice echoing in the woods, "Good, good, good, good, good, good, good!" as he drove off, leaving behind a half-naked, 143-pound seventeen-year-old young man that stood only five feet, seven inches, in thin, cold, muddy, and stormy weather. He didn't have a pair of hiker's boots to run in.

As he looked at his watch until he could not hear the jeep's motor in the distance, five minutes had passed, so he now knew that he had only one hour and five minutes left. But Kristoff knew he could not let this be a downfall for him as he gripped tightly to his knives in both of his hands and took off running in full speed. As he was running in full speed, his knives were cutting branches off trees. The buck knife in his right hand had lost its tip, flying into his forehead, but he did not know that that had happened. All he knew was that those branches were hitting him in the face, head, chest, and legs, sticking into his feet.

Private Kristoff made it to the road in three and a half minutes. He looked down the muddy dirt road and wondered how he would be able to prove that he indeed came in the direction that he was ordered to come. Finally, he got a piece of a tree limb and spiked his knives through it, then twisted some limbo as a rope and made a small plow. After that, he started running with it tied around his waist. As he was running and looking back at it, he knew that it was okay to concentrate on his running in full motion for at least seven miles, killing twelve minutes. He then ran half-full speed for ten minutes, eleven minutes, and then back to full speed for nineteen minutes, killing twenty-two and a half miles without knowing it.

He looked at his watch as he was running in half-full speed, then noticed the camp in the distance, with only his watch counting down. He put his running in full speed, dragging that plow behind him, proving that he came back in the direction that the drill instructor had ordered him to come. As he made it to the camp, he ran past all the other bunkhouses, with some soldiers waking up and looking and laughing at him. But that did not stop him, and he made it to his bunkhouse. He just stood there with his backpack, T-shirt, a pair of boxer shorts, a pair of socks on his feet, and two big buck knives, one in each hand. He was muddy and bloody from head to feet and had a homemade plow behind him.

Sergeant Ibdam pulled up behind him in his jeep, revving the engine up twice. Then the sergeant got out of the jeep, turning it off, and went around in front of him, standing at attention, as did Private Kristoff, who then saluted Sergeant Ibdam. Then, Sergeant Ibdam walked off, going inside. He was in there for two hours, and when he came back out, he noticed that Private Kristoff had not moved a muscle or blinked an eye, even as other soldiers were mocking him and laughing at him.

The drill instructor yelled out, saluting Private Kristoff, saying, "At ease, soldier!"

Kristoff took off his backpack, the two buck knives, the watch, and the small homemade plow that he had made, and then he saluted and walked off. After he left them on the ground and got on the porch of his bunkhouse, another soldier asked, "Why didn't they give you some clothes and shoes to do this in?"

He just pointed at the backpack. The other soldier opened it up and pulled out a pair of boots, socks, pants, and shirt. The drill instructor then took him to see the nurse, and the nurse took the tip of the buck knife out of his forehead, placing eight stitches to close his wound.

Private First Class Kristoff went to the mess hall to eat. He saw one table that was empty, and he went over and sat down, then started eating his breakfast. As he was eating, three big lance corporals came to the table, and one of them asked, "Private, this is our table. Why are you sitting here?"

He just sat there and did not respond to them.

The soldier on the right said to the soldier in the middle, "Jason, this boy seems to be ignoring you. He ain't paying you any attention. Look at him, he's just still eating!"

Jason got angry and started yelling, "You fucking freak! Get your ass from our table! Did you hear me, boy?"

Private Kristoff still just sat there; he wasn't paying these three soldiers any attention.

The soldier on Jason's left side then said, "Come on, Jason, leave the kid alone. Let him eat—"

Before he could finish his sentence, Jason replied angrily, "Bret, shut the fuck up! Close your goddamn mouth before I close it for you! Now, listen, Private, get your ass away from our table!"

Private Kristoff did not blink an eye. He just stayed there so calm, until the three soldiers that stood in front of him were more nervous than he was. Bret and Kyle tried to pull Jason from the table as the other soldiers and drill instructors were watching them; that was when Jason flipped the table, yelling at the top of his lungs, "You fucking mute! Get your ass away from our table!" As the table was turning over, Private Kristoff caught his milk and water before they spilled out or hit the floor, but his food was everywhere. Private Kristoff just stared into Jason's eyes as he slowly sat on the floor in an Indian position, picking up his spoon, fork, and knife, and then he began eating his breakfast.

Jason, Bret, and Kyle said at the same time, "What the fuck is this? This boy is a goddamn retard!"

Jason then continued by himself, "Ain't you, boy? You're a damn retard!"

One of the drill instructors felt sorry for Private First Class Kristoff, and he was about to stand up; that was when drill instructor Sergeant Ibdam placed his hand on that drill instructor's left shoulder, directing him back to his seat. Sergeant Ibdam stood up, fixing his tie and placing his hat on his head, and walked slowly over there. He stood on the right side of Bret. Jason, Bret, and Kyle started walking backward, and that was when Sergeant Ibdam shouted at once, "Stop! Watch! And understand! Attention!"

Private Kristoff jumped up to his feet so fast without touching anything on the floor. The drill instructor leaned forward to Kristoff's left ear and said, "I'll let you have them one day, but not right now. Meet me outside tomorrow at 0300 hours. Raise you left eyebrow if you understand."

Kristoff raised his left eyebrow.

Sergeant Ibdam stood back, his attention still on Private Kristoff, and replied, "You're excused, soldier. At Ease."

Private Kristoff saluted Sergeant Ibdam and walked off, leaving him with Jason, Kyle, and Bret just standing there, saluting Sergeant Ibdam as well.

The sergeant said to them, "Clean this mess up. And that is an order! You have your table now."

They began cleaning the mess they made, but they were still confused and shocked about Private Kristoff eating off the floor like an animal using eating utensils.

The next morning, at 0230, Private Kristoff got up and fully dressed and went outside. He stood there in attention, with his hand up in a salute, waiting to be recognized as the soldier that he was. He knew that the drill instructor told him to be there at 0300, but being thirty minutes early, he also knew, would get his body temperature used to the weather. He was in this position for two and a half hours, while the other dorms' soldiers were shaken out of their sleep in their dorms by other lance corporals, to be trained by their drill instructors. The other soldiers could not believe what they were seeing as they looked at the private standing there in his combat uniform, with a hiking backpack and a duffel bag lying on the ground at his right side as he was in a salute.

The drill instructor walked into the dorm, and hearing all the soldiers muttering, he yelled out, "Stay as you are! Let me see what you idiots are looking at. I really would like to know. Enlighten me!"

One of the soldiers was about to tell him what they were look-ing at, but the drill instructor said loudly, "Silent, soldier!" as he continued walking to the window, seeing Private First Class Kristoff standing there at attention in a saluting position, with his backpack on his right side. The drill instructor said to the soldiers, "Don't move, you maggots! You just stand there until he leaves, since you want to know what he is doing there."

It was now 1000, and these soldiers had missed breakfast as they had been in this position, undressed, for at least six hours. These soldiers knew that that soldier must be hungry, because he had been like that when they woke up. They knew if they hadn't eaten, then he sure as hell hadn't.

One of the lance corporals asked, "Permission to speak, sir."

The drill instructor replied, "Permission granted."

The lance corporal said, "Sir, we haven't had breakfast, and it is now making its way to 1100, sir. How long do we have to wait until this soldier makes a move? He's still standing there like a statue."

The drill instructor replied, "My order was what, Lance Corporal?"

The lance corporal said, "For us to stand in our position until we see him leave, sir."

The drill instructor replied to the lance corporal, "Well, Lance Corporal, I still can see him standing there, right?"

The lance corporal said, "Sir, yes, sir."

The drill instructor then said, "Then you keep standing there, Lance Corporal."

It was now twelve noon. The soldiers that were watching him had not moved since five thirty this morning, and they hadn't even brushed their teeth, washed their face, used the bathroom, or eaten any breakfast. About thirteen soldiers had pissed and shit on them-selves for not being able to move all those hours. They were wonder-ing how this soldier standing out there in the cold was holding up, or was he going through the same thing they were going through inside?

Fifteen minutes past twelve, the soldier out there saw drill instructor Sergeant Ibdam come out of Company C dorm, putting his hat on. He walked past Private Kristoff standing there at attention in a salute as he walked to the jeep. As he started up the jeep by reaching inside of it, he looked at Private Kristoff. The other soldiers were watching this in a great pondering of the mind and were very puzzled. The drill instructor then stood up in attention and saluted Private Kristoff, yelling out loud in a commanding voice, "Move it, move it, move it! Move it on the double, soldier!"

Private Kristoff reached down on his right, picking up his duffel bag and running to the jeep's trailer, placing his duffel bag on it and sitting himself there in an Indian position. He hit the trailer twice; that was when Sergeant Ibdam pulled off, circling the parking lot, leaving the campus ground with Private Kristoff. As the other soldiers in Company D dorm watched him leave, they were still standing in position. They had been in this position for at least six and a half hours now when the lance corporal said, "Permission to speak, sir."

The drill instructor replied, "Permission granted."

The lance corporal asked, "Permission to at ease, sir, since the private that was standing at the flagpole has left with drill instructor Sergeant Ibdam, sir?"

The drill instructor said, "Permission to at ease is granted, Lance Corporal."

The lance corporal responded, "You maggots heard the drill instructor. At ease!"

They all were holding themselves and yelling at one another to get out of the other's way.

Sergeant Ibdam drove for about thirty-five or forty minutes off the road, continuing driving five miles through the woods. The jeep then came to a halt, but the engine was still running. Sergeant Ibdam came to the bumper of the jeep and said in a loud voice, "Move it, soldier!"

Private Kristoff jumped off the trailer, grabbing his duffel bag at the same time, landing on his feet and standing at attention. He then saluted Sergeant Ibdam. The drill instructor said, "Don't ask any questions, and if you do, you're dead. Don't let them see you. If you do, you're dead. Don't wake them up, and if you do, you're dead. Follow your instruction to the letter, 'coz if you don't, you're dead.

Bring them back home alive without a scratch on them. If you don't, you're dead."

After the drill instructor gave him his instruction and saluted, he walked off. Private Kristoff was still standing at attention as Sergeant Ibdam stood up at the driver's side of the jeep. The sergeant said to him, "If you understand, raise your left eyebrow." By then he was climbing in the jeep, putting it in gear, then said out loud, his voice echoing in the distance as he was driving off, "At ease! At ease, at ease, at ease, at ease, at ease..."

Private Kristoff bent over, looking through his duffel bag, trying to find something to eat because he hadn't had anything to eat all day. He knelt down on his knees with tears in his eyes for being hungry. He started feeling sorry for himself, and that was when he heard those words echoing in the distance among the trees: "No pity, no pity, no pity, no pity, no pity, no pity..."

He said in a low voice, very pissed off, replying, "Man, this is some bullshit. I haven't eaten or drunk anything in fifteen hours."

His stomach was growling as if he had two lions inside. He just sat there next to his duffel bag, finding a balled-up sleeping bag, two big buck knives, a hatchet, a flint, and some night vision goggles. He pushed the duffel bag away from him very violent, saying, "What the fuck am I supposed to do with this shit? I'm only seventeen years old." He was about to say something else, tears coming out of his eyes, but then he saw a piece of paper folded up. Private Kristoff picked up the paper and opened it, and it read, "This is your survivor kit. Keep it with you at all times."

Kristoff stood up after he counted to ten, then paced and stuck a stick in the ground, marking his spot. He started walking in a circle until he made it back to that stick he stuck on the ground. He noticed that he still had at least five hours of daylight left to clean up at least half of this circle, then get himself some firewood to make a fire. He went into his duffel bag and took out his night vision goggles and placed them on his face, then he put his two buck knives and hatchet in their holsters and started walking. He walked for an hour and a half, two at the most. He knew that he was about a good three miles from his camp. He stopped by this big tree and looked up at it and started climbing it halfway. As he was sitting there as patiently as he could, his stomach was growling like crazy. He looked at his stomach and said, "It won't be long, my friend. Be patient."

It was around 0130, and he was watching this five-point buck walking in his direction. He knew that he had to be very still, very quiet, very skillful in order to have something to eat. He sat there patiently for almost forty-five to fifty minutes, camouflaging himself like a chameleon, just waiting for this five-point buck to come under his tree. As the buck was getting close, Kristoff slowly stopped moving, making sure that the buck did not hear or see him. The buck looked back for a second, then back in front of him, and then on each side of him. Kristoff just watched and waited patiently on him, because he knew that this was his meal. The buck was slowly walking and eating as he came under Kristoff's tree. Kristoff could reach out and touch this buck with his hand, but he waited until the buck raised up his head to look forward. As soon as the buck was concentrating in front of him, Kristoff sank his right-hand buck knife inside of that buck's whole side until his whole entire hand with his knife was inside of this buck. The buck was trying to run, but Kristoff's hand and knife were stopping him, and as soon as Kristoff took his hand and knife out of him, the buck tried to run but couldn't. He just fell on his left side, with his two front legs the only things moving. That was when Kristoff took his knife across the buck's throat, finishing killing him.

Kristoff said to the buck, "Sorry, big guy. It was either you or me." He was cut the buck's head and four legs off, all the way up to his hips, and ripped it open, pulling out all his guts and blood and placing it a little higher than the ground so that the other wild animals could have something to tussle over before they could make it to him.

Kristoff made it back to his camp, where he went and found some stones, small, medium, and large. He dug a hole using his hatchet and buck knife. After digging the pit, he put some dry leaves and kindling in it, striking a rock for the flint, making a spark that ignited a fire. As the fire was burning hot and good, Kristoff started skinning and cleaning that buck. He cut off a nice piece off the buck and placed it over the fire. He saw that it was breaking dawn, and he welcomed it. His deer was cooking, so he took off to explore the area six miles out from his camp.

He found a freshwater stream and a big lake. He knew that his hunger was about to end. Kristoff knew that inside his duffel bag, he had this plastic on each end of it, and the shoulder strap had soft plastic on each one too. He just nodded at the freshwater stream and walked off, going back to his camp. He knew that his deer meat had been cooking for about three and a half hours, and he knew that he had to put some food in his stomach very soon. As he knelt himself down and took a pinch off his deer, tasting it, he knew that it tasted good for a first-time cook. He knew that he had this all good, but he didn't have anything to drink; however, he knew where to get some water. As he started ripping those plastic circles off the inside of his duffel bag and the long soft plastic off the handles, he now estimated that it was, at the most, 0600, and he still hadn't really eaten in twenty-seven hours. He took the rest of the deer meat with him and made it back to the stream. He cut up the rest of the deer meat in direct pieces and washed it in the stream, and when he stood up, that was when he noticed a hollow tree branch about the size of the small part of his leg. Kristoff said to himself, "I can use you. Appreciate it, nature. You really know how to help a soldier in need."

He then placed that hollow branch into the stream, filling it up to the top, checking to see if it would leak out after covering the bottom of it. Strange enough, the water only came out between his fingers, so he used his sharp buck knife and saved a piece off as he took the plastic circles, sliding them inside the hollow branch and placing another piece of wood at the bottom plugging. He looked at it and saw that it was working very well, as if it were made for it. Kristoff knew that this was about two gallons and a half. As he was about to leave, he saw about twenty to twenty-five ducks landing in the lake. He started taking off his clothes until he was buck naked. He kept crawling on his elbows as slowly as he could, making it to the water, then took a deep, concentrated breath, swimming underwater. As he got closer to the ducks, he went deeper down into the lake to keep from disturbing them. As he was directly right under the ducks, he started swimming up toward them very fast. He made it to them before they could fly off; that was when he grabbed three of them, pulling them under the water and scaring the other ducks off. As he swam with them in his hands, he broke their legs and wings off. When he got out of the water, he just snapped their necks. He cleaned and washed them very well.

So now he had deer and duck meat to eat, but how would he keep them fresh until he had to leave? He knew that this was going to be hard to do, but he was just glad that he had some food to eat.

On his way back to his camp, with water to drink and clean food, he was batting a thousand with the food and water supply. Thirty eight minutes later, Kristoff made it back to his campsite. He was so hungry he just dropped his clean meat and water at his duffel bag. He cut a nice chunk of deer meat off his rotisserie. He knew that some spices would have been better, but he had to make do with what he had at this moment.

After he had eaten and was full, nighttime had come upon him, and so he lay down thinking about some shelter, as it was getting colder and colder outside. He headed off, going to sleep around his campfire. He slept for well over nine and a half hours, ten at the most. He figured that it was 1100 when he woke up. He warmed up and took a nice chunk of meat and then placed one of the ducks on the rotisserie. Kristoff looked around his area, at some trees, and marked them so he could remember the one that he'd be using to build himself a shelter with. After picking his trees, he pulled out his hatchet and start cutting them down, those that he had marked. He cut small-, medium-, and large-size trees, sixteen large-size trees. He trimmed the limbs off the trees and piled them up, then he twisted some of the limbs like a rope and tied it around the trees and then pulled them to his camp eight at a time, piling them up in a stack on the side where they'd be used for the shelter.

He could smell his duck cooking, and it was smelling delicious to him, especially since he hadn't eaten in over five hours or so. But he knew that his work was first.

As he was knocking the limbs off the trees to make a log out of it, he heard a watch beeping sound. He stopped cutting the limbs and stood up very quietly, trying to locate the beeping sound. As Kristoff did, that was when he knew that he was right over it. He knelt down and moved the pile of brushes that was part of the rubbish that he placed there over three days ago. After removing most of the rubbish, he found the watch that his drill instructor Sergeant Ibdam had before he left him out there three days ago. He looked at the time, and it was 1643. He measured off his marks to build his shelter, and when he finished, he made sure that his rotisserie cooker was surrounded by his shelter, as were his stove and heater. He took his big buck knives and hatchet and dug twelve holes for his small-size trees to serve as braces to hold his logs steady in place. He dug the holes deeper than his arm could go, and he then placed one of the small trees in one—it was a tight fit. He took one of the big rocks out of the rotisserie pit and started banging it on the top of the log, nailing it into the ground. After he nailed all his small braces into the ground, he started picking his logs, putting them in their brace and building the right side of his shelter. It took twelve logs to complete each wall of his little shelter. He then looked at his watch and noticed that it was 1922.

He took a drink of his water slowly, sitting down in front of his rotisserie stove, and tasted a piece of his duck. He liked the taste of it, and he knew he would have plenty of time to eat; fixing his shelter was the most important part of his mission. As he finished all the walls of his shelter, he looked up at the part where the roof should be. He placed his attention to that very spot and put a great deal of concentration on it. He sat down and looked at his watch, and then ate his dinner.

As he was eating, he heard some noise in the dark woods. Kristoff slowly eased his left hand into his duffel bag and grabbed his night vision goggles and both of his buck knives. He put his night vision goggles on very slowly and stood up, looking around to see what or who was moving around out here. Then he saw three big skunks and two little skunks out searching for some food. He just turned around, going back to his shelter to finish eating so that he could get himself some rest, because tomorrow morning was going to be a little hectic.

He had two main missions on his mind; the first one was him fixing his roof and door, the second one protecting himself from the wild animals or anyone who was hunting them and might make a mistake, thinking he was an animal as they trespassed on his little wooded property. He set the alarm on his watch to wake him up at 0500. As he lay down on his homemade cot inside his shelter without a roof and a front door, he was about to feel sorry for himself again. He jumped up in attention and yelled out at the top of his voice, which echoed with each word he was saying "I'm, I'm, I'm, I'm, I'm, I'm, I'm, I'm, I'm...only, only, only, only, only, only... fucking, fucking, fucking, fucking, fucking, fucking, fucking...seventeen, seventeen, seventeen, seventeen, seventeen, seventeen, seventeen, seventeen, seventeen...years, years, years, years, years, years, years...old, old, old, old, old, old, old, old, old!"

He stared in the dark and listened, waiting for an answer, until he just burst out in laughter and said out loud, his words echoing, "No Pity, No Pity, No Pity, No Pity, No Pity, No Pity, No Pity... that, that, that, that, that, that, that, that...is, is, is, is, is, is, is...me, me, me, me, me, me, me, me, me, me...Robert, Robert, Robert, Robert, Robert...'No, No, No, No, No, No, No, No, No...Pity, Pity, Pity, Pity, Pity, Pity, Pity'...Kristoff, Kristoff, Kristoff, Kristoff, Kristoff, Kristoff!"

He just lay back down very easily and slowly looked at the sky, at all those stars, and yelled out loud again, his voice still echoing, "No Pity, No Pity, No Pity, No Pity, No Pity, No Pity!"

Then softly to himself once again, "Private First Class Robert 'No Pity' Kristoff, stop feeling sorry for yourself, man. You're a soldier. You're a protector of this whole country. Remember that, soldier." And he just smiled to himself and dozed off to sleep. The watch alarm started beeping, waking him up at 0500.

He sat up, rubbing his face and head with both hands, making a growling sound. He picked up his water bottle and took a nice, big swig out of it and swished it around in his mouth, then spit it out; he then took another swig and two large bites off his duck meat and picked up one of his smaller homemade canteen and walked off.

After walking for nearly an hour and a half, he saw a bunch of vines hanging out of the trees. He then climbed up the tree, cutting the vines as long as he could get them. After cutting at least seventy-five or eighty of them, he climbed back down from the tree and barely tied each end together, dragging all of them back to his campsite. As he walked toward the front of his shelter, he saw those same five skunks that he had seen last night with his night vision goggles. He let his vines go very gently as he slowly walked toward his cooked duck, cutting five nice pieces off for each of them. He tossed it to them very easily, and they started eating and looking at him. He looked at his watch and noticed that it was 0932. He went to cut down thirty really small trees and their little branches off and wrapped them together at the top, then threaded them over and under on one side. And then he flipped it over, threading the other side over and under, and tied it at the end. He repeated it almost at the end and wrapped the bottom part. His roof had been made. He picked up one end and leaned it up against the shelter, then tied a vine on each side and one in the middle so that he could pull it to the other side. He used all his might pushing it a piece of the way on the top of his shelter; he took the three sticks with the vine tied to the end of it and threw it to the other side. He then jogged around to the other side and started pulling it evenly as it was on the top of his shelter. He took a few good breaths and swigs of cold water, looking at the well-done job. The roof hung about seven to eight inches off the shelter, which was okay, because he needed for it to be like that so that he could stick some sticks in the ground and tie it down really steadily. He took most of the rubbish that was lying around his shelter and started throwing it on the top of his shelter. He then cut down four more medium-size trees and dug their holes, banging on them after, thereby forcing them in their holes. He then placed logs between them, making another small front wall.

As he put that together nice and tight, he yelled out loud, his voice echoing in response, "Perfect, perfect, perfect, perfect, perfect, perfect…" One of the skunks just looked at him for about ten or eleven seconds and started eating what Kristoff gave them.

Kristoff then walked inside of his shelter and came back to his doorway, looking out, just observing everything that he had accomplished. He went to gather some more wood and small kindling and piled them up in the corner of his shelter. Kristoff looked at his watch and noticed that it was 1600. He knew that he had other work needed to be done, like making a door for his shelter. He laid ten very long small trees side by side and started threading the vines over and under at the top, and he then eased it over to the other side, threading it over and under. Next, he went to the bottom of the door and threaded it over and under, then flipped it on the other side and threaded it over and under, and then in the middle, making it steady. He made some loops on the side of the door and placed a small tree through it and tied it to the post of the shelter. The door closed very well.

He felt a breeze coming under the bottom part of his shelter. He went outside and got some rubbish, spreading it tightly under the bottom logs, stopping the breeze. To hold it in place at all times, he went out and cut down three nice-size trees, placing them at the bottom of the shelter. His shelter had warmed up so nicely and quickly he decided to crack his door open to let it cool off in there.

Kristoff looked at his watch again and noticed that it was 2113. So he cut off a nice piece of duck meat and started eating. Kristoff now wondered what to do next to better his shelter. After getting full, he looked at his watch and noticed that it was 2200. He went outside again and cut three pieces of thick tree bark off the tree; that was when he saw this tree stump on its side, with roots coming from it. He took it with him by placing it on his shoulder. As he made it back, it was almost 2400. He took all of it inside with him and set it on his dirt floor. He got on his homemade cot with his sleeping bag as a mattress and started evening out the tree barks, scraping them out, making little dishes for the five little skunks earlier. When he finished scraping them out and wiping them with his shirt, the chipped particles of wood were out of them, and he then lay back on his cot and went to sleep. His watch was still set at 0500 so that he could be awakened.

Later, the watch alarm woke No Pity up at 0500. He sat up, rubbing his face, and poured some water into his left hand, splashing it on his face. After drying off his face with his shirt, he then took a small swig out of it, swishing it around in his mouth. He placed a few kindling in the rotisserie pit, warming himself some deer meat. He then looked at the little wooden dishes that he made for the five little skunks. He stated to himself while walking toward the door, "Man, these little jokers might be gone!" But when he opened the door, all five of them were balled up, trying to keep warm, as a little snow had fallen down. No Pity warmed their meat up and placed it in each of their little dish. As he slowly walked toward them, the three big ones raised their heads up, looking at him. No Pity said softly to them, "Take it easy. I'm not going to hurt you. I'm just bringing y'all something to eat." He then lay all their combination food-and-water dish down in front of them. One of the skunks immediately started eating their food as No Pity said softly, "There you go, little one, there you go."

He slowly started walking backward, going back into his shelter so he could eat something in a dish that he also made for himself. He now had those little skunks on his mind. He knew they needed a place to sleep in, just like he had a place to sleep in, so he quickly finished eating and went outside, looking around. Then he got a brainstorm idea of how to make a shelter for his little friends. He got some big tree branches and chopped them clean by removing all the leaves and sticks that were on them. He bent the limbs in sections, forcing each end into the ground so deeply, until its brace was secured. He then got the small leafy branches and put them on the top, side, and back of this little shelter. No Pity could not believe his own eyes, at what his mind had thought of. He really believed initially that this wouldn't work, but it did. And even better. He stripped the leaves off the branches and laid them as bedding for their little shelters. After finishing the first one, No Pity knew that it wouldn't take long to build these little shelters. He looked at his watch, and it was only 0816. No Pity looked at the little skunks as they looked at him. And he said to the little skunks, "Y'all will have your own shelters, so don't worry, little ones."

That was when the two biggest ones went into the shelter and turned around inside as they stuck their heads outside by side, looking at the other three. No Pity now knew that these were the parents watching over their children. He said to the parents, "I understand," moving his left eyebrows. No Pity started building the other shelters, fixing them just like he did the first one, as the little ones were playing out front. An hour and ten or twelve minutes went by, and No Pity had finished fixing their little shelters. He put their beddings in and said, "All right, you little ones, your house is ready." They acted as if they understood and started going inside their little shelters. No Pity placed their dishes inside with them, right in their door way. No Pity just smiled and went into his shelter.

As he sat there, he took his buck knife and scraped off the bark of five nice sticks, and when he was finished, he took a burnt piece of kindling out of the rotisserie pit and started writing names on the clean-shaved wood with it. The first one with the parents read, "Gotcha 'N Shevil," and their three sons with the names of "Skin'em," "Bite 'em," and "Kill'em." He placed their names up on their shelters, saying, "Here y'all go, little ones. Pop, your name is Gotcha. Mom, your name is Shevil." Then he left their shelter and went to Skin'em, saying, "You're Skin'em," and then went to Bite'em's shelter and said, "You're Bite'em," after which he then went to Kill'em's shelter and knelt down, saying, "You're Kill'em."

He knelt down on his left knee, making a little whistling sound to calling all of them out. At first, they didn't come out. So he did it again, but they still didn't come out. He made the little whistling sound again, then said, "Gotcha, Shevil, Skin'em, Bite'em, and Kill'em…" As he finished saying their names, they all came out of their shelters and looked up at him. He smiled at them and said, "I am No Pity. My name is No Pity. I just want y'all to know that. So you can go back inside of your shelter." They all turned around and went inside. Their shelters were lined up in a row in front of his shelter.

Kristoff then went back inside and put his coat and his night vision goggles on, not knowing how long he was going to be gone. He had his hatchet, his duffel bag, and his two buck knives, which were razor sharp and ready for anything that came his way. He looked at his watch and noticed that it was 1141. As he was leaving, Gotcha, Shevil, Skin'em, Bite'em, and Kill'em watched him. He just looked at them and said, "Go back inside. I'll be back." And they did, and he kept walking.

While he was walking, he found two big tin cans and seven medium-size cans, which he placed inside the duffel bag. He went to the freshwater stream and collected some water. He took all the tin cans out of his duffel bag and cut the top out of them and keeping then can and its' tops. He washed them out very good and placed them back into his bag. He walked over to the lake to see if he could spot some food, although he did have more than enough. He noticed that the snow was beginning to fall, and he did not know how much they were going to be getting. No Pity just looked up, down, and all around, saying "No Pity. No, No, No, No, No, No, No, No, No… Fucking, Fucking, Fucking, Fucking, Fucking…Pity, Pity, Pity, Pity, Pity, Pity, Pity, Pity…"

He was about to pick up his duffel bag when he noticed a big-ass rabbit eating closely by a bush about sixty yards from him. He pulled his camouflage hood over his head and face and tied the string so that it wouldn't come off. Now, before he started off, he looked at his watch and saw that it was 1335. He then slid all the way to this rabbit. As he was about to snatch the rabbit, his watch alarm started beeping, scaring the rabbit off. He said, "Shit! I almost had the fucker!" He just got up and looked down at his watch, noticing that it was almost 1700. So he headed off toward his shelter, but going in a different direction.

As he was walking, he saw three deer running across his path. He wanted them, but he knew that he could not catch them. He just continued walking with those loud-clanking tin cans in his duffel bag. No Pity got close to his camp, and as soon as he did, Gotcha, Shevil, Skin'em, Bite'em, and Kill'em were making a growling noise, coming out of their shelters. No Pity stopped in his step as Gotcha, Shevil, Skin'em, Bite'em, and Kill'em came running out and stopped in their step, looking at him. He took his hood off his head and face;

they then knew that it was him. He just smiled and said, "Okay, soldiers. It's just me. At ease. Return to your shelters."

They did exactly what he said.

He went inside of his shelter and looked at his watch, noticing that an hour and twenty-nine minutes had passed by. He put holes inside of the big tin cans and four in the medium-size tin cans. He put a little water in it and cut up some deer meat and crushed some acorns that he picked up on the way back to his shelter. After warming up the deer meat and placing the crushed acorns on it, he then went outside and got the skunks' dishes. They came out of there shelters and followed him into his shelter, where he fixed their dishes. He said, "All right, soldiers, let's move out."

Gotcha and Shevil went out of the door first, with Skin'em, Bite'em, and Kill'em right behind them. Skin'em, Bite'em, and Kill'em went into their shelters first as No Pity placed their food-and-water dish in behind them.

No Pity made a little whistling sound and said, "Gotcha, Shevil, Skin'em, Bite'em, and Kill'em, out." They all came out, and he continued, "Good job soldiers. At ease."

They all went back in, and he just walked off, going back inside. No Pity knew that he had lost track of the days since he had been out here in these woods. He didn't even know what his face looked like anymore. He felt a large beard on his face and how his hair had grown longer. He didn't know when his drill instructor was going to come and say, "At ease, soldier!" The only thing that he was sure of was that it was now the wintertime of 1957. The month and day had slipped away from him, but he didn't care, as he was out here making the woods his home, a lake his bathtub, a stream his water supply, five skunks his protectors, and other animals his food, and a home-made shelter for his home. He was very well in a blessing stage, as he had pity on himself when he first came out here but now had none.

Winter was hitting them real hard. No Pity got up out of his warm bed and looked out door, seeing the snow covering the shelters of Gotcha, Shevil, Skin'em, Bite'em, and Kill'em. He stacked all his firewood in a neat stack so he could bring his soldiers inside with him. As he tried to open his door, the snow would not let it open widely like it should. He said to himself, "I got a plan for you. Just wait and see." Then he went in front of the shelters of Gotcha, Shevil, Skin'em, Bite'em, and Kill'em and said, "Out front!" And the skunks all came out of their shelters. No Pity picked up their dish and added, "Come on, soldiers. Follow me."

They all followed behind No Pity, going into his shelter. He set their dishes in certain spots, with their names above it. He then put some food and water in each one. His shelter was a nice-size place for all six of them, but his little soldiers knew that their job was to give him some protection like he was protecting them. No Pity went outside to his pile of long small trees and vines and lined thirty-eight little trees for a porch shelter. As he fixed it and had it very secured together, he looked around to see what could be used to remove the snow from his doorway. That was when he thought about the tree bark. He took his buck knives and hatchet and knocked two big, long, and thick pieces off the tree. He then took his buck knife out and drilled a hole in it, making a scoop out both of them. As he started pushing the snow out of the way, he realized it was working very well; he just smiled and said, "Fucking right, boy. Get this shit done, son. Put some work in!"

After he cleared it out of the way, the ground was a little muddy, but that would not stop him from completing his mission for his little soldiers. He went to get two medium-size trees out of the pile and made two holes in the ground, forcing the trees in them by banging on top. When he was sure they were steady in the ground, he got another medium-size tree to push the porch shelter up, letting it rest on top of the post. He then went to pull some of the rubbish brushes that were still on those branches and threw them on top to keep the rain and snow from coming through so fast. No Pity then placed two medium-size trees in an X, crossing each other, and another medium-size tree going in between them, bracing up against the top and the ground. He ran seven vines across it very tightly, and he then started sticking branches with their leaves in between the vines, building a wall. After doing both sides, he knew it was going to work. The snow that fell in while he was building the wall had already melted.

No Pity went out front and picked up each of the skunks' shelters. After bringing them in, he then went back out to get their beddings. He placed a lot of rubbish around the bottom of the walls so that no breeze could come under it. He knew he had to stop the air from coming in the front way, so he used three deer hides as a curtain to their front door. The rubbish was placed on the ground walkway. No Pity kept walking back and forth on it, jumping up and down. He then opened up his front door after working five and a half hours on this mission. He went to his soldiers and said, "Gotcha, Shevil, Skin'em, Bite'em, and Kill'em, let's move it, soldiers!" picking up their dishes and their name tags. "Follow me, soldiers." They did, and he put their dishes in front of their shelters. They looked at him, and he said, "You're welcome, soldiers. Now, at ease." They all went into their warm shelters, leaving the door open.

As soon as he made it inside, No Pity got his main rock, which he used to sharpen his knives and hatchet. After sharpening them for at least ten minutes each, he then got his night vision goggles, cleaning them off and testing them for its vision. No Pity set his watch for 0130 so that he could wake up and go hunting for some food. His food supply was getting a little low, but he knew that was not a problem. No Pity lay down and stared at the wall and all around his shelter. Before falling asleep, he looked out his door and saw Gotcha checking on his children, Skin'em, Bite'em, and Kill'em. Shevil had her head peeking out of the doorway. They both looked at No Pity, who nodded at them, watching Gotcha walk in their shelter.

Later, as No Pity was in a deep sleep, he had a nightmare, making him sleep twenty minutes past his wake-up call. As he was in deep sleep, he was hollering and screaming, waking up his little soldiers. Gotcha ran out of his shelter, with Kill'em following behind him. Gotcha and Kill'em were both looking at No Pity, seeing that his danger was not on the outside of him. They just watched him, until his hand came off his homemade cot. Gotcha eased over to his hand and struck it with his little claw, waking No Pity out of his nightmare, with his watch alarm just beeping, though it was now twenty-five minutes past his wake-up time. He tapped his watch, cutting its alarm off, as Gotcha and Kill'em still looked at him. He looked back at them and at Shevil. Skin'em and Bite'em were at the front door, with their backs to the entrance into his shelter. No Pity looked back at Gotcha and Kill'em and said, "Good job, soldiers. Thank you. At ease. Good job."

Gotcha and Kill'em then walked off side by side, with Shevil, Skin'em, and Bite'em leading the way, all of them going back into their shelters.

No Pity got up and got dressed in the stuff that was going to keep him warm. As he walked past his little soldiers' shelters, he said, "All right, soldiers, man your post and stand your ground!"

As he went under the curtain, leaving his shelter, something told him to look back, and so he did. That was when he saw his soldiers lined up in a row two feet apart from one another. He said, his echo hitting the trees, "Good, good, good, good, good, good, good…"

The break of dawn was coming, and the snow was falling a little heavier at 0445. No Pity was walking past a tree with ropelike vines hanging down from it. He tugged at it to see how strong it was. He noticed that it was very strong. He took some of the crushed-up acorns out of his pocket, which he kept in a tin can, and then spread some in a circle, and he then put some leaves and broken twigs slightly on top of it and let it snow a little on it as well. He then made a noose out of the vine and secured it nicely so that it couldn't be seen by any animals. No Pity climbed the tree and secured himself very comfortably up on a limb. He reached out and grabbed ahold of that vine, cutting it, and tied the other end around a stick. He then sat there, waiting to see can if an animal could find the food that he left for it to eat. As he looked down at his watch, he noticed an eight-point buck working his way toward him. This buck was so goddamn big he thought to himself he didn't know if he'd be able to snatch his ass up if he did get in the noose. No Pity just sat there and waited, and waited, and waited. He wouldn't dare move up in this tree, as he knew this buck was the biggest he had ever seen in his young life. He had sat there for well over three hours, and the eight-point buck had made it to the tree and was eating right under him. The buck used his front left hoof and nose to remove the snow and kindling away from the crushed acorn, then, all of a sudden, No Pity jumped out of the tree backward, away from the buck. The buck's left front leg came out of the noose, but its neck was caught in it. No Pity wrapped the vine around another tree and watched the buck dangle viciously on the vine, trying to get loose. No Pity picked up a nice tree branch and made a very pointy tip and stuck it into the buck's stomach as he was still fighting him and making a noise.

No Pity then took one of his boot strings out of his boot and tied it to his big buck knife on the end of a stick, sticking it inside of the buck's neck, cutting his throat, killing him. The buck stopped moving after a while, and No Pity then took his knife out of the buck's neck and laid it down on the ground. He was very tired after wrestling with this buck. He knelt down beside the stick with his knife tied to the end of it and untied it, wiping it clean by using the snow. He kicked the snow out of the way while taking his knife back out and stuck it in the buck's neck. He then brought it all the way down the center of his stomach until he made it to the end, his whole entire guts rolling out of him. He cut all four legs and head off this buck and then skinned him. After skinning him, he then spread out the buck's guts all around the area that he was in. As he finished, he put the buck's hide in the snow and rubbed snow all over it, cleaning the blood off. He balled up the hide and placed it in his duffel bag. He cut up the rest into big pieces and placed it in his duffel bag with the hide. He started walking, going back to his shelter, and as he was, he found two big plastic bags wrapped around a tree branch. He unwrapped it and turned it inside out, putting his meat in one and his hide in the other.

On his way back to his shelter, he snagged two rabbits and five raccoons. He looked at his watch and noticed that it read 1441. He knew that his soldiers hadn't eaten breakfast or lunch, because he hadn't eaten anything himself. He went to the stream and lake, where he washed the meat and hide of the buck, the two rabbits, and the five raccoons. He knew this was enough meat to hold him again for a while. As he headed to his shelter again, the snow had lightened up a little. When he made it to his shelter, out in the front, he could smell that his soldiers had let loose their scent. He noticed, too, that the snow on the ground had been disturbed very bad, and some blood drops were all in the snow as well. He just smiled and said to them, "Good job, soldiers. At ease!"

They all came walking toward him as he was meeting them. When they made it to him, that was when he saw a note in Gotcha's mouth. He knelt down and took the note. He opened it up, and it read, "Soldier, I have a mission for you. Your mission is to bring them boys home. Don't ask any questions. If you do, you're dead. And if you understand, raise your left eyebrow."

No Pity raised his left eyebrow and started walking inside, saying, "Let's go, soldiers! Good job. Good job, soldiers!"

As they made it inside, that was when Kill'em brought another note to No Pity. No Pity said, "What's this, soldier Kill'em? Where did you get this from?"

He knew that his little soldier couldn't speak, but he also knew that these soldiers were true to him. He opened the note up and read it out loud to his soldiers. "Your journey is over, soldier, and the last mission that you're about to go on will either kill you or make you stronger. Personally, I think it's going to kill you, Private First Class Robert 'No Pity' Kristoff."

No Pity balled up the notes and threw them in the rotisserie pit. He then warmed up his soldiers something to eat and drink. He went to their shelter and got their dishes and put enough food and water in each for them because he knew they hadn't eaten all day, and neither had he. They ate and drank and sat near the rotisserie pit. After he and his soldiers had eaten, his soldiers started leaving one at a time, with Gotcha and Shevil both looking at him. He reached down and rubbed on them as if they were kittens. They then went to their shelter.

No Pity set his watch to wake him up at 0100, and when the hour came and the alarm woke him up, he got up and told his soldiers to stand guard. He left and went looking for the place where the human soldiers were located. He had walked about twenty-three and a half miles in these woods when he found a log cabin. He saw two soldiers outside and one inside, so he eased back to set a plan to remove these guys or kill them if they had any hostage or hostages. He made it back to his shelter, but his soldiers did not meet him. He did his little whistle and called them by name, but they still didn't appear. He said to them, "Move it, soldiers! Move it on the double! Gotcha, Shevil, Skin'em, Bite'em, and Kill'em, out front, soldiers!" Still, not one of them came out. He went in his shelter and saw this note on their shelter: "This will kill them or it will kill you. The lake is a very big place. Get there!"

He took off running in full speed in the woods, with both of his buck knives out, one in each hand. He made a wide path, yelling out loud, his voice echoing as he called out his soldiers' names, "Gotcha, Gotcha, Gotcha, Gotcha, Gotcha, Gotcha…Shevil, Shevil, Shevil, Shevil, Shevil, Shevil, Shevil…Skin'em, Skin'em, Skin'em, Skin'em, Skin'em, Skin'em, Skin'em, Skin'em…Bite'em, Bite'em, Bite'em, Bite'em, Bite'em, Bite'em, Bite'em…Kill'em, Kill'em, Kill'em, Kill'em, Kill'em, Kill'em, Kill'em…I'm, I'm, I'm, I'm, I'm, I'm, I'm, I'm…coming, coming, coming, coming, coming, coming, coming… soldiers, soldiers, soldiers, soldiers, soldiers, soldiers, soldiers…"

As he got close to the lake, running across the stream, he saw this thing in the middle of the water. He jumped in, quickly, swimming full speed just as he saw the bundle going under the water. When he got very close, that was when he went under. The water was very, very cold, but he refused to allow his soldiers to die, even if it cost him his life. He caught them before they hit the bottom, and made it back up at the top, saying, "Hold on, soldiers. I got y'all now. Just hold on, soldiers."

He made it to the land, his ass freezing off, and tried to untie this net that they were bundled up in. He cut the net open with his buck knife, and as it split apart, his soldiers did not budge; they just lay there, stiff, frozen. He picked them up and cuddled them in his arm and took them back to their shelters like the soldiers that they were.

No Pity made it back to his shelter with Gotcha, Shevil, Skin'em, Bite'em, and Kill'em. He took them inside and tried to warm them up, to see if they would come back to life. But they didn't. He left them inside and went out to clear the snow off five spots side by side for their shelters. After cleaning their spots and digging their graves, he went in, grabbed their little bodies, and put them inside their graves. He covered them with stones and brushed the snow off each one. He then placed their shelters over them, with a plaque that read, "To a family of brave soldiers. You'll be missed. RIP, my true soldiers, Gotcha, Shevil, Skin'em, Bite'em, and Kill'em." He said a prayer for his soldiers, and then he saluted them, saying, "At ease, soldiers. Good job, good job, soldiers." After, he turned around and went inside to dry off and to dry his clothes and shoes as well.

He did not know how long he had been in these woods, living off the land itself and not caring about the days that had gone by. He hadn't seen a movie or listened to the radio. He had only seen three people, and that was off distance. But anyway, he hadn't been around people in a long, long time. No Pity just lay down on his homemade cot and stared at his rotisserie pit. A hunger pang came across him. He got up and put a pot of water on the pit and let it boil until it was about to run over. He then put some cut-up meat in it, trying to make himself some stew, but without the rest of the vegetables. After it was smelling good, he took it off the fire and ate it very slowly, thinking about his little soldiers.

He looked down at his watch, setting its alarm to go off at 0315. He then fell asleep. An hour had passed when he was awakened by a noise outside his shelter. He slowly got up, putting his night vision goggles on and grabbing his two big buck knives, putting one in each hand. He put on his boots and tied them up very easily. He then eased through his door, going to the outside, on the walkway. He had made it to the curtain hanging down when he saw this deer eating over there by grave site where Gotcha, Shevil, Skin'em, Bite'em, and Kill'em were buried. No Pity was so damn quiet as he sank his right hand's buck knife in the middle of that deer's spine, and his left hand's buck knife went into the skull, killing it on the spot. He said, "Not on my watch! I got y'all's back, soldiers." He saluted them and added, "At ease, soldiers."

No Pity looked around and saw some movement, and he knew it was not an animal. He knew then they ran this deer over to where he was as a decoy. They were the same three that he had seen at the cabin about two and a half or three miles from his shelter.

No Pity said, "I've been in here for a very long goddamn time, and now you want to come around and play? Okay, I'll play with y'all's asses!"

He was about to walk off when he saw a note on his door, with a knife through it. He took it down and opened it, reading, "At ease, soldier. It's time for you to come back now. You've been out there long enough, soldier. You come back and bring those three soldiers back with you. You have four days to bring those three back without a scratch. If you don't, you're dead. If you understand, raise your left eyebrow."

No Pity raised his left eyebrow and put the fire out in his rotisserie pit and went to his little soldiers' grave site and saluted them, saying, "You'll never be forgotten." After that, he took off running in full speed.

He got his buck knives in his hands, and the third knife, the one that was in that note, was in a holster. He was running in full speed, and it was now almost 0435. He stopped running when he could see smoke in the distance through his night vision goggles; plus, he could smell the scent of burning wood. The snow was still falling heavily. No Pity set up a post and shelter by piling up a bunch of branches, making it look like a big bush. The snow was camouflaging him up in it. He came out of his little hideaway before daylight and took off running, going to his shelter to get something to lay these guys on and cover them up. When he made it back to his shelter, he looked at his walkway roof and knew this could hold all three of the dudes. He took all the animal hide that he had and the hot stones that he had chipped up, putting them in tin cans, then he bent the top of the can to keep the rocks from coming out. He then wrapped them up really good as he knew that his job was a very hard task. He then yelled out, his voice echoing among the trees, "No Pity, No Pity, No Pity, No Pity, No Pity, No Pity, No Pity..."

He went inside his shelter and looked at his watch; it read 1152. He said, "Nap time, No Pity. Get yourself some rest, because you have three and a half days to get them and yourself back. Now relax and get some sleep." Then he set his watch to 1845.

He slept a good while, then his alarm woke him up. He got up and put his night vision goggles on. He then went to his little soldiers' grave site for the last time. He knelt down on his left knee and put a last prayer of respect to his loyal little soldiers. He stood up at attention and saluted them, saying, "Very good job, soldiers. Very good. At ease now, soldiers."

He tied a vine in two loops for each arm and placed his arms in each loop, then he took off running, saluting back at his little soldiers' graves as his voice echoed among the trees in the distance as he said, "No Pity, No Pity, No Pity, No Pity, No Pity, No Pity, No Pity…" He pulled this thing with both of his buck knives out as his night vision goggles guided him through the dark woods and snow. He knew that these guys were not going to come willingly, but then he thought, *Hey, my name is No Pity, so I'm not going to show any pity. This ten-foot-by-seven-foot wood sleigh can carry four people, but I only have three.*

When he made it back to the tree, he realized he now would have to pull them out one by one. His first thought was to take one of the red-hot rocks in the can and make some sparks flash. He did this for about fifty-three minutes until he could see two of them come out of the cabin.

One of the soldiers said to the other soldier, "You chickenshit, get your ass out there and see what it is. I'll be watching over you."

The soldier walked down the stairs, heading toward No Pity and his sparks. He kept making the sparks even as the soldier got seven to eight feet from him. The bushes were getting thicker and thicker for that soldier. The bushes were so thick he decided to turn around. He said, "This is some bullsh——"

No Pity grabbed him by the back of his jacket, wrapping a vine around his neck. He then yelled, his voice echoing, "help, help, help, help, help, help, help…me, me, me, me, me, me, me, me, me, me, me, me…" No Pity put this soldier's whole entire jacket around his face, mouth, and head, muffling his every word as he hog-tied this soldier.

He heard the other soldier yelling out, "Bret, Bret, Bret, Brett, Bret, Bret, Bret, Bret, Brett…this, this, this, this, this…is, is, is, is, is, is, is, is, is…Jason, Jason, Jason, Jason, Jason…where, where, where, where, where, where, where…are, are, are, are, are…you, you, you, you, you, you, you, you, you, you…?"

No Pity's face was covered as he got Bret very silent and very still.

Jason said again loudly, "Bret, Bret, Bret, Bret, Bret, Bret, Bret… where, where, where, where, where, where…are, are, are, are, are, are, are, are, are…you, you, you, you, you, you, you…?"

No Pity, imitating Bret's voice, replied in a whisper, "Over here…over here…"

Jason asked, "Where? I can't see you!"

No Pity said, again imitating Bret's voice, "Over here, Jason. I'm over here."

Jason said, "Where? Where are you?"

No Pity was now just a few inches behind him and said in a whisper, "Right here, Jason."

It was so damn dark Jason could not see No Pity as No Pity placed a looped vine over his arms and threw him to the ground, flipping him on his stomach. He wrapped up his ankles and gagged his mouth too. He put Jason on the sleigh and covered him up alongside Bret, and he had both of their faces and heads covered so they couldn't see him. He knew he had one more soldier left. He knew that Kyle was not a rough guy, as Jason and Bret were, but he couldn't have any pity.

No Pity knew that the wind was blowing very hard out here. He knew that he had to put those candles out. He couldn't let Kyle see him, so No Pity broke all the windows in the cabin, making it pitch-black dark inside. Kyle was so afraid he ran out of the cabin, and No Pity caught him before he made it to the steps, yelling for help and for No Pity not to kill him. Kyle was still begging for his life as No Pity put a window curtain around his face, head, and mouth, muffling his words. No Pity then hog-tied him, like he did the other two soldiers. He took Kyle to the sleigh and laid him with Bret and Jason. They all were muttering at the same time.

No Pity looked at his watch, and it read 2125. He started walking, then went into a jog. As he got clear from most part of the wood, he took the last nine vines and wrapped six of them very tightly around the sleigh, twisting the other three together. He put it around his waist and with the ones on his shoulders. He looked at his watch and said in a loud voice echoing, "No Pity, No Pity, No Pity, No Pity, No Pity, No Pity…" Jason, Bret, and Kyle muttered something together.

No Pity took off running, dragging them on the homemade sleigh. He was running in full speed.

When he made it seventy-five yards from their dorm, he stopped and then started walking, looking at his watch. He had three and a half hours or four left before the break of dawn., he realized. He then started jogging once again, then going into full speed. When he made it to Jason, Bret, and Kyle's dorm, he picked Jason off the sleigh, and then Bret and Kyle, all three still muttering. No Pity looked at his watch again and saw that he had to keep them out there for at least another hour.

He knew he had sat down with them for an hour and that time was up. He drew his fist back and hit Jason on the chin, knocking him out. He picked him up and carried him inside to his bunk and laid him down very gently, without waking a soul. He then went back out and lifted Kyle up, hitting him on his chin, knocking him out. Then he carried him inside to his bunk. After, he went back out a third time and got Bret, hitting him on his chin too, thereby knocking him out. He then carried him to his bunk without waking anyone or allowing anyone to see him. Once outside, he picked up the sleigh and carried it out to the flagpole, standing there at attention, in a salute.

Private First Class Kristoff stood six foot one and weighed at 218 1/2 pounds, with wild hair and a beard. He didn't know that he had been gone for a little over a year. And he just stood there, waiting for his drill instructor, since he was an hour early.

He looked at his watch and noticed that it was 0500. He could hear all the muttering from other soldiers yelling for their drill instructor.

Drill instructor Sergeant Ibdam pulled up in his jeep right in front of Private First Class Kristoff. He stepped out of the jeep and stood at attention, face-to-face with Private First Class Kristoff, and said out loud, "Code name, soldier."

Kristoff said out loud, "No Pity, sir!"

Sergeant Ibdam asked, "Who?"

Kristoff said, "No Pity, sir!"

The other soldiers in their company dorms all heard and watched this as Sergeant Ibdam said, "I can't hear you!"

Kristoff said at the top of his lungs, "No Pity, sir!"

Sergeant Ibdam said out loud, "At ease, No Pity. Now go and get cleaned up. Move it! Move it!"

Private First Class Kristoff ran and saluted Sergeant Ibdam; he was going to get cleaned up and get a haircut and a shave before eating breakfast.

No Pity got out of the shower and got some scissors and an electric shaver, shaving his beard clean off his face. He went to the barber and sat in the chair, not saying a word; he just sat there very still. The barber cut his hair off and then took the cape off his neck, saying, "All done, soldier."

No Pity said, "Thank you, sir," and walked out of the door. The barber looked puzzled because he knew that this kid looked familiar to him, but he knew that kid to be five foot seven or five foot eight and weigh at 140 pounds, give or take a few pounds. Although he knew that he hadn't seen this kid in a while now, this guy here was six foot two and weighed at 225 pounds, give or take a few pounds.

No Pity made it to the mess hall and got his tray, then went back to the same table where Jason, Bret, and Kyle sat at to eat. The other drill instructors and soldiers were sitting there quietly, watching him. The only one who really knew who this soldier's identity was was drill instructor Sergeant Ibdam.

Jason, Bret, and Kyle came in and went to the table. They stood there looking at him. Jason said, "Excuse us, soldier. This is lance corporals' table only. You have to be excused from this table."

Private First Class Robert "No Pity" Kristoff raised up his head and looked at all three of them in the eyes and saw all kinds of scratches, bite marks, and cuts. He noticed their arms and hands and saw the same type of wounds. He now knew that they were the ones who murdered his little soldiers.

No Pity said, "Good job. Good job, soldiers."

Jason asked, "What? What did you say, soldier?"

No Pity responded, "I said, good job. Good job, soldiers."

Jason smiled and said, "Thank you, Private. Now you're dismissed from this here table."

No Pity said, "I wasn't talking to you three shit-eaters. I'm talking about the battle marks that my five brave little soldiers did to you fuckers. Gotcha, Shevil, Skin'em, Bite'em, and Kill'em, good job, soldiers." He then saluted to their battle with these shit-eaters. No Pity continued, "Now I must do to you three motherfuckers what y'all did to them." Suddenly, he jumped up very quickly and was about to start fighting Jason, Bret, and Kyle when a voice loudly said, "Attention!"

Everybody in the mess hall stood up at once. You could not hear a sound—not even the cooks in the kitchen were making a sound. The only sound that could be heard was the sound the footsteps of this person who had yelled "Attention!" made as he walked toward the table where Bret, Jason, Kyle, and Private First Class Kristoff were. Private Kristoff was standing in a salute. Jason, Bret, Kyle, and the rest of the soldiers were wondering why Private Kristoff was standing there, saluting.

Drill instructor Sergeant Ibdam eventually made it to them and stood in front of Private First Class Kristoff, saying very loudly, "What is your code name, soldier?"

"Private First Class Robert 'No Pity' Kristoff, sir!"

Sergeant Ibdam asked, again, in a very loud voice, "WHAT IS YOUR CODE NAME, SOLDIER?"

Private Kristoff responded just as loudly, "NO PITY, SIR!"

Sergeant Ibdam asked in the most demanding tone of voice, "Private Kristoff, what is your code name?"

Private Kristoff said, "Private First Class Robert 'No Pity' Kristoff, sir!"

Drill instructor Sergeant Ibdam then said very loudly, "Corporal Robert 'No Pity' Kristoff, at ease, soldier!"

Corporal Robert "No Pity" Kristoff responded, "Sir, yes, sir!"

Sergeant Ibdam then turned his attention to Lance Corporals Nelson, Smith, and Phillips, asking, "What is the problem, soldiers?" in a very commanding voice.

Lance Corporal Jason Nelson said, "Sir, there is no problem, sir."

Sergeant Ibdam responded, "Do you have some beef with Corporal Kristoff, Lance Corporal Nelson?"

Lance Corporal Nelson said, "Sir, no, sir."

Sergeant Ibdam replied, "All right, then, soldiers, sit your asses down and eat your slop, or I shall release you and your two friends here in a cage faraway out, and it will be no pity, do you understand me?"

All three lance corporals said at the same time, "Sir, yes, sir."

Sergeant Ibdam said, "Good," as he turned his attention back to Corporal No Pity Kristoff, who was still standing and saluting. He then said in a loud tone voice, raising his left eyebrow to him, "Corporal No Pity Kristoff, no pity, soldier. Remember who do deserves the pity and who doesn't deserve the pity. Do you understand, soldier?"

Corporal No Pity Kristoff answered, "Sir, yes, sir." Sergeant Ibdam then saluted him Corporal No Pity Kristoff, releasing his salute immediately as he walked off, adding very loudly, "At ease, soldiers! As you were!"

Corporal No Pity Kristoff sat down in his seat and started eating his breakfast as Lance Corporals Nelson, Smith, and Phillips just stood there, waiting for Corporal No Pity Kristoff to give them the okay to be seated. Corporal No Pity Kristoff barely looked up as he was still eating his food, watching all three of them just standing there. Fifteen minutes went by, and Corporal No Pity Kristoff finished eating his meal. Lance Corporals Nelson, Smith, and Phillips were still standing there and hadn't eaten a bite of their food. As Corporal No Pity Kristoff stood up and was about to walk off, he said in a low, commanding voice, "You three have three minutes to eat and be back in the barracks. Do you understand, Lance Corporals?"

They all said at the same time, very loudly, "Sir, yes, sir."

Kristoff said, "I can't hear you!" in a loud voice.

They all yelled out in a very loud voice, at the top of their lungs, "YES, SIR, CORPORAL NO PITY, SIR!"

Corporal No Pity answered, "At ease, Lance Corporals."

His left eyebrow was raised when he went past Sergeant Ibdam, going to get his corporal uniform with his rank on it.

CHAPTER 2

A year and a half had gone by. Corporal No Pity Kristoff was nine-teen years old. His training was so strange, but his attitude and tem-per never changed. Sergeant Ibdam had known there was something very special about this soldier even on his first day of boot camp. His corporal status had improved so deeply, until Sergeant Ibdam was promoted to first captain from drill instructor sergeant, and he wanted Corporal No Pity Kristoff to take his place as drill instructor.

Sergeant Ibdam stood up in his doorway and yelled out loud, "Attention!" The whole dorm got quiet. Sergeant Ibdam continued, "Corporal No Pity, come to my office ASAP, on the double." Then he said to the others, "As you were!"

Corporal No Pity was at his door before he could sit down in his chair. Sergeant Ibdam thought to himself, *Well, I'd be damned!* He then finally made it down to his chair. Corporal No Pity was standing as he was saluting, then said, "Corporal No Pity Kristoff reporting, sir!"

Sergeant Ibdam said, "At ease, Corporal, and have a seat. Don't talk, just listen, until I ask you to speak. Do you understand, Corporal?"

Corporal No Pity responded, "Sir, yes, sir."

Sergeant Ibdam said, "Corporal Kristoff, I'm being promoted to first captain, and I want to put a recommendation in for you to take my position as drill instructor. You're more qualified to fill this rank and then some, Corporal. You know what it takes, and you have what it takes. So, Corporal, tell me, would you like to fill this position? Because I can make it happen."

Corporal No Pity Kristoff replied, "Sir, permission to speak, sir."

Sergeant Ibdam said, "Permission granted."

Corporal No Pity Kristoff said, "Sir, I am honored, but the training that you had for me was to end problems and not sit in one place to see if a person was going to protect and rescue our boys and girls and bring them back home. I appreciate the thought, sir, but you know what my intentions, duties, and job are all about. It would be nice for someone, but not for me."

Sergeant Ibdam answered, "I understand, soldier. You're excused."

Sergeant Ibdam knew deep in his heart that Corporal No Pity was going to turn that promotion. Sergeant Ibdam really could make that happen for Corporal Robert "No Pity" Kristoff, but Corporal Kristoff turned it down because his calling was way higher than the journey of being a drill instructor. Sergeant Ibdam put a black strip across Corporal Robert "No Pity" Kristoff's name, and under it also was written, "Do not order, per First Captain Ibdam."

First Captain Ibdam finished packing up his belongings, with Corporal No Pity Kristoff's words ringing inside of his head, his wanting to be that soldier that makes a difference in the world. As he was leaving his office, he knew that he had a better chance of helping his soldiers under his command. First Captain Ibdam was told by other commanding officers about the wars that they had been in and were still going through as they stood at that moment. Little did they know First Captain Ibdam wasn't that person you'd want to wrestle with or even use threating words toward. They thought First Captain Ibdam was wet between the ears when it came to calling shots over soldiers that were putting their lives out there for one another as well as for their country. First Captain Ibdam just sat there, listening to his colleagues tell him things that he already knew; little did they know, First Captain Ibdam knew more about them and their past.

He thought to himself, *If only these sons of bitches knew who I really am. But that chapter of my life is sealed. This life history of mine will give people an everlasting nightmare and stuff to talk about, and then they'll understand why they call me by the name Ibdam.*

First Captain Ibdam eased away from them without them knowing that he had left. One of the other commanding officers said, "Where did the first captain go. He was just here a second ago, as we were talking to him?"

Another commanding officer said, "He was standing right here as you were talking, George. How could he leave when we were right here with him? The man has pulled a Harry Houdini act, but better!"

They were standing there puzzled and muttering to themselves, and then they walked off a little astounded about the way he just disappeared right before their eyes.

Now, First Captain Ibdam had moved all his things into his new office. His secretary came to his door, saluting and saying, "First Captain, sir, Colonel Bradford Blackstone is on line 3."

He said, "At ease, Sergeant. I'll take it." He saluted her as she backed out of the doorway, closing his door. He picked up his phone receiver and said, "Yes, Colonel Blackstone. This is First Captain Ibdam speaking, sir."

Colonel Blackstone said, "Captain, I need for you to report to General Sherman Huckybees's office at once. I'll be there to meet you." He then hung up the phone before First Captain Ibdam could say a word to him.

First Captain Ibdam got up and went out of his office, where he said to his secretary, Sergeant Freely, "Take some messages for me and let them know that I'll be out probably for the rest of the day." She saluted him, and he saluted her back as he was walking out the door. Millions of things were running through his thoughts. He did not have the slightest idea what they wanted to talk to him about; he just walked faster, saluting all the soldiers and their ranking officers. As he made it to the building where the general and colonel were stationed at the base, he immediately went to the receptionist, saying, "I'm First Captain Ibdam, and I was ordered to report to meet Colonel Blackstone in General Huckybees's office."

She said, "Just a minute, sir. Let me call and tell them that you're here." She picked up the phone and pushed the number to General Huckybees's office, then said, "General Huckybees, sir, I have First Captain Ibdam down here to see you and Colonel Blackstone, sir."

He stood there for not one second longer, for the receptionist then said, "Go on up to the fourth floor, room number 231, sir."

He said, "Thank you, ma'am," as he walked off, going toward the elevator. First Captain Ibdam was up in the elevator, going to see the general and the colonel, for what reason, he didn't know, and his heart was beating faster and faster along with the thoughts racing through his mind like the rushing waters of the Niagara Falls. He just shrugged it off when he got out of the elevator to meet with the general and the colonel. He saw the number on the door that said, "General Sherman Huckybees, 231."

He opened the door and went up to his secretary, saying as she saluted him, "I'm First Captain Ibdam. I'm here to report to General Huckybees and Colonel Blackstone."

She said, "They both are waiting for you, sir. Go on in, sir."

First Captain Ibdam walked in, where he saluted General Huckybees and Colonel Blackstone, saying, "First Captain Ibdam reporting, sir."

General Huckybees said, "At ease, soldier. Have a seat, please."

He sat down and did not ask any questions; he would not dare question a general, his superior officer. The thing that was really racing in his thoughts, though, was, *Why have I been called here to see them?* He was very puzzled, but he just kept his mouth closed and his mind open. Whatever it was, it had to be important.

The general and the colonel stood up, and so did First Captain Ibdam. The three of them then walked into this conference room that belonged to the general. At the big table, there were only three chairs.

General Huckybees said, "Men, have a seat. What I'm about to show you is very much confidential. This is for your eyes only. Do you two understand?"

They both said at the same time, "Sir, yes, sir."

He said, "Good," cutting the lights off and the projector's slides on. General Huckybees said to both men, "Gentlemen, what you're looking at are five dead bodies hanging upside down, being eaten by two 250-pound hungry lions. Believe it or not, gentlemen, out intel tells us that these people were alive as they were being eaten."

Colonel Blackstone asked, "General, sir, what are we looking at? At the very bottom, sir?"

The general said, "You really want to know, Colonel?" General Huckybees clicked the clicker to the projector for the next slide to show. "This is what you're looking at. Colonel Blackstone. That was blood, human intestine, and body parts. All that you see is probably from multiple people. This is not from one person, gentlemen. Look at the clothes that were ripped off them by these lions..."

Colonel Blackstone asked, "Is that U—"

But he was cut off by General Huckybees, who said, "Yes, that was a United States Marine Corps uniform. They have our men, and a few of our allied men, too, over there, and a couple of news reporters. I don't know if they're dead or alive over there. Our intel tells us nothing about their situation. We just know that they are there in that place that you see. Any questions?"

Colonel Blackstone asked, "General, sir, what do you want from us? If they're dead, then what can we actually do for them without sacrificing our soldiers' lives for this cause?"

General Huckybees responded, "I don't give a shit if our soldiers are dead or alive. I want them home, especially the live ones."

Colonel Blackstone said, "General, sir, if your intel cannot give you a for-sure thing that our soldiers, our allied soldiers, and those two news reporters are alive, then I don't see why we should put our soldiers in jeopardy, only to have them be mistreated like those soldiers, sir."

General Huckybees then asked, "Then tell me, Colonel Blackstone, what if those soldiers and news reporters are very much alive and are about to be treated like these ones in this here film? What if they are just watching what is being done to their friends and praying for help, wondering why in the hell we ain't trying a fucking thing to get them out? I want to at least try, Colonel!"

The colonel said, "It's not as easy as said and done, General Huckybees. I am more than willing to go get them out. It's just I'll feel much better if we know that they're alive, sir."

First Captain Ibdam suddenly said, "Permission to speak, sir."

The general said, "Permission granted."

First Captain Ibdam continued, "Give me eighteen men and seventy-two hours to get them out and seventy-two hours to get back home. I'll get them out, sir."

Colonel Blackstone replied, "How in the fuc———"

But then the general said loudly, "Shut the fuck up, Colonel Blackstone!" He then turned to the first captain. "Go ahead, son. How would you be able to do that, Captain?"

First Captain Ibdam said, "General Huckybees, sir, with all due respect, don't ask, just tell me to do it. Every question sometimes doesn't have or need and answer, just results, sir."

As the general stared into the captain's eyes, the captain stared back into his too. They stared at each other for well over four minutes. When they apparently were finished staring each other down, General Huckybees asked, "You need eighteen men and seventy-two hours and you can bring those people out of there?"

Captain Ibdam answered, "General Huckybees, sir, don't ask no question. Just tell me to bring them home. Sir, your command is my order, and my order is their families' wishes and prayers, sir. Just give me the command, eighteen men, and seventy-two hours and it'll be done, sir."

General Huckybees got on the phone, saying, "General Sherman Huckybees here, and I'm sending First Captain Ibdam to do whatever he wishes. Don't question him. As a matter of fact, just leave the premises without locking any of the doors. And that's an order, sergeant!" The general then hung up the phone and said to the captain, "You have everything at your disposal, anything and everything, without any questions asked. Now, go get our soldiers and bring them home, soldier! Now that's an order!"

. First Captain Ibdam got up and saluted both superiors and walked out of the general's office.

Colonel Blackstone said, "General, sir, you know something that I don't know about this first captain. The reason that I say this is, he said he only needs eighteen soldiers and seventy-two hours to go get them out and bring them home. That is a bunch of bullshit, and you know it is, General."

The general replied, "You know what the real bullshit is, Colonel? There is no fucking way that this first captain can fail."

The colonel said, "General, there is no goddamn way in hell that this captain can pull this shit off, and you know it, sir! I believe that these soldiers will be landing into these gorillas' hands. I ask you, General, how can he and eighteen men pull this shit off in seventy-two hours, sir?"

The general replied, "Now, you listen to me, Colonel. You're the one who's full of bullshit if you don't believe in your own soldiers. You better understand this also, Colonel: those soldiers and news reporters have been missing for well over a year, and we just got this intel a week ago, letting us know that some of our soldiers are being tortured over there. Even if they are dead, and even if we lose a couple of soldiers in that fight, at least we can say that we tried, Colonel. But you have to give a fucking boot to say that you've given a goddamn thing for our soldiers and their families. So you ask, Do I believe that First Captain Ibdam and his soldiers can bring them back? I say yes, and I'd be damned if I feel or say otherwise about this captain and his soldiers."

Colonel Blackstone just sat there quietly, thinking to himself in discomfort about the conversation that he was having with his general about the captain and his eighteen soldiers. He knew that those nineteen men would be walking in a death trap. The place was called Hell's Valley, and whoever went there knew that its name spoke for itself. This place had a hell of a smell—it smelled like nothing but death, with dead animals and dead bodies spread out all over the place, as if they were fertilizing the ground. Bodies up in trees, leaning up against trees, and hanging off tree limbs. Why would this captain want to go there? he wondered. And most of all, why would this general send these soldiers out to a place such as this?

As he stood up slowly, Colonel Blackstone muttered to himself, saying, "I'd be damned..."

General Huckybees asked, "You have something to say, Colonel Blackstone?"

Colonel Blackstone replied, "Sir, no, sir, General." Then he asked, "Am I dismissed, General?" Then a salute.

"Yes, you're dismissed, Colonel," the general said.

Colonel Blackstone walked out of the conference room, leaving the general in there by himself, the general still staring at the slides. He stared harder at the slides, pondering how cruel and gruesome they must be to anyone who saw them. He believed he was looking at the worst of the worst mass killing he had ever heard of, read about, or seen. He said softly to himself, "Why did I agree to send these soldiers to their death? Why couldn't I say, 'No fucking way that I'll send only you and eighteen men'? How could I be so naive of this subject? I'm sending these soldiers in a place that's called Hell's Valley, which has all kinds of dead animals and dead people in its midst. But I cannot stop it, as my order is already being carried out as I think. Colonel Blackstone was right, but we need our soldiers home. At least we put an effort to bring them back."

General Huckybees then turned off the projector, turned the lights back on, and walked to his window, looking through the blinds and saying "God, be with your soldiers, and let them bring the others home alive." He let the blinds go back to closed. He just stood there, staring at the close blinds. His phone was ringing. It had been ringing for at least three minutes, until it finally broke him out of the trance that he was in. He picked up the phone and said, "This is General Huckybees." He paused for a few seconds, listening. Then he said, "I'll be there at 1400, and I'll hear and see what you have." Then he hung up the phone.

Now, First Captain Ibdam had made it to the armory. When he went inside, there was not one person in the unit. He was in there all by himself. He chose the weapons that he and his soldiers were going to be needing for this suicide mission. The captain knew this was a suicide mission, what he was taking these soldiers and himself to. But little did the general and colonel know that his eighteen men had already been handpicked a long time ago. These eighteen men knew exactly what it took to make it in this here mission. After he picked out all the weapons needed for their arsenal, he then made eighteen notes and placed them in separate envelopes with only the soldiers' last names on it. Also added was a note: "For your eyes only."

The captain went to the company dorm that these soldiers were in; he didn't want one single person to see him place these envelopes in these soldiers' possession. Captain Ibdam went into the files of the soldiers that he had handpicked to go on the mission with him, knowing that he could not do this without losing any of these soldiers. He cleared their files as if they had never even been at this camp, and that also included their beds once they came to their new unit. He then left and went to his office, cutting the lights of the radio off so he could concentrate on this mission and get some thoughts in.

The only noise that was in the background was the sound of the drill instructors and the marching soldiers, and not one of them was off-key. He knew it had been a long time since he went into battle, but he knew that his ass was very much healthy. He said to himself, "First Captain Charles 'Ibdam' Patterson, you stand at six foot three and weigh 210 pounds, are meaner than a hundred sons of bitches! Poisonous snakes move out of your way when you come toward them, because I Be Bad is in your name."

He stood there in the dark at attention. He then cut on his desk lamp and called the identification building so they could make nineteen dog tags with names and numbers as follows: C-Apocalypse, 1-Lowlife, 2-Rattler, 3-Shadow, 4-Tornado, 5-Flood, 6-Illusionist, 7-Consequence, 8-Evil, 9-Eliminate, 10-Fatal, 11-Furious, 12-Destroyer, 13-Hectic, 14-Hocus-Pocus, 15-Maniac, 16-Nuclear, 17-Polarize, and 18-Animosity. "Did you get all that, Sergeant?" the first captain asked.

The sergeant replied, "Sir, yes, sir. Now, when will you be picking these up, sir?"

He said, "In three hours, Sergeant."

Sergeant Kingster said, "Sir, it'll take me at least five hours at the most to do all these tags, sir."

The captain said, "Sergeant Kingster, you have three hours and a half to have those dog tags ready for me. Am I clear to you about this order?"

Sergeant Kingster replied, "Crystal, sir."

"Good," said First Captain Ibdam. Then he hung up the phone.

Now that he had the dog tags in order, he went to have an old bunkhouse with twenty-nine to thirty-three rooms in it closed down for him and his soldiers and their supplies, and he had it marked off-limits to everyone. To all official personnel, no matter their ranks and serial numbers. They would do their own laundry, the cooking, and the cleaning. Going off base and making phone calls would have their own personal standards and rules. Those soldiers who had been chosen did not have a clue what was in store for them. The unit was called the No-Name Unit.

When the soldiers made it back to their barracks, they opened up their lockers to get their shower clothes, and that was when they saw the envelopes in their lockers' box. Only certain chosen ones got an envelope, and some of them looked around to see if everyone had the same thing in their box. The outside of the envelope read, "For your eyes only," in big red letters. So they cuffed the letter as if nothing happened. None of the soldiers knew who put this in their lockers.

First Captain Ibdam, meanwhile, left out of his office, going to the identification unit to pick up the soldiers' dog tags, especially made for them. Sergeant Kingster was sitting at his desk, inventorying the dog tags, stating who ordered them and how many. First Captain Ibdam said, "Sergeant Kingster, son, I advise you not to continue writing. This was done for your eyes only." He went around the counter and took the dog tags and paper with his name on it.

Sergeant Kingster asked, "What if someone asks about these missing tags? And then what am I supposed to say, sir?"

He said, "You won't say anything, soldier."

He left the building, going to his unit to await for his hand-picked soldiers. He had already placed each of their dog tag on the door of the room they were going to be sleeping in.

Now, after all the soldiers had finished taking their showers back at the barracks, they separated themselves from the others without them noticing that they had left. Their drill instructors and corporals did not know too. None of the soldiers knew who all had one of these envelopes or if it was just him who got one. Each of the soldiers felt as if he was the only one that got one. The envelopes gave all of them each a Pacific Standard Time to report to their new building, which was called the No-Name Unit, and for them to go into their own rooms.

As all eighteen of them made it to each of their rooms, a note was slid under their doors. The note requested the size of their clothes, shoes, hats, gloves, and neck, and a measuring tape then went under the door as well so they could give their proper neck size. After they had finished measuring their sizes, they then slid the note back under the door. After, as they sat in their rooms, the commander of their squad knew that they had to be hungry, so he had menus slid under their doors, telling them to circle anything they liked to eat or drink. The soldiers were smiling because they had never seen a menu like this one before. This one had food that they had not had in four to five years, and some could not have afforded a meal like this at a restaurant. They wanted to say something to their neighbor next door, but they were not allowed to do that, as it was part of the rules. These soldiers realized they needed a key to open their doors from the inside, and now they were wondering how in the hell they were going to get out to go and eat.

The intercom came on in their rooms, saying, "You'll be issued keys later with some standards."

First Captain Ibdam pushed the mail intercom button so that he could talk to them as a team but also as an individual. The mail intercom allowed him to speak to each room one at a time. When the speakers in their room came on, that was when this voice on it said, "I am Captain Apocalypse, your captain. You are my team, under my command at all times. You all will follow my orders at all times. I will not allow any insubordination from this team, because we all are honorable soldiers. Now, this unit is not like any other unit that you've heard of or been in before, so don't try to figure it out. Just let it be what it is. This unit will not allow you to see one another's skin complexion and not even each other's faces. Your names have been turned into the number of the room that you're in and the code name that is on the back of it. So whatever your name was before coming to this unit, you'll never be called that name again until you no longer belong to this team, and it won't be in existence for you to tell anyone. That is why this unit is called the No-Name Unit.

"I welcome you all, handpicked soldiers that I've chosen to my unit. I know that you soldiers are hungry, and so am I. We'll be eating soon. Now, however, before you come out to eat, I want you to be fully dressed in your black uniform, and that includes your mechanical voice detector and ski mask. I don't care if you come to breakfast, lunch, or supper—you better have that uniform on. A key is being placed under your door, and the key that has the word *right* on it is the key that will let you in the room, and the key that has the word *left* on it is the one that will let you out of the room. You'll have your own personal table and chair where you'll eat all your meals. We have a conference room, where we do all our debriefing and meetings. Remember, whenever you come out of your room, you must have your full uniform on, and that also means your mechanical voice detector. You are allowed to come and go from your rooms, but you're not allowed to have any social contact at all with the other bunkhouses. While you're eating, there'll be a big box in front of each of your rooms, and in those boxes is everything that you'll need to live in here. It has more than you'll ever imagine can be in it. You are soldiers, you are brothers, and you are as one, as a team. You have to believe in one another, as each one of us has to depend on the next person as a team member. I am your captain, and you all are sergeants—meaning, you all listen to me and not to one another. We have been chosen for some very special missions, and we are here to serve the country and not men, you can leave this building and this compound, but you must use the underground tunnel.

"Now, I would like to explain that menu to you. The reason that your menu has those meals like is that we never know if this will be our last meal, and when I say 'our last meal,' I'm talking about mine as well, because I'll be in that time with you soldiers, because we are a team. Now, since all that has been out of the way, you all will see a black wire coming out of your wall, and if you agree to the terms of this unit and the mission that is upon us, then unplug your wire."

One minute later, the wires were disconnected, the lights then going off, meaning that they were in agreement with all the terms of the unit and its mission. Room number 10, with the code name Sergeant Furious Light, was still on.

Captain Apocalypse said, "I see that you're in disagreement with the unit's terms. Is that correct, soldier?"

Number 10, Sergeant Furious, said in his mechanical voice, "No disrespect, Captain Apocalypse, sir, but my wire has been removed before you finished that part of your rules, sir. I am more than willing to do my part and then some, sir. Captain, sir, I do believe that your end is indeed a malfunction as to my decision to be under your command, sir."

Captain Apocalypse tapped on the switchboard's light with the number 10, and that was when the light went out. Captain Apocalypse said, "You're right, soldier, the malfunction was on my end. Now, Sergeant Furious, continue to listen like you never listened before.

"I am one of you, and you all are me. For the last part of this here briefing, about your uniform, I have to make something clear, and that is about your dog tags. Your dog tags have to be protected at all costs. If anyone gets your dog tag, then they'll have the key to all our brothers, and we can't allow that to happen to this unit. Your brothers and I will be dead, dead, dead. And if you're dead, then we'll have to kill the poor sons of bitches who have it, because this is something that has got to be protected as if your lives were depending on it.

"Now, I want all of you to stand outside your door, and I'll see you all in ten minutes. Thank for your attention and your support, soldiers. At ease, soldiers, and may God be with us all on all our suicide missions. We are the No-Name Unit soldiers!"

Captain Apocalypse came down right at his ten-minute mark, on the dot, to meet his team as they were standing in front of their doors, with their ski mask on. Captain Apocalypse said, "Attention!" All the soldiers stood in a salute. Captain Apocalypse continued, "When I call your number and code name off, step forward in that order, and after I release you, go find your seat and table. When you finish your meal, make sure that your brotherly soldiers are ready to go. Understand?"

All of them said at once, at the same time, as if they were robots, "Sir, yes, sir!"

Captain Apocalypse said, "Number 1, Sergeant Lowlife; number 2, Sergeant Rattler; number 3, Sergeant Shadow; number 4, Sergeant Tornado; number 5, Sergeant Flood; number 6, Sergeant Illusionist; number 7, Sergeant Consequence; number 8, Sergeant Evil; number 9, Sergeant Eliminate; number 10, Sergeant Fatal; number 11, Sergeant Furious; number 12, Sergeant Destroyer; number 13, Sergeant Hectic; number 14, Sergeant Hocus-Pocus; number 15, Sergeant Maniac; number 16, Sergeant Nuclear; number 17, Sergeant Polarize; and number 18, Sergeant Animosity. At ease, soldiers! Now, go eat. Move it! Move it! Move it!"

The soldiers lined up in a single file as their platters came from behind this wall, where they then found their tables with one comfortable seat. The table had everything a café or restaurant had on them.

The captain was the last one in the line. His seat and table were in the middle of all his sergeants. All nineteen soldiers had their ski mask on their faces, so none of them knew what the next soldier's skin complexion looked like. They didn't know what the next soldier's skin complexion looked like. All they saw were just clothes, the same exact thing that they all were wearing. The only obvious difference between them were their heights, weights, and sizes, and that was good enough for them and their captain. After they all finished eating, they all stood up at their tables without moving an inch.

Captain Apocalypse was still eating his meal, so the soldiers just stood there at attention for eight to twelve minutes at the most. When Captain Apocalypse finished drinking out of his cup, he reached into his pocket and pulled out a few dollars, laying it on the table. The other soldiers saw this, and they all did the same thing and stood back up in attention.

Captain Apocalypse said, "Good job, soldiers. At ease! Now, as you may notice at your door, there is a very, very big box in front of it on a flatbed dolly. Put the dolly back outside the door. Now, let's move it! Move it! Move it!"

All eighteen soldiers went to their assigned rooms to take all their stuff out of their boxes. They all then set the dollies back outside of their doors.

After, the captain laid out for them the proper way of wearing their uniform in its entirety. Captain Apocalypse said, "We will be fully dressed in our gear as we go over our plan of attack. I know you hear my voice in a mechanical mount, and you'll get onto it as well as I'll get used to yours. Now, I want you all to go get fully dressed into your unit uniforms, and after you're geared up, wait for my command. Now, move it! Move it! Move it!"

They all ran to their rooms and got fully geared up, and then stood up inside. Captain Apocalypse hit the main intercom button and said, "If you all can hear me, hit your green button."

All green lights lit up.

Captain Apocalypse continued, "Number 1, Sergeant Lowlife, tell me how you are geared up."

Sergeant Lowlife's mechanical voice said, "My darkest fatigue uniform, my shock-resistant combat boots, my mechanical voice detector, my stocking cap, my ski mask over it, my first pair of gloves, my leather gloves over them, and my watch."

Captain Apocalypse said, "Is there anyone geared up differently from Sergeant Lowlife? If you are, hit the green button and leave your room right now."

All their doors opened and closed at the same time.

Captain Apocalypse said on the intercom, "Good. Stay as you are."

Captain Apocalypse came and stood in front of them, saying, "As you soldiers can see, there is something sitting up on your tables. Look how I'm wearing all my arsenal. If you understand, then I advise you soldiers to get geared up right now. Move it! Move it! Move it!"

As they were getting geared up, Captain Apocalypse commented, "Good. Now, I want you to look in your backpack. There you'll see all your ammunitions already loaded in their clips, ready to go. Each rifle has a scope. You know where all the safety on your firearms is at, but we do not lock and load until we reach our destination. My safety and your safety is very important, and we don't want to place it in a friendly fire of our own weapons."

After the captain finished his talk, he marched all of them to their conference room, saying, "We're about to go on our first mission to a place called Hell's Valley, and what you're about to see will be very gruesome to the stomach. I'm warning you now, and after you see this, then I'll ask you that one main question. So have a seat and pay very close attention to this intel."

He turned off the lights and used his clicker to turn the projector on. The No-Name Unit soldiers saw those soldiers in the country of Congo, Belgian Congo, torturing American soldiers along with two news reporters. The No-Name Unit watched these slides and saw two full-grown lions ripping up and eating these people alive. After three and half hours of them watching, they were debriefed on the intel and the plan that would be executed in going in and bringing those soldiers out of there.

Sergeant Illusionist said in his mechanical voice, "Permission to speak, Captain Apocalypse."

Captain Apocalypse replied, "Permission granted."

Sergeant Illusionist asked, "What if they're dead? Can we still bring them home, sir?"

Captain Apocalypse said, "If you all agree with Sergeant Illusionist, I want all of you one at a time to tap the table three times. Starts now."

The other seventeen soldiers agreed with their brotherly soldier.

Captain Apocalypse then said, "All right, soldiers, it'll be our mission to bring all of them home, dead or alive. I want you to know that we have at least three hundred and seventy-two or seventy-five soldiers standing in our way. Are you ready for this warfare, soldier? This guerilla warfare will not go unsuccessful—do I make myself clear, soldiers?"

All said at once, "Sir, yes, sir, Captain Apocalypse!"

Captain Apocalypse said, "Then let it be done. Move out!"

They all put their night vision goggles on and started walking in a single file as they made their way to the basement door. Captain Apocalypse said, "Halt, soldiers! This door leads to a tunnel, and the tunnel is eight miles long. When it comes to an end, that is when you will see this line stop at, and we'll walk at least five yards. That is when we will take an elevator down to our cargo plane, and once we're inside, I'll give another order on what we will have to do. Any questions?"

Sergeant Tornado asked, "Are we going to run double time down this tunnel for the eight miles, sir?"

Captain Apocalypse said, "No, soldier, we won't have to do that. We have our own Harley 250cc that gets up to 120 miles per hour. We'll be there in no time, soldier. Any other question?"

There was just silence among them all, so Captain Apocalypse continued, "Once we go through this door, there is no turning back. You have seen what these people can do if you get caught. If you get caught, then we all get caught. We shall die for who we are, and we *are* soldiers! If you want to change your mind, you can, and none of us will see you any other way because they don't know who you are or what you look like. Anybody want out, just leave now."

Everybody was still lined up and ready to go.

Captain Apocalypse said, "Now, let us bring our people home, soldiers!"

They all then jogged out of the doorway, going to their own Harley with their number on it. It was very dark in the tunnel that they had to use their night vision goggles. They then drove for about twenty-eight minutes, making it to the end of the tunnel. The captain got off his Harley first, and the rest followed. The elevator could not hold all of them at one time, so they went nine at a time. When they all made it down to the cargo plane, Captain Apocalypse said, "What you see here is a Lockheed C-5 Galaxy plane. And inside of it, we have a Sea Stallion helicopter that is carrying a device and a quarter-truck with eighteen more units of Harley 250cc. Now, let us load up and go get our people from those who are holding them."

All nineteen soldiers loaded up on the Lockheed C-5 Galaxy, knowing that this mission could be their first and their last. They stood there in a salute as the door was raised, and when it was closed, Captain Apocalypse said, "All right, Sergeants, I want all of you soldiers to take your positions."

They all took their positions and strapped themselves in their standing posts. They then heard one of the mechanical voices saying, "I'm your pilot, the Big Badass Wolf." And another mechanical voice said, "I'm also your pilot, the Boogeyman. So buckle up and we'll be at your destination in twenty to two hours."

As the plane got off the ground so smoothly, Captain Apocalypse said, "Unstrap yourselves and look up over your head. There you'll see a very long insulated leather gun case. In that case you will have one .45 automatic, one M1 Garand, one M79 grenade launcher, one AK-47, seventy-five pineapple hand grenades, one .30-caliber tommy gun, and one Japanese Arisaka 97 sniper rifle. All of them go on your back before your smaller backpack goes on. Now, in your backpack you'll see your clips in there. For each gun you have twenty clips ready to go for each. Your clip will go over the weapons on your back. I want you soldiers to know we're the only ones who know that we're over here. So what we have to do is to be vigilant in our missions. Here is your personal walkie-talkie each. They can reach up to fifteen to twenty miles. You'll also have a code button to press to report. Now, this plane will land sixty miles from our drop zone, then we will climb abroad on the Sea Stallion and fly fifty-five miles from the hot spot of our mission. You will take the Harley, and I'll keep the deuce and a quarter and I'll park a mile from the hot spot. When it's the time for me to come, I'll be waiting on y'all's call. The Boogeyman and the Big Badass Wolf will take care of the chopper and plane. Are we clear on this mission, soldiers?"

All of them said at the same time, "Sir, yes, sir."

The plane landed, and everybody got out of the Lockheed C-5 Galaxy and took the Sea Stallion out of the C-5 Galaxy. They flew it fifty-five miles and landed five miles from the hot spot. The chopper landed, and the doors opened up, with Captain Apocalypse saying, "Not yet, soldiers. As soon as it hits dark, then we move. We'll have approximately eleven and a half hours to get there, go into a battle with these murdering sons of bitches. We want to show these fuckers that we love our country and our people. This will let the rest of those motherfuckers know that they're fucking with the best. Now, set your watches to 0525. After that, we will meet back here and get back to our chopper and then to our plane, and then we go home, soldiers. We have to get our soldiers, Sergeants! Am I clear, Sergeants?"

All of them said at the same time, "Sir, yes, sir, Captain!"

Captain Apocalypse said, "I CAN'T HEAR YOU!"

They all said, very loudly, this time, "SIR, YES, SIR, CAPTAIN APOCALYPSE, SIR!"

Captain Apocalypse said, "Here is y'all's positions once you get there, and I want you all to report by clicking me your number on the walkie-talkie. I want each of you to count to 'three Mississippi' before you click after one person, and I want all of y'all to do that in order of your number. Now, after I get all of y'alls clicks, then I'll click four, then two, then three. Then I want y'all to let it storm with bullets on those sons-of-bitches soldiers."

Captain Apocalypse looked down at his watch and said out loud, "MOVE OUT! MOVE IT! MOVE, MOVE IT!"

They climbed on their Harleys with their night vision goggles on, cranking up their Harleys, coming out of the Sea Stallion helicopter. They were not riding on the road; they were riding through the woods and tall bushes in all black. About twenty-six minutes later, they had made it to their position on their Harleys. They walked about seventeen yards, and that was when they saw about forty to fifty Congo soldiers sitting over there, laughing and having fun. They all clicked one at a time, checking in with the captain after counting three Mississippi. Captain Apocalypse hit his buttons 4-2-3. "The No-Name Unit" opened hell's fire on those Congo soldiers as they fired back at the No-Name Unit. This battle just began. It was 1824, but as all those shots were fired, a lot of people would've thought that we were firing. All those soldiers fought against them as if they were rookies or they were very good at what they did. They knew this wasn't ground zero, where they were holding the soldiers at. So they continued marching in a horseshoe formation, and they could see in the distance where twelve or fourteen people were hanging off this giant homemade horse-thing. As they came closer, gunshots rang out at them. Now they understood why they called this place Hell's Valley. They returned fire at them, backing their cases up, but they were surrounded and pinned down. And that was when number

12, Sergeant Destroyer, got hit in the gut and in the right shoulder. Numbers 11 and 13 both were yelling in their mechanical voice, "Twelve down, Twelve down!"

Captain Apocalypse said in a commanding, mechanical voice, "NO FUCKING PITY, SOLDIER! NOW, GET OUR SOLDIERS OUT OF THERE AND BRING THEM HOME! NOW THAT'S AN ORDER!"

Eleven said, "You heard him—NO PITY! NO FUCKING PITY!"

Little did Eleven know that Captain Apocalypse wasn't talking to them about having no pity; he was in fact calling Sergeant Destroyer, with the real code name of No Pity, which he was the one who gave him. Sergeant Destroyer waited until Eleven and Thirteen went back to their shooting position, because he knew that Captain Apocalypse had been telling him to get these soldiers out, as well as the ones they were fighting for now. He dragged a Congo soldier in his place and circled about nine Congo soldiers, killing them by shooting them all in the head, neck, back, stomach, chest, and face. He saw some fire coming out of the ground when he eased over there, and threw three pineapple hand grenades in there, killing five more of the Congo soldiers. He then climbed a tree halfway to the top with his Japanese Arisaka 37 sniper rifle, shooting and killing the main soldiers in those towers. He killed four gunmen, then three inside the gates and five outside it.

He turned his attention back to where the No-Name Unit was still under fire, and he eased out of the tree, watching these Congo soldiers still firing wildly up in the trees, wanting to hit the sniper. Sergeant Destroyer went into his duffel bag and took out his Thompson .30-caliber tommy gun and his AK-47, walking up and killing ten or twelve more of the Congo soldiers. He went back to his duffel bag, and before he got there, he saw three soldiers standing around it, one of them kicking it with his feet, and when they looked up and noticed him, Sergeant Destroyer shot each of them at least twenty times with his AK-47. He then climbed back up in the tree, looking at his teammates still in their position. He saw three people firing still at them, and he then shot one in the neck, the second one in the heart, and the third one in the temple. He got on his radio and said in a mechanical voice, "This is number 12, Sergeant Destroyer.

It's clear. You can come in. Your path has been cleared. Look sixty-five yards up and high a little to the left very carefully, then you'll see me. Click if you all can see me."

They all clicked, and he returned their clicks. Now they knew it was truly him.

When they made it, they saw about eighty to a hundred bodies. They saw him in the tree, and number 6 and number 15 climbed up in another tree as well; just like number 12, they were snipers. Numbers 6 and 15 took their sniper rifle out and their M79 grenades launchers and their AK-47, with twenty pineapple hand grenades. Seven had a Thompson .30-caliber tommy gun with a grenade launcher. Two of them took their M79 and forty pineapple hand grenades.

The hell's fire went on for about two and a half hours or a little more. The last two Congo soldiers were still alive, and with them were the 250-pound lions. Number 12 heard and saw them, and he said in his mechanical voice, "No PITY!" killing both of the lions by shooting them in the head. They all hit their buttons, letting the captain know that everything was all clear. These soldiers were walking in a bloody mud with body parts and bones all around them, the stench of death heavy in the air. The soldiers that they came to get were there along with a hundred more soldiers from other countries, and the news reporters. They took all these people out of this place as prisoners of war, taking them to safety so they could be picked up.

They could hear their captain coming with the deuce and a quarter-truck. They knew they had at least two hours to get off this no-man's territorial place. Captain Apocalypse backed the truck in as numbers 4 and 18 let the gate down, the other soldiers standing guard for Captain Apocalypse. After loading all of them up, the Big Badass Wolf pulled down a homemade steel door that they made to protect those suffering soldiers and news reporters. The Big Badass Wolf was sitting back there with three M79 grenade launcher. The Boogeyman was at the Sea Stallion, waiting for them to make it as he was ready to go. All of them got on their Harleys and escorted Captain Apocalypse back to the chopper. It was six at the back, three on each side, and six in the front of him. They all were going about seventy miles per hour.

When they made it to the Sea Stallion helicopter, Captain Apocalypse backed the truck into the chopper, all the Harleys going in, nine on each side. The Big Badass Wolf jumped out off the truck and got up front in the chopper, closing the back door to the Sea Stallion. Twenty-nine minutes later, the chopper made it to the Lockheed C-5 Galaxy. The No-Name Unit would not forget about the bodies that they had seen on their way back to the chopper. They knew Captain Apocalypse and the Big Badass Wolf had gone through a battle themselves, because there were at least forty dead bodies lying there. The Big Badass Wolf and the Boogeyman took the C-5 Galaxy off the ground, and as soon as they were up in the air, the other Congo soldiers were pulling up to stop them. But they were twenty-six minutes too damn late. They had now seventy-seven hours to make it home.

Captain Apocalypse got some food and water and gave it to the soldiers. One of the American soldiers wanted to take Captain Apocalypse's ski mask off, but he stopped him, saying, "Soldier, you're not allowed to see any of our faces. I know you want to know who we are. We are somebody, but nobody knows. We don't have names, so don't worry or be afraid." He explained this to the soldier in a mechanical voice.

As they came over the Pacific Ocean, they found a big open land on Hawaii Island and landed Lockheed C-5 Galaxy there. The Big Badass Wolf and the Boogeyman let the door down on the C-5 Galaxy, and then that of the Sea Stallion. Captain Apocalypse then backed the deuce and a quarter out of the Sea Stallion, leaving the Big Badass Wolf and the Boogeyman back at the plane and chopper. Captain Apocalypse and his sergeants made it to the main hospital as people looked at them, wondering what was going on. The police had not said anything to them, noticing that these were United States soldiers. When they finally made it to the hospital, the doctors, nurses, and other staff members ran out with gurneys, taking all the soldiers inside the hospital, with police officers helping them.

Captain Apocalypse got back in his truck, and his sergeants got on their Harleys, leaving all those people inside the hospital. They pulled up in front of the police station and went in to talk to the chief of police. All the people that were standing out there started fearing for their lives because they thought the soldiers were terrorists. About twenty-nine to thirty police officers ran out of the police station, and two police helicopters were up in the air. As the police were being placed in formation, the American soldiers stood there with blood and cuts all on them, waist-high. They were not panicking like the police officers; they were just standing there, knowing that they could not fire on these police officers.

Captain Apocalypse said in a loud, mechanical voice, "Attention!" All his sergeants stood up in a salute at their captain. Captain Apocalypse continued, "I am Captain Apocalypse, and these are my sergeants. We were the United States Marines. I am looking for Chief Chou."

Chief Chou responded, "I am he. What can I do for you?" Fear was all on his face.

Captain Apocalypse said, "Take this note to your head supervisor of authority, and I'm pretty sure that they are waiting for this information. Call them and they'll call the United States, the mainland, and I'm positive that the United States would be here before they could hang the phone up."

Chief Chou said, "Then who shall I say gave me this intel? Who are you? Why can't you relay this information to your authority?"

Captain Apocalypse responded, "Maybe I should, but, Chief Chou, I can't report my name to you besides the one that I have given you. For your second question, I got a soldier with a gunshot wound to the guts and shoulder, and I have taken him to the hospital before he dies. And for your last question, I can relay this information if I choose, but I landed in your land and the prisoners of war that have been in Belgian Congo are in your hospital, all a hundred and fifteen or sixteen, give or take a few bags of human remain and clothes with plenty of names on them. We have to go now. We have done our part, so please, do your part for your country. I'm sure that some of those prisoners of war are some of yours as well." He then turned around, saying in a loud, mechanical voice, "At ease, soldiers. Mount up!"

As they started up their Harleys, the captain started up his truck and pulled off, the Harleys escorting him. All the people were standing there in shock, as they hadn't seen anything like this before in real life—maybe on TV, but not in person like this. Chief Chou called the authority's number, and those people called the Navy base, and the Navy base talked to the authority. They sent multiple people to the hospital along with news reporters reporting live, and the Navy base connected with the authority in the United States, the mainland, and told them what had just happened. The United States authority said, "We are on our way."

All the authorities wanted to know who in the hell had brought these people here. Police Chief Chou, his officers, and some of the civilians tried to explain it to them, but they still did not believe them. The chief, his officers, and those civilians knew what they heard and saw this was done in broad daylight. The news reporters wondered why these people did not call and report this incident that they were claiming.

Chief Chou said, "How can you get on the phone when it's happening in a span of a split second? And these guys are fully armed, covered in what may or may not be blood and guts all over them, and dressed as if they were some terrorists but giving you the right information about his authority. He and the eighteen soldiers that were with him, I do believe they could've killed all of us without any injury to them. So you ask me why I did not report it as it was happening?"

One of the officers inside was taking pictures while they were standing out there, talking, and he took pictures until they left. He came out and said, "Chief Chou, I have all that on my camera. I have everything on it. I took the pictures because I didn't want this to go undocumented for the books."

Chief Chou took the camera and gave it to the reporter, saying, "Report this! You'll see what we have all seen, and you'll see why I did what I did. You'll be shocked just as we were in the state of shock, with chills running over our bodies."

The news reporter left with the camera, and when he finished developing the films, that was when he opened the door and was about to reply, "Hey, you re—,"

All of a sudden, there was a person dressed in all black from head to toe, with a mechanical voice, standing six foot five and weighing 280 pounds, with guns, hand grenades, and bloodlike stains on his clothing. The film developer looked for everybody else, but they were not within sight. The person that sounded mechanical said, "You have something that belongs to me. May I have it, please?"

The film developer gave him the pictures and the camera. Then, the developer heard a noise behind him, so he took a quick look, and when he turned back around, he was gone. The developer still didn't know what happened to the other people that were working just prior to him developing those films, all of ten minutes.

Five minutes after the Boogeyman left, all the other people came out of their hiding places, as they were instructed to do or die. The Boogeyman was back at the plane before Captain Apocalypse and the No-Name Unit soldiers, and as they made it back, the Boogeyman said to his captain, "Captain Apocalypse, this is for you, sir, and there isn't anything else, and if there is, then I'll do my sworn duties as the name that I uphold, sir."

Captain Apocalypse responded, "It's nothing else, and I do believe that you would do it to soldier. Now, let us go home and get number 12 to bed so that he can get some rest before our next mission.

CHAPTER 3

It was August 1, 1958, fourteen months later, and the No-Name Unit was out training for their next mission. Sergeant Destroyer's bullet wounds had healed completely, as if they did not affect him at all. As they were all out training, their walkie-talkies were clicking for all of them to report in. Captain Apocalypse knew who it was but never saw the face of the person who gave them the intel for their mission.

All nineteen of them made it inside and went into their rooms to get cleaned up. That was when they saw this big ten-by-ten yellow manila envelope on their tables. The captain went to his table and stood there, saying in his mechanical voice, "Team, we have a mission ahead of us, and I know that you all are hungry, so be patient and you'll be eating a small snack soon."

As the team went back into their room, Captain Apocalypse picked up the dining room phone and said, "This is Captain Apocalypse, your captain. I need for you all to place a nice snack on these tables ASAP. Thank you, soldiers, for your service." He then hung up the phone, leaving the dining room area with their envelopes still on the tables.

When the soldiers came back to eat, they saw a basket sitting next to their table on the left and a food tray sitting on the right, with their meals and whatever they were drinking on that tray. Each soldier took their envelope off the table at the same time they were sitting down to eat. As they finished eating, they all took their envelopes out of their baskets and reported to their conference room. Captain Apocalypse turned the lights off and turned the slide projector on, the slides showing the pictures of the US Embassy in Quezon City in the Philippines. As they watched this film, they also showed men and women with bullet holes in their bodies and heads. They saw thirteen to seventeen men and twelve to fifteen women all who are shot up with bullets. Some of them had half of their heads blown off. This bloody bath was a war that happened inside The US Embassy. They saw bloody prints of shoes and boots all through the embassy. There was so much blood, so many bodies, that you could not avoid stepping in or on the bodies to investigate what the terrorists were after in the embassy.

Captain Apocalypse said in his mechanical voice, "Open up your envelopes and you'll see what they came after and took. We have to retrieve what they stole and annihilate anyone who participated in this act of terrorism. The first two that are going into this mission to find us a command post will be Sergeant Big Badass Wolf and Sergeant Boogeyman. You two are going to get a fresh start on these people that we're after. We have three people that we can get and give us the location to their place. These people do not care about themselves, so we know that they don't care about killing us and civilians out there in the streets. I want the Big Badass Wolf and the Boogeyman to find us a command post in the city so we can set up and watch these three in order to find their location and destroy it and them altogether. We will deploy at 0100. Get yourself together. We will be using silencers on all our weapons and the reason is that we have to have it done quickly, quietly, and sufficiently. We don't want any hostages on this mission. Do I make myself clear, team?"

All of them said at the same time in a mechanical voice, "Sir, yes, sir! Captain Apocalypse, sir."

Captain Apocalypse said, "Move out!"

They all got up from the briefing room table and went to the tunnel door and lined up in a single file, waiting for their captain. Captain Apocalypse opened the door to the tunnel as he went first, pulling his night vision googles on his face, climbing on his Harley, as did the rest of the team. They made it to the end of the tunnel and got on the elevator shaft that now could carry all of them down at once. Sergeant Big Badass Wolf and Sergeant Boogeyman took the deuce and a quarter out of the Sea Stallion as it was not a part of this mission. As the team came down to the Lockheed C-5 Galaxy, Sergeant Big Badass Wolf and Sergeant Boogeyman were waiting for them, saluting Captain Apocalypse. They turned around and saluted the flag at the end of the elevator shaft. Captain Apocalypse said, "Load up and let's go get what needs to be gotten!"

All of them loaded up, and the Boogeyman and the Big Badass Wolf took off into the air, flying high on their way to Quezon City in the Philippines.

Captain Apocalypse said, "The paperwork that these people have stolen is very important. These papers have some information on the whereabouts of a prototype of an aircraft carrier that is carrying some sarin nerve gas. This prototype is in the USS *Enterprise*, the first nuclear-powered aircraft carrier. We have to take it back, as I said earlier, and also those who took those papers and stole this thing have to be annihilated."

They all were concentrating on their plane as Sergeant Boogeyman came in the back and said, "Captain Apocalypse, we'll be landing in thirty-one hours."

Captain Apocalypse replied, "Here are your and Sergeant Big Badass Wolf's plans once we get there, Sergeant."

Sergeant Boogeyman saluted him and went back there as they meditated on it very carefully.

Captain Apocalypse picked up two small bags and took them up front, giving one to the Big Badass Wolf and the other one to the Boogeyman. He said, "These are silencers for each of your weapons. You do know what to do with them, right, soldiers?" The captain then walked back and gave the rest of the soldiers their silencers, saying to them, "Be sure that the silencers are on all your guns once we land, and if they don't fit, then let me know."

They had flown twenty-eight to thirty hours when the Boogeyman said, "We're about to land, so buckle up, team."

As they landed on the Philippine Islands, the C-5 Galaxy then took the Sea Stallion out of it, along with their Harleys 250cc inside of it, and took off, going to the US Naval Base Subic Bay. The No-Name Unit flew for at least forty-five to fifty minutes, and it was about to get dark out. It was 1822 when they finally went inside the Navy Base so they could be recognized and briefed on what they needed to know. Captain Apocalypse with his twenty soldiers stood at attention to the admiral of the fleet, Admiral Kenneth "Powerhouse" Sloan III.

Admiral Sloan said, "Gentlemen, at ease, and I do mean *at ease*, soldiers. You can remove your face gear now as your secret's safe with us."

Captain Apocalypse then said in a mechanical voice, "Admiral Sloan, sir. We thank you for the vote of confidence, but we are what you're seeing, sir. These are our faces, sir."

Admiral Sloan replied, "Captain, we understand that your and your team's identities need to be kept from the world, but not from your superior officer, soldier."

Captain Apocalypse said, "Admiral Sloan, sir, I am Captain Apocalypse, and all these men are my sergeants. The only persons who know what they look like and who they are are my sergeants, and it'll remain like that, Admiral Sloan, sir. As I said, I am Captain Apocalypse, and these here eighteen soldiers are my sergeants, and we'll be on your rosters as of now until we finish our mission and leave you. You will cooperate with us, sir. Here is your roll call. Call them out and they'll step forward, sir!"

Admiral Sloan said, "Sergeant Lowlife, Sergeant Rattler, Sergeant Shadow, Sergeant Tornado, Sergeant Illusionist, Sergeant Consequence, Sergeant Evil, Sergeant Eliminate, Sergeant Fatal, Sergeant Furious, Sergeant Destroyer, Sergeant Hectic, Sergeant Hocus-Pocus, Sergeant Maniac, Sergeant Nuclear, Sergeant Polarize, Sergeant Animosity, Sergeant Boogeyman, and Sergeant Big Badass Wolf."

Admiral Sloan looked at this roll call log and at his crew, then back at the roll call log and at his crew again, and said to Captain Apocalypse, "What are these names all about? And what unit are you and your crew on back at your home base in the USA?"

Captain Apocalypse replied, "We are from the No-Name Unit, sir. You'll be getting a phone call in a few seconds, sir."

Admiral Sloan said, "How in the hell do you know that, uh…uh…uh…?"

"Captain Apocalypse, sir."

Admiral Sloan then continued, "How do you know that, Captain Apocalypse?"

Captain Apocalypse said, "Because we touch down on your turf and you're busy holding me from doing what we have been sent here to do. Your job is to tell us to bring your aircraft carrier back at all costs and not one question asked. What you really need to understand is what you actually don't understand. I am not going to go over your head, sir, because I respect all my ranking superiors, but some very dangerous people have stolen something from you and your country, and we're here to get it back from them or destroy it. What is your poison, sir?"

Admiral Sloan was about to speak, but Vice Admiral Timothy "Be Still" Skyler said, "Admiral Sloan, the phone is for you, sir. It's the US calling."

Admiral Sloan received the phone and asked, "This is Admiral Sloan. What can I do for you, sir?" As the admiral of the fleet was on the phone, he kept saying over and over and over, "Yes, sir. Yes, sir. I understand, sir. No problem, sir. No questions also, sir. No, sir. I do understand, Commander in Chief. Yes, sir. Thank you, sir. Goodbye, sir."

As the admiral of the fleet passed the phone back to Vice Admiral Skyler, he said to Captain Apocalypse "Captain Apocalypse, "Please accept my deepest apologies with a thousand pardons. I apologize for my questionable curiosity toward you and your team. Please do accept my humble apology. Room 185 is open to you and your men, and you will not be disturbed, sir."

Captain Apocalypse and his twenty men saluted Admiral Sloan at the same time as he said, "Thank you, Admiral Sloan, sir. You won't be disappointed, sir." They all then left the presence of the admiral of the fleet, with Captain Apocalypse leading them.

Vice Admiral Skyler asked, "Admiral Sloan, what is this all about, sir?"

Admiral Sloan said, "These soldiers are without a name but the names on this here roster. These guys are some who don't ask questions no matter how dangerous their mission is. They just want the order and go carry it out. They are the commander in chief's right hand, and they don't let the left hand know what the right hand is doing. So whoever they are, we should just be very thankful that they're on our side, because we most definitely do not want these soldiers to be our enemies."

Vice Admiral Skyler said, "Admiral Sloan, these guys are not above you, sir. Why did you allow this insubordination, sir? You're an admiral, and he's just a captain, sir."

Admiral Sloan replied, "With the words you're using toward these soldiers, Vice Admiral, you're being insubordinate, because though he is just a captain, he's a captain our commander in chief salutes and lets loose to the United States' problems. If there is a guerilla warfare with any type of combat, then they're the ones who seek and destroy that problem as if it never happened. Look at their names, because that lists their specialties. Now, Vice Admiral Skyler, are we clear on this, that it never happened and we never saw anything? If you look at the chart listing them, then you'll see that they aren't in this country."

Admiral Sloan just dropped his head as his vice admiral watched. He was about to say something when Admiral Sloan said loudly, "It's over, Vice Admiral. It's over! Leave it alone before you get court-martialed. It's over son. It's over." He then closed the door behind him.

The vice admiral thought to himself, *Who in the hell are these people? Who is their ranking superior? What the hell?* He, too, left, but going in a different direction.

Captain Apocalypse and his team, meanwhile, were in the conference room with their plans and speaking in their mechanical voices. Captain Apocalypse said, "Sergeant Boogeyman and Sergeant Big Badass Wolf, I want you two to go in the city and find us a command post on the highest ground possible. Once you get it situated, clean it up so we won't trip over anything. I'll then have Sergeant Illusionist, Sergeant Shadow, and Sergeant Hocus-Pocus follow these three perpetrators, and once everything is set up, then you let them know so that they can keep an eye on them. Do you five understand the assignment?"

They all saluted the captain, letting him know that they understood their duties. As they all left the conference room, going to their Harleys with the pictures of the three perpetrators from the intel, the captain said, "Hey, don't let these guys see y'all, and, Sergeant Boogeyman and Sergeant Big Badass Wolf, keep an eye on them. You can't afford to let them fade away from you. Now, let's get these motherfuckers!"

Captain Apocalypse then said, "Sergeant Animosity, Sergeant Fatal, and Sergeant Consequence, I want you three to go into the sewer and find all these streets and mark the manhole covers so that we know where we're at on our location. See how much water and sludge are in it so we can clean some of it out to keep from messing up our Harleys. We will be using it as part of our getaway. If you need more help, then we can manage that also, so you three go start on that now."

Captain Apocalypse then debriefed the other thirteen soldiers on what they were going to be doing for the next seven hours. He said, "We're going to the embassy, and I want you all not to be seen. We have to go and take a look at what we're up against. I want to go through this with a fine-tooth comb. Don't leave anything unturned or unnoticed. This place was indeed a massacre. So each one take this picture and look at what you can see, then I want you all to tell me if you learn anything. If you see what I see and learn what I've learned, then we all know what to do. So mount up and let's move out."

As Captain Apocalypse turned off the lights and the slide projector, all thirteen of them left out, with Captain Apocalypse leading the way. It was 0330 when they went to the embassy through dark alleys on their Harleys. Very few people saw this, but they thought they were just members of those little young punk gangs that needed to be home and ready for school the next morning.

When they made it to the embassy, Captain Apocalypse ordered Sergeant Evil, Sergeant Lowlife, Sergeant Nuclear, Sergeant Tornado, and Sergeant Destroyer secure the premises; Sergeant Destroyer and Sergeant Evil got on top of the embassy as Sergeant Nuclear,

Sergeant Lowlife, and Sergeant Tornado took ground level. Captain Apocalypse, Sergeant Polarize, Sergeant Hectic, Sergeant Furious, Sergeant Maniac, Sergeant Eliminate, Sergeant Flood, and Sergeant Rattler then all went inside.

They all had been there for at least three hours and forty-five minutes, and they could see that dawn had caught up with them. They brought all their Harleys inside as Captain Apocalypse got on his walkie-talkie, saying, "All of you who are out in the field, dig in deep like a tick on a hound. Report every thirty minutes until we meet back up. Clear."

As he cleared himself, each one took turns sleeping and standing guard in their little squad. They had to fight hunger pangs as they could smell the aroma of food in the air but couldn't give up their position.

Meanwhile, the Big Badass Wolf and the Boogeyman watched one of the three guys all day, seeing where he went until he did a disappearing act for at least six and a half hours. He was wondering what the hell this asshole could be doing off the grid for six and a half hours. Hell, for even just an hour! That had to be one boring-ass day for this guy. He noticed that this guy was wearing different clothes, but this did not break his concentration on this dude.

It was now 1423, and the soldiers were wondering when they would eat. Captain Apocalypse knew that they were hungry and were just keeping quiet about it, so Captain Apocalypse said on the walkie-talkie, "I know that you soldiers are hungry, as am I, but we have things to do and some of us cannot get to any food without giving up our positions. So when one eats, then we all eat." He clicked off the walkie-talkie after that.

Later, Captain Apocalypse and his crew got all the databases that they had found. Sergeant Destroyer found a folder upside down as if someone had been running with it and dropped it. He looked at it and saw that these papers had the names of five University of the Philippines scientists on it. Two of these scientists were multilingual, speaking Tagalog, Japanese, and Russian. One spoke English and Tagalog, and the other two spoke Tagalog only. After the sergeant had looked at it, he went to Captain Apocalypse and said, "Captain, I just found this upside down. Look very closely at their names, occupations, and specialties. I do believe that our terrorists were searching for some translators for this big-ass weapon, sir."

Captain Apocalypse replied, "We need to put somebody on these five ASAP because they are the ones that can make these fuckers' mission possible. Good job, Sergeant Destroyer." Captain Apocalypse then added, "Sergeant Boogeyman and Sergeant Big Badass Wolf, respond ASAP!"

Sergeant Boogeyman picked up his walkie-talkie and said, "This is the Boogeyman. I'm here, Captain Apocalypse."

Captain Apocalypse told him, "We have found five scientists that work at the University of the Philippines, which is on R-7 Highway near Quezon Memorial Circle. Can you find that location with those strong eyes in the position you're in? Can you spot it from the distance you two are at?"

Sergeant Boogeyman said, "Let me see, Captain. You said it's on R-7 near Quezon Memorial Circle, right, sir?"

Captain Apocalypse replied, "Yes."

Sergeant Boogeyman then went silent for a minute or a minute and a half, then said, "Captain Apocalypse, that is affirmative, sir. I have eyes on both sides and the front, but not as clear as it should be, and I also cannot see around the back at all, sir."

Captain Apocalypse said, "Well, we cannot win them all, Sergeant. Just watch what you can watch."

When they both signed off on the walkie-talkie, the Big Badass Wolf said, "Captain Apocalypse, this is Sergeant Big Badass Wolf. I can get a closer look without being seen or giving up our position, to see what position we can take to see if those targets are still there or not."

Captain Apocalypse said, "Check it out and report ASAP." Then they both signed off.

The Big Badass Wolf then took off on his journey. As he got down to the basement of the building of their command post, he saw two policemen sitting on the hood of their cars as if they were taking a break. He, too, just sat there, listening to them talk in Tagalog. They were not trying to leave anytime soon, it appeared. By the time he had sat there for twenty-eight to thirty minutes, he thought to himself, *Man, I got to get these little sons of bitches out of my way, but how? I guess there comes a time when a person has to leave their lives behind for a day or two. Don't kill them, Big Badass Wolf. Just put up with them for a second.*

As he was about to kidnap them, that was when they were both called back to the police station. The Big Badass Wolf whispered, "Saved by the police radio," as they left, and the Big Badass Wolf went forward with his journey. When he got closer to see everything, all while he was deep into the darkest spot and couldn't be seen, he saw some newspaper on the newsstand with his high-powered binoculars, and it showed those five scientists in their lab coats. Though he couldn't read the writing, he knew it got to be the people that Captain Apocalypse was talking about. The Big Badass Wolf raised him up on the walkie-talkie, saying, "Captain Apocalypse, this is the Big Badass Wolf, and I'm reporting that your five people may have already been taken, sir."

Captain Apocalypse asked, "Can you confirm that, Sergeant?"

Sergeant Big Badass Wolf said, "Well, Captain, sir, I see five people in lab coats, and they are on the front page of the newspaper, and the number 3 under it with the words must say days. I cannot make out the language of the writing."

Captain Apocalypse ordered, "Stand guard." He then got on the embassy phone, calling back to US Naval Base Subic Bay, saying, "May I speak to Admiral Sloan?"

Admiral Sloan replied, "This is Admiral Sloan. What can I do for you, Captain?"

Captain Apocalypse asked, "Do you know if any scientists from the University of the Philippines are missing, sir?"

Admiral Sloan said, "Yes, three days ago now. Why do you ask? I'm sorry, Captain. I mean—"

Captain Apocalypse reassured him, "No need to apologize, sir. But we have a big problem. I'll fill you in when we return at 2000." He hung up the phone, and Captain Apocalypse got back on his walkie-talkie with the Big Badass Wolf and said, "Sergeant Big Badass

Wolf, it's them. Finish your setup for the command post. Now, stand down on the five scientists and continue with the person of interest."

Sergeant Big Badass Wolf responded, "Affirmative, sir. Signing off."

As the Big Badass Wolf made his way back to the basement of the building, the Boogeyman said, "Big Badass Wolf, this is the Boogeyman. Keep walking and don't look back. Don't make any sudden movements. Just keep walking until you come into the darkest area. Click your button twice if you understand."

The Big Badass Wolf clicked his button twice.

Sergeant Boogeyman continued, "Good. Now, once you get him in the dark, take him with you. Click your button if you agree."

The Big Badass Wolf clicked his button twice as he continued walking, making it back to the basement of the command post. The Big Badass Wolf kept walking very slowly, as if he didn't know that this police was behind him. As he was getting deeper into the basement, the police officer was getting a little afraid, but he refused to call this in to his superior. He stopped his car immediately and jumped out, speaking in Tagalog to the Big Badass Wolf. The Big Badass Wolf stopped and the officer said something else, but the Big Badass Wolf still did not understand what he said; he just put his hands high in the air as he stood there. The officer kept yelling in Tagalog as the Big Badass Wolf started walking backward until he made it to the police car. He then leaned forward and placed his face and body onto the car.

The police officer took out his handcuff, and the Big Badass Wolf could hear it jingling. When the officer put his hands on the Big Badass Wolf to cuff him, that was when the Big Badass Wolf said, "Sorry, little guy, but you have to sacrifice yourself for your country," in a mechanical voice. He then maneuvered himself about, throwing the police officer up against the car, making him drop his gun and knocking him out without breaking his jaw. The Big Badass Wolf stood at six foot one and weighed at 285 pounds, while this officer was five foot two and weighed 152 at the most.

After the Big Badass Wolf put the cuff on him and gagged his mouth, he drove his car deeper into the basement, hiding it from anyone who might come in here. He hid the car well and picked up the officer, carrying him up ten floors and placing him in one of the office rooms. The Big Badass Wolf went on up to the very last floor, on the twenty-fifth floor of this condemned building. As he made it up top, the Boogeyman said, "Can it be useful?"

The Big Badass Wolf replied, "The car and radio can be useful. We can drive through the streets and people will avoid us, and we'd be able to ride past places and check them out."

The Boogeyman just nodded his approval as he started back looking through his telescope and high-powered binoculars. He was looking at this guy still just wandering out there, not knowing that he was being watched. The Big Badass Wolf raised the captain on the radio. "Captain Apocalypse, this is the Big Badass Wolf, sir."

Captain Apocalypse replied, "This is the captain. Go ahead, Big Badass Wolf."

The Big Badass Wolf said, "Captain Apocalypse, we have a very important star that we need to keep in the sky and let it glow at the end like it should, sir. We just need a book to let it rest under its own story, sir."

Captain Apocalypse responded, "Understand. You will have everything you need in order to make it to the end, Sergeant. And good job, soldiers." Then he got off the walkie-talkie.

Captain Apocalypse then said to Sergeant Hectic and Sergeant Maniac, "When the lights go off, I want you two to take to Sergeant Big Badass Wolf and Sergeant Boogeyman the whole entire living supplies. Do you need instructions on what needs to be done and how it's supposed to be done?"

They both said at the same time, "Understand, Captain Apocalypse, sir."

Captain Apocalypse looked at his watch and saw that it was now 2212. He pushed his button, 4-3-3, and all the soldiers that were in their positions understood that was code for them to move out and return to the base. The Big Badass Wolf and The Boogeyman had to stay where they were at, however, as they had company and had these three guys under surveillance. As the others made it back to Subic Bay, Admiral Sloan met them at the door.

Captain Apocalypse said, "Admiral Sloan, sir, I need some supplies, if it is okay with you, sir."

Admiral Sloan replied, "Captain Apocalypse, anything and everything you want is at your disposal. Whatever you need, it's yours with no questions asked. Take whatever you need. I have everything you want, I'm sure of that, Captain."

Captain Apocalypse said, "Thanks, Admiral Sloan, sir. May I call you Admiral Powerhouse, sir?"

Admiral Sloan concurred. "Sure, Captain. You can call me that."

Captain Apocalypse threw up a salute, as did his eighteen sergeants, and all of them said at once, "Thank you, Admiral Powerhouse, sir." They then started marching off in a single file behind Captain Apocalypse.

Admiral Sloan said to Vice Admiral Skyler, "Whatever those soldiers are about to do will be marked down in history and talked about for a very long time. This will be the story to tell other soldiers about whenever they need an uplift. Do you agree, Vice Admiral Be Still?"

He said, "Sir, yes, sir, Admiral Powerhouse, sir."

They both then left smiling, going in the same direction.

As Captain Apocalypse and his team, meanwhile, were walking off, Captain Apocalypse said, "Sergeant Hectic and Sergeant Maniac, get one of those big warehouse trucks and load it up with a sleeping cot, a fan, a miniature freezer, a hot plate, a television set, a radio, and lots of groceries and take it to the Big Badass Wolf and the Boogeyman. Let them also know that we will be there later, and while you're there, take the manhole lid up and let it be halfway off, then find a barricade to place over it so that it'll be our way to the headquarters and so we can leave our Harleys in the sewer. Do you understand, Sergeants?"

They both said at the same time, "Sir, yes, sir, Captain Apocalypse, sir!" then left to collect the things that they were told to get.

Four and a half hours passed by, and Sergeant Hectic and Sergeant Maniac had picked everything that was on the list and had loaded them up on the truck to take to the Big Badass Wolf and the Boogeyman. They then took off in the truck as Sergeant Hectic escorted Sergeant Maniac on his Harley. Sergeant Maniac said on his walkie-talkie, "Sergeant Boogeyman, this is Sergeant Maniac. Pick up."

Sergeant Boogeyman said, "This is the Boogeyman, Sergeant Maniac. Go ahead."

Sergeant Maniac continued, "I have a truckful of supplies that you need, and Sergeant Hectic and I are five minutes away in a Subic Bay base truck. I need one of y'all to come down and help unload it."

Sergeant Boogeyman said, "The Big Badass Wolf will come down to help." He then signed off his walkie-talkie.

Minutes later, they finally made it to the command post. They had already called ahead to Sergeant Boogeyman and Sergeant Big Badass Wolf so they wouldn't get fired upon. Sergeant Hectic pulled up on his Harley, riding with his night vision goggles on, and gave Sergeant Maniac the okay to come inside. They parked the truck and Harley and could see the Big Badass Wolf walking toward them to help them unload this truck and take everything up a flight of stairs because the elevator was out of order. They knew it would take them a while to get everything up there if they had to do it this way.

Sergeant Manic got on his walkie-talkie and said, "Captain Apocalypse, this is Sergeant Maniac."

Captain Apocalypse replied, "This is Captain Apocalypse. Go ahead, Sergeant Maniac."

Sergeant Maniac informed him, "Sir, the elevator is out of order here, but I believe Sergeant Consequence and Sergeant Nuclear can fix it if you send them, sir. They both know how to make electrical things work, even on a bootleg level. They also are two good-ass electricians. We have here an out-of-order elevator, and I'm positive that they can fix it, sir, if you can send them down here."

Captain Apocalypse said, "If they can, then you'll have them ASAP."

They both signed off their walkie-talkies after that.

Captain Apocalypse asked Sergeant Consequence and Sergeant Nuclear, "Do either of you know how to rewire an elevator so that we can use it with our supplies?"

They both said, "Sir, yes, sir."

Sergeant Consequence said, "Sir, we were the ones who fixed our elevator shaft back at the unit. Yes, we can have this done probably by an hour or two at the most."

Captain Apocalypse said, "I'll take a little electricity for a room with no windows on the same floor as our command post. Can you make that happen?"

They both said, "Yes, sir, Captain Apocalypse."

Captain Apocalypse ordered them, "Move out." They then left, going to the command post very fast, as time was not on their side. They only acted in the dark, but two could go in the daytime as it was the specialties for which they had been trained for their missions.

Sergeant Consequence and Sergeant Nuclear made it to the command post to meet up with Sergeant Maniac and Sergeant Hectic. They went to the box of the building and saw that it had some hot wires still in connection to the power source. Sergeant Nuclear ripped a hundred feet of wire out of the wall and coiled it up, then spliced it for Sergeant Consequence and Sergeant Consequence. He then ran it into the box as they both looked at each other and at Sergeant Maniac and Sergeant Hectic. He said, "Put your stuff on the elevator." When they did, Sergeant Nuclear said, "Going up!"

As the stuff was going up, Sergeant Hectic went to Sergeant Boogeyman and Sergeant Big Badass Wolf. "It's on its way," Sergeant Nuclear said on his walkie-talkie to Sergeant Boogeyman and Sergeant Big Badass Wolf. "The elevator is now working, and some of the things are already on their way up. The rest will be coming."

The Big Badass Wolf helped unload the elevator, while Sergeant Boogeyman still watched their target's every move.

In the meantime, Sergeant Hectic went out on the street and removed the manhole cover off the sewer, placing a barricade over it. He then clicked his button to let Captain Apocalypse know that it was done. Captain Apocalypse clicked back to him. Sergeant Hectic came back inside and finished helping them carry the rest of the supplies up to the top floor. The Big Badass Wolf, Sergeant Hectic, Sergeant Maniac, Sergeant Consequence, and Sergeant Nuclear fixed the room up with the cot, freezer, TV, hot plate, and radio. Sergeant

Big Badass Wolf went to the tenth floor and escorted the police officer up to that room, as he was very afraid of these guys, who looked like terrorists and that were fucking giants.

When they opened the door to let him in his room, his little fear left him, especially when he saw how it looked. He still wanted his freedom, but he knew that they weren't going to give it to him. He couldn't understand why they hadn't spoken to him, as if they couldn't understand what he was saying to them. The officer came out of the corner of the room and put his hands up in a praying position and bowed his head, apparently thanking them as they all did the same thing. They all were eating as Sergeant Boogeyman watched their target. He looked through the telescope and through his high-powered binoculars, watching their subjects, since now two of them had met up. The Boogeyman was still watching when this police officer walked over there and gave them a big envelope, and the passenger of that van gave him some peso for what he gave them.

The Boogeyman said, "We got a crooked police in this game. We have to find us a translator that can speak Tagalog."

As he talked to the group about what he had just seen, Captain Apocalypse and the rest of the team came in with other needed equipment. They went to the six big long tables and laid out their briefing plans on what they were about to be doing.

Sergeant Boogeyman asked, "Permission to speak, Captain."

Captain Apocalypse replied, "Permission granted."

Sergeant Boogeyman said, "Captain, as we had these two perps on surveillance, a police officer went to their van and gave them a big envelope, and the perps gave him a sum of money."

Captain Apocalypse said, "Pick this rotten, sorry bastard up and bring his ass here and let us see how much this officer knows! Don't hurt him, though, just bring this fucker to me. As a matter of a fact, just leave that piece of shit where he's at, because if they don't see him, then there is no telling what will happen. Now, if we let him go, then he might tell. We already have one police officer, and we don't need another one. So just keep watching and following all the movement out there."

Captain Apocalypse and seven sergeants went to the room where they had the police officer in. He had been there now for two days. The officer knew they were not going to be killing him, as Captain Apocalypse just stared at him.

The officer asked in little but understandable English, "What have me done to you?"

Captain Apocalypse said in his mechanical voice, "Don't be afraid, Officer. Now, what did you say, Officer?"

The officer asked again, "What have me done to you? I do nothin' wrong."

Captain Apocalypse replied, "You did nothing wrong, Officer. We are soldiers who protect people and country. There are some very bad people in your country that are trying to kill billions of people, and we are here to stop them."

The other soldiers heard their captain talking to the officer, so they came closer to listen to them.

The officer said, "Me here to protect me people also. I am good police. Me no bad police."

Captain Apocalypse asked him, "What is your name?" pointing at himself then at the officer.

The officer responded, "Injema-Kin, Officer Injema-Kin."

Captain Apocalypse said, "Officer Injema-Kin, sir, we just want you to be as comfortable as we can allow you to be. Rest assured you will be returned to your job with a recommendation and paid status. You just keep all this to yourself, okay, sir?"

Officer Injema-Kin replied, "Yeah, sir, me understand. Me understand."

Captain Apocalypse looked at Sergeant Fatal and said, "Take his clothes and his car, and I want Sergeant Polarize in the trunk while you're driving. Take a tape recorder with you, and you both record your every move as you see Sergeant Fatal coming and going. Do you two understand your mission?"

Sergeant Fatal and Sergeant Polarize both said at the same time, "Sir, yes, sir."

Officer Injema-Kin gave Sergeant Fatal his uniform and went to sit down on his cot and started watching television, laughing at the show that was on. Captain Apocalypse knew that this officer was not trouble, as he figured when he first heard that Sergeant Big Badass Wolf and Sergeant Boogeyman had him in their custody. Sergeant Big Badass Wolf and Sergeant Boogeyman did not know that this officer could speak broken English and that he could speak and understand a little English until Captain Apocalypse was speaking to him. Before they left the room that Officer Injema-Kin was in, Captain Apocalypse walked in and whispered something to him, and he stood up and saluted him. Captain Apocalypse saluted him back and hugged him, then shook his hand and walked out of the door. His sergeants did not say a word; they would never question their captain, as he would never questioned them on their call whenever they made a judgment call.

Sergeant Fatal put on Officer Injema-Kin's uniform as he and Sergeant Polarize left with the police car, hearing the dispatcher speaking Tagalog, and not knowing what they were saying. They rode around by the place Sergeant Boogeyman told them they saw this guy was at for almost six hours. As they drove in the dark with their night vision goggles on, they went four miles per hour. Sergeant Fatal saw about ten or twelve men standing in a group in one spot. They truly didn't know that Sergeant Fatal could see them as clear as daylight moving around over there in the darkness. As they drove, he counted twelve over here in this spot, nine in this spot, seventeen over here in this area, five in a little shelter in front of it, four on each side of the building. He drove for a few more feet, then stopped the car as if something were wrong with it. As he got out and popped the hood open, Sergeant Polarize counted the ones on the top of the roof, making out from twenty to twenty-five people up there. Three were at the basement door as about thirty of them climbed up this thing that looked like a protection wall. It looked like they were preparing themselves for a firefight.

Sergeant Polarize clicked his walkie-talkie's button twice very fast as Sergeant Fatal made the engine start from under the hood. He then got in his car as a van with a bullet hole on the side fender came passing by very slowly. Sergeant Fatal turned his emergency lights and siren on, driving off very fast. Sergeant Polarize was looking at the windows in the building, watching people looking out of the windows. Sergeant Fatal drove in the direction of a rough type of place, but he detoured, going to his command post. He secretly made it back without another police seeing him in this car, knowing that the other officers might be looking for Officer Injema-Kin. Sergeant Fatal and Sergeant Polarize went up top and reported to their briefing table.

Sergeant Fatal said, "Captain Apocalypse, sir, we counted over a hundred people protecting the outside of this building, and Sergeant Polarize counted at least thirty climbing some kind of a protection wall that they got in there. He also counted plenty of them looking out of the windows as we were leaving. I estimate that there are at least two hundred to two hundred and fifty bad people in and out of that building, sir."

Captain Apocalypse replied, "Our intel tells us that it is exactly that many people, but we also have found a corrupt cop on the force. We need to find out if he is recruiting others or is doing this alone. Sergeant Boogeyman, know who he is, and I want you, Sergeant Boogeyman, to find out whom this guy is with after we take over their operation. He will be your subject."

As Sergeant Boogeyman saluted Captain Apocalypse. As he went back to watching their target, Captain Apocalypse said, "Sergeant Fatal, Sergeant Consequences, and Sergeant Animosity, did y'all find me an end to the tunnel?"

Sergeant Animosity said, "Yes, sir, Captain Apocalypse, sir. There are three ways, and a fourth one is way out there, probably at a landfill, sir. But we can come out right in the middle of our target, as you can see a big slab of concrete with a manhole sits on top of it. You can see it with our surveillance. You have six people sitting on it, sir."

Captain Apocalypse said, "With the manhole in front of our command post, can we use it to come up at the university without being seen coming out of it?"

Sergeant Fatal responded, "Sir, there is not one person out there at this time. Take a look now, sir."

As Captain Apocalypse looked through the binocular and the telescope, he said, "Good job, Sergeant Fatal. Now, what about the innocent bystanders and their homes or stores? Would they be in the line of fire when we engage in this battle with those terrorists? I don't want those terrorists to get off one shot outside that building. Am I clear, Sergeants?"

They all said, "Crystal, sir. Crystal clear."

"All right, team," Captain Apocalypse said. "We need to do the following to make sure that everything works out as we've planned. We have five scientists in that building somewhere, and we also know that they have this prototype aircraft carrier loaded with sarin nerve gas and had nuclear power. Although it's a prototype, it still works as if it were built to go right now. We have to remove them and take that carrier back from Russia and North Korea as they want this prototype and these scientists who are bilingual and multilingual. Whoever they are, they got the right people that can tell them what they need to know about that carrier. Now, I need for you, Sergeant Tornado, Sergeant Shadow, Sergeant Polarize, Sergeant Illusionist, Sergeant Fatal, Sergeant Hectic, Sergeant Nuclear, Sergeant Furious, Sergeant Lowlife, Sergeant Eliminate, Sergeant Hocus-Pocus, and Sergeant Consequence, to go into the sewer and use your Harleys and push all that stuff to the end of the drains. Sergeant Animosity will lead you to the end of the path. Any questions?"

No response as they all left to go clean the sewer out.

As they were cleaning the sewer, the terrorists, meanwhile, had one of the male scientists hanging up by his own necktie tied around his wrist and pulled above his head, questioning him in all types of languages, but he did not speak, just hung there next to seven dead bodies before them, which were already smelling. They had tortured him now for four and a half hours, trying to make him talk.

The Russian general Riftto Yurkwizo said, "Since he won't talk to us, then I know whom he will talk to."

General Yurkwizo said to his comrade Yuerfwkoff, "Go and bring me the little one."

As Comrade Yuerfwkoff went to get Dr. Ickieto Pheli's son, General Yurkwizo said, "He will talk for this little one. This is his son."

Dr. Pheli's son was only nine years old, and he was yelling in Tagalog to his father for help, and when his father saw him, in all the pain he had battled, his father yelled now at the Russian general in Tagalog. But the general just laughed at him. Dr. Pheli was crying now, too, and replied in Tagalog, not understanding a word that the Russian general was trying to make him understand. The Russian general said, "Comrade Yuerfwkoff, when I ask a question and he doesn't talk, start cutting down his forehead like this, between the eyes, until he talks. And if he does not talk, then we continue, until he dies. Do you understand your order, Comrade Yuerfwkoff?"

Comrade Yuerfwkoff had barely begun cutting Dr. Pheli when General Yurkwizo said loudly, making everybody jump, "Deeper, Comrade Yuerfwkoff, go deeper!"

Comrade Yuerfwkoff then went deeper, all the way to Dr. Pheli's skull, splitting the skin on his face in half. Dr. Pheli's son bowed his head, stopping up his ears, as his father was screaming for help and mercy in Tagalog as he was in pain. Dr. Pheli's son was yelling something in Tagalog at the general, but General Yurkwizo only laughed at the little boy. When Comrade Yuerfwkoff had his razor-sharp knife sliding down the center of his face to his lips, General Yurkwizo was just watching and said, "Dr. Pheli, you refuse to tell us what this translation is, huh? Well, you will die before you tell us?"

Dr. Pheli said over and over and over in Tagalog, not knowing what they were saying to him. One of the terrorists said to the general, "We got information that these five scientists are bilingual and multilingual."

The general looked at the other generals from Japan and North Korea, then said, "Let's see if he will talk before he dies."

He then said very loudly, "YUERFWKOFF!"

And Comrade Yuerfwkoff cut Dr. Pheli's lips and between his bottom gum, stopping at his throat and starting at the top of his chest plate, blood pouring out of Dr. Pheli as his son was begging for his father's life in Tagalog. His father said something to him in Tagalog, making him smile, but he was still crying, although he and his father both had stopped screaming from all the pain that Comrade Yuerfwkoff was dealing him with. Dr. Pheli felt the razor-sharp knife making its way down to his stomach. He wanted to scream, but he had assured his son that if he wouldn't scream, then he wouldn't scream. Dr. Pheli felt his life slipping away as blood ran down his face and his body, and his lips were split in half. The knife then started cutting through Dr. Pheli's stomach, to his intestines, and blood was gushing out of him, splashing onto Comrade Yuerfwkoff and pooling on the floor.

Just before dying, Dr. Pheli said in Tagalog to his son, and his son said something in Tagalog back to him. His father had just died in front of him. General Yurkwizo pulled out his pistol and grabbed Dr. Pheli's son by the hair, saying, "Like father, like son." He then shot Dr. Pheli's son in the head, blowing his brains out and killing him instantly. He then said, "You four better come up with the answers that we need by tomorrow night, or you will be treated like the rest that you see up here. I will see you four tomorrow. Now, take them out of here!"

Meanwhile, Captain Apocalypse had just set up their briefing table and said on the radio, "Is the sewer ready?"

Sergeant Consequence clicked his button three times, and Captain Apocalypse ordered, "Return to the base for briefing."

They all then turned their Harleys around, going back to the command post, and as they made it back, Captain Apocalypse said, "We are going to take care of the four people on the rooftop first. I want nothing but a one-shot deal. One to the head, neck, or heart, with through-and-through action. Make sure that they don't fall off the building too. Sergeant Rattler, Sergeant Evil, Sergeant Destroyer, and Sergeant Animosity, I want you four to snipe these guys first and then assist us on the ground. I want Sergeant Shadow, Sergeant Flood, Sergeant Illusionist, Sergeant Hocus-Pocus, Sergeant Boogeyman, and Sergeant Big Badass Wolf to get in the midst of them as the rest of us surround these fuckers and blow their shit to smithereens. These sons of bitches won't know what hit their asses! We need to find a way to get our inside troops in to make this work out like it should."

Sergeant Boogeyman asked, "Permission to speak, Captain."

Captain Apocalypse said, "Permission granted."

Sergeant Boogeyman continued, "Captain, sir, the police officer that we had seen receiving money from those people in that van after they had kidnapped those women about three days ago…Captain, I do believe that officer was watching the compound for them, to make sure that nobody entered the premises. Those 'Keep Away,' 'Restricted,' 'Dangerous,' 'Stay Off,' or 'Violators Will Be Prosecuted' signs don't work too well if a police officer isn't there, and as along as an officer is there, then nobody is going to go over there, because they don't want to go to jail. What's needed is for someone—me—who knows what this cop looks like very closely to snatch his ass up for a few minutes until the troops are settled inside the compound."

Captain Apocalypse said, "Let us use Officer Injema-Kin to talk to this officer and have him make him leave his post there so that the ground troops can enter the compound."

All twenty members of the team just nodded in agreement with Captain Apocalypse. As they went to Officer Injema-Kin's door and opened it, Captain Apocalypse said, "Officer Injema-Kin, we need your help in saving a lot of people, as I told you earlier. I need for you to call this officer on your car radio and try to get him to leave the spot he's at for at least five or six minutes. Can you do that for us, Officer?"

Officer Injema-Kin replied, "Me try as hard as me can, okay? Okay. Me will do that."

Sergeant Lowlife went on the watch, looking at the police car sitting idly there, the officer watching the big building that had been condemned, with a big fence around it. As Sergeant Lowlife zoomed in, he gave a nod at Captain Apocalypse, and in turn Captain Apocalypse said, "Move out, team!"

They all left with Captain Apocalypse.

Sergeant Big Badass Wolf went to get the police car that Officer Injema-Kin drove, and when the Big Badass Wolf made it back with the car, he got out of it. Officer Injema-Kin got in and said, "Me have to speak not like this. He doesn't know how to talk like me."

Captain Apocalypse just nodded as Officer Injema-Kin started talking in Tagalog on the radio. The other officer did not pick up. Officer Injema-Kin said something, again in Tagalog, over and over and over for two minutes, and finally the officer picked up, breathing very hard, trying to catch his breath. Officer Injema-Kin talked in Tagalog for thirty-five or thirty-six seconds, and the other officer said something back to him. Officer Injema-Kin said something back to him, hitting the dashboard of his car and yelling at him. He then got quiet and was still holding the button on his car radio, yelling and screaming, his car screeching off.

Sergeant Lowlife said on his walkie-talkie, "He's gone, sir. Your inside troop can go, sir."

Captain Apocalypse pointed as Sergeant Big Badass Wolf, Sergeant Boogeyman, Sergeant Shadow, Sergeant Illusionist, Sergeant Flood, and Sergeant Hocus-Pocus got into the sewer, climbing on their Harleys, going to that big concrete slab with that sewer manhole on top. They made it there safely, and as they were inside the fence, Sergeant Lowlife and Sergeant Tornado watched them get out of the sewer, putting themselves in their position. They were all dug deep like a tick on a dog and camouflaged themselves into their surroundings. All six of them were spread out about twenty yards away from one another. They placed a mark over their positions, and the only ones that knew that mark were members of their team, and they, too, were the only ones that could see it with their night vision googles.

Captain Apocalypse said, "Sergeant Big Badass Wolf, Sergeant Boogeyman, Sergeant Illusionist, Sergeant Hocus-Pocus, Sergeant Flood, and Sergeant Shadow, are y'all ready? Click your button twice."

They all clicked their buttons two times each, and Captain Apocalypse said, "I'll click three-one-three when you start your mission. Remember, one shot only, and I mean no mercy, soldiers, no mercy at all. I do want the hostages taken alive, so don't kill them, as we are on a need-to-know basis of who's really controlling this operation, because this carrier is somewhere out there. Are we clear, Sergeants?"

And they all responded, "Sir, yes, sir!"

Sergeant Lowlife said on the walkie-talkie, "The officer is back, and he is about to park in the same spot."

The officer did park in the same spot, looking over at the building in the fence to see if there had been any movement around over there, but everything was as it was. He now looked at some photos and looked over at the place, then back at the photos, only to see nothing wrong over there. He then got back into his car and picked up the radio, calling Officer Injema-Kin. He tried to reach him a few more times, and when he was about to throw the radio in his car, Officer Injema-Kin answered in Tagalog, hitting himself with an open palm to his forehead, laughing, then said something in Tagalog, continuing laughing as he put the CB up. He said, "It's no his wife and son, like me say it is. Him need me, where me at, and me told him work in bad neighborhood on drug case."

Captain Apocalypse just saluted him as they all went back up to the top floor, where Sergeant Lowlife was watching his teammates watch this corrupt officer look at the area. Captain Apocalypse, Officer Injema-Kin, and the rest of the team made it back up top with Sergeant Lowlife, and they all went to the big debriefing table. They did not put Officer Injema-Kin in his room or order him out from the debriefing table; they just let him stand there at the briefing.

Captain Apocalypse said, "Officer Injema-Kin, I want you to stay posted here. Here is a walkie-talkie. And follow me." He then turned to Sergeant Lowlife. "Let Officer Injema-Kin stand post here." Sergeant Lowlife left that post, going to the briefing table.

Captain Apocalypse asked, "Officer Injema-Kin, do you see that officer at his car? The one you spoke to earlier?"

Officer Injema-Kin said, "Yeah, sir."

Captain Apocalypse ordered, "If you see any movement, let us know, okay?"

Officer Injema-Kin replied, "Okay."

Captain Apocalypse then said, "All right, Sergeants, we are about to step into a mission, and I want us out and safe as soon as possible. As I said earlier, the four on the roof have to go first, and then after that team, we all are going to hit those sons of bitches on the inside by giving those fuckers a new asshole! Remember, one shot down and it'll be so dark they won't know what hit their asses until it's already too late, their bodies lying beside those of their buddies.

It is that time. I want Sergeant Animosity, Sergeant Polarize, and Sergeant Nuclear on the right side of the building. Sergeant Maniac, Sergeant Hectic, Sergeant Furious, and Sergeant Fatal, on the back side of the building. Sergeant Eliminate, Sergeant Evil, and Sergeant Consequence, take the left side of the building. Now, I want Sergeant Destroyer, Sergeant Lowlife, Sergeant Rattler, and Sergeant Tornado to take the front with me. Put your silencers on your AK-47, M16, Japanese Arisaka 97, and the .45, and make sure you have seven clips for each weapon. And make every shot count, soldiers. After the ground crew has been annihilated, then I want Sergeant Destroyer, Sergeant Animosity, Sergeant Evil, and Sergeant Rattler to go to the roof and annihilate anyone who comes and anyone who tries to leave. Understood?"

They all just saluted Captain Apocalypse.

The captain then said, "ALL RIGHT, THEN, MOVE OUT!"

Before Captain Apocalypse walked out, he went over to where Officer Injema-Kin was and whispered in his ear, "You're a soldier, son, so don't feel left out. You're playing a major role for us out here while we're in this danger, and we're very much appreciative of your assistance. Your mother and father will be proud of you for saving their country and others." He then embraced him and shook his hand, then saluted him, walking off to catch up with his team.

Officer Injema-Kin just smiled, looking over his teammates out there in all that danger. He knew that these guys really didn't need him, but they made him a part of the good cause that they were doing. As Captain Apocalypse and his team made it to their position, officer Injema-Kin saw when they arrived, but a second or two later, they all just disappeared. He could not tell what was what out there, as everything was just the same when they went there. He couldn't tell if anything was added to that place, as it was filled with fifteen big, grown-ass men. He could not really see them when he looked very, very, very hard, and he really did not know if he was looking at them or something that was just in his imagination.

About three and a half hours had passed by when he heard his radio click three-one-three. He then saw flashes of shots being fired, hitting the terrorists in the head, neck, or heart. He watched bodies falling. It was 0210, and a war zone was going on up on La Mesa Ecopark on the Manila highway called the Skyway. The corrupt police officer, who was watching the terrorists' backs, did not know what was going on right under his nose, or in his face. The terrorists were whispering for one another, trying to figure out what was going on. All they were hearing was just a small *Pfft* sound, and they did not know that death was taking their friends, and them, until it was too fucking late to realize what was going on. The whole entire ground crew had been annihilated, and Officer Injema-Kin noticed that it took his team forty-three minutes to remove the outside terrorists without the corrupt officer ever knowing that his "friends" had been neutralized. He still thought he was watching over them.

Captain Apocalypse said, "It's time to annihilate the terrorists on the inside of the building and free those five scientists! Sergeant Rattler, Sergeant Evil, Sergeant Destroyer, and Sergeant Animosity, take y'all position up on the roof!"

Each one of them took a corner as they clicked the button on their walkie-talkies. They looked around on the ground crew and saw that it was very still, with no movement from anyone but the members of the No-Name Unit.

"Sergeant Lowlife, you take the basement and hit the fuse box and turn off all the power. I see that it's light out here, so cut the power. Sergeant Shadow, Sergeant Tornado, and Sergeant Illusionist, I want you three to take the fifth floor. Sergeant Flood, Sergeant Consequence, and Sergeant Eliminate, I want you three to take the fourth floor. Sergeant Fatal, Sergeant Furious, and Sergeant Hectic, I want you three to take the third floor. Sergeant Maniac, Sergeant Nuclear, and Sergeant Hocus-Pocus, I want you three to take the second floor. Sergeant Polarize, Sergeant Boogeyman, and Sergeant Big Badass Wolf, you three come with me on the first floor. Move out!" he whispered.

As the lights went out, there was a bunch of muttering heard, in Tagalog. Also, the Russian general Yurkwizo and his comrade Yuerfwkoff were trying to run out of their room when Sergeant Boogeyman shot Comrade Yuerfwkoff in the head, blowing his brains out all on his general. He then shot the general in the left kneecap and both hands. Meanwhile, Captain Apocalypse shot the generals of Japan and North Korea in both of their arms. They then took the dead hostages down and placed them with the terrorists.

Sergeant Polarize went into this room and saw three naked women lying in the bed, their hands tied above their heads and their legs spread-eagle and tied down. One woman was bleeding very badly between the legs as two terrorists were lying on top of them. Sergeant Polarize eased to the first terrorist and shot him point-blank in the head, blowing his brain out, and then shot the other one in the temple. He took them off the women and laid them on the floor. He waited for three minutes, and then two more terrorists came in. He shot them both in the heart, and as he removed them, four terrorists came in, speaking in Tagalog. He shot one in the head, the other in the heart, while the other two saw the flashes and tried to run. He shot them both in the back of their heads. As he was about to stand, another terrorist came in, speaking in Russian, and he shot him twice in the mouth and once in the heart.

All the sergeants cleared their floors, and Captain Apocalypse said, "Sergeant Lowlife, turn the cover back on in ten second."

Sergeant Lowlife replied, "I read you loud and clear, Captain Apocalypse."

Sergeant Lowlife started counting, and then all the lights popped back on, revealing all the dead bodies, the Russian, Japanese, and North Korean generals, hanging by the tip that was a part of their uniforms.

Now, as Sergeant Polarize was about to untie the naked women, they seemed afraid, yelling in Tagalog, but he couldn't understand what they were saying. He figured these women thought he was going there to do very bad things to them. Sergeant Polarize put his finger up to his mouth and pointed at the bad guys, who were dead, on the floor. He then cut them lose from the bed and gave them the terrorists' pants and shirts for them to cover their little bodies with. As they thanked him in Tagalog, he heard some banging on a locked door. One of the women said something, this time not in, Tagalog "Friend, friend, friend, friend!" pointing at the door. He slowly walked over there, and they were holding on tight to him, as they were very scared. He walked over the dead bodies of the terrorists and forced the door open. Two women were at the door, naked and screaming for help. The other girls, it seemed, were afraid of these women. These two women did not have one scratch or blood on them, unlike the rest of the women. The other women had burn marks, cut marks, and bruises all over their little bodies, and two of the women were bleeding between the legs. Sergeant Polarize saw a Russian and a Japanese female uniform lying on the floor, with panties and bras lying near them. Sergeant Polarize shot both of the women in their calves, crippling them, and the other females got up and walked past them, spitting on their asses.

The Russian girl said in a very pained voice, "I…I…I…I am a Russian captain with diplomatic immunity. You cannot do this to me!"

The female Japanese sergeant just yelled out at the top of her lungs.

Sergeant Polarize took the women out and covered their naked bodies, then locked the Russian and Japanese girls in the room so they wouldn't get away.

As they went past the captain and his crew, stepping over dead bodies everywhere they stepped, Sergeant Lowlife came out of the basement with four scientists—this after killing the nine terrorists who were watching over the scientists. He then said, "All cleared in hell."

Sergeant Hocus-Pocus replied, "Affirmative on the second floor."

Sergeant Fatal said, "Third is cleared."

Sergeant Flood said, "The same for the fourth floor."

And Sergeant Shadow said too, "The same as for the fifth floor."

Sergeant Polarize the told the captain, "Captain Apocalypse, I got this Russian captain, and I am guessing that this is her general, I don't know, but I have her locked up with a Japanese sergeant. Maybe they two can tell us where our prize is located."

Captain Apocalypse and the other soldiers saw the dead scientists had been tortured, as the females had their breasts removed, their clitoris mutilated, and their virginal walls spread open with safety pins. Captain Apocalypse said, "Sergeant Flood and Sergeant Shadow, take these four scientists outside, but don't let that corrupt police officer see them." He added, "Sergeant Big Badass Wolf and Sergeant Boogeyman, go get that corrupt police officer out there. We have three and a half hours before 0600 and the break of dawn. Now go get that shit-eater, Sergeants."

As they left to go and get him, there was not one person in sight. The Big Badass Wolf jumped off the second floor of a store, landing on the roof of the officer's squad car and denting in a part of the roof. The officer said something in Tagalog, yelling out very loud as he was getting out of the car very fast to look at the roof of his car. He was still yelling when he saw the Big Badass Wolf standing up there with an AK-47 in his hand, and more guns too, and blood dripping off him onto his car. He slowly backed up, looking at him as the Big Badass Wolf was still staring him down. The corrupt officer reached slowly for his gun as he was still backing up, bumping into the Boogeyman. He turned around and saw the Boogeyman standing, and as soon as his hand tried to bring his gun out of its holster, the Big Badass Wolf grabbed his right hand, breaking his wrist and cuffing him up with his own cuff.

The Big Badass Wolf threw him down on the ground and put his right hand in the back of the collar of his shirt, picking his top part up, choking him, all while the Boogeyman grabbed both of his pant legs as they took him inside and gave him to Captain Apocalypse, as it was requested by him. The corrupt police officer saw all his dead friends' bodies everywhere. He was shaking, scared, as these two big giants carried him past these bodies out on the ground. They made it inside the building, where he started screaming and yelling in Tagalog. But nobody really cared about what he was yelling about.

Captain Apocalypse said, "Put him up here with the rest of these sorry motherfuckers."

The corrupt officer vomited everything that he had eaten that day, and possibly the day before, when he saw all of the dead bodies, blood, guts, and brain matter all on the walls and floors. The smell of the dead bodies had him gagging, too, as he couldn't hold his breath long enough.

Captain Apocalypse ordered, "Throw that piece of shit in this, in all this, face-first so he could taste what he made happen on his watch. They threw him facedown in all this blood and guts alongside the nine-year-old little boy the general had murdered. His face stayed in it until he was blowing bubbles, at which time Captain Apocalypse pulled his face out of it, blood and guts gushing out of his mouth. His face was covered with blood, intestine, urine, and feces. He was coughing and spitting it out of his mouth as well.

Captain Apocalypse said, "Take the bodies of the innocent out of here, and take them to the hospital so that they can be treated respectfully. But as for these motherfuckers, they are going to talk no matter what they think or how tough they think they are, so go get the truck and three ambulances and take the innocent people to the hospital."

Captain Apocalypse hung the Russian general's captain next to him, and she said, "I have diplomatic immunity!"

Captain Apocalypse said in his mechanical voice, "I don't give a fuck about your diplomatic immunity, and I don't give a rat's ass about you! What you have done to these poor peoples is what I *do* care about. Now, I am going to ask your general a question, and if he doesn't answer in five seconds, then I'll hurt you and her real bad. And I do mean *very* bad. Now, General Yurkwizo, where is the USS *Enterprise*?"

Captain Apocalypse pulled out his big buck knife and pushed it inside of the general's captain's left shoulder, and it went all the way through it. He took Sergeant Shadow's buck knife and pushed it all the way through the Japanese girl's left shoulder. He took Sergeant Lowlife's buck knife and pushed it all the way through the left shoulder of the corrupt police officer. And he took Sergeant Fatal's buck knife and pushed it all the way through the general's right kneecap.

Captain Apocalypse then asked again, "General Yurkwizo, where is the USS *Enterprise*?"

Captain Apocalypse took Sergeant Tornado's buck knife and pushed it all the way through the right shoulder of the general's female captain. He took Sergeant Hectic's buck knife and pushed it all the way through the Japanese girl's right shoulder. He took

Sergeant Nuclear's buck knife and pushed it all the way through the corrupt police officer's right shoulder. He then took Sergeant Flood's buck knife and pushed it all the way through General Yurkwizo left kneecap.

Captain Apocalypse asked again, "General Yurkwizo, where is the USS *Enterprise?*"

Captain Apocalypse took Sergeant Hocus-Pocus's buck knife and pushed it all the way through the center part of the Russian girl's arm, disconnecting her elbow as she was screaming out loud. He took Sergeant Eliminate's buck knife and pushed it all the way through the center part of the Japanese girl's arm, disconnecting her elbow as she was shouting something that they didn't understand. Also, the two women had peed and shit themselves, which they all saw as they didn't have any clothes on at all. Captain Apocalypse took Sergeant Rattler's buck knife and pushed it all the way through the corrupt police officer's right ankle. He then took Sergeant Maniac's buck knife and pushed it all the way through General Yurkwizo's right ankle. All of them were screaming and yelling for him to stop.

Captain Apocalypse asked again, "General Yurkwizo, where is the USS *Enterprise?*"

Captain Apocalypse took Sergeant Animosity's buck knife and pushed it all the way through the center of the female Russian captain's right arm, disconnecting her left elbow. She was screaming in response, "I'll tell you! I'll tell you what you want to know. I-I-I-I'll tell you! Please stop! I'll tell you!"

Captain Apocalypse asked, "Where is the USS *Enterprise?*"

As she was about to answer, the Russian General suddenly said, "I will tell too, if you let me live too."

"Where is it?" Captain Apocalypse asked.

General Yurkwizo answered, "V-V-Vice Admiral T-T-Timothy Skyler has it stored for us in Clark Air Force Base. He said you damn people would not ever look for it over there. It's there in between the two retired aircraft carriers. Just look!"

Captain Apocalypse had Sergeant Illusionist call over there to verify if it was there. Sergeant Illusionist said, "Captain Apocalypse wants to know if you can check and see if the USS Enterprise is sitting on your dock."

Captain Dwight Sledge said, "Are you talking about the one that came missing?"

Sergeant Illusionist replied, "Sir, will you just check for him, please?"

He was gone for about four and a half minutes and then came back out of breath, saying, "Sir, it's here. It's there, sir!"

Sergeant Illusionist hung up on him and went to tell Captain Apocalypse that it was there in one piece.

General Yurkwizo said, "It is there, right? It is there, right, Comrade? It's there?"

Captain Apocalypse pulled out his .45 auto and shot the Russian girl in the head, blowing her brains out. Then he shot the Japanese girl in the head, blowing her brains out as well. He then looked at the corrupt police officer and shot him in the mouth, which blew the back of his head and neck out. Captain Apocalypse killed them instantly as the Russian general said, "I'll live, will I? I will live, will I not, Comrade? Do I live, Comrade?"

Captain Apocalypse responded, "Sergeant Animosity, three... one...three..."

Sergeant Animosity pulled out his .45 auto and shot General Yurkwizo between the eyes, killing him instantly; he just hung there, dead with his whole team inside and out.

Captain Apocalypse went out to help load the people on the truck, and he saw this forty-eight-year-old lady's name tag on her lab coat, and it had a "K. Injema-Kin." He now knew that it got to be the officer's mother, who worked as a scientist at the university. He waved up toward the command post. Officer Injema-Kin then jumped in his police car and made it to them. He escorted the truck and ambulances to the hospital along with the team. The hospital people came out and took the people inside, emptying the truck with all the dead bodies of those innocent ones. The people that were alive shook their hands, while the lady K. Injema-Kin hugged all of them. And when she hugged Captain Apocalypse, he hugged her little four-foot-nine and 112-pound body back and whispered mechanically in her ear, saying, "Don't say anything, please. Don't say anything. I'm proud of you!" He pulled her bra and let it pop her in the back like her father's son used to do to her.

Captain Apocalypse turned around as she tried to pull him back, but he kept walking, getting up in the truck as it was pulling off at the same time. He looked in the mirror at her as they were driving off, and he looked at her as he was still waving, and she was waving back. They went back to the command post and took their stuff out and put them on the truck. They then set dynamite all around the condemned building, making it to the sewer at the same time. At the very top, the middle, and the bottom. Captain Apocalypse let the dynamite go off, blowing up the whole entire command post.

The police came to see what had happened, and they saw this big building had finally come down. They looked around as Officer Injema-Kin went back to his car to radio for a fire truck. That was when he saw a big envelope on the driver's-side seat. He picked it up, and it had 150,000 pesos, and also papers on a terrorist organization and about a corrupt police officer as well as a corrupt vice admiral, Timothy Skyler. The note read, "Don't worry, this is your reward from us for your assistance. Now, take your chief and captain as well as the rest of the police force to the place where we terrorized the terrorists, as it has a note from us giving the information that you need about this slaughterhouse. Good luck, Sergeant Injema-Kin."

Officer Injema-Kin knew that they'd never be able to clear all this mess up, so he relayed it in Tagalog to his superior when they got in their cars and drove off. Daybreak had come at 0700 when they saw all the dead bodies of those terrorists. Officer Injema-Kin told them about it in Tagalog and took them to the hospital to show them the ones that were tortured and the ones that were safe and alive. His superior was proud of Officer Injema-Kin for saving these people's lives and bringing the dead innocent bodies to be buried and treated with respect. The Philippine authorities all made statements to the media, saying that these terrorists from Russia, Japan, and North Korea had turned on one another and killed one another off. Officer—excuse me—Sergeant Injema-Kin killed the last two, they said, and that also included one of their own, but he was a corrupt officer.

Captain Apocalypse heard on the radio, in Tagalog, how they were giving Sergeant Injema-Kin all kinds of gratitude for his bravery. He just smiled under his ski mask. When Captain Apocalypse and his team made it back to US Naval Base Subic Bay, they were still soaked and dripping blood, and as they walked, they left bloody boot prints behind them. Admiral of the fleet Sloan and his vice admiral, Skyler, came out of the back and saw them standing all bloody, with stuff hanging off them that looked like intestines.

Admiral Sloan said, "Captain Apocalypse, what is this? Why are you looking like this and tracking all this blood everywhere?"

Captain Apocalypse said, "Take your post, Sergeants," and they all surrounded Admiral Sloan and Vice Admiral Skyler.

Admiral Sloan said, "Captain Apocalypse, what is this all about? What are you doing? Stand down!"

Captain Apocalypse said, "Sorry, Admiral Sloan, sir. We can't do that. You have a traitor in your midst, and we want him."

Admiral Sloan said, "All my seamen are loyal, and they are true to their country. Now stand down, soldiers!"

Captain Apocalypse and his team had them in a circle, with nowhere to go, and they were still standing there, not saying a word. Admiral Sloan said, "Are we just going to stand here in silence, or are we going to talk about what's going on here?"

Captain Apocalypse pulled out his .45 auto, and so did his soldiers, and Admiral Sloan said out loud, "Woah! Just hold on a fucking second here. What the hell is the shit? The fun is fun, and now I give you soldiers a goddamn direct order to stand the fuck down. Now!"

Captain Apocalypse said, "I told you that we can't do that, Admiral. We were sent to do a job, and our job isn't finished. Isn't that right, Vice Admiral Skyler?"

Admiral Sloan said, "Whatever you have to talk to him about, you talk to me, Captain Apocalypse. You don't have the authority to question my vice admiral!"

Captain Apocalypse responded, "You are right, if I were under those types of command, sir. My order is to find the people who are terrorizing us, and once I get these terrorists, then it's my job to find the truth. Your vice admiral has placed you and your seamen in jeopardy, as well as our country and other countries too, as he is a terrorist himself."

Vice Admiral Skyler said, "Admiral Sloan, sir, don't believe this bunch of hogwash!"

Admiral Sloan said, "Captain, I understand that you and your team are good soldiers, and your team as well as yourself put your lives on the line, but I do believe you got this all wrong. Now, stand down."

Captain Apocalypse responded, "Vice Admiral Skyler, you're not going to come with us to answer to your treason against your country and as well as to your brothers of arms?"

Vice Admiral Skyler was about to reply when Admiral Sloan shouted, "ENOUGH! I have heard just about enough of this bullshit! I have had enough of this goddamn insubordination! This bullshit has to end now, and whatever you soldiers think my vice admiral has done, you better have some fucking proof, because your asses, no matter if I can see your faces or not, will be court-martialed. I will see to it and make it happen. Somebody will tell me who in the hell you and your men are under all that shit."

Captain Apocalypse wasn't worried about anything this admiral had just stated, whether he had proof or not. He reached inside his backpack and pulled out a blood-soaked file folder and walked it over to the admiral, saying, "Thank you for your vote of confidence, Admiral Sloan. Here is your proof of evidence, sir."

Admiral Sloan said, "What the hell is this shit, Captain?"

Captain Apocalypse said, "Open it up and you'll find out where your USS *Enterprise* is located and who hid it there and who was selling it to the terrorists. Plenty of people were murdered, lots of terrorists died, a nine-year-old child was murdered, and we made it to save the last four of the five scientists that were kidnapped, as one was murdered in front of his son. We got your aircraft carrier back, sir. Your vice admiral, Vice Admiral Skyler, is the bad bookend to your books. I strongly advise you to find yourself another vice admiral that is faithful and loyal to us all, sir."

Admiral Sloan looked at the folder and at Vice Admiral Skyler with great disbelief and said, "Why did you do this shit, Skyler? Why?"

Vice Admiral Skyler said, "People like you are weak, too damn weak to run this country and this unit with thousands of loyal soldiers under your command. I am so fucking sick of hearing your fucking shit about when you were my age and younger. Your ass is sixty-one years old. You need to retire and allow us young minds to run this fucking world like we should!"

Admiral Sloan was a lot older than his vice admiral, Captain Apocalypse realized as he looked at the size and difference.

Admiral Sloan said, "Vice Admiral Timothy Skyler, you're under arrest for the charge of treason."

Vice Admiral Skyler said, "You and what fucking Army, old man? Captain Apocalypse doesn't have the authority to arrest me, and you sure in hell are not going to put your hands on me. I will not allow an old pea-brain of a man to touch me—"

Before he could finish talking, Captain Apocalypse shot Vice Admiral Skyler with his .45 auto in both of his kneecaps, making him hit the floor and yelling and screaming in pain. "T-t-t-that son of a bitch shot me, Admiral! He shot me! You saw him shoot me, Admiral, didn't you?"

Admiral Sloan said, "I did not see that. You got shot by your terrorist buddies by giving them to Captain Apocalypse and his team, and they brought you here to be court-martialed. Isn't that right, Captain Apocalypse?"

Captain Apocalypse nodded and said, "Sir, yes, sir."

The vice admiral said in pain, "T-that's a lie!"

Admiral Sloan said, "It's our words against yours, son. Now, who do you think they are going to believe? You, a traitor in espionage and treason, or soldiers of war for the country?"

Admiral Sloan shook Captain Apocalypse's hand as his team saluted Admiral Sloan. Admiral Sloan said, "At ease, soldiers! Good job, soldiers!"

Then they said all at once, "Thank you, Admiral Powerhouse, sir!"

He just smiled and said, "You all are welcome, and the Philippines, the United States, Russia, Japan, and North Korea, as well as other countries, and their citizens thank you."

They all started walking out the door and getting on their Harleys, then rode them up on the Sea Stallion. The Sea Stallion was about to fly back to the Philippine island where they landed the Lockheed C-5 Galaxy. As the chopper made it to the plane, all of them rolled the chopper inside the C-5 plane and closed its door. It then took off back to the United States. They were heading back home with their mission having been well executed, and they knew they had made a great difference to their country.

Twenty-nine hours later, they had landed on their home turf and were back at their base and ready for their next mission to be handed to them.

CHAPTER 4

It was June 11, 1965, eight years after the No-Name Unit came off a major mission. They went on small missions that only took a day for them to bring things under control. Captain Apocalypse and his team did not actually care, but they knew that they were used to battling badass terrorist type of people that were threatening their country as well as other countries. Captain Apocalypse and his sergeants neutralized several little countries without shedding a lot of the blood of their enemies. They always made their little pact and their little motto before going out to their mission. They never underestimated their opponents when they went to battle with their asses.

This particular day, as they were about to go out to do their training, an envelope came down Captain Apocalypse's mail slot. It read "Urgent" in big red letters. Captain Apocalypse hit the intercom button for the whole team to hear and said, "Team, report to the debriefing room ASAP!"

Five minutes later, all his sergeants were in the debriefing room, in their chairs, waiting for Captain Apocalypse. Captain Apocalypse entered the room, and all the soldiers stood at the same time at attention as Captain Apocalypse said, "At ease, soldiers."

They all sat down. Captain Apocalypse turned the lights off and turned the slide projector on, saying, "Team, we have another one of these 'Simple Simon' missions that will only take a few or maybe five hours and we'll be on our way back home. This mission is over in a small area of townspeople in South Vietnam where some very bad peoples are terrorizing their little village because they refuse to participate in their regime. They have killed over two to three hundred people. They have murdered men, women, and children, as well as the elders. They have asked our country to assist them, and they'll finish what we leave them as leftover. This little place is in Saigon, a little compound where this general, Bien Lo, and his little badass soldiers are itching for a scratch, and we are going to scratch their asses with the worst pain they have ever felt. We have a safe house with these people here. It's a family of five, with a cellar that we can use as our command post to operate in. The woman of the house is Mrs. Qs Long, and she's about forty or forty-two, and she is waiting for our arrival. So you know what we have to do, and let's go do it. Let's wipe these murdering sons of bitches off the map ASAP and come back home! Are you ready, team?"

All of them stood up at attention, saluting Captain Apocalypse.

Captain Apocalypse said, "Let's move out, team!"

They all went to the basement door, going to their Harleys in the tunnel, making their way to the end as they got on the elevator shaft. As they got off the elevator shaft, the Big Badass Wolf and the Boogeyman saluted them. They then lined up in single file next to them, saluting Captain Apocalypse, who saluted them and said, "At ease." They all then loaded up on the C-5 Galaxy.

As the door was closing, the Boogeyman said, "Where to land, Captain?"

Captain Apocalypse replied, "We are going to take the plane to Da Nang Air Base in South Vietnam and go way under the radar."

Sergeant Boogeyman said, "Yes, sir, Captain Apocalypse, sir." He then went back up front to help the Big Badass Wolf take off, as always, very smoothly, to their mission.

They flew for fifty-three hours and sixteen minutes before they landed at Da Nang Air Base, getting greeted by General Stanley "Too Cool" Foster. General Foster said, "Welcome, Captain Apocalypse and team. We have your ride sitting out and waiting for you. I want you to use my helicopter for as long as it's necessary for you to use, but I am positive that you won't need that, Captain."

Captain Apocalypse and his sergeants saluted General Foster, then went back out of the door. As they were leaving, everybody on the base was looking at them, wondering who the fuck these god-damn guys were.

General Foster's lieutenant general Bobby "Hawkeye" Blade said, "General Foster, who in the hell are those goddamn guys there? Shit, those fuckers look like some goddamn terrorists!"

General Foster said, "Son, those motherfuckers are not some goddamn terrorists. They are the fucking terrorists' worst fucking nightmare! Those terrorists that they are after are some shithead terrorists, but these soldiers are the terrorists that we can count on, as they can sniff those wannabe bad sons of bitches out and remove them from their lives. So yes, they are the worst of the worst of terrorists. You can't see their faces or hear their normal voices. They are your terrorists, my terrorists, the whole goddamn world's terrorists. The bad and the worst, but good goddamn terrorists, Lieutenant General."

The lieutenant general replied, "Well, I feel safe already, sir."

General Foster said, "You got that shit right. You got that right."

They both just watched them load up on the general's Huey helicopter, which was fully loaded, and disappear in midair.

The groundskeeper came back in with a clipboard bearing Captain Apocalypse's and his sergeants' names on it and gave it to the lieutenant general. "I was told to give this to you, sir."

The lieutenant general said, "What is this, soldier?"

He said, "I guess it is their names, sir."

The lieutenant general then asked, "What do you mean, soldier? You guess it's their names?"

He said, "Look at it, sir."

The lieutenant general snatched the clipboard out of his hands and read, "Captain Apocalypse, Sergeant Lowlife, Sergeant Rattler, Sergeant Flood, Sergeant Illusionist, Sergeant Tornado, Sergeant Hocus-Pocus, Sergeant Shadow, Sergeant Fatal, Sergeant Furious, Sergeant Animosity, Sergeant Maniac, Sergeant Big Badass Wolf, Sergeant Boogeyman, Sergeant Destroyer, Sergeant Evil, Sergeant Eliminate, Sergeant Hectic, Sergeant Polarize, Sergeant Nuclear, and Sergeant Consequence. General Foster, what kind of names are these?"

General Foster said, "Did I have any questions for him or them? No, Lieutenant General, I did not ask them anything about their names, because it is their names." He started walking off, saying, "Lieutenant General, you better remember that as well." He waved goodbye at him and shook his head at his thoughts about these soldiers.

Two hours passed by and Captain Apocalypse and his team made it to Saigon, in a town called Tre Long, where they landed the general's helicopter. The people were shocked and scared as the captain came out to greet them and saluted them. He said, "I'm Captain Jenkins, and you must be Captain Apocalypse. I'll debrief you on how to get to Mrs. Qs Long's house, and you can hide your chopper here and double-time on feet for about a mile. Here is Mrs. Qs's picture, so you'll know what she looks like. Do you have any questions for me, sir?"

Captain Apocalypse said, "You said that it is a place where we can hide this chopper at, right?"

He said, "Yes, you can't miss it because Mrs. Long will be out there, pretending to be a field-worker, and you will land it next to an open patch of all those tall woods next to the field."

Captain Apocalypse said, "That is all, Captain Jenkins." He walked off, saluting as they were heading to their destination in Saigon.

They flew for another twenty-three minutes, then the Big Badass Wolf and the Boogeyman saw Mrs. Qs Long in the field as they landed the chopper in the middle of a crop circle. They got out of the helicopter, walking toward Mrs. Long, to whom Captain Apocalypse said, "Mrs. Qs Long, I am Captain Apocalypse, and these are my sergeants. We are here to assist you, ma'am."

Mrs. Qs Long said, "I am she," looking at them in the dark. She added, "Follow me and I will show you my house."

They all walked in silence through the woods off the road to keep from being seen by spies for the North Vietnamese leader Cho San Hue and his general Bien Lo. They walked for about fifty minutes to an hour. When all of them made it to her house, they saw her husband and three children. Her husband jumped up, saying "Why here? Why you here?" Her children were looking very scared and frightened by their appearance.

Mrs. Long said something to her husband in Vietnamese, and he got very quiet and sat down, as did her children. Captain Apocalypse and his sergeants knew then that this woman was in charge of this household.

Captain Apocalypse said, "Show us the room that we can use to have this little briefing for this mission at, please," in his mechanical voice.

Mrs. Long replied, "Follow me." She then escorted them to a hideaway shelter in one part of her house.

When she left, Captain Apocalypse said, "We will be at the site in an hour and be out in three. Set your watches for three hours."

The team set their watches, and Captain Apocalypse continued, "Sergeant Flood, I want you to stay here and watch over this family until we get back, because we don't know if anyone has received information about Mrs. Long and her family helping us. I need for you to protect the innocent people. Do you understand, Sergeant?"

Sergeant Flood replied, "Yes, sir, Captain Apocalypse."

They all went back up for the team to step outside. Captain Apocalypse said to Mrs. Long, "I am going to leave Sergeant Flood here with you and your family. He is going to stay just in case someone has thought you helped us."

She said, "Understand. I understand."

Captain Apocalypse and his team went on out, leaving Sergeant Flood behind, at 2220, going to these wicked soldiers who had murdered over two to three hundred innocent people. They did not want Mrs. Long, her husband, and their three young children to be murdered by these fucking homegrown terrorists. These children were too young to die this way. The eldest was twelve, then a ten-year-old, and also a seven-years-old.

After a forty-eight-minute walk, Captain Apocalypse and his sergeants made it about thirty yards from their target, the compound Lon Nol shared with his seventy-five to eighty little soldiers. Captain Apocalypse said, "Sergeant Evil, Sergeant Nuclear, Sergeant Big Badass Wolf, and Sergeant Tornado, go on the west side of them and wait for my command. Sergeant Furious, Sergeant Animosity, Sergeant Consequence, and Sergeant Lowlife, you four take the east side of them and you four wait for my command. Sergeant Illusionist, Sergeant Fatal, Sergeant Eliminate, and Sergeant Hocus-Pocus, you four take on the north side and you four wait for my command. Sergeant Boogeyman, Sergeant Hectic, Sergeant Maniac, and Sergeant Polarize, you four take the south side of the compound and wait for my command. Now, Sergeant Rattler, Sergeant Destroyer, Sergeant Shadow, and I will be your snipers as well as your backup if anything gets too rough out here. Do you all understand?"

They all saluted him and headed to their position along with their sniper rifles, watching over them. They got in their position and had barely gotten settled in when Sergeant Furious saw two soldiers creeping upon the right side of him, where he was sitting up in this big-ass tree. He whispered in his walkie-talkie, "Captain Apocalypse, we have two Vietnamese soldiers coming up on my right."

Captain Apocalypse said, "All of y'all look around and watch closely and carefully and tell me what you see. If you see anything, click your buttons once."

Everything went silent as they all were watching.

Forty-two seconds later, they all saw these North Vietnamese soldiers sneaking up behind them. They knew they were there in their compound, and they all hit their buttons. Captain Apocalypse said, "Rain on these motherfuckers! Kill all these sons of bitches!"

Captain Apocalypse and his team used silencers on all their weapons, but they still were combat weapons, killing the North Vietnamese soldiers before they even knew what was going on. The North Vietnamese were open-fired upon by Captain Apocalypse and his team. The North Vietnamese soldiers never saw Captain Apocalypse, Sergeant Destroyer, Sergeant Furious, and Sergeant Shadow in those big-ass trees sniping them with their AK-47 so fast. The people heard only one set of guns being fired.

Sergeant Flood cut all the lights off in the house and said, "Everybody get down! Stay down and don't move!" in his mechanical voice.

Mrs. Qs Long whispered in her seven-year-old daughter's ear, "Jeu Te, run, run to the door and open it."

Jeu Te ran to the door and unlocked it just as Sergeant Flood said in his mechanical voice, "Come back here, kid. Don't do that!" He was going after her into the light when he saw this jeep in the back of the house. Sergeant Flood rushed over there to get Jeu Te when he heard a loud gunshot in the house, and then another loud shot. He felt numb all over his five-foot-eleven and 219-pound body as he hit the floor very hard and could not move, his ears still ringing in his head. The lights came on at once, and his night vision goggles were still on his eyes, blinding him. He could not see or take them off. He felt somebody tugging on his neck, pulling up his ski mask off. He was paralyzed from head to feet. He could not stop them.

Then he heard Mrs. Qs Long's voice saying "Son, good-ass shot. You broke his ass down like the terrorist he is. Captain Lon Nol's going to be proud of his little soldier."

Her stepson said, "Mama, do you want me to kill him? I'll kill him good."

She said, "No, Lin Ti Sue, let him live, because he has questions that need to be answered."

Lin Ti Sue just stood over him with his gun as his father took his mask and the mechanical voice off him and said, "All your friends are dead, and you soon you will be too." He threw his ski mask, voice detector, stocking cap, and night vision goggles on his face. Sergeant Flood still could hear gunfire ablaze, and he knew they were still battling with those North Vietnamese soldiers. He had been lying there for about eight to twelve minutes when about ten North Vietnamese soldiers came in and circled Sergeant Flood. Captain Lon Nol looked at him and spit on him, saying, "Fucking American people always getting in others' business. So now we teach American people not to fuck with soldiers. Get him up and bring him to our house of horror. He has information we need."

They saw that both of his legs were half-gone, and Captain Lon Nol said, "Don't let him die yet until we get our information. Let's go now."

They could not hear any more shots being fired in the distance, so they threw Sergeant Flood in the back of their truck without his ski mask, guns, voice detector, stocking cap, and night vision goggles. All the North Vietnamese soldiers spit on him on the back of the truck.

After Captain Apocalypse and his team had annihilated over two hundred North Vietnamese soldiers, one was still alive, laughing out loud, knowing that death was about to take him any moment. Captain Apocalypse and his team walked over there, where he was lying on his back, still laughing at them. As Captain Apocalypse and his nineteen sergeants pointed their guns at him at point-blank range, the Vietnamese soldier said, "We just need..." *Cough cough, cough cough.* "We...we just need one of your..." *Cough cough.* "Your team..." He started laughing again as Captain Apocalypse and his team emptied their AK-47s at point-blank range. With their silencers on, no one could hear the sound of over two hundred rounds hitting the soldier's whole entire body, making it disappear. The only thing that was left were pieces of his clothing, one thousand puzzle pieces. After annihilating this son of a bitch, they all ran full speed back to Mrs. Qs Long's house, which by then was riddled with bullet holes, with a dead seven-year-old little girl and her husband, a bullet wound going through and through his right side. He son was still holding the gun. Mrs. Long was beaten up pretty bad, with a cut on her face.

Captain Apocalypse and his team saw Sergeant Flood's ski mask, stocking cap, voice detector, night vision goggles, and emptied guns lying in a whole lot of blood.

Captain Apocalypse asked, "Where is my sergeant?"

Qs and her son did not say a word.

Captain Apocalypse asked again, "I *said*, goddammit, where is my sergeant?"

Still no word.

Captain Apocalypse said, "I am going to say it one more time, where is my fucking sergeant?"

They just dropped their heads.

As he was about to pull out his pistol on Qs, her twelve-year-old son tried to raise his gun up on Captain Apocalypse, but Sergeant

Boogeyman snatched the gun out of his hands and pushed him on the forehead, making him flip once and land on his side.

His mother said, "We don't know where he's at. They took him after shooting him, killing my daughter and husband, and beating me up. We don't know where he went. They took him. They took him!"

Captain Apocalypse picked up Sergeant Flood's stuff and said, "Let's go find our brother, soldiers. Do you all agree?"

They all saluted him as they all walked out of the door to find Sergeant Flood. They split up in four groups of five and were ordered to kill only and trust no one and to report in ten hours by the field where the general's chopper was. They walked around, asking if any of the people had seen a truck full of North Vietnamese soldiers with an American soldier on the back of it with them. Some said no, some would not speak to them, some would not get involved, while some could not understand their words to them. Captain Apocalypse and his team just walked from night to day and then to night again, and still they couldn't find a soul to tell them that they saw anything. Captain Apocalypse knew that these were South Vietnamese people and that they would not treat them like they were strangers, as they were allies to the United States, because the United States had sent them over here to stop this mass slaughter of innocent men, women, children, and elders.

All of them made it back to the chopper, and Captain Apocalypse said, "We have lost one of ours, soldiers, and I am not going to rest until we bring him back, dead or alive. But now we have to leave. Salute this country and don't ever forget that it took one of us."

As they walked in those tall weeds and got into the helicopter, the North Vietnamese had it surrounded, shooting at them like they were sitting ducks. Those North Vietnamese shooting through the bushes made it sound like Fourth of July, and they all jumped out of the chopper, firing back heavily and throwing pineapple hand grenades at them. They were shooting in all directions, and then one direction stopped firing at them, on the left side, and then the right side stopped firing at them, but the back side still did. When those shots died away completely, Captain Apocalypse and his team didn't know what made them stop; he just knew they were ambushed. The helicopter had hundreds and hundreds of bullet holes in it. Sergeant Rattler was lying on the ground with his forearm missing from his right side, lying next to him.

Sergeant Illusionist said, "Captain Apocalypse, we have Sergeant Rattler down, sir!"

Captain Apocalypse replied, "Put him in the chopper and get his arm, now! Put him in the chopper now!"

As they put him, his arm, and his gun in the chopper, Captain Apocalypse noticed that it was two missing instead of one. He said, "Numbers! I want numbers now!"

The No-Name Unit said, "One, two, three, four…six, seven, eight, nine, ten, eleven…thirteen, fourteen, fifteen, sixteen, seventeen, eighteen, nineteen, twenty."

Sergeant Furious said, "Sergeant Destroyer, Captain, it's Sergeant Destroyer!"

Captain Apocalypse said, "Sergeant Destroyer, if you are alive, click your code as well as my code ASAP!"

Sergeant Destroyer pushed his code and Captain Apocalypse's code, No Pity and Ibdam respectively. Captain Apocalypse said, "Stand your ass down, soldier, and get your goddamn ass to this chopper! Stop with the fucking pity, soldier! No pity, no fucking pity!"

Sergeant Destroyer was lying on his back with five bullet holes going through his stomach, a chunk of meat out of his right arm and left leg, and a bullet hole to his left hand, and the right side of his ski mask and stocking cap were split from his jaw down to his neck. He came walking out of the midst of sixty-five to seventy dead North Vietnamese soldiers that he had annihilated for trying to kill his team. Sergeant Big Badass Wolf and Sergeant Boogeyman were about to jump out of the chopper to help him when Captain Apocalypse said, "He doesn't need any help. Leave him alone, soldiers."

Sergeant Destroyer was using his gun and a North Vietnamese gun as a crutch to make it to the chopper. He got in and threw the North Vietnamese gun down as Captain Apocalypse said, "Let's go home, soldiers. Let's go home."

They took off in the general's helicopter, going back to Da Nang Air Base in a Huey full of bullet holes. As they landed the chopper, General Foster watched them landing in and smoking very badly, with bullet holes so big he could put his fist through them. He came out running, old as he was, still helping them out of the chopper. He said, "Captain Apocalypse, I saw twenty-one of y'all leave here, and now only twenty came back. Do you need us, Captain?"

General Foster saw two were injured, and he said again, "Captain Apocalypse, is there anything that you need for me to do for you?"

Captain Apocalypse replied, "General, sir, it's better for you not to get involved in this, but we did survive to live and see another day. I would like to recruit three of your best medical staff, if you can spare them, and I would like to swear them in under the penalty of espionage and treason if they violate this unit. That's if you'll allow me, sir, and if it is possible for us to have them, sir."

General Forster said, "Yes, it is possible. And consider it done. What happened to just a 'Simple Simon' mission, Captain Apocalypse?"

Captain Apocalypse said, "Only the insects on the walls know, General, only the insects on the walls know that answer."

The medical staff, including doctors, loaded up on the Lockheed C-5 Galaxy plane for Sergeant Rattler and Sergeant Destroyer. Captain Apocalypse and his sergeants saluted General Foster, getting on the plane as the door closed and taking off while General Foster was watching them disappear in the dark night sky. Captain Apocalypse got up and went into the back, where the doctors were tending to Sergeant Destroyer and Sergeant Rattler. He went over to Sergeant Destroyer and said, "I had a gut feeling that it was you out there annihilating those fucking North Vietnamese soldiers." Sergeant Destroyer moved his left eyebrow as Captain Apocalypse (Sergeant Ibdam) continued, "We all thank you, Sergeant Robert 'No Pity' Kristoff, the Destroyer." He then whispered in his right ear, "You saved all our lives, and you brought us home. All of us."

Sergeant Destroyer said, "I didn't bring all of us back, Captain. I did not bring all of us back. I failed you, sir. I failed." He then went to sleep.

Captain Apocalypse wiped the blood streaming off the deep slash to his face, replying in a whisper in his ear, "You didn't fail, soldier. You didn't fail. Fight for your life now, soldier. You have to fight for yourself. Don't show pity to death. Do you hear me, soldier? Don't show no fucking pity to death."

Captain Apocalypse went back up front with the rest of the soldier and said, "They're going to be all right, soldiers. They'll be all right."

The Lockheed C-5 Galaxy plane made it back to their base with one missing in action and two injured and in the care of three medical doctors who were now part of their team. After they were put in their rooms, Captain Apocalypse turned on their intercom buttons and he said, "I want all the soldiers of the No-Name Unit and the staff to report out front of the eating area."

They all came down.

Captain Apocalypse said, "We have two badly wounded soldiers in their rooms, and we have to pull our shit together to watch over them. I want us all to spend a day in their rooms with our brothers. The medical staff will be in and out at all times, plus the medical staff need their rest so they will be able to tend to our teammates properly. So, medical staff, get some sleep too. I want y'all to spend at least eight hours a day with them. Are there any questions?"

Not one person said a word. Their thoughts were on their brothers there with them, fighting for their lives, but they also wondered about the things that Sergeant Flood must be going through back in that country that was not his. They all were wondering why they ain't talking about getting him cut of there from those murdering motherfuckers who had kidnapped him for protecting a family that tried to help them. They killed a seven-year-old little girl that could not have harmed them even if she tried. They put three big rounds in her little head and chest, killing her instantly.

Since no one had any questions, Captain Apocalypse said, "Okay, you all can go now, and I thank you, staff, for agreeing to help us."

They all just saluted him, going back to their patients.

The whole unit was in deep thought, but they knew that this was their job, and they knew that they had some good side as well as bad ones, as this was what this job offered. This was not a case of what-if to these soldiers. The job that they faced was very dangerous, but now this had become personal to them. Their thoughts were on their teammates and on revenge for what those North Vietnamese did to them. "No guts, no glory" was what was keeping them.

Captain Apocalypse was walking around the unit when he saw five sergeants in Sergeant Destroyer's room and seven in Sergeant Rattler's room, standing around them in a circle of protection. Sergeant Hectic was the spokesman of the group. "We will carry you. We will die for you. We will kill for you. We will battle for you. We will do whatever you wish for you."

They did not expect for Sergeant Rattler to respond, but he said, "I want my own revenge. I am a soldier, and I want to die a soldier. Train me to use my only arm, as this shit isn't…" *Cough cough cough.* "Over." *Cough cough cough.* The MT laid him down, giving him a morphine shot as blood was still coming out of his arm. They all just went on their left knee and vowed to their brothers. They still did not get a chance to hear or see what he looked like. Captain Apocalypse was watching his sergeants checking on one another as a whole, and he could not be any prouder for handpicking all these soldiers. All the remaining sergeants were standing at the three doors of their unit. They were at number 2, number 5, and number 12. They were just standing there like statues as Captain Apocalypse saluted them and said, "Good job, soldiers. Damn good goddamn job."

The MTs had never experienced this type of brotherly love before. They knew that this team would die for one another, and they were proud to be a part of them, as they had sworn under the penalty of espionage and treason for revealing anything about this unit or the soldiers. As they sat there in their unit, all kinds of things came from the bigwigs up top. The commander in chief wrote them, which the captain read, "Captain Apocalypse and team, I am so sorry. I myself and my family send our condolence, as well as the people of this country. You are my right hand, and now it's time for us to leave well enough alone, Captain Apocalypse. Please do inform me on what you want from your country for all you and your team have done. Signed, CIC."

Captain Apocalypse went up to his office upstairs, where he hit the main intercom button so that everyone in this unit could hear what he was about to say to the CIC. The phone rang for about four times, then Captain Apocalypse said, "I am Captain Apocalypse. I would like to speak to my boss, the commander in chief, President Richard C. Crawford II."

The CIC said, "This is the CIC. How can I help you, Captain Apocalypse?"

Captain Apocalypse replied, "President Crawford, sir, your soldiers and I knew what we were up against when we took this role. We don't have any complaints, and if we complain even once, then you remove us from this project, sir. Many soldiers have died, and many allies to our country have been tortured for assisting us. We cannot let these terrorists think that we don't have what it takes to remove their asses out of the innocent people's way. We are the ones who make you not seen but give the credit to, and it'll never be on you, sir. We belong to you and your country and we do as you wish, but we cannot allow those people to think that we are not the ones who can stop them and put them in their place, and that is in the ground. And plus, sir, they still have one of my soldiers over there. Dead or alive, I want him back. No, let me rephrase that: the soldiers and I want him back, sir. So, sir, I ask you with bravery and honor to not stop this unit until we are dead and to show that we died for the right reason for our country. I have a sergeant that just lost half of his arm, and he wants us as a team to train him to use his good arm. And my other sergeant killed almost seventy North Vietnamese soldiers by himself, and he lives to tell about it. Now, this is what you really would actually do to us?"

President Crawford said, "Captain Apocalypse, continue as you wish, and Godspeed." Then he hung up the phone.

Captain Apocalypse sat at his desk and got back on the phone, saying, "Will you please connect me with the director of the CIA, please, ma'am?"

She said, "Please hold on, sir. And may I ask who's calling?"

He said, "Yes, I am Captain Apocalypse."

She said, "Please hold."

He was on the phone for at least three minutes, then a voice came on the line and said, "I'm the director's secretary. How may I help you?"

Captain Apocalypse said in his mechanical voice, "Yes, I am Captain Apocalypse, and I would like to speak to the director."

She said, "Sir, I cannot do that. Sorry, sir."

He said, "Look, missus, miss, or whoever you may be, you have ten seconds to connect me to the director, and you have already lost four seconds of it. I am the captain of a very special force, and I need to talk with him."

She said, "Again, I'm sorry, sir, but I still cannot connect you, and I will not accept your threats very likely."

Captain Apocalypse said, again in his mechanical voice, "Ma'am, missus, or miss, I'm sorry too, but I want you to pack all your shit at your desk and get up and start walking, because you'll be fired in sixty seconds after I hang this phone up on you."

She said, "You better stop this before this line gets traced and you'll be arrested for—"

Captain Apocalypse hung up before she could finish her sentence to him.

She said, "Hanging up the phone while I'm talking. What's his fucking problem, with him disguising his voice and threatening me and my job?"

As she was cleaning up her desktop, three CIA agents came into the director's office, and one of them said to the secretary, "Mrs. Janice Storm?"

She said, "Yes. May I help you agents?"

He said, "Ma'am, I am Agent Greg Hammerson, and we were told to escort you out of the building because you're fired."

As she was about to reply, the phone rang, and Agent Hammerson said, "You can answer that, Mrs. Storm."

She said, "Mrs. Storm. This is Director Fredrick Jefferson's office. How may I help you?"

Captain Apocalypse said again in his mechanical voice, "I am Captain Apocalypse. I would like to speak to your director, please."

She said, "I have warned you once about these obscene phone calls, whoever you are. As a matter of fact, I have here somebody you can talk with. Here, talk to him with your funny voice."

She gave the phone receiver to Agent Hammerson, who said, "I am Agent Hammerson." Agent Hammerson kept on replying, "Yes, sir, Captain," "I hear you, Captain," "I have no problem, Captain," "I am very sorry for the misunderstanding, Captain," "The whole building apologizes for this employee," "Yes, sir, Captain, we should screen them with diligence, sir," "I understand."

As he continued talking with Captain Apocalypse, she was in shock, replying, "I did not know! Please understand! I did not have clue that this call was important! Please allow me—"

Before she could finish, one of the other agents said to her, all while Agent Hammerson was still talking to Captain Apocalypse, "Ma'am, be quiet."

Agent Hammerson said, "It is done, sir. We thank you and your team for a job well done." He then buzzed Captain Apocalypse to the director.

Agent Hammerson said to his other two agents, "Take Mrs. Janice Storm to the mail room. She's demoted. And dock her pay for six months right now for disrespecting a ranking authority of this country."

She was very much confused because she did not know that this phone call was real. She said, "I really did not—"

Before she could finish, Agent Hammerson said, "Mrs. Storm, all calls that come in here are very much screened, because that is our job. How do you think we know what is going on here? Plus, we were told to fire you at first, but Captain Apocalypse asked for that to not happen, and that was his wish, so thank him for you to be still working at all. After he found out that you have three children to feed and you are a single mother with a deceased husband, he felt bad for you. Your pay will not be docked, but you will be demoted to a lesser job, ma'am."

They walked her out of the office as another lady sat in her seat.

Captain Apocalypse said to the director, Fredrick Jefferson, "Sir, if you can, I would like for some person-to-person intel on a mission that I myself and my team went on a few days ago. Please do not ask for anyone to assist you as I need for you to do this on your own. I don't understand what went wrong, but it did happen, and now I'm looking for answers. So will you please give me some intel on Mrs. Qs Long and her husband? The North Vietnamese leader is Cho San Hue, and his captain is Lon Nol. When you find this out, call me back at this number, 299-810-0000, and I'll be up at any time."

Director Jefferson said, "I'll take care of that ASAP." They then both hung up their phones.

Captain Apocalypse was just sitting there, contemplating about what went wrong on their Simple Simon mission, because there wasn't anything simple about that mission. He knew losing a soldier was way worth having an injured soldier. Captain Apocalypse knew that they were not immortal and that they could die on any of the missions that they went on. They went on at least nine to ten Simple Simon missions, and not one single soldier was injured, but this Simple Simon mission was not a simple one. Two got injured, and one was missing in action.

Captain Apocalypse was in the dark office of his and heard everything on the intercom. He said, "This is not fucking over by a long shot. I won't die until I find out what happened on this fucking mission. I'd be goddamned if I let this fucking shit die or go unnoticed. Whoever is involved will die in these hands of mine with an angry revenge." He just lay back in his chair, staring at the ceiling.

Now it's May 19, 1966. Sergeant Destroyer was healing from his multiple bullet wounds and cuts, feeling 85 percent better, while Sergeant Rattler was still having problems accepting his one arm. He was getting very frustrated of what he was trying to accomplish. He had learned how to eat, write, and load his weapons as well as reload his clips faster than anyone and probably anything. As far as putting his sniper rifle into position to take aim and brace, it was still a serious task for him. His AK-47, shotgun, tommy gun, and M16 were just the same as his sniper rifle. He looked at the part of his arm where his forearm and hand used to be, and he just thought, What could he actually do about it? He was staring very hard and smiled behind his ski mask and stocking cap. He then pushed his code and Captain Apocalypse's code.

Captain Apocalypse said, "Go ahead, Sergeant Rattler."

Sergeant Rattler said, "I really need to talk to you, sir, when you find some spare time."

Captain Apocalypse said, "I always have time for my team soldier. I'd be at you in five minutes." But he was just sitting in the dark, still contemplating.

It had been eleven months since that mission took place, but he really was angry at the madness that came across him and his team, and he decided he was going to annihilate the madness that possessed the ones that did this to him and his team. Captain Apocalypse said, "I am Captain Apocalypse, searching and seeking to annihilate and destroy madness. Anything that sleeps, speaks, crawls, and eats. I am Captain Angry Apocalypse." He walked out of the door still staring into the darkness of no return. His real code name, the one given by his general and country, was Ibdam, and the comment was, "Did he really actually do this shit in our fucking armed service? This damn young man is a nuisance!"

That word *nuisance* had been ringing in his head from the age of nineteen until now. Being a forty-one-year-old leader of the most elite handpicked squad ever molded and produced the same way as him was what he had wanted for years. Captain Apocalypse never doubted his team, as they did everything that he expected them and then some.

He made it down to where Sergeant Rattler was, out at the target range, firing off shots as if he had not lost his arm. "Captain Apocalypse, I see that you still have what it takes to come up on us to see where our titles stand, sir," said Sergeant Rattler.

Captain Apocalypse replied, "Sergeant Rattler, what is going on here? How are you doing that, soldier?"

Sergeant Rattler said, "Captain Apocalypse, sir, I refuse to feel sorry for myself and accept pity when I know that I am stronger than that, sir. Sergeant Destroyer went to kill all those motherfuckers as if he were invisible or immortal or he just didn't give a shit about himself. He put his goddamn life in danger for us all, and that is who I admire the most, sir. He could have died if it weren't for you, sir, and that has been in my head, my heart, and my mind, to actually see what I saw that day. You told Sergeant Big Badass Wolf and Sergeant Boogeyman to get back in the chopper because he did not need their help. I did not understand why at that time, but I did earlier, so that is why I am like this now, sir."

Captain Apocalypse said, "Continue on, soldier. At ease, Sergeant Rattler. As you were." He walked off, going back to his office, the gunshots echoing as Captain Apocalypse said very loudly, getting the attention of Sergeant Rattler, "Sergeant, Sergeant, Sergeant, Sergeant, Sergeant, Sergeant…Rattler, Rattler, Rattler, Rattler, Rattler, Rattler, Rattler, Rattler…your, your, your, your, your, your, your…new, new, new, new, new, new, new, new…code name, code name, code name, code name, code name, code name, code name…is, is, is, is, is, is, is, is, is…Doom! Doom! Doom! Doom! Doom! Doom! Doom!"

Sergeant Rattler, now Sergeant Doom, grabbed his bazooka and blew up his target to smithereens. It was in thousands of thousands of pieces, his shot even destroying everything that was fifty yards around his target as the ground shook with a small vibration. Captain Apocalypse hit the ground hard and fast. As the dust was settling down, he saw Sergeant Doom still kneeling down on his left knee, holding the bazooka on his left shoulder with a homemade device braced on his arm where his forearm used to be.

Captain Apocalypse got off the ground and said, "'What the fuck was that?" That thing had his ears ringing as he dusted himself off, walking away, looking at Sergeant Rattler (Sergeant Doom).

Captain Apocalypse just nodded, knowing that he and his team were not immortal but were some die-hard-ass sons of bitches.

He walked around, noticing the other soldiers going through training and testing their abilities, putting them to the maximum that it could go. They were running two hundred yards from one end and back and to the other end and back again and then jogged half their speed around the track. They did this four times in good timing, then picked up their weapons and loaded them, hitting their targets in the heads, necks, and hearts as they fired from the ground and then up on their knees and then standing. They then walked in a stretched-out line in order, hitting their targets in the heads, necks, and hearts. Captain Apocalypse watched them hit the ground and pick up their bazookas, blowing everything away as they got up and stretched in order, going to the lake and going under the water for at least twenty-five minutes, then easing up at the same time for about forty-five seconds for air, then back under as they made it to the other side and out of the water at the same time.

Sergeant Destroyer and Sergeant Rattler both were right there with their team, as if they were never wounded in their little battle. Captain Apocalypse was just watching his soldiers and standing up in a salute. The team was about to continue on while they were on the other side when Sergeant Hectic saw Captain Apocalypse standing over there, saluting them. He stood up and saluted him back, as did the rest of them. They were having an invisible war with themselves, stopping, and all of them entered the water at the same time, going under at the same time as well. They were under for thirty-three minutes and came up for air to catch their breath for twenty-eight seconds, then went back under again. They all came out and ran up to him in full speed and stopped at attention at the same time in front of him, saluting him.

Captain Apocalypse said, "Damn good training, soldiers. Good job. At ease. I know that you all are doing just fine. I am very much in an understanding stage. Take the rest of the day off. Move out!"

They all walked off, heading toward the unit to take a shower for themselves and eat some lunch. As the team was walking in, they heard a big booming sound, and when they turned around, they saw a big chunk missing out of the ground, and also missing was the deuce and a quarter truck that used to sit on that spot. All they could see was a whole lot of pieces that used to be a truck everywhere they looked.

Captain Apocalypse thought to himself, *We won't be needing that anytime soon.* He then laid that bazooka down on the ground, walking behind his team going inside.

It was now February 24, 1967, two years after Sergeant Flood was captured and two years after the battle on their mission that caused Sergeant Rattler his arm and wounded Sergeant Destroyer almost to death. Captain Apocalypse was sitting in his office and pushing the main intercom button and said, "All soldiers—and I do mean *all* soldiers—to meet in the debriefing room ASAP!"

All of them had been in the debriefing room, sitting quietly in their assigned seat, for fifteen minutes when Sergeant Big Badass Wolf and Sergeant Boogeyman came in. They both stood at an end of the table, and two minutes later, Captain Apocalypse opened the door. Sergeant Big Badass Wolf and Sergeant Boogeyman said at the same time in their mechanical voice, "Attention!"

They all stood up as Captain Apocalypse said, "At ease, soldiers. Have a seat. This is a briefing that we all shall talk about, and I will not make this decision alone. I have to include you in this mission's decision on a voluntary thing. You have the right to say yeah or nay in this mission. Now, team, I have racked my brains over and over and over trying to figure out what happened on our Simple Simon mission, and I still have not figured it out until today. Our plan was executed the way it was supposed to, but goddammit, something went very wrong. Shit, I'm still having headaches about this shit. I went over our briefing so many fucking times until I lost a goddamn count of it. I did replay after replay, but the bullshit was still blocking me from what I was searching for, until I have come to one fucking conclusion on that damn mission. My answer is to go back over there to that goddamn country and find Sergeant Flood, dead or alive, and bring him back home at all costs. We did leave him, and we left him over there, and I want our teammate back. We will go unannounced and find out what happened. I talked with an intelligence agent at the CIA for some information on every ally over there, and I received this package yesterday. I refused to open it until we all are at this here table. I don't give a rat's ass what it says, because either way I want to go do a diligent search for Sergeant Flood. This briefing is truly an unauthorized mission, and we will not have any assistance whether we need it or not. And it is not like we ever use it, anyway."

Captain Apocalypse opened the envelope and pulled the pictures and intel out of it about the requested information. Captain Apocalypse looked at it for seven minutes, then passed it around the table to all his sergeants. They saw that their safe house was in the intel, but without any direct information. The names that were on the list included the leader Cho San Hue, General Bien Lo, Captain Lon Nol, Lieutenant Lo Hap, and Sergeant Turtle Dragon. "None of these people knew of our mission and about our safe house, where a little girl was killed, a husband was shot, and our host was beaten very badly. All those houses couldn't have heard our shots even, because of our silencers. Those fucking North Vietnamese came in some way in order to battle with us, as they had all those other houses surrounded, and probably were holding those other families as hostages to stop them from talking to us. They want our way of training and our way of doing things on our missions. Those fucking North Vietnamese soldiers needed one of us, and they got one of us. I do believe that Sergeant Flood is still alive, and even if he is not, I still want him back. Whether he is dead or alive. Then somebody will tell us where Cho San Hue, Bien Lo, Lon Nol, Lo Hap, and Turtle Dragon are. This bullshit has to be reckoned with. Now, team, the question is, Are you all aboard for this mission?"

They all picked up their gavels and hit the table one at a time according to their number. The MTs hit the table as well. Captain Apocalypse then said, "Agreed." He then turned off the lights and cut the slide projector on from, showing photos and info on that Simple Simon mission. They looked at all the houses and people that stayed in them; it was showing men, women, and children.

Captain Apocalypse said, "We have fifteen houses circling this compound in the middle, and we're going to give them a taste of their own medicine. I want twenty-three United States soldiers' uniforms of mainly 2, 3, and 4 x's. Boots sizes 7 to 12 for each uniform. Get black ski masks and M16 with blanks in them. I want some heavy-duty tape that sticks real good.

"We're going to snatch up some North Vietnamese soldiers and dress them like United States soldiers. When they see them, we can then rest assured whom we're up against, and their asses, not knowing who these soldiers are, will sure in hell kill them, not knowing they are one of them.

"Now, as for our position, I am going to give you your position and you study them and burn the info when you finish. All of us will be using bazookas in this mission. Now, listen carefully. Sergeant Maniac, Sergeant Tornado, and Sergeant Polarize, I want you three to take the four houses on the north side of the middle of that compound, and I want you to wait for my mark. Sergeant Fatal, Sergeant Shadow, and Sergeant Consequence, I want you three to take the four houses on the east side of the middle of that compound and you three wait for my mark. Sergeant Nuclear, Sergeant Furious, and Sergeant Lowlife, I want you three to take the four houses on the west side of the middle of that compound, and you three wait for my mark as well. Sergeant Hocus-Pocus, Sergeant Eliminate, and Sergeant Illusionist, I want you three to take the three houses on the south side of the middle of that compound, and you three wait for my mark.

"Now, we got three towers with two guys in each tower. I want Sergeant Destroyer, Sergeant Hectic, and Sergeant Evil to take sniper rifles and eliminate them first before our battle begins. I want you to wait until you hear this." *Click click click.* "And hit them in the heads, necks, or hearts. And then I want Sergeant Hectic and Sergeant Evil to take over those towers. Sergeant Destroyer, I want you to take the ground with Sergeant Animosity and start at that compound in the middle of those houses. When we come flying in, bring hell to these goddamn North Vietnamese soldiers.

"I am going to call General Foster and ask him if we can borrow two of the baddest equipment on his lot. I want Sergeant Big Badass Wolf, Sergeant Boogeyman, and Sergeant Rattler to take the plane *Puff, the Magic Dragon*, and I want Sergeant Rattler to handle the Gatling guns on both sides as Sergeant Big Badass Wolf and Sergeant Boogeyman fly like hell into their asses. And Sergeant Big Badass Wolf, Sergeant Boogeyman, and Sergeant Rattler, make the inventor of the Gatling guns proud and make him look up from his grave and cheer y'all on. I want you three to wait for my mark especially. I will be flying solo in the Cobra attack chopper. I want all of you ground crew to wear this new thing that we have, which is called M1951, and a bulletproof armor, and I want you to bring at least eight more just in case we find Sergeant Flood alive. I want some guns in his hands also.

"When we hit these sons of bitches, I don't want a stone left standing. Tear that motherfucker down to the goddamn ground and make them pick that shit up to find their goddamn friends, if they can, after we finish with their asses. Are we clear about our mission?"

Everybody stood up at the same time and saluted Captain Apocalypse.

Captain Apocalypse said, "Sergeant Big Badass Wolf and Sergeant Boogeyman, go down and get the C-5 Galaxy ready and remove the Sea Stallion from it as we won't be needing it, because when we get back to Da Nang Air Base, we'll be taking *Puff, the Magic Dragon*, better known as Spooky, with those Gatling guns and the Cobra attack chopper with us, and we will return them to General Fredrick Foster after we finish.

"Now, we will be leaving early tomorrow at 0400, and we want to land at 0100, and maybe a small brief to make sure we are ready. Plus, I want to peep the scenery before we make our move. I want you all to know that this mission might end badly, but I don't know for who.

"All right, team, move out and get some rest and study your plans to the maximum and burn them in your rooms."

As they were leaving, Captain Apocalypse said to his MTs, "You can go if you like, and if you don't, you still have your jobs when we get back. This mission isn't for everybody. Do you understand? So are you three in on this mission?"

They all said, "Yes, sir, Captain Apocalypse, sir."

One of them continued, "We're a part of this team. We're your medical team, so yes, Captain Apocalypse, we're in, sir."

Captain Apocalypse said, "Then go get suited up, as your suits are in your personal rooms."

As they left, Captain Apocalypse picked up his phone and called General Fredrick Foster on his hotline. The phone rang twice, then General Foster picked up and said, "You got General Foster here, Mr. President. How can I help you, sir?"

Captain Apocalypse said in his mechanical voice, "General Foster, this is Captain Apocalypse, not the president, sir. I am calling for two very important pieces of your equipment."

General Foster replied, "Captain Apocalypse, how are you and your men doing? I'm sorry for what happened, and I know it's hard to lose a man under your watch. What can I do for you, Captain?"

Captain Apocalypse said, "Sir, I need your permission and blessing to enter into your territory so that I can take care of some unfinished business. I need also to borrow two of your important equipment."

General Foster said, "I can do both, but the part about the equipment, you have to be frank with me, okay?"

Captain Apocalypse said, "General Foster, I am frank. I need your *Puff, the Magic Dragon* with two Gatling guns, one on each side, and have it fully loaded for my fliers and gunman, if you can. I also would like to borrow the Cobra attack chopper, if you can do that as well. I am being frank with you, sir. Can you make that happen?"

General Foster laughed out loud for about five seconds and said, "Shit, Captain, I thought you wanted my damn wife! Shit, *Frank*, it's yours whenever you need it. The Cobra attack can be flown by one man if you're not scared of it. I flew that motherfucker in so many battles by myself, probably before you were born or when you were just a snot-nosed kid. I'll let my ground crew off that day until you leave, and off again when it wis over with. It's all yours, Captain Apocalypse."

Captain Apocalypse said, "General Foster, sir, I still have to be frank with you, sir."

General Foster said, "Permission to speak, *Frank*."

Captain Apocalypse said, "General Foster, this mission—"

General Foster cut Captain Apocalypse off by replying, "What I don't know won't hurt me, Captain Apocalypse. I know nothing. This here conversation never took place. You and your team never landed here the first, second, third—"

General Foster was cut short in his sentence as well by Captain Apocalypse saying, "Understood, General Spooky." They both laughed and then hung up their phones on each other.

General Foster stood up and looked out of his window and said at old Spooky, "Spooky, old boy, you're about to go into a battle that you'll never forget. Make this old man proud." General Foster hit his intercom button and told his secretary to send for his machinery mechanic.

Eight minutes went past before his machinery mechanic came in and saluted General Foster and said, "You sent for me, sir?"

General Foster said, "Yes, Lance Corporal Williamson. I need for you to take *Puff, the Magic Dragon* up for a test run, and after you give it a rough and tough run, then I want you to fill the tanks and put a Gatling gun on each side and load that boy up with extra ammos. After you finish that, then I want the same for the Cobra attack chopper, and load that son of a bitch with everything that goes into it."

Lance Corporal Williamson said, "Yes, sir, General Foster, sir." He saluted the general, going out of the door to do as he was instructed.

General Foster knew it was about to be hell, and he was glad that he wasn't the one that fucked with these soldiers, who didn't know the meaning of dying, or care about dying. General Foster said to himself, "Whoever these poor sons of bitches are that fucked with this goddamn team, may the Lord have mercy on your souls, because these boys are about to show y'all asses the true meaning of what hell looks like. What hell does to you while being in it. And who doesn't want to be in its domain."

He shook his head, picking up a cigar and lighting it, and stared at himself standing between *Puff, the Magic Dragon* and the Cobra attack Helicopter.

Captain Apocalypse, meanwhile, walked back to his quarter and lay down to get himself some rest. As he was lying there in the dark, he said, "Sergeant Flood, whether you're dead or alive, we're coming to get you, soldier. Hold on and we will find you no matter what. I want you to know that we are bringing death with us—no, we are bringing death and hell with us. So hold on to your last breath. Leader Cho San Hue, General Bien Lo, Captain Lon Nol, Lieutenant Lo Hap, and Sergeant Turtle Dragon, all your days have been numbered, and it's time to exit this life you're living, says me, the one that can make that happen. I *am* Captain Apocalypse!"

In Vietnam, General Bien Lo was watching his captain torture Sergeant Flood. He said, "General, he is not talking, sir. We have burned his hair off, broken two of his ribs, broken his jaw, broken his nose, pulled out seventeen of his teeth, and we even fed him rats to eat, and his left eye is blind, sir. What else can we do to this damn stupid American for invading our country? So stop feeling bad for this damn American and let's kill him!"

Sergeant Flood had pissed and shit all over himself. Vomit was coming all out of his mouth as they all were taking turn pissing and spitting on him. Sergeant Turtle Dragon was on her period, and she lifted her dress and pulled her panties off, sitting on his face, rubbing her pussy blood all over his face. The general and captain were laughing at her for doing this to him, while three big tigers were trying to get through those bars to get him.

General Bien Lo said, "We give him two more days, and if he does not talk or is dead, then we kill him."

Sergeant Turtle Dragon stuck a cotton ball up in her bloody pussy and got it soaked and wet. She said, "This is from my country, stupid American soldier!" She pushed it in his mouth, and he gagged off it, trying to spit it out as she said, "Aww, he doesn't like my pussy, General."

The males all left Sergeant Turtle Dragon in there with him. She said, "Tell me about your friends and you live." She was squeezing his dick and nuts as she said this, licking his cuts.

Sergeant Flood looked at her as she got up in his face, and he was whispering something. She put her right ear up to his mouth, but then his side teeth gnashed on her ear, biting it off. She screamed as loud as she could. Sergeant Flood chewed on her ear, staring up at the ceiling, as the others rushed in and rushed her out of the room. He spit out her ear and smiled, saying, "Captain Apocalypse, sir, I am here, still alive and maintaining my vows for the No-Name Unit. We are a team of justice who do our best to stop any injustice in any country. I am alive, sir. I know you're coming. I am not dead, and if I am dead by the time you arrive, then just take me home."

Sergeant Flood was not feeling sorry for himself; he was feeling sorry for the ones that were about to receive the worst of the worst pain that could ever be given to a person. The pain that they were about to endure was way shorter than his. Sergeant Flood had not let those who tortured him know that he was paralyzed from the waist down. All the insect soup, molded bread, and dead rats that they fed him did not bother him, though he pretended that it did. He ate it to keep himself alive as a survivor. The three big tigers were smelling his blood as well as the blood from Sergeant Turtle Dragon's pussy that she spread on him, plus her blood from his biting off her right ear.

In the United States, it was now 0400 as they all were lined up at the tunnel door right along with the MTs. They climbed on the back of the Harleys with their teammates, going to the elevator shaft to go to C-5 Galaxy plane. They made it to the elevator shaft and were going to the plane, where Sergeant Big Badass Wolf and Sergeant Boogeyman were waiting for them, standing at attention. They, too, all stood up at attention as Captain Apocalypse said, "At ease, soldiers. Let's move out."

They all loaded up on the plane as it slowly started moving as smooth as always. The plane left the ground, taking them back to the mission they decided to call Death Mission, back to South Vietnam, to get those who presented themselves to be South Vietnamese when they were North Vietnamese soldiers.

When Captain Apocalypse and his team made it back to Da Nang Air Base in South Vietnam, Lance Corporal Williamson landed them in and watched the team unload themselves off the plane, marching in single file following behind Captain Apocalypse, as he was going inside to meet the general. General Foster met them. They saluted him as Captain Apocalypse said in his mechanical voice, "General Foster, sir."

General Foster said, "Everything is ready for you, Captain Apocalypse."

Captain Apocalypse replied, "Thank you, General Foster, sir."

They all were saluting him when General Foster said, "Room 417, and it is yours, Captain. Now, at ease and go and get your soldier, Captain Apocalypse!"

They all walked off, and as they did, Captain Apocalypse said, "I need to borrow your Red Cross food truck with a little food in it. I need something almost like a deuce and a quarter with twenty-three pairs of handcuffs and shackles."

General Foster said, "Done, done, done, Captain. Those items will be in the truck when you get out to it." He looked at some of his medical staff walking with them, and they now were being treated like members of their team. He was very proud and honored to see them being treated like they belonged to that group.

As they made it to the debriefing room, Captain Apocalypse said, "Everybody have a seat. Now, we need to go get twenty-three North Vietnamese soldiers and sacrifice their asses to their own people. I want Sergeant Illusionist, Sergeant Boogeyman, Sergeant Big Badass Wolf, Sergeant Shadow, and Sergeant Hocus-Pocus. Go get the truck and put the food in it and go to this trail line that is call Ho Chi Minh, where the North Vietnamese soldiers have been sneaking into South Vietnam. Use the food as bait and pretend that the truck broke down with South Vietnam food supplies and they'll feel as if it were for them. When the North Vietnamese tries to take it, then snatch their asses up, cuff them, shackle them, and gag them. Take a tranquilizer gun with you because we need them healthy. Are you five clear about this mission?"

They all stood up, saluting the captain, as Captain Apocalypse said, "Move out!"

As they left, going to the truck, Sergeant Shadow got in the driver's side, while the other four went under the truck and hid themselves. They were driving to the Saigon trail line. Sergeant Shadow had his ski mask off but was still dressed in the rest of his uniform and equipment. Sergeant Big Badass Wolf, Sergeant Illusionist, Sergeant Boogeyman, and Sergeant Hocus-Pocus had never seen Sergeant Shadow's face. They drove for forty minutes, and when he was about to park the truck, he tooted the horn and pulled over slowly on the side next to the wooded area and stopped for a split second. Sergeant Big Badass Wolf, Sergeant Boogeyman, Sergeant Illusionist, and Sergeant Hocus-Pocus let go of the truck and rolled in the woods. Sergeant Shadow jumped out of the truck and kicked the tires as if something were wrong. He started unloading some of the boxes and then walked off, putting on his mask. They waited for their targets to start coming, as they knew that somebody was watching.

An hour went by when they finally saw seven North Vietnamese walking down the trail, heading toward the truck. As they got closer, four more came running to it fast, as did the first seven ran with them as they looked the truck over. They then started going through the boxes, and that was when Sergeant Boogeyman, Sergeant Big Badass Wolf, Sergeant Illusionist, Sergeant Hocus-Pocus, and Sergeant Shadow hit their fucking asses with those tranquilizer guns, knocking their asses out while some were trying to run. Sergeant Shadow, Sergeant Illusionist, and Sergeant Big Badass Wolf handcuffed them, shackled them, gagged them, and threw their asses in the truck. They went back into the woods for another fifty minutes, and six more guys came down. Four of them were soldiers with guns, and they hit the ones in the back of the line first, then the fourth one, and the rest of them fell to the ground. As they were cuffing and shackling and were about to gag these six, that was when three more ran to the truck. As they got close, Sergeant Boogeyman and Sergeant Hocus-Pocus hit all of them twice with the tranquilizer gun, stopping them in their step.

Now two hours had passed, and ten North Vietnamese soldiers were coming to the truck with their guns pointed at the truck. They split up as they only needed four of them. Sergeant Illusionist and Sergeant Shadow were hitting them with the tranquilizer gun, and Sergeant Boogeyman, Sergeant Big Badass Wolf, and Sergeant Hocus-Pocus were killing them with their AK-47 with the silencers on them. They loaded all of them in the truck along with the food, and then they drove off, going back to the base, pulling the truck in the hangar of the warehouse.

Captain Apocalypse and his team came out there to Sergeant Illusionist, Sergeant Big Badass Wolf, Sergeant Hocus-Pocus, Sergeant Shadow, and Sergeant Boogeyman and said, "Are there any injuries? I want all of you to speak."

They responded in their mechanical voice, "We're okay, Doc." They then walked off.

One of the crew said, "Captain Apocalypse, we have four dead North Vietnamese soldiers also in the back, sir."

Captain Apocalypse responded, "Good job, damn good fucking job. Sergeant Destroyer, take the uniform off one of those dead sons of bitches and dress up in it. Then go to our friend's place to see how they have been doing since the last we were here, and to see if she needs anything after they killed her seven-year-old daughter. Go ahead now, Sergeant Destroyer. As for the rest of us, we will take the clothes off these live ones and place them in our uniforms and dress them like American soldiers. We will let it hit dark at 1600, then we will wake their fucking asses up with some smelling salt as we dress them up like American soldiers and put the black ski masks on their faces to have them look similar to us. After we get them fully dressed like United States soldiers, we then put those M16s in their hands and tape them to their hands with blanks in their clips. As we're done doing this to those North Vietnamese soldiers, Sergeant Destroyer, wearing the uniform of one of the North Vietnamese soldiers, will sneak around and cut corners, going through the woods, trying not to be seen."

Later, when he made it to Mrs. Qs Long's house, Sergeant Destroyer went behind and into and through the cellar door. He was easing through the house, and when he was about to go in to surprise her with his present and to let her know that they were back and that they needed her house again, that was when he heard a male voice saying to her, "Turtle Dragon, your hair can hide your missing ear. That American soldier is going to die tomorrow, and you can ask the general if you can be the one that can kill him and feed him to his tigers."

She said, "I will kill that son of a bitch good for biting off my ear."

He said, "I will see you tonight at the center. Take headache medicine and you will be okay and ready tonight. Later, Mrs. Qs Long, my Turtle Dragon."

As he left her, Sergeant Destroyer heard the voice of a fourteen-year-old boy say, "Turtle Dragon, you okay now, right?"

She said, "Yes, Tran Pham, I'm okay. You helped me captured that stupid American by shooting him in the legs for us. Now, get me some more water, please, soldier. Our leader, Cho San Hue, and General Bien Lo will definitely be proud of you, Tran Pham. Now, get me some water, please."

As he went into the other room, Sergeant Destroyer eased out of the cellar and up behind Tran Pham, grabbing him around his little neck and picking him off the floor. He pulled out his big-ass buck knife and cut Tran Pham's throat, blood gushing out of him. After he died in the arm of Sergeant Destroyer, Sergeant Destroyer easily set Tran Pham's body upward and then cut his head completely off his neck. Sergeant Destroyer stood up on his six-foot-one and 230-pound body, with Tran Pham's five-foot-three, 136-pound dead body lying by his feet. Tran Pham's head was in his left hand, his fingers in Tran Pham's mouth, holding it up.

Mrs. Qs Long, who really was Sergeant Turtle Dragon, said, "Come on, Tran Pham, I am hurting here. What is taking you a long time?"

Tran Pham couldn't say anything because he was dead. Sergeant Destroyer set Tran Pham's head down and picked up his little body, then threw it across his left shoulder. He knelt down and picked his head back up with his left hand and eased into the front part of the house, where he saw Mrs. Qs lying on the couch with nothing but her panties on, facing the back of the couch.

Mrs. Qs said, "Come on, boy, I need water."

Sergeant Destroyer threw his little body on top of her while her face was facing the back of the couch.

She said, "Shit, boy, I don't fuck little boys. Get off me and give me water!" She was just lying there in her panties and no bra. She said again, "You need no pussy, Tran Pham. I'm too old for you, and I got a headache."

His little dead body was still lying on the top of her.

She said, "Okay, you want pussy? I'll give you pussy!" She reached between them, pulling off her little blue panties and throwing them on the floor. She then reached into his little pants, not knowing that he was dead with no head, because she was still facing the back of the couch. She put her left leg up on the back of the couch while playing with Tran Pham's little dick, rubbing it up against her pussy lips.

Sergeant Destroyer just watched her as she said, "See? You don't want pussy—you can't get stiff! Now, get off me, Tran Pham!" She then felt something trickle down her neck, so she said, "You have wastewater on me!" She did not know that Sergeant Destroyer was dripping Tran Pham's blood on her as she brought her left hand up and wiped the side of her neck, still lying there with her little four-foot-eleven, 106-pound butt naked body. Sergeant Destroyer was still standing there as she put her left hand on her left hip and said, "Look, boy, you have to stop dripping this water on me!" She wiped again and again, the couch getting soaked with his blood; that was when she caught an attitude, forcing herself, trying to get him off her. She said, "Get up! You're too heavy! Get off me, Tran."

She still didn't know that he was dead and it was dead weight that was on her. She tried her best to push him off her as she said, "You get up now. Get! Off! Meeeeee!" His little body hit the floor hard, knocking over her medicine tray. She was laughing at him with his blood all over her little body and hand. She then put her fingers with his blood on them inside of her pussy, pulling her pussy walls open. She said, "You still can have some if you give me water."

Sergeant Destroyer was still standing there with Tran Pham's head in his hand. She turned on her back with a towel over her face, covering her eyes, and put her right leg on the back of the couch, her left leg on the floor. Her little legs were now spread-eagle, with her right hand rubbing and playing inside of her pussy. She said, "Come on, Tran. I need you, since you want it. Come on. I'll make it ready for you. I'll be your first woman." She then put her left hand on the back of his dead body as Sergeant Destroyer was still standing there, just watching her.

She said, "I won't tell your daddy that I gave you pussy. He's too old for me, anyway, but you're young and strong, and I am sorry for killing your little sister, but we had to make it look like we weren't involved with this shit. So stop being a little boy and come and get this pussy! Your daddy is torturing that stupid American, and you can torture my pussy!" She was still playing inside of herself.

As her left hand made it up to Tran Pham's neck, where his head used to be, she put her hand inside of his neck part and said, "What is this, boy? W-w-wh—"

She snatched the towel off her face with both hands, blinking fast, trying to focus her eyes. That was when she saw this six-foot-one, 230-pound man that she had seen two years ago standing over her as she started screaming. That was when he put his knee into her little chest really hard, knocking the wind out of her as she was looking into Tran Pham's dead eyes. Sergeant Destroyer was still holding his head in his hand. He put Tran Pham's blood in both of her eyes and set it on her face as he got his left hand around her throat. He put the little boy's head on the floor and picked up her panties, putting them in her mouth to gag her. Then he tied her mouth with the towel that she had and took Tran Pham's belt off. Then he flipped her on her stomach, tying her hands behind her back. He picked her up by her long hair, pulling some of it out, and sat her upright on the couch and just looked at her. She was muttering, trying to talk, and he was just standing there.

He then picked up Tran Pham's headless body and put it on the couch next to her, who was trying to scream. He picked up Tran Pham's head and spread her legs open wide and put Tran Pham's head between her legs, his eyes looking up at her as she was trying to scream. The blood from his neck was running down to her pussy, and still she was trying her best to scream. He knew that she was very important to this mission and he had tortured her enough. He also knew that she knew where Sergeant Flood was, because she also had tortured him.

Sergeant Destroyer ripped Tran Pham's shirt off his dead body and snatched Turtle Dragon's ass off the couch, throwing it on the floor onto her back and putting his size 14 boot in between her legs, pressing hard on her clitoris. She was trying her best to scream, her eyes wide open, since she was in deep pain. And he was looking into her eyes. He tied her feet up and pushed them hard to the floor as he stepped on top of her. Tears were steadily pouring out of her eyes. He then went to get two bedsheets and put them on the floor, doubling them up. He picked her up by the hair off the floor and dragged her naked body to the sheets, picking her up from the floor and throwing her on the sheets so hard the whole floor vibrated with her little body, blood coming out of the side of her head. By then, tears and blood were flowing together from her face, all while she was still trying to talk. She knew this was not Sergeant Flood, but she also knew this was one of his friends, one of those she had captured and tortured at their circle compound.

Sergeant Destroyer rolled her ass up in those sheets, tying the head part first with her hair mixed with, it and then he went to tie up her feet, making it look like a cocoon. He looked at Tran Pham's head and body on the floor and went into the kitchen area to look for a plastic bag to put Tran Pham's head in. He looked into the garbage can and found one as a rope hanging on the wall. He took that back into the front part of the house. He put Tran Pham's head into the plastic bag and put the rope all around Mrs. Turtle Dragon's little body while she was wrapped up in two bedsheets. He looked at his watch and picked up her little body, throwing it over his right shoulder, and knelt down. He then picked up Tran Pham's head in that plastic bag off the floor and went out the cellar door with them. He noticed the blood coming through the sheets and knew that other people would notice it too if they saw it. He got a bunch of bushes and thicket and made one big bush.

When he finally walked out with her, it was about to get dark, but it was still kind of light out. He saw this South Vietnamese soldier get out of his jeep and go into a store as he threw Mrs. Turtle Dragon's bushed-up body in the back section and Tran Pham's head on the seat with him. As he was driving off, the soldier came back out to see him drive off, and he noticed that it was a soldier just like him. He now knew that this was a North Vietnamese soldier who was a perpetrator as a South Vietnamese soldier, since he just waved at him, and he waved back. He had General Bien Lo's sergeant in the back of this jeep, and she knew where Sergeant Flood was located. She was in the back of his jeep, wrapped up in sheets and covered with bushes, with her little soldier Tran Pham's head in a plastic bag. He looked at his watch and saw that it was 1400. He continued driving, making it back to the base, and pulled up in the warehouse hangar, then closed the door back down. He then got out of the jeep and went inside and to the debriefing room, where Captain Apocalypse and his teammates were in.

He just stood there at attention, saluting the captain.

Captain Apocalypse saluted him back, and Sergeant Destroyer said, "Permission to speak, Captain?"

Captain Apocalypse replied, "Permission granted, Sergeant Destroyer."

Sergeant Destroyer said, "Sergeant Flood is still alive, Captain Apocalypse. They were talking about killing him in one more day, sir, if he doesn't talk."

Captain Apocalypse said, "Do you have any evidence or pr—"

He was about to say *proof* when they saw all this blood coming off him, just dripping like a water faucet. One of the MTs ran over to him and said, "Are you hurt? Are you injured? Where are your injuries, Sergeant?"

He said in his mechanical voice, "I'm okay, MTs. I'm not hurt. But the two that I have in the back are, though. Captain Apocalypse, we need to take a walk to the warehouse."

While they were walking to get ready to go out the side door, General Foster saw bloody boot prints and blood droppings all on his tiled floor. He said, "Captain Apocalypse, is everything okay?"

Captain Apocalypse turned around with respect as they all saluted General Foster. Captain Apocalypse said in his mechanical voice, "Everything is fine, General. Would you like to meet an old enemy of yours, sir? If so, come with me."

General Foster walked next to Captain Apocalypse as they exited through the side door of the warehouse, cutting the lights on. They then walked to a small South Vietnamese soldier's jeep as Sergeant Destroyer said to them all, "Stop right here, please," leaving them about six or seven feet away from the jeep. He then picked the plastic bag off the front seat. He held it up and ripped it open, revealing Tran Pham's head. He said, "This is the son of a bitch who shot Sergeant Flood in both legs, rendering him unable to fight for himself." He threw the head of a fourteen-year-old boy at his feet. "That seven-year-old girl was not his sister. She was just collateral damage to their game." Sergeant Destroyer then added, "Now, you want to see proof that our brother is still alive? I have that proof right here, sir." He reached in the back of the jeep and picked up a big bundle of bushes, throwing it on the concrete floor next to Tran Pham's head.

The MTs were sick at the stomach as this kid's head was staring up at them with his dead eyes.

General Foster said, "Killing him is not going to give you and your team an upper hand on these sons of bitches. Who's going to tell you where he is and that he's still alive?" General Foster walked to the big bush. "What is that? The body of th—"

The bush started to move and mutter, with General Foster and the MTs jumping in fear.

General Foster was about to grab the bush when it moved again and muttered a muffled sound. General Foster just stared at it and said, "What is that, Sergeant Destroyer?"

Sergeant Destroyer responded by unwrapping the bushes and throwing it out of the way, and all they saw were some bloody bed-sheets moving, a muffled muttering sound coming from it, as if it were trying to talk.

"Now, this person here is the North Vietnamese leader Cho San Hue's sergeant with the name of Turtle Dragon." When he removed the sheets, Captain Apocalypse and the team saw Mrs. Qs Long, the hostess of their safe house.

Captain Apocalypse walked over there as they removed the sheets and saw that she was buck-ass naked. He knelt down and looked at her, pulling out his big-ass buck knife and putting it between the towel and her face. He started cutting the towel. They saw that Sergeant Destroyer did not have any pity on her, as she was bruised up very badly, tears pouring down her face. She looked very frightened, just staring up at all of them.

Captain Apocalypse said, "By the time this towel gets cut away from your face, you better tell me where my goddamn soldier is, and he better not be dead. If you understand me, blink your fucking eyes two times. Now, Mrs. Qs Long, or shall I say Mrs. Turtle Dragon? Now, where is my sergeant?"

She still couldn't talk as the towel was still on her mouth.

Captain Apocalypse said, "She is your responsibility. Do your job, soldier."

Sergeant Destroyer picked her buck-naked body up by her hair as she pissed everywhere. He hit her so hard she was farting and shitting all on the floor as the buck knife was still between the towel and her face, cutting her jaw. Sergeant Destroyer turned her on her back as she was trying to talk but she couldn't as the towel and knife were not letting her.

Captain Apocalypse said, "Look here, Turtle Dragon. Where is my sergeant? And is he dead or alive?" He had cut half of the towel, looking up at Sergeant Destroyer. He had cut it halfway off her face, but she still couldn't say a word except muffled mutterings.

Captain Apocalypse said, "Sergeant Destroyer, you know what to do."

Sergeant Destroyer walked up to her, looking down at her, and then stomped her in the stomach and her left and right shoulders, dislocating them out of their sockets. She was about to faint. Captain Apocalypse cut the towel off her face, cutting her jaw open, and popped a smelling salt under her nose, asking, "Do you want to live, or do you want to die, Mrs. Turtle Dragon? It's your call. Now, tell us where Sergeant Flood is. And he better be alive!"

She was in pain and coughing up blood, replying, "H-h-he-he…" *Cough cough cough.* "He is…is…is…" *Cough cough cough, cough cough.*

"Where is he, Turtle Dragon?" Captain Apocalypse asked again.

She said, "In the circle of our compound. H-h-h-he is in a torture chamber in room number 304. Please don't k-k-k-kill me! I'm sorry. I'm so sorry, Captain Apocalypso! P-p-p-please don't kill me, pleassssssse!"

Captain Apocalypse stood up and looked down at her and said, "You are hereby being 'DET-U-CEXE for EG-ANO-IPSE and NO-SA-ERT!'"

Sergeant Destroyer eased her off the floor and cut her feet loose with his big-ass buck knife. He also cut Tran Pham's belt from her wrist. She said, "Tha—"

But Sergeant Destroyer pushed his big-ass buck knife from the back of her neck all the way through her throat and pulled it back out of her neck and throat, placing it back in its holster without wiping her blood off it. She was gagging, with blood coming out of her mouth, throat, and the back of her neck, her little naked body hitting the floor very hard.

General Foster said, "What the hell? I thought you weren't going to kill her?"

Captain Apocalypse said, "I didn't, General Foster."

They circled her and did not pay this dead body any attention as Captain Apocalypse said, "Okay, everybody know their positions and assignments, correct?"

Everybody saluted him.

Captain Apocalypse continued, "All right, move out!"

General Foster said to himself, "I am truly glad that I am on these guys' side. God forbid if I ever become an enemy of the United States."

Captain Apocalypse was walking next to the general and said, "Sir, I had to do what had to be done. She was supposed to be an ally, but she wasn't, so I had to remove this part of your problem. And now the rest will know not to fuck with you or your boys, and if they do, then you call me no matter what, sir." He then went to climb into the Cobra attack helicopter as the others jumped on *Puff, the Magic Dragon* in the darkness. Night had just begun to fall.

Captain Apocalypse said on his walkie-talkie, "Ground team, make sure that you have your bazookas and wait for my mark and you will see it. I'm out."

Puff, the Magic Dragon took off, as did the truck with twenty-three North Vietnamese soldiers dressed like United States soldiers with black ski masks on their faces and an M16 taped tightly in their hands, their mouths gagged. Sergeant Boogeyman, Sergeant Big Badass Wolf, and Sergeant Rattler flew that plane so low in the dark. People heard it but didn't understand it. Then, Sergeant Evil,

Sergeant Nuclear, Sergeant Tornado, Sergeant Furious, Sergeant Consequence, Sergeant Lowlife, Sergeant Illusionist, Sergeant Fatal, Sergeant Eliminate, Sergeant Hocus-Pocus, Sergeant Maniac, Sergeant Polarize, Sergeant Destroyer, and Sergeant Hectic all jumped out of the plane, going to their position.

The Big Badass Wolf said, "Captain Apocalypse, this is the Big Badass Wolf. Come in."

Captain Apocalypse said, "Go ahead, Sergeant Big Badass Wolf."

Sergeant Big Badass Wolf replied, "The drop has been made, sir."

Captain Apocalypse said, "Good job. Is everybody in their positions? If so, code me now."

All their codes came in.

While the truck was parked, it was 2039. Sergeant Shadow and Sergeant Animosity pushed their buttons, 1-4-2, then ran to their positions as the North Vietnamese soldiers took about three to four minutes to wake up. All of them were confused and in a whole new state of mind as they came out of the truck, walking, trying to figure out how they got there and who put the guns in their hands and why they couldn't talk. They were walking to go get help from the true perpetrators who pretended to be South Vietnamese people. They came out of their homes yelling, "American soldiers, American soldiers! Kill them, kill them all!" They then open-fired on them.

The team just watched this unfold.

The ones that tried to run were gunned down and shot in their backs. Little children were shooting them and stabbing them with knife and throwing gasoline on them, setting them on fire after. There were no innocent people in this neighborhood, it appeared.

Sergeant Animosity said, "Captain Apocalypse, this is Sergeant Animosity, sir."

Captain Apocalypse said, "Go ahead, Sergeant Animosity."

Sergeant Animosity said, "All these people in this neighborhood are North Vietnamese soldiers, sir. They all are working together, sir."

Captain Apocalypse said, "That was what I figured, Sergeant Animosity. To all my team, be ready."

Click click click. Sergeant Destroyer, Sergeant Hectic, and Sergeant Evil sniped the gun tower guards in the head, neck, or heart, then Sergeant Hectic and Sergeant Evil took over the gun towers and clicked their buttons. Captain Apocalypse responded. Sergeant Destroyer and Sergeant Animosity were on the ground as Captain Apocalypse said, "I want Sergeant Flood out of that damn place. I want him home! Did you hear me, No Pity? And I mean no goddamn pity! Get him out, soldiers! No fucking pity! No goddamn pity! No, bring us all back home, and that is a goddamn order, soldier! No fucking pity!"

Captain Apocalypse came flying in Cobra attack chopper, hitting houses after houses, the bazookas knocking houses after houses down as people were running out of them. The bazookas were sending them into many pieces up in the air. Then the air support came, with Sergeant Big Badass Wolf, Sergeant Boogeyman, and Sergeant Rattler bringing *Puff, the Magic Dragon*, with Sergeant Rattler blazing the Gatling gun. Bullets went through their heads and bodies.

Sergeant Destroyer, meanwhile, eased himself into the building and found the fuse box, knocking the power and generator out, making it pitch-black inside. He was walking around with his night vision goggles on, his AK-47 killing soldier after soldier. He was looking for room 304. The North Vietnamese soldiers couldn't see their way through this darkness, and Sergeant Destroyer killed them by the pack, their brains, teeth, and guts, as well as their blood, hitting the walls and spreading on them. He had multiple bulletproof M1951 on, and some to put on Sergeant Flood when he found him. He killed three North Vietnamese at the door with 304 on it. He went in, and a couple of shots were fired as he shot both of them in their heads seven or eight times each. The three big tigers were growling mad and trying to get at them, and he shot them, just waving his AK-47 from side to side, killing them. He walked backward and knelt down to keep from looking at Sergeant Flood's face and gave him ski mask, his voice detector, and said, "Here, put these on, Sergeant."

After Sergeant Flood put on his voice detector, ski mask, and night vision goggles, he said, "Sergeant Destroyer, I am paralyzed from the waist down, man. I cannot walk, so save yourself before both of us get killed."

Sergeant Destroyer pushed his walkie-talkie button and said, "Captain Apocalypse, I got Sergeant Flood, sir, and he is alive but paralyzed from the waist down, sir."

Captain Apocalypse said, "If he can shoot, then give him a goddamn gun and bring us home *now*! I said, no goddamn pity, soldier! No fucking pity! Now move it, Sergeant! No goddamn pity!"

Sergeant Destroyer tied Sergeant Flood's wrist together and put M1951 bulletproof jackets on his back and side and on top of his head and gave him two .45 automatic pistols with silencers on them. He then put his head between his arms and placed Sergeant Flood on his back. Sergeant Flood said, "Just leave me, Sergeant Destroyer. I won't blame you, because you and the team tried. Let me die, please."

Sergeant Destroyer replied, "I will not ever repeat what you just said to me. Now, take these fucking .45s and let me know when you need a reload. Now, are you *fucking* ready?"

Sergeant Flood said, "LET'S KILL OR BE KILLED!"

Sergeant Destroyer said, "I! Am! So! Fucking! Pity!" He ran out the door, going backward and forward, then backward and forward, as Sergeant Flood said, "Clip!"

Sergeant Destroyer reloaded him as they went backward and forward and backward and then forward and then backward again. Sergeant Flood said, "Clip!" as they made it to the door. They turned backward, killing the ones coming toward them as the little light gave them away, but they made it out. Sergeant Destroyer put, like, five dead bodies up against the door as the North Vietnamese soldiers were trying to get out of it.

Sergeant Evil, who was echoed by Sergeant Hectic, said, "Sergeant Destroyer has Sergeant Flood, and they have made it safe to the ground, sir."

Captain Apocalypse's code came on the walkie-talkie, 3-4-2, as Captain Apocalypse came flying in with the Cobra attack chopper. Sergeant Big Badass Wolf, Sergeant Boogeyman, and Sergeant Rattler later came thundering on *Puff, the Magic Dragon*, truly destroying everything in their path. Sergeant Hectic and Sergeant Evil left the towers when Captain Apocalypse was knocking them down. Sergeant Destroyer said, "Clear! All clear, Captain Apocalypse!"

Captain Apocalypse replied, "Hard air attack to ground attack. DON'T LEAVE ANY ONE THING STANDING. BRING DOOM, DOOM, DOOM! I AM CAPTAIN APOCALYPSE, AND I AM BRING DOOM TO EVERYTHING!"

They knocked holes in the ground, the houses and buildings not there anymore, as leader Cho San Hue, General Bien Lo, Captain Lon Nol, and Lieutenant Lo Hap and their soldiers went to where they thought they would never go. They were blown to smithereens. The North Vietnamese soldiers who penetrated into the South Vietnamese regime had been annihilated without a trace. The Cobra chopper and *Puff, the Magic Dragon* did one more round on this compound, till there wasn't a nail or screw that could be found. They knew that not one body would ever be found in this area. The Cobra attack chopper and *Puff, the Magic Dragon* were flying off together, disappearing in the night skies. The other South Vietnamese citizens knew that those people were no more to terrorize them, as those American soldiers did not come close to putting a scratch on their place or them, as if they knew who to hit and who were truly the bad people.

Sergeant Hectic and Sergeant Evil got into the truck in the front as Sergeant Maniac, Sergeant Destroyer, and Sergeant Illusionist covered the doors. They made it back to the base and got out of the Cobra, *Puff, the Magic Dragon*, and the truck and walked toward their Lockheed C-5 Galaxy plane. Then General Foster came jogging out there, and they all saluted him, including Sergeant Flood.

General Foster said, "Did you get your man, Captain Apocalypse?"

Captain Apocalypse nodded, replying "Yes, General Foster, I did. It's twenty that went, and twenty-one came back. I tha—"

General Foster cut his sentence off by replying "Don't. No need for that, soldier. I thank you for finding what I did not see for years. So I tha—"

Captain Apocalypse cut his sentence off too and said, "Whenever you need me, General, I'll come, sir." He saluted the general, and the rest of the team saluted him too as they stepped up to the C-5

Galaxy plane. Before the door closed, he heard their real voices replying, "Thank you, General Fredrick 'Spooky' Foster, sir!" As the door closed, he saluted them, the plane then doing a disappearing act in the night skies, going back to the United States. General Foster heard all the kinds of sirens going off as they went toward the compound.

General Foster said, "You will find not one single person or their remains, as they have been annihilated and buried in the hell that created them. Not one single body will be found." He laughed, going back inside, saying, "I'm glad that it's not me they're after." And he continued laughing.

As they were flying, the MTs were doctoring on Sergeant Flood. He was very talkative and holding conversation with his little tortured body. A man that stood five foot eleven and used to weigh at 212 pounds was now five foot eleven and weighed at 132 pounds, but still alive. They flew for another ten hours and finally made it home to their unit, where the MTs took him to their little hospital room, looking him over, feeding him, and bathing him. They knew their mission was very top-notch, and they would do anything for these soldiers as they would not leave one another, and if it had to happen, then they would go get him at all costs.

All the sergeants were led by Captain Apocalypse into his room, where they stood in front of him in salute, and as he saluted them back, Sergeant Flood said, "Captain Apocalypse, I need to tell you and the team something. When Sergeant Destroyer put me on his back to carry me out, I—"

Captain Apocalypse cut him off. "Whatever was said, and whatever you thought, that's between you and Sergeant Destroyer. We don't need to know what you or he knows, as we all have things to say when it comes our way, and that's just it, things that need to be said. We're just glad you're here back with the team until we all are no more. So your prayers were your prayers, just our prayers were ours, and by that I mean no fucking pity!"

They all stood at attention.

"Now, you soldiers get some rest before our next mission. Now, at ease, soldiers!"

CHAPTER 5

It was now September 25, 1972, five years after the mission that the No-Name Unit called Death Mission, one that was supposed to have been a Simple Simon mission, until the North Vietnamese injured Sergeant Rattler and kidnapped and tortured Sergeant Flood. The North Vietnamese soldiers did an outstanding job penetrating fifteen families as if they were South Vietnamese families. It took a very intelligent person to plan out a layout like this, without General Foster and his servicemen ever knowing anything about it. Captain Apocalypse had banged his brains trying to figure out how in the hell three or four hundred North Vietnamese soldiers could infiltrate that well without being noticed, although they caught them and anni-hilated their asses without a trace. Captain Apocalypse knew that the Death Mission might not be over, although they got who they wanted.

He sat back in his chair and stared into the darkness and hit the intercom button. He said, "I want all soldiers to meet up in the debriefing room for a meeting. I do mean now, ASAP."

All the team members were in the debriefing room when Captain Apocalypse came in, saying, "Remove your night vision goggles, please. The lights will be on, as it's time for a meeting about what we need to come to an agreement on. This is a part of you as well as me. This has been bothering me on a level that will not escape my mind. Now, the first topic of this meeting is about Sergeant Flood and Sergeant Rattler. Sergeant Flood and Sergeant Rattler were moved to another section of our unit, and we will have them as our RSAD, which stands for 'research, seek, and destroy.' By them being RSAD, they'll be our eyes, ears, and nose. When it comes to our missions, we will need somebody out there that'll be able to pinpoint us away if we get stuck in one of our missions. Does anybody disagree?"

Sergeant Rattler asked, "Permission to speak, sir."

Captain Apocalypse replied, "Permission granted."

Sergeant Rattler said, "Sir, I am not dead, and neither is Sergeant Flood. We don't want to just sit here in this unit and watch all of you go out with those motherfuckers trying to kill all of you. We all do well together, so please don't count us out, sir."

Captain Apocalypse said, "Wherever we go, you two are coming with us, but the battle part of the mission, you two won't be in, and that's another part of this debriefing, why I am calling this mission. Since nobody has any objection on the first topic, now let's take it to the second topic. I know there're only nineteen of us that'll be going into the battle now, as Sergeant Flood and Sergeant Rattler will now act as our RSADs. With that, we have some new recruits coming to join us. They are you, but way younger. We need them, and they need us, so they can continue our legacy when we are all dead and gone. I have fourteen of them, and they are you and you are them. I handpicked them, just like I handpicked you. I want y'all to take them in this training camp. These young soldiers don't smile, and they don't ask questions. They do as they are told, and they are looking forward to being teamed with the best. They haven't been on missions such as these, but I have allowed a protégé to keep them company as they receive some homegrown problems in Texas, Mississippi, Michigan, Wisconsin, Ohio, New York, Montana, and a few more states, where they were very successful. They can be your children or some sort of relative. Take them, teach them, and train them. I have outfits for you with your initials on them, so please wear them very proudly, team. Any questions?"

There was no response.

"Now, as for the last topic. Why we need Sergeant Rattler and Sergeant Flood as our eyes, ears, and nose, and why those young soldiers, it's that I got an itch that can't be scratched. That itch is on my brain. I don't know why it's bothering me so goddamn much. Team, what we did in South Vietnam, in Saigon, is wrecking the shit out of me. Now, we got our soldier back and all, and we annihilated the motherfuckers who did this to him—sorry for bringing up the past, team—but I cannot be at rest for that as I believe it's not over in that country. See, the problem that I have seen to is a steel fucking wall that stands six thousand feet high, and I cannot overcome it.

"Did you ever ask yourself, How did that many fucking soldiers move in undetectable like that? I understand a couple of families, but a whole little town, a community? All of them were North Vietnamese soldiers. Men, women, and children. We need to find that person that was so goddamn intelligent enough to pull that shit off and fool General Foster. I know that he would not jeopardize life for these murdering sons of bitches. This fucking North Vietnamese authority must have an intelligencer to have made that bullshit last all those fucking years before we wrecked their goddamn asses. Now, we removed their leader, Cho San Hue, and his general Bien Lo, his captain Lon Nol, his lieutenant Lo Hap, and his sergeant Mrs. Qs Long, or as they called her, Turtle Dragon. We removed their whole little circle, but I have a gut feeling that we are about to have the worst nightmare ever, or we can make it out as a daydream, which I do prefer. The North Vietnamese know that it wasn't General Foster's soldiers who did that, but they do know that we used his equipment to make this mission possible. We really need to sit and think, because I want us to feel the same thing about our missions.

"I will end this meeting by asking, How did those North Vietnamese soldiers and their authority plant themselves in there unnoticed? Ask yourself that question. They probably knew that we were coming, and you better believe the thought that we were destined to lose since there were twenty-one of us. Remember, that North Vietnamese soldier said that they only needed one of us, and they got one of us. But we took him back. Sergeant Turtle Dragon knew our count time, and while we landed the chopper, they had already been waiting for us there as well. Just ask yourself that question. Now, you all are excused, soldiers."

They all left the briefing room puzzled by the question that Captain Apocalypse had asked them.

Captain Apocalypse got on the phone and called to North Vietnam, to Saigon, to speak to General Foster. His private hotline rang about four times before someone picked up and said, "Lieutenant Colonel Kerry Foster, how can I help you?"

Captain Apocalypse hung up the phone without speaking.

General Foster then said, "What are you doing with my phone?" as he walked into his office.

His son said, "It rang four times, and so I answered. It's just a phone, Dad."

He said, "No, it's not just a phone. That's just phone right there, but this one is not *just* a phone. Who was it?"

He just said, "They hung up."

As he was talking, the phone rang again. General Foster picked up this time and said, "You got General Fredrick Foster here. How can I help you?"

Captain Apocalypse said in his mechanical voice, "It's me, sir, and I am sending you a tracking device. It won't be detected by anything. It's new, and I want you to put your innermost trust in someone from your medical team and give them my information, just in case anything ever happen to you. I know you keep the peace talk over there and you've been having it for years. But since that fight we had, I have been thinking that our fight isn't over there yet, sir."

As Captain Apocalypse and General Foster were talking, the wife of his son, Lieutenant Colonel Foster, came in the door and stood next to her husband. General Foster said, "I understand, sir, and I will make that happen, sir. Yes, sir. Thank you, sir. Goodbye, sir."

As he hung the phone up on Captain Apocalypse, he said to his son, Lieutenant Colonel Kerry Foster, "Who is this beautiful young lady you have, son?"

He said, "Dad, I told you over three and a half years ago that I got married. Did you forget?"

The general said, "I'm sorry, son, I thought you told me that you were engaged to a young lady, but never married. Either way..." He walked over there to them and said, "Congratulations, son. What's her name?"

He said, "She's your daughter-in-law, Dad, so why don't you ask her yourself?" with a smile on his face.

General Foster said, "You're right, son. How rude of me! Sweetheart, I'm Kerry's father, and I'm the general of this outfit, as my son has probably told you a lot about me, and now I am sorry for not asking you. What's your name, sweetheart?"

She said in very well-spoken English and Vietnamese, "My name is Kim Ly Foster, and it's Foster by marriage, General, sir."

General Foster said, "Cut that *general* and *sir* crap, sweetheart. You can call me Fredrick."

She said, "With all due to respect to my husband, I prefer to call you Dad also, if it's okay with you?"

He said, "Sweetheart, I'm okay with that, and it will be an honor to be in your glory with my son. Now, let me give you two a celebration that you two will never forget! You know what, Kim? I haven't seen Kerry since he was twenty years old, and here he is, out of an outstanding college, married with a beautiful wife, and took up the torch of his old man and is a lieutenant colonel. I'm proud of him, Kim, and I thank you for being a part of this. One more question please?"

She said, "Sure, Dad," as she was holding his hands.

General Foster asked, "How long have you two known each other?"

She said, "He helped me with my algebra when I was eighteen and he was twenty. We dated for four and half years and got engaged when we both signed up for the Army. We did three and half years together in the Army, and when he was twenty-seven and I twenty-six, we got pregnant and I did not know. I got shot by the enemy and lost the pleasure of getting pregnant ever again. So here I am, thirty-nine and childless." She had tears in her eyes for having lost their only child.

General Foster hugged them both, saying, "I'm sorry. I'm so sorry. No more questions, okay? I'm sorry, sweetheart. I'm sorry, son." After a brief silence, he continued, "Let's go celebrate your success."

"Thanks, Dad," both of them said at the same time.

They all walked out of his office, going out of the general administration building, where his office was in, and his driver pulled up and picked them up. General Foster and his son, Kerry, both were still in active force, but Kerry's wife, Kim, was not.

They went to a high-class restaurant to celebrate their marriage and his son's rank in the service. As they were waiting for their dinner, Kerry said, "I heard that you had some problems over here some years ago, Dad. I was in Iraq when I heard about it, but they never put me through. I knew, though, just how tough you are, and if something was wrong, you would've found a way to get word out. Right, Dad?"

He said, "Yes. But that war wasn't by me or orchestrated by me. Some South Vietnamese soldiers went to war against some terrorist group. I could not get involved, and I'm sure that the police put everything in control that night."

His son said, "There was a lot of death that night. With you being a general of this outfit here, won't you be a target for these people?"

The general said, "Kerry, son, we're here to celebrate, not have a conversation about a war. Your wife wants to hear other things besides us conversing about stuff like this, huh, sweetheart?"

Kim smiled beautifully and said, "Yes," very softly.

When their dinner came, they ate and talked.

General Foster asked before their dessert came, "Are you two going to stay, or are you going back to Iraq, where your station is at? How long can you stay?"

Kerry said, "We can only stay for a couple of days, and then we'll be on our way back to Iraq."

His father said, "I understand. So let us three make the best of it. Where are you staying?"

Kerry said, "At the Majestic Hotel. It seems kind of nice there, but not as grand as I wish it could be for me and the wife."

The general responded, "You two can stay at my house with me. It's only me, and I can use the company in that big house of mine."

After they finished their dessert, they sat around, just chitchatting, then they finally got up. General Foster paid the bill and left a tip for the waiters. The hostess that seated them said with a smile at the general, "You come back, General."

He said, "I will, but only to see you, beautiful." She blushed at that and smiled.

Kerry said, "I see that the old man still got it, the old man still got it!" as they went out to get their car.

His driver said, "Where to, General?"

He said, "Home, Chou. Take us home."

As they got in the car, Kerry said, "Can we see that place that they call Smithereens, Dad? I would like to see how the terrorists wrecked Tre Long, that little village."

General Foster said, "Chou, take us by Tre Long."

He replied, "Yes, General."

As he drove for twenty-three minutes, they came up on nothing; all they saw was a big-ass hole in the ground where something used to be. He saw eighteen little houses that looked like holes and a big hole in the middle of it, but the surrounding places hadn't sustained any damage at all.

Lieutenant Colonel Foster said, "Stop the car, Chou. I would like to take a look around."

As they all got out of the car, Kim said, "General, I mean Dad, were there houses here?"

He said, "To my understanding, there were. When I heard the air raid sound going off, I put all my boys on alert and called to Washington, and they told me to stay neutral as we're not to get involved with any of this because of the peace talks. I wanted to involve myself, but I couldn't break protocol."

She said, "The authorities said they couldn't find a trace of anybody or anything that's remotely similar to a body when they investigated this place. They said that when they came, there was only smoke going up in the air, without any fire burning."

General Foster replied, "I heard the same thing, sweetheart," as he got back in the car. "Come on, enough of this. Let's go home."

Kerry put his arm around Kim and walked her to the car. She got in it and said, "This place smells like death, and it looks like hell. It feels real strange to be here. Can we go home now?"

General Foster said, "Let's go, Chou," and he drove off, going to their hotel first to pick up their things.

When they made it to Majestic Hotel, Chou and Kerry got out of the car to go get their luggage. General Foster saw Kim shaking really bad, so he said, "Sweetheart, I hope you're okay. I shouldn't have allowed the driver to take you over there to see that. I felt the same way that you're feeling when I came over here the third night after it was over."

She said, "I am okay, Dad. That was why I did not rejoin, because of stuff like this. I'm okay."

After Kerry and the driver made it back to the car and put their luggage in the back, they both got inside and drove off, going to General Foster's house. They drove for seventeen minutes before making it to his house. They then went inside. The driver showed them the room where they'd be sleeping. They all had a nightcap and went to their rooms.

As the driver was walking around in the house, checking up on things, like he always did, he heard moaning and groaning coming from the couple's bedroom. He just kept walking, going to the other part of the house. He then went to the kitchen to fix himself something to eat before going to sleep.

Kim came into the kitchen with just her little panties on. As she turned the lights on, Chou saw her topless. She put her hands over her breasts and said, "I'm sorry, I thought everybody was asleep." She then went to put a robe on and came back to the kitchen, smiling, and said, "I am so sorry."

Chou said, smiling as well, getting out of his chair, "It's okay. I've had many wives, and I'm getting too old to try to keep up now." He then waved, saying, "Good night."

She replied, "Wait! Can I ask you something, please?"

He stopped and said, "Sure, you can."

She asked, "Did you know any of the people who stayed in Tre Long village?"

He said, "No ma'am, I didn't. I've been the general's driver before we came over here, before he took over. Wherever he goes, I go. I've been driving for him now for twenty-four years, and we've been here for twenty-one years."

She said, "Okay. Thank you." She was then looking at the refrigerator.

He said, "Can I ask you a question, please?"

She said, "Sure, you can."

She thought he was going to ask her about sex or something since he saw her half-naked body, but he said, "That mark on your arm, did you hurt that in the war that you were in? If you were my daughter, I wouldn't have allowed you to fight a man's battle. I just couldn't allow that. But you fought for your country as a brave woman."

She said, "Thank you, Chou. I appreciate the fatherly thoughts of concern."

He walked off and said, "Good night, Mrs. Kim Foster."

She then finished making her and her husband a snack after having sex.

Meanwhile, Captain Apocalypse was just sitting in the dark, as always, contemplating on his new recruits, the two soldiers that he had appointed as RSAD, his main team, and that goddamn thorn in his side, the one that kept him up about that mission of death they went on a little over five years ago. He put the detection device in an airmail package about the size of a shoebox, certified for the general personally, from the country of Hong Kong, so that those North or South Vietnamese wouldn't know that he got an air package from the United States.

As he was in the office, his phone rang, and he knew it had to be somebody very important in order to call this number. He picked up, and a mechanical voice said, "Captain Apocalypse, this your lieutenant Obliterate. The four teen soldiers are ready to come in, sir."

Captain Apocalypse said, "I'll send Sergeant Big Badass Wolf and Sergeant Boogeyman to come and get you and the crew. We all are a one-man concept. I am the captain and you are my lieutenant, Lieutenant Obliterate. Are we in an agreement on this, sir?"

Lieutenant Obliterate replied, "Sir, you made me who I am, and I thank you for giving me that opportunity to watch over your crew here. I am honored to get your call replying that you are ready for me and the team that you left me in charge of, sir."

Captain Apocalypse said, "The Sea Stallion should touch down at 1310 and have y'all back here at 1745, with your rooms ready."

As Lieutenant Obliterate was about to reply, Captain Apocalypse's other line buzzed. He said, "I have a phone call coming through. I'll talk to you and fill you in on everything when you get here, Lieutenant, okay?"

Lieutenant Obliterate said, "Yes, sir, Captain Apocalypse, sir," as they hung the phone up.

Captain Apocalypse pushed his other line's button and said in his mechanical voice, "You have me, General Spooky, sir. How can I assist you, sir?"

General Foster said, "I have the package and this other little thing that looks like a walkie-talkie. What is it? If it is a walkie-talkie, how in the hell can we talk this far apart?"

Captain Apocalypse said, "I got your single loud and clear. Now, as far as the walkie-talkie goes, remember this code if you're ever in some danger. My code is, push that button three times and count one Mississippi, two Mississippi, three Mississippi, then you press the button four times and count the same Mississippi and push the button two times and count the same Mississippi. Don't let anybody see you push that button even though they can see it in your possession, because they'll still not know what it is. I will come, General, sir."

General Foster said, "I know you will, Captain Apocalypse. Oh yeah, Captain Apocalypse, my son came here a day ago with his beautiful Oriental wife. They make a lovely couple. I was so glad to hear, or shall I say see, my son. He's a lieutenant colonel, Lieutenant Colonel Kerry Foster. His little wife is a firecracker. Her name is Kim Ly Foster. They may have to adopt in order to have children, though, because she was pregnant and shot without knowing that she was pregnant, and now they can't have children."

Captain Apocalypse said, "Sorry to hear that, General, sir."

General Foster said, "It's okay. I'm glad that I can spend two days with them before they go back to Hong Kong, where his ground is at, and maybe I'll surprise him and stay a month. Or maybe I'll retire."

He laughed on his end before he said, "I want you to know that being in your service has been a great honor, Captain Apocalypse. You and your team really need to be commended for your the bravery for this country and many others."

Captain Apocalypse said, "We all thank you for recognizing us, and that'll never be forgotten. I'll be sure to tell the team what you said, General Spooky, sir. Oh, I forgot to give you your congratulations, sir."

General Foster asked, "For what? What are you giving me congratulations for?"

As Captain Apocalypse was hanging the phone up, he said, "For receiving your five stars, sir." He then hung the phone up on General Foster.

General Foster just laughed at him for knowing that he was about to be promoted to a five-star general and he didn't have to be there any longer.

Later, Lieutenant Colonel Kerry Foster and his wife, Kim, came to the base and went to General Foster's office. As they went in, they saluted his father, as they both were in their uniforms. Kerry said, "Dad, you about to go somewhere? I came here to spend some more time with you before we leave tomorrow."

He said, "I have to go get my blood pressure checked and give blood to see what may test positive of my health, although I am healthier than a young mule. Stay here and I'll be back some." He then walked out of the door.

When he made it to the doctor, he said, "What I am about to ask you is between you and me, understand?"

The doctor replied, "Yes, sir, General Foster!"

General Foster gave him a little microchip and said, "Put it in a place that nobody can detect if they tried."

The doctor said, "If I do, it'll hurt like hell for a few days, but it'll be in you until you get it removed yourself. So take off your shirt and lie on your back and stretch your left arm out, and I'll use your excess elbow skin and put it in there."

General Foster said, "Let's do it, then, Doc."

As the doctor placed that detection device inside of the general's arm, he said, "It's there, General, and your secret's safe with me."

The general then left, going back to his office, and did not see his son or his daughter-in-law. He just stood there for about a minute, then he got ready to turn around, out his door, to leave; that was when he heard some moving and bumping in his little sleeping quarter. He was walking slowly to the door when he heard a lady's voice say, "I think somebody is coming. I think your father is coming!"

He said, "Come on, it'll be a while before he gets back."

He was at his door then. He pulled the door open fast and saw Kerry's wife straddled on top of him as his hands were on her breasts. She fell forward on top of him and put her left hand at the back of her, hiding his dick, which was up inside of her.

The general closed the door very quickly and said, "I'll be outside when you two are finished." He then left outside of his entire office.

Ten minutes later, they came out, and Kim said, "Sorry, sir."

He said, "No need to apologize, you two. It's only human. I am sorry for walking in on you two, though."

Kerry said, "It's okay, Dad. We're all very much old enough not to do that, but that was a spur of the moment."

General Foster just smiled and said, "Come on, Lieutenant Colonel, let's get you two some lunch."

They got in the car, going to the restaurant.

Meanwhile, as Captain Apocalypse was sitting at his desk, Sergeant Boogeyman said, "Captain Apocalypse, this is Sergeant Boogeyman."

Captain Apocalypse responded, "Go ahead, Sergeant Boogeyman."

Sergeant Boogeyman said, "Cargo's safe and sound, sir. We're landing as we speak."

Captain Apocalypse said, "I'll be there in five. And send them all to the debriefing room. Let them know that they need to turn their Harleys facing the elevator shaft."

Sergeant Boogeyman said, "I got you, Captain. I'm clear."

As the plane landed and cut off, Sergeant Boogeyman said, "Five bikes and two people up until all bikes are on the floor. And Captain Apocalypse wants all of you at the debriefing room. The room can't be missed. The first and only door on that floor on your left side. Now move!"

As they all unloaded off the Lockheed C-5 Galaxy plane, they got up on the elevator shaft with the Harley 250cc. Captain Apocalypse appointed Sergeant Maniac at the tunnel's door and Sergeant Consequence at the debriefing door, with the instruction not to talk, not to question, not show their face except only to Captain Apocalypse. They should never, ever see his face. Captain Apocalypse's protégé did not know what Captain Apocalypse looked like, nor did he know what these fourteen soldiers under his command looked like. Captain Apocalypse knew all of them by face and name, but once they went under their transformation, they all looked alike. These soldier knew Captain Apocalypse, not by that name, but by his drill instructor name. They did not know, though, that they were still under his command.

Captain Apocalypse flashed his flashlight once, calling Lieutenant Obliterate. He came in, and Captain Apocalypse said, "I'm not demoting you, as it may seem, Lieutenant Obliterate, but your rank as a lieutenant has to be dismissed until I'm removed and then you take over the crew. Understood?"

Lieutenant Obliterate said, "Understood, Captain Apocalypse, sir."

"Sergeant Obliterate, your number is 21," the captain said. "Sergeant Maniac and Sergeant Consequence, send the rest of them to their rooms and I'll speak to all of them at one time. Understood?"

They saluted him and said, "All of you will go up top in the order that you're in now. Now move it."

They all went to their rooms with all their stuff in it.

Captain Apocalypse said, "Team, I am Captain Apocalypse, your captain. The name of the room you're in is your name, and your code name is on your dog tag. So take a look at it and keep and protect it at all costs, just like you do your brother soldiers. The same rules apply here just like in the other—of course, besides a few things different. Your meal is not your average meal. We eat as if it were our last meal. You have everything a normal house will have. You eat at your own table. You can go out to our training ground, but you can't associate with those from the other barracks. The unit is better known as the No-Name Unit, meaning, this unit can never be spoken of even when you go home, and if you do, then you'll be executed for espionage and treason. All of you are now sergeants, and this will be that until you die or get promoted. The only person that can give you an order is me. No other ranking officer can give you an order. I am the only one that can 'at ease' you or to tell you to stand down. But take note: this doesn't give you the okay to disrespect any ranking member or anybody who doesn't rank. You and your teammates will know the same thing before we go on our missions. I am always with you when we go. If you all agree with what I have said, remove your green wire."

All of them removed their green wire, agreeing with Captain Apocalypse.

Captain Apocalypse continued, "Lieutenant Obliterate is gone now, so don't miss him too long, because you'll see him one day again."

The lieutenant was sitting in there with Captain Apocalypse as Captain Apocalypse was talking to them. Captain Apocalypse said, "I'll be there in eight minutes, and I'll put you on my roll call with the No-Name Unit, so at ease until I come down. Your keys explain to you what they do, so stay put until I get there."

Captain Apocalypse cut the intercom off and said to Lieutenant Obliterate, "Lieutenant, your name has to change, so please choose a name for the record, okay?"

He said, "Yes, sir, Captain Apocalypse, sir. You can now call me Sergeant Wrath, Captain Apocalypse."

Captain Apocalypse said, "I understand, Sergeant Wrath. Go and join your team. But do not let them see you arriving, okay, Sergeant?"

Sergeant Wrath said, "I understand, Captain Apocalypse." He then left Captain Apocalypse's presence, going to his room. He made it down there and went into room M-14, code-named Sergeant Wrath.

Captain Apocalypse came down and said, "All new recruits, attention!"

All of them came running down the stairs, lining up in single file, stretched out. "As Captain Apocalypse says your number and code name, step forward, and do not forget it, ever!"

The captain started, "Now, A-1, Sergeant Red Rum; B-2, Sergeant Viper; C-3, Sergeant Death; D-4, Sergeant Executioner; E-5, Sergeant Vicious; F-6, Sergeant Torture; G-7, Sergeant Horrific; H-8, Sergeant Graveyard; I-9, Sergeant Undertaker; J-10, Sergeant Chaos; K-11, Sergeant Venomous; L-12, Sergeant Grim Reaper; M-13, Sergeant Night Terror; N-14, Sergeant Wrath; and O-15, Sergeant Body Snatcher. All of you are my sergeants, and I am your captain. Now go back to your room and get ready to go on your training. M-13, Sergeant Night Terror, step forward."

As Sergeant Night Terror stepped forward, Captain Apocalypse said some words to him for at least three to five minutes. Then he said, "Sergeant Night Terror, step back into the line. Now you all can go."

They all saluted him and said, "Yes, sir, Captain Apocalypse, sir!" They all then ran to their room and back out to train.

As they were training, Captain Apocalypse was watching his old team train his new team with honor and bravery. They were having an invisible war and hand-to-hand combat training. Captain Apocalypse knew his new group of fifteen plus the eighteen and him were truly a deadly combination. Captain Apocalypse wanted to see if his guys really had what it took to avoid authority and if the authority could sneak-attack them and catch them, day or night.

He picked up his phone and called the White House, where the president seat had changed from President Richard C. Crawford II to the new commander in chief, President Gregory S. Ackerson. The president was his boss.

The phone rang twice, and President Ackerson said, "Captain Apocalypse, my right hand, this is your left hand. How can I help you, Captain?"

Captain Apocalypse said, "Am I and my team still at your good grace, sir?"

He said, "You sure in the hell are! How can I help you?"

Captain Apocalypse said, "I want to put my team up against some people to see if our new recruits are ready for anything you throw at them. Can I have your approval on anything we do? And if they get caught, then they are caught, but don't let them get time in jail or prison in any state or federal prison, sir."

President Ackerson said, "What is your wish?"

Captain Apocalypse said, "All my guys will not have live ammos in their weapons, but they will have smoke bombs to use for escape from authority only, and I will not allow them to hurt a soul. I want them to work together as a team, and we will let them, our opponents, go home safe and sound. They can call the Army National Guards if they like. It will also give them a training as well."

President Ackerson said, "What state do you want this to be, Captain Apocalypse?"

He said, "Sir, I want it to be a surprise to the world news, as I want it to seem as if we are running from the US, but in reality, we're not, until you come out of there."

President Ackerson said, "Go, son," hanging up the phone.

Captain Apocalypse looked at his map and picked Denver, Colorado, and said on the intercom, "I want y'all to meet me in the debriefing room ASAP."

As they all came and sat at the big table, Captain Apocalypse said, "I have a mission for this team, and it is a dangerous job, and the reason that it is going to be dangerous is that you are not allowed to fire real ammos at your opponents, although they will be firing live ammos at you. I want there to be a statewide, nationwide, and worldwide manhunt on you. Now, if you get caught, then you'll be off the team, so you better count on your teammates. I want all new recruits to participate except for Sergeant Wrath, because I got something special for him. President Ackerson knows all of what is going on, and you all know what's going on, but the people in Boulder County don't know, so it's a daylight thing, and the old crew will back you up on this mission. I am splitting you in two groups of seven each, and I want you to hit the biggest two. And I want you to record the money that you take and put it up so that I can pick it up and turn it back to the rightful authority. You better not keep even a wrap out of that money. Am I clear?"

They all said, "Crystal, Captain Apocalypse, sir!"

He said, "All right, team 1 will be Sergeant Red Rum, Sergeant Viper, Sergeant Death, Sergeant Executioner, Sergeant Vicious, Sergeant Torture, and Sergeant Horrific. Team 2 are Sergeant Graveyard, Sergeant Undertaker, Sergeant Chaos, Sergeant Venomous, Sergeant Grim Reaper, Sergeant Night Terror, and Sergeant Body Snatcher. All your guns will be by blanks, no live ammo at all. Am I clear?"

They all said, "Crystal, sir!"

Captain Apocalypse continued, "Now, you'll have over four to five police authorities looking for you and trying to hunt you down and bring you in, dead or alive. The FBI also will be involved, along with the Army National Guard, and probably some Good Samaritan citizens that know how to shoot a gun. They'll be on houses, bikes, and jeep types of vehicles. The one thing that you can do is capture them, and once they're captured, we will send somebody for them. Are we clear?"

They all said, "Crystal clear, Captain Apocalypse, sir."

He said, "Take their guns, cars, or whatever they're using to apprehend you and put it up. So, new recruits, the old recruits will be grading you, and this will tell me that you all have what it take to be a part of this team. So go do this and make it to your mark so you can battle with them on your territory. And your territorial is this whole goddamn fucking world. So go get it and protect your country and citizens from bad people. Now, move out!"

They stayed in the briefing room, planning their shit out as this: one person to cut the power, one person to take the video camera, one person to stand at the vault, two people at the inside door, and two people in getaway cars with the money in it. The rest will be on their Harleys as their getaway ride, but they all would meet up by leaving the cars so they could find them. They all stood up and marched in single file and stood at attention in front of Captain

Apocalypse, who said, "Go do it, then, and come home soldier. Be a team as a team was watching over you. No move out!"

They all left, getting on the Sea Stallion as Sergeant Big Badass Wolf and Sergeant Boogeyman flew under the radar and landed their chopper on government property. The soldiers were riding their Harley 250cc on back roads, putting their marks on it. They were at least forty-five to fifty-five miles away from the woods, and an extra twenty-four miles from the Sea Stallion. They made it to the town at 0500 and waited for the banks to open at 0900. But they were not going to hit it before that, because the bank manager was the one who got the combination to the vault.

At 1000, they all hit their walkie-talkie buttons to hit at the same time. As they did, they hit the power circuits to the bank and at the police station, which would give them at least five minutes before it could be noticed. They took the camera videos and took at least 2.9 million dollars out of the bank, recording it on with a home video camera. They had all the people tied up without any injuries, and they were almost out of town on the way out.

A county deputy pulled the car over and came to the car, and soon he saw how this guy was dressed. He pulled his gun out and said, "Put your fucking hands in the air. Put your hands out of the car, where I can see them!"

As he complied with the officer, that was when Sergeant Chaos came out of the trunk and took him by surprise. By then the dispatch was reporting their teammate. They took the officer and his car and placed him in a well-lit-up cove for his protection. They then spread out and were guided by the backup crew, following their every order. As they came to the woods, they set up shop. But they were being shot at as they were camouflaging themselves like the woods.

The Army National Guard disappeared, and the officers were shooting in distance as the other officers were telling them to report, but they couldn't. They started calling the FBI and asking for help from the State Highway Patrol and other law enforcement units to assist them. It was getting bigger and bigger, and the helicopters were saying, "We don't see any movement in these woods. Maybe if we come close to the ground, maybe we can."

As they came closer, Sergeant Big Badass Wolf took the chopper and brought it to the rescue of four of their team players. They took those officers and four FBI agents and carried them to safety. The whole law enforcement was taken single-handedly by fourteen soldiers who took over two banks and returned the money. They then used the helicopter to take the first seven back, and as they came back for the other seven, they heard that they were pinned down. They were under fire as Sergeant Body Snatcher eased out of his tree, grabbed one of the officers, and cuffed him. He tied his tie around his mouth. He walked behind five of them and made them drop their guns and cuff them together and gagged them, then took their walkie-talkies. He climbed the tree with their binoculars and disguised his voice, saying in multiple voices, "We're hit! We're hit! Help us! We're pinned down!"

As those last nine were still moving around, they heard all kinds of gunshots, but it was Sergeant Body Snatcher making the gunfire sound off like that as he snatched them up one at a time. The last one backed up after seeing all of them cuffed and gagged. They tried to warn him to look behind, but it was too late, because Sergeant Body Snatcher had him in a choke hold and threw him to the ground, cuffing him and unloading his gun. He then pulled out his walkie-talkie and said, "All clear, team! Make it to the house of wings. I'm coming in."

He took off running, going to his Harley, and all of them were driving up in the Sea Stallion. Sergeant Body Snatcher was standing there, looking out the door, making sure nobody was left to follow him. All of them were on the Sea Stallion as the news and police choppers were sitting in a row along with an FBI chopper. Ten of the twelve officers that were blocking the roads and highway got a call from the CIA director, Mr. Fredrick Jefferson, who said, "I am the CIA director, Fredrick Jefferson, send some men out in those woods and release all those law enforcers. Tell them that we appreciate their cooperation as our special team has to go to real training. Our men are not allowed to shoot or hurt your people, just render them helpless, and they did. We are sorry for this conduct, and we do appreciate it. Your money is accounted for."

The governor said, "Then why didn't you inform us about this simulation?"

CIA's Mr. Jefferson said, "We made it real to your law enforcers, Governor Brian Ferguson. We have to make sure that our guys know how to avoid terrorists when being attacked. So send someone fast to release our brothers of the law enforcement. I thank you, and most of all, your country thanks you. Goodbye, sir. Oh, Mr. Ferguson, this here conversation never took place, and neither did that action your state just went through. Goodbye, sir." He hung up the phone on Governor Ferguson. Governor Ferguson called for someone to go and release the officers of the FBI, the Army National Guards, and the Good Samaritan citizens. They had nothing to prove that this took place, just like people claimed to see a UFO. The damn FBI couldn't believe that an ordinary group of people had the power and knew how to pull this shit off.

As the state troopers were getting in their cars and helicopters, the sheriff said, "What about filing a report on this shit? This shit has to be investigated."

The FBI director said, "It's over, and it has been investigated. The money is in your car with the tape, and I know that it's there because I took it out of my fucking helicopter and put it in your car. And you better put all of it back, unless I hit your goddamn ass for bank robbery. Now, take this damn thing up and let's go. All agents, move out!" They all left them in the same spot, wondering what the fuck happened.

The sheriff said to a state trooper, "How in the hell can fourteen men take heavily armed officers without firing a shot and win a battle such as this one? This fucking shit is not possible! One of these motherfuckers should be lying somewhere dead. As a matter of fact, where are the fucking dogs?"

A voice came on the radio and said, "Sheriff, come up here on the hill, sir."

As he made it up on the hill, that was when he saw these dogs all tied on the same rope, with their owner tied with them to a tree, gagged. The dogs' mouths were tied also so they would not bark. The

169

sheriff and state trooper said at the same time, "Now, who in the hell are these goddamn people?"

The state trooper said, "These boys are just playing a game with us, and that's a training that we will never forget as long as we live. Just leave it alone, Sheriff Karl, and I'll leave it alone."

Sheriff Karl said, "You got it, Kenny. This shit never happened. I'll see you."

They then both got in their cars, driving off.

The whole world had watched this as the news was reporting this chaos that was going on. They were not aware, though, that that was just a drill for the soldiers, but it was very much real for the officers, the Good Samaritan citizens, the state troopers that actually did not know, like state trooper Kenny, and Sheriff Karl. They kept it under their helmets.

As the team made it back to the unit, they marched in single file, going inside and lining up at attention. Captain Apocalypse, Sergeant Wrath, Sergeant Flood, Sergeant Rattler, and the MTs were there to greet them. Captain Apocalypse said, "Good goddamn job, soldier. Well-executed plan! You all worked as a team. Good job! Now go get cleaned and get yourself some food. Does any of you have any questions. Sergeant Night Terror, step forward now."

Sergeant Night Terror stepped forward, and Captain Apocalypse then said something in his ear. The other team members knew this was the second time this had happened. Captain Apocalypse stepped backward and said, "Sergeant Night Terror, step back in line." He stepped back in line, and Captain Apocalypse continued, "At ease and move out!"

The sergeants ran to their rooms, as did Sergeant Flood, Sergeant Rattler, and Sergeant Wrath. Captain Apocalypse went to his office, going over the news footage that he received from Sergeant Big Badass Wolf and Sergeant Boogeyman. He watched it and the bank robberies and noticed his new recruits did not hurt a soul. Captain Apocalypse said, "I really need to find out why I am feeling the way I am feeling. How in the hell could that many fucking North Vietnamese soldiers infiltrate as South Vietnamese soldiers and citizens?"

Captain Apocalypse knew that Sergeant Destroyer had put on the uniform of one of the captured North Vietnamese soldiers, and a South Vietnamese soldier allowed him to take his jeep. This soldier had to be a North Vietnamese. Captain Apocalypse did not want to alarm anyone about this, because this might fuck up the peace talks between the two of them.

Captain Apocalypse said on the intercom, "To all soldiers, when finished eating and resting, get back to training for six hours, nonstop. I would like to see Sergeant Rattler and Sergeant Flood in the debriefing room, now, if you are finished with your meal." He then just sat bark, collecting all his paperwork. He went to the debriefing room with all his paperwork, and they all saluted Captain Apocalypse.

Captain Apocalypse said, "At ease, soldiers! Sergeant Flood and Sergeant Rattler, I have a brain-picker here, and we need to figure out why in the hell I am still stuck in South Vietnam. Now, we need to study these intel very closely. So let's get started!"

As they were looking at these papers, going over them, the other team members were out there, training. They were in the debriefing room for well over five and a half hours, nonstop. Captain Apocalypse was looking at the pictures, and they all kept looking at the slides on the projector.

Sergeant Rattler said, "Going to the latrine, sir."

Captain Apocalypse just nodded as he was about to leave the room, still looking at the slide. That was when he saw something in the wooded area where Sergeant Boogeyman, Sergeant Big Badass Wolf, Sergeant Shadow, Sergeant Hocus-Pocus, and Sergeant Illusionist had parked the Red Cross truck, by this trail line called Ho Chi Minh. Some soldiers were all up in the trees too. He said, "Captain Apocalypse, did you see that?"

Captain Apocalypse said, "See what, Sergeant Rattler?"

He said, "That!"

Captain Apocalypse asked, "What? What did you see, Sergeant?"

Sergeant Rattler said, "Magnify that projector and look at that trail again, sir. It's North Vietnamese soldiers dressed like South Vietnamese soldiers, sir, before they came off the trail, as the North

Vietnamese soldiers were watching over them as they left. Your two real South Vietnamese soldiers were standing at a point, watching that trail, but the two that were standing there later were two North Vietnamese soldiers. The truck that was picking them up was South Vietnamese, and they did not know that they were indeed North Vietnamese soldiers. Why question them when they are wearing the same uniform and speaking the same language?"

Captain Apocalypse looked hard at Sergeant Rattler, as he was talking. Then he said, "You're right, Sergeant Rattler, you're right. I see exactly what you're saying. We have been infiltrated long enough. We have to plug that hole in that gap for life and make sure that no other damn South Vietnamese crosses that line. Ho Chi Minh has to close in order not to have another battle like we had years ago."

They broke the meeting up knowing what it was all about. They saw how it was possible for them to pull that off like they did.

Captain Apocalypse said to himself, "We have to close that trail. It must be foolproof, plan-proof, and soldier-proof." He was staring into the darkness, as always.

A month and a half went by, and Captain Apocalypse was sitting in his office when an envelope came down his mail slot with big letters saying, "Urgent." He opened it up and read the letter. After reading it, Captain Apocalypse said, "All soldiers—and I do mean *all* soldiers—please report to the debriefing rom ASAP!"

They all came into the debriefing room as Sergeant Big Badass Wolf and Sergeant Boogeyman were standing up, and as Captain Apocalypse was coming through the door, they said, "Attention!"

Everybody stood up, saluting him, as Captain Apocalypse said, "At ease. Please be seated. We have a very important mission to go on, and this time, we will not consider this as a Simple Simon mission. We will make every mission that we go on as 'our death mission.' We will be ODM. Now, this ODM will take us to Iran. We have five soldiers and three news reporters lost in the city of Tehran, which is very populated. I need these main sergeants to go in and get them, and the rest will be as a wall as well as a gate for them. Now, the ones that are going inside the city are Sergeant Big Badass Wolf, Sergeant Boogeyman, Sergeant Illusionist, Sergeant Hocus-Pocus, Sergeant

Shadow, Sergeant Night Terror, and Sergeant Body Snatcher. Take an armored personnel carrier in with you and be sure to paint it in their form and use paint that has a fluorescent color in it with their company's name in their language so we don't have to stick out like a sore thumb. This has to be done at night, when the inside team hits. After that's done, you all make it to the Caspian Sea, where the Sea Stallion will be ready to go fly us to the desert, where we'll be landing the C-5 Galaxy. I don't want a big scene with our death mission because we do know that those Iranians fight together. We don't want that whole entire city's population, Sergeants. We want those eight people out of there without being noticed. If you have to kill a few of their soldiers or anyone who sees you, then you have to do what you have to do, no matter what. Do you all understand our death mission?"

All of them stood up and saluted Captain Apocalypse as he then said, "All right, soldiers, then move out, soldiers, and load up."

They all were about to leave as Captain Apocalypse said, "Halt, soldiers! Sergeant Night Terror, step forward."

Sergeant Night Terror stepped forward and then to his left ear for about twenty-five seconds, then leaned back. The captain then said, "Step back in line. You all are dismissed. I'll see you on the plane."

Captain Apocalypse went to their garage and got their armored personnel carrier and loaded it up in the Sea Stallion, which they then placed in the Lockheed C-5 Galaxy. With all of them loaded up, he saluted before the door closed. Sergeant Boogeyman and Sergeant Big Badass Wolf took off smoothly, as they always did, going up in their air to Iran. Captain Apocalypse was just sitting there, and he said, "Sergeant Night Terror, step forward."

Sergeant Night Terror stood up and stepped to Captain Apocalypse and saluted him. Captain Apocalypse leaned to his left side for at least fifteen or sixteen seconds and then stood back upright and saluted him back, saying, "At ease and as you were." He went back and sat back down.

After flying for nearly twenty-eight to thirty hours, the Lockheed C-5 Galaxy landed in Baghdad, where they all unloaded the Sea Stallion out of the Galaxy and loaded back up on the Sea Stallion to fly to Iran's capital, Tehran. As they flew off, going to Tehran in the country of Iran, Captain Apocalypse said, "Sergeant Night Terror, step forward, soldier."

Sergeant Night Terror stepped forward and stood there at attention for at least five minutes while saluting Captain Apocalypse. Captain Apocalypse said, "Return to your sea, Sergeant."

An hour and fifteen or seventeen minutes went by. It was 2240 when they landed the Sea Stallion at the head coast of the Caspian Sea. Captain Apocalypse said, "Sergeant Big Badass Wolf and Sergeant Boogeyman, turn the Stallion around, toward the hard point of ground, so the inside team can drive it straight off the Stallion and back in it when they come back, so we can get a clean getaway if we have to. But remember, I don't want any mess."

As they turned the Stallion around and kept the blades running, Sergeant Big Badass Wolf and Sergeant Boogeyman came back around the back. Captain Apocalypse said, "Sergeant Boogeyman, Sergeant Big Badass Wolf, Sergeant Illusionist, Sergeant Hocus-Pocus, Sergeant Shadow, Sergeant Night Terror, and Sergeant Body Snatcher, you seven have these names for a reason, and I want it to be clean, because Sergeant Big Badass Wolf and Sergeant Boogeyman will use our ride back home. Sergeant Destroyer and Sergeant Grim Reaper, get on your Harleys and tailgate them from the side off in the distance as if you two were not part of them. Whatever you soldiers do, don't make any noise. Not one fucking sound! Shoot those fuckers in the mouth or neck to hold them quiet, and do not let their bodies be found until a week or two later. We will be back in the air and on our way back home when they realize that we took our package from them. Do you all understand?"

They all stood up and saluted Captain Apocalypse as Captain Apocalypse said, "All right, soldiers, move out! Ground team, take your positions."

And they all spread out into their positions. Sergeant Boogeyman, Sergeant Big Badass Wolf, Sergeant Illusionist, Sergeant Shadow, Sergeant Shadow, Sergeant Hocus-Pocus, and Sergeant Night Terror drove off in the armored personnel carrier to Tehran to pick up the seven captured Americans. The truck looked just like the

Iranian soldiers' truck. Nighttime gave them the advantage for their mission.

As they made it there, Sergeant Boogeyman set his watch at two minutes before it started. He then went to the power box, cutting the lights out on the second floor of this building where they were holding the hostages. As soon as the lights went out, three of the Iranian soldiers were walking down the hallway. And Sergeant Illusionist shot them in the neck and mouth. Sergeant Big Badass Wolf went into the room, killing eight of them while they were talking in the dark. He then released the seven people, leading them down the hall, just as Sergeant Shadow and Sergeant Hocus-Pocus killed fourteen or fifteen of them who were trying to find their way through the darkness. Sergeant Body Snatcher had four on his side die with their guns still in their hands, not having fired them, then two on the right corner, tied up, and five on the left side, tied up as well, as if they were still standing guard. He then hit his walkie-talkie and said, "Come on out. The path is clear."

As they came out, they put the seven in the armored personnel carrier. Then they were driving through the night as an Iranian police was trailing them and tried to pull them over. That was when Sergeant Destroyer and Sergeant Grim Reaper drove past on their Harleys, shooting them in the neck and sitting them up in their car as if they had just stopped for a minute or two. They then got back on their Harleys, protecting the truck, although it was armored.

Sergeant Boogeyman said to Captain Apocalypse, "Sergeant Boogeyman to Captain Apocalypse."

Captain Apocalypse responded, "Go ahead, Sergeant Boogeyman."

Sergeant Boogeyman said, "We all are on our way back with the cargo along with our wings, sir. We are three minutes out, and we can already see you, sir."

Captain Apocalypse said, "Come on in and we're ready. The gates of hell are waiting for you!"

The truck came in and slowly pulled up inside the Sea Stallion. Sergeant Big Badass Wolf and Sergeant Boogeyman then jumped out of the truck, leaving the seven people and Sergeant Hocus-Pocus,

Sergeant Illusionist, Sergeant Shadow, Sergeant Body Snatcher, and Sergeant Night Terror in the back with their guns, protecting them. Sergeant Night Terror was standing over Sergeant Illusionist, Sergeant Shadow, Sergeant Body Snatcher, and Sergeant Hocus-Pocus, who were kneeling down toward the door, ready to die for these seven people. Sergeant Night Terror had his AK-47 in his right hand, his M16 in his left hand, and three pineapple hand grenades on a string hanging out of his mouth, with a 9mm in his shoulder holster on the left side. The Sea Stallion took off, going back to Baghdad, where the C-5 Galaxy was ready on the runway to take off.

An hour and fifteen minutes went by when they finally made it to the Baghdad airstrip, cutting the Sea Stallion off as the propellers stopped rotating. They rolled the Sea Stallion inside the C-5 Galaxy plane as the armored personnel carrier and people were still in the Sea Stallion. Captain Apocalypse opened the door of that armored vehicle and said, "All soldiers out!" All of them came out, except for Sergeant Night Terror. Captain Apocalypse saw him standing there with his AK-47 in his right hand, his M16 in his left hand, and three pineapple hand grenades on a string hanging from his mouth with his 9mm in his holster on the left side guarding those seven people. Captain Apocalypse jumped up in the armored truck and saluted him and leaned to his left side for thirty-three seconds, then stood up at attention and said, "Good job, soldier."

Captain Apocalypse jumped back out of the truck and locked the door as the plane took off. They flew for thirty-nine and a half hours, making it back to the United States at the Washington, DC, airport, letting the door down on the C-5 Galaxy. The airport police, fire trucks, and medical team came driving fast to their plane, just as they opened the door and saw Sergeant Night Terror standing guard over the seven rescued hostages, prisoners of the Iranian soldiers. The officers for the airport were so scared when they were about to pull their guns on him.

Captain Apocalypse said, "Holster your weapons, Officers. That man will kill you and won't lose any sleep over it. His job is at my command, so holster your weapons now. It is safe now, Sergeant Night Terror. You can let them out." He then walked to the edge of the truck and jumped down, helping the five men and two women off the truck. Captain Apocalypse said, "Call the authorities and tell them that you have them in your presence." They all climbed back in the C-5 Galaxy plane, taking off, going back to their unit. After they landed back at their unit, they got off the plane. As they were about to go in, Captain Apocalypse said, "Sergeant Night Terror, step forward, soldier." He stepped forward, saluting Captain Apocalypse. Captain Apocalypse leaned forward to his left ear for ten seconds and leaned back up, saying, "At ease, soldiers. Take it in and get yourselves something to eat and some rest. And good job, soldiers. Damn good fucking job. Now, move out!"

They all went to, and Captain Apocalypse was very proud of his team as he went in behind them. His medical team was proud to be with this team.

It was a year later, March 22, 1974. Captain Apocalypse was sitting in his office, at his desk, going over his paperwork. His walkie-talkie button was being pushed with his code, 3-4-2, and he saw the tracking device leave Da Nang Air Base, going into North Vietnam. Captain Apocalypse's phone rang as he was looking at the map and the tracking device. Captain Apocalypse picked up the phone as a voice said, "General Foster has been kidnapped, and somebody killed Chou, his driver. They shot him at point-blank range in the face and head at least four or five times. They overkilled him, sir."

Captain Apocalypse said in his mechanical voice, "Hang up now!"

As that person hung up the phone, Captain Apocalypse sat in his chair, at his desk, and then got up, pushed his intercom button, and said, "All—and I do mean *all*—soldiers report to the debriefing room now!"

As they all made it to the debriefing room, they sat in their assigned seats. Captain Apocalypse came inside the door, and Sergeant Big Badass Wolf and Sergeant Boogeyman said, "Attention!"

All of them stood up, saluting Captain Apocalypse, who said, "At ease, soldiers. As you were. Now we got a serious dilemma here, and if you are in agreement, then we will do this off the record, because this is not open to anyone besides us. The United States does not know that this person is missing, but we know that he is. We know who got him, and we have to get him back. He is alive, that much I can tell you.

"A general in South Vietnam has been kidnapped by some North Vietnamese soldiers, by order of the leader of the North Vietnamese. We killed him about seven years ago. His name was Cho San Hue. We killed him and his ranking officers for penetrating as South Vietnamese soldiers after killing the families of those homes along with the circle inside it. We went to take that circle back, but it was hell to do, and they took one of us and tortured him, then injured another. So we went to claim what was ours. I guess they believe that General Foster has had a hand in that mission. He let us borrow his Cobra attack chopper and *Puff, the Magic Dragon*. Our hostess was an infiltrate as well. Her name was Qs Long, but she was also known as Sergeant Turtle Dragon for Cho San Hue. I don't know who called for this to happen to him, but what we need to do is to go get him out of North Vietnam at all costs. This is what we call our death mission. You can stay back and the old team and I would not mind, and if some from the old team do not want to go, then I'll understand that too. The question is, Are you in an agreement to go on this death mission?"

All of them stood up and saluted Captain Apocalypse, as Captain Apocalypse then said, "Then it must be done."

As they all sat back down, Captain Apocalypse continued, "Sergeant Night Terror, step forward, soldier."

Sergeant Night Terror stepped forward, and Captain Apocalypse said, "You are off the team. Now, get your ass out of my fucking sight. And I mean now. Get! Out! Now!"

When Sergeant Night Terror left the meeting, the other members of the team did not say a word, because they kept seeing Captain Apocalypse keep talking to him.

Captain Apocalypse said, "Now, back to business. Here is a detection device, and this is where it's located in North Vietnam, at Hanoi, at Hoa Lo Prison, which they call the Hanoi Hilton. This place has SAM-5 and SAM-7 suffice-to-air missiles. This place is ready for any air raid and ground assault. Our job is to get in there and disengage that missile. Hanoi will knock anything that is not theirs out of the air. General Foster is in one of the cells in that prison, and we must get him very quickly and close that trail up so goddamn tight that when anything tries to cross it, then their fucking assess will be just a memory. We will not attack these motherfuckers by air, because they will be waiting for that to happen. We are going to bring hand-to-fucking-hand combat on their asses. We will kill every son of a bitch that is not us or on our team.

"Now, here is your mission position. When we get to South Vietnam, we will take the Harleys to the Ho Chi Minh trail. I want you to bring all your weapons with their silencers and your crossbow. And you will have a garrote. You will wear your M1951 bulletproof jacket. In your duffel bag of arsenal, each of you should put twenty-five smoke grenades, twenty-five tear gas canisters, CS gas, and keep two antivenom in your pocket for a quick pull if you need it. And also twenty-one Claymores. Now, it's a one-day hike to Nang Kihnag from the Ho Chi Minh trail and back to the Da Nang Air Base. We will sit there with him until our president gets that shit smoothed out.

"Listen carefully now. Sergeant Big Badass Wolf, Sergeant Boogeyman, Sergeant Evil, Sergeant Illusionist, Sergeant Hocus-Pocus, Sergeant Lowlife, Sergeant Destroyer, Sergeant Hectic, Sergeant Nuclear, Sergeant Eliminate, Sergeant Wrath, Sergeant Body Snatcher, Sergeant Death, Sergeant Grave Yard, Sergeant Torture, and Sergeant Chaos, all of you will go in and get him out of there, and you will know where to go. Trust me, with your Starlight night vision goggles, you will know exactly where to go when you come back out, because we all will be placing Claymores all on the ground and in the trees up and down the Ho Chi Minh trail. Whoever tries to follow us or come through at a later time will get their asses blown to smithereens!

"This mission will start at 1900, and we'll be out of the whole city, back on the trail, at 2100 or 2200, then back at the base at 2245 or 2245 with the general. Are you ready, soldiers?"

They all said, "Sir, yes, sir," in their mechanical voice.

Captain Apocalypse said, "Go to your room and study those papers and learn them by hard and then burn them when you finish. You have until next week, Wednesday. Now, clear out!"

As they all left, Captain Apocalypse went to his office and opened up his door. Sergeant Night Terror stood up, saluting Captain Apocalypse. Captain Apocalypse said, "Sergeant Night Terror, you ready for this mission, soldier?"

Sergeant Night Terror said in his mechanical voice, "Ready to die, sir!"

Captain Apocalypse said, "Then I will die with you, soldier." Then he continued, "Have a seat, Sergeant. The mission is a death mission, and this mission is in North Vietnam, and I am going to fly you over there personally. I want you to infiltrate as a prison guard and find this general. He is General Foster, who is about to be a five-star general. We have to get him back before this country knows that he has been kidnaped by the North Vietnamese soldiers. We have some North Vietnamese soldiers' uniforms put up back at the base. The prison is in Hanoi, and the prison's name is Hoa La Prison, with the nickname of Hanoi Hilton. Your guard's name will be Sien Yi Tiu. You will be in there for one week, and we will be there at 2245, so have your plan ready for us to come and get you two, and let him know that we are on our way. Now go out to your Harley and I'll be behind you."

They both left his office, going to the tunnel door, getting on their Harleys when Sergeant Big Badass Wolf and Sergeant Boogeyman said, "Where to, Captain Apocalypse?"

He replied, "Take us to South Vietnam."

They all got in the G5 Galaxy, going back to South Vietnam.

Captain Apocalypse said, "We're going to dress you out, and we have a jeep for you also. You can drive right in there, and we will be there in one week, soldier. Just give me a week."

They made it to South Vietnam with nobody knowing that they had made it there. Captain Apocalypse ordered Sergeant Big Badass Wolf and Sergeant Boogeyman to remain in the plane and ready to go as soon as he got back. Captain Apocalypse took Sergeant Night Terror to the warehouse and took the old uniform of one of the North Vietnamese soldiers, then gave him the keys of the jeep with the dead body of a South Vietnamese who was in the Da Nang Air Base morgue; he had just died within two hours of their arrival. He drove off with his dead passenger, who was a lieutenant of the South Vietnamese soldiers.

A lot of South Vietnamese people were yelling at him, very angry, but he just kept driving, going north.

Captain Apocalypse, meanwhile, got back on the C-5 Galaxy as Sergeant Big Badass Wolf and Sergeant Boogeyman took off very smoothly, going back home. As they made it back home at their unit, the team was out there, training for their mission. Captain Apocalypse, Sergeant Boogeyman, and Sergeant Big Badass Wolf joined them in their attacks. They fought for well over seven to eight hours, give or take an extra half-hour. They were about to start over when Captain Apocalypse said, "Enough, soldiers! Enough! Now, get some rest and get yourself some dinner."

The whole team laid their weapons down at the same time as smoke and tear gas smell were all up in the air. These soldiers did not have on a mask to keep the tear gas from bothering them. Their stocking cap and ski mask must have stopped it some sort of away, or maybe they had something to support them to breathe.

Now, as Sergeant Night Terror was inside North Vietnam, a prison guard was walking around, jiggling his keys and speaking Vietnamese. All the other North Vietnamese guards had heard a lot of bad, cruel, and ruthless shit about Officer Sien Yic Tiu. One of the North Vietnamese guards took him to General Foster's cell, and it had another American soldier in there dead of starvation.

General Foster said, "You goddamn people need to bury this man, as he is dead and his body is going to rot in here!"

Officer Sien Yi Tiu could understand his words very well, and he translated in North Vietnamese, and they both laughed at the dead soldier. Officer Sien Yi Tiu then said, again in North Vietnamese, "He'll die like all stinky Americans!" They both laughed again.

General Foster said, "You sons of bitches, what do you want from me? I don't know a goddamn thing. Why do you have that shit on your face? Show your goddamn self, you sorry-ass pissant! You motherfuckers know that I'm a goddamn general!"

They both left the cell door where General Foster was in, just as General Foster said, "Come back here, you motherfucker, and get my soldier out of here and bury him right!"

But they just kept on walking and talking.

This guard that was walking with Sien Yi Tiu saw this beautiful girl and an American man walking with her, and he said to her in North Vietnamese, "This is Sergeant Sien Yi Tiu and Sergeant Sien Yi Tiu. This is Lieutenant Kim Ly, who is also known as Golden Lion. She devours things!"

She stared at him, and he smiled at her.

The American looked at him and said, "What is the cover on your face for?"

Kim Ly replied, "He is our torture man, who will tell us what the fuck the general knows. I can't believe he thought you were his son, and I your wife. He doesn't know shit! He can't ever see us, you understand, don't you, Vince?"

He said, "Yes, I understand."

She then said to Sergeant Sien Yi Tiu and the other guard in North Vietnamese that she'd see them when it was over. She then saluted him and walked off.

The sergeant officer now knew the leech who had the general kidnapped. He walked around, studying everybody and everything. As he walked outside with his North Vietnamese guard with him, he saw three big-ass beehives lined up in a low branch, swarming everywhere. The sergeant officer was just looking at both of them, just laughing, speaking in North Vietnamese. This guard was showing Sergeant Sien Yi Tiu all the escape routes that he would need when he took General Foster out of here. He had counted two hundred and seventy to seventy-five soldiers, give or take, and the people in the area as well; they'd give the count of three hundred and ninety-five people.

As he was walking still, he saw this nice, armored car for Lieutenant Kim Ly, who was really Golden Lion.

Officer Sergeant Sien Yi Tiu said in North Vietnamese, "She likes you, I see." Then he said in messed-up English, "Dey murder her mother in South Vietnam. Her mother was Mrs. Qs Long. Dey call her Sergeant Turtle Dragon. Dey thought dey kill leader Cho San Hue, but it his son, Cho To Hue, and dat make leader very mad."

Sergeant Officer Sien Yi Tiu said, "American die in two days."

They went to the first floor, which was an empty cell, next to the dayroom. And the key fit perfectly.

Three days later, it was Wednesday afternoon in North Vietnam when they brought General Foster to that last room for torture. They also brought the dead American soldier, at his request.

General Foster said, "What can you do to him? He is dead already!"

Sergeant Sien Yi Tiu walked over there to him and slapped him so hard, making him hit the floor, where he knelt down and replied in North Vietnamese. As the general was trying to talk, he eased the right side of his face and said in a whisper, "General, I am an American soldier. Captain Apocalypse and team are coming for us. Just play along, sir, and I'm sorry." Then he said out loud in North Vietnamese, "Stupid American." And they all laughed. He then hit and kicked the general, putting his foot all on his neck.

The general protested that it was hurting him, saying, "I…I…I…" *Cough cough cough.* "P-p-please…" *Cough cough cough.* "I know nothing…" *Cough cough cough.*

Sergeant Sien Yi Tiu said in North Vietnamese, "Leave him. I know how to make the soldier talk."

He went to get a big plastic bag and went to those three big beehives, putting it in the plastic bag. He got a car battery and some gas that'd kill you for taking in too much of it, and he rigged up their mask so that the gas could go straight into their system.

Nighttime came. It was 2244, and his watch was beeping. He stopped it from beeping and said in broken English, "General, your time is up." He then continued, "Turn off the lights so my two favorite watchers can see what will happen to any American that fucks with our leader, Cho San Hue." He passed out the gas mask and put some Starlight night vision goggles on the general, saying, "The light is about to go!" Then, three lights hit the building.

Sergeant Night Terror arranged the gas canisters, setting all three of them off as those people were laughing, at least at first, and then they started coughing and trying to run. But they bumped into one another and the walls as the sergeant then shook those bees up in the bag, guiding General Foster out of that side door, with this dead American soldier on his shoulder. As the door opened, he shot two North Vietnamese guards in the head, killing them instantly with his 9mm, his silencer on it. He then cut the bag open and threw it on the other North Vietnamese soldiers, who could not shoot because the bees were stinging them as they were roaming and dying from the gas.

He then met up with Sergeant Big Badass Wolf, Sergeant Boogeyman, Sergeant Evil, Sergeant Illusionist, Sergeant Hocus-pocus, Sergeant Lowlife, Sergeant Destroyer, Sergeant Hectic, Sergeant Nuclear, Sergeant Eliminate, Sergeant Wrath, Sergeant Body Snatcher, Sergeant Death, Sergeant Graveyard, Sergeant Torture, and Sergeant Chaos, then covered his face and said in his mechanical voice, "I need you, Sergeant Big Badass Wolf. I have two murdered bodies to get out of there. It's important to our mission."

They went on, killing ten to fourteen North Vietnamese prison guards and picking up the body of Kim Ly, who was known as Lieutenant Golden Lion, and the American man that was with her. They made it out and got in her car, then drove to the area of Nang Khang, where the Ho Chi Minh trail was.

Later, Sergeant Wrath said, "General Foster, everything in bright colors can only be seen with your special-light night vision goggles on, so please don't take them off for anything." As they were setting more Claymores out for those who were about to follow him, the North Vietnamese tried to cut the surface-to-air-missiles SAM-5 and SAM-7 as they blew up, making it feel like an earthquake. As they made it to the wood and putting General Foster on the back of one of those Harleys with the rest following them beside of Sergeant Snatcher, Sergeant Big Badass Wolf, Sergeant Destroyer, Sergeant Boogeyman, Sergeant Death, Sergeant Evil, Sergeant Animosity,

Sergeant Consequence, Sergeant Grim Reaper, Sergeant Red Rum, Sergeant Vicious, and Sergeant Horrific as they were battling with the North Vietnamese soldiers killing them as the North Vietnamese was up in the air as Sergeant Rattler came out of nowhere and aim that bazooka up at the chopper blowing it to smithereens and a small plane with a Gatling gun on it as they all ran and got on their Harleys with Sergeant Rattler on the back of Sergeant Red Rum.

Captain Apocalypse said, "No fucking pity, goddammit! I MEAN NO FUCKING PITY!"

As the rest of them went on ahead, Sergeant Destroyer turned around without them knowing and went back to close the line down on Ho Chi Minh by destroying it and killing at least forty-five North Vietnamese soldiers. He then got on his Harley, where a North Vietnamese soldier that was hiding up in a tree jumped out of it and pushed his knife inside of Sergeant Destroyer's eye. Sergeant Destroyer pushed him down with that knife still in his eye, looked down at him, and took one of the Claymores from his bag. He then took the knife out of his eye, still looking at the North Vietnamese soldier as he gutted him so fucking fast, with the Vietnamese soldier still alive. Sergeant Destroyer put that land mine in his open stomach and put the Vietnamese soldier's right hand on it, as it was inside of him. He cranked up his Harley and sped off very fast with just one eye.

As he was riding off, he could hear a lot of land mines going off. He was at the end of the Ho Chi Minh trail, where he then went to the Da Nang Air Base. All the soldiers and the South Vietnamese soldiers, along with three thousand more United States soldiers, were there, standing guard, as Sergeant Destroyer parked his Harley next to the rest of them inside the C-5 Galaxy plane and came back, walking out, standing at attention.

Sergeant Night Terror said, "Permission to speak to you, Captain Apocalypse."

Captain Apocalypse replied, "Permission granted."

Sergeant Night Terror said, "We have the two responsible for the general's kidnapping, sir. These are the two who did it, sir." He then threw them on the ground in front of the general. He noticed that the man was an American, but he could not tell about the woman, because the gas and the bees had kind of disfigured her.

Captain Apocalypse said, "Pick them up."

Sergeant Big Badass Wolf and Sergeant Night Terror picked them up and carried them inside, throwing them on the floor side by side on their back, at General Foster's feet. General Foster said, "You killers! You killers! You fucking murderers! You killed my goddamn son and his wife! Why did you do that? Why? Please tell me why!"

Sergeant Night Terror said, "General Foster, sir, they did not do this. I—"

His explanation was cut short as he snatched an M16 out of the hand of one of his soldiers. The No-Name Unit did not pull their weapons at all because they respected ranks, as they were told to. General Foster was still holding the gun on Sergeant Night Terror. "Why? Why? Why did you kill my son and his wife, soldier?" He was crying so hard, looking at them, as if he were a little kid.

Sergeant Night Terror said, "Permission to speak, General Foster."

General Foster replied, "Speak, soldier."

Sergeant Night Terror went on, "General, this is not your son, sir, and neither is that his wife. This man is a traitor to us all as he worked with this lady to seek revenge on you because she thought you had something to do with killing her mother."

General Foster asked, "Her mother? What the fuck you talking about, soldier?"

Sergeant Night Terror continued, "Her mother was a lady by the name of Mrs. Qs Lang, who they called Sergeant Turtle Dragon, whoever she was. And it was not the leader Clio San Hue who died here. It was his son. Your son is a lieutenant colonel, but he is in Washington, DC. He was in Iranian custody, included in those that we took out of there almost two years ago. Please go make that call, sir. On my life, if it's not true, then you can kill me for killing one of my superior officers. Just go call, please. MPs, place me under arrest until the truth comes."

One of the MPs said, "We are not—"

Captain Apocalypse said, cutting their sentence off. "You heard my soldier. Do it, goddammit. Do it now!"

They put the cuff on Sergeant Night Terror as General Foster went into his office. He was gone for twenty-seven or thirty minutes. General Foster then came back and dropped the gun at his feet, then went to his knees, replying in tears, "Please, please, please forgive me, son. I'm so, so, so, so very sorry, son. Please! Please! Please, I beg for you forgiveness, son. Please forgive me."

The MPs were taking the cuff off Sergeant Night Terror as Sergeant Night Terror went on his knees with the general, saying, "Come on, General. It's okay, sir. I came to die for you, and I'll die to protect you. And if I ever hurt you, then I'll die for that too." General Foster hugged him tight as he helped the general off the floor. The general bowed with a smile on his face as Captain Apocalypse raised his left eyebrow and said, "Good job! I's be damned, soldier! You did a fucking good goddamn job. Now, sleep, son. Get some sleep."

As he closed his right eye and went to sleep, Captain Apocalypse went out to the team, who were standing there at attention. He said, "He doesn't want y'all to show any pity, and he knows how y'all feel about him. So at ease, soldiers. Good fucking job on our death mission."

Later, they all went to their rooms to get cleaned up.

Captain Apocalypse went to his office and sat up in the dark, thinking about the first time that he ever met Sergeant Destroyer, Robert Kristoff, who became No Pity and a destroyer. He had to be a cat to have nine lives, or perhaps he was just too fucking stubborn to die.

Captain Apocalypse just sat there in the darkness, staring at the ceiling, wondering what their next mission was going to be.

CHAPTER 6

Six years and four months later and it was July 11, 1980. The captain knew that his original team had gotten up in their ages, and three of his original soldiers were physically injured. Sergeant Flood was paralyzed from the waist down, Sergeant Rattler's left arm was missing from the elbow down, and Sergeant Destroyer had lost his left eye. He was at his desk, looking through all the missions that he and his team had gone on. He was just sitting there, since he knew that he himself had aged as well. He didn't want to let go of the team, but he knew that an experienced young captain needed to take over. The team had been on other missions and had defused several hostage-taking situations. The No-Name Unit tried fighting against the Hezbollah terrorists, who were killing and kidnapping men, women, and children. A year and a month after that mission, they then were back on call to go to another country.

He was still holding on to him as he sat the general on the chair. Sergeant Destroyer walked up to Captain Apocalypse and asked, while Captain Apocalypse was standing next to the general, "Permission to speak, Captain?"

Captain Apocalypse replied, "Permission granted, Sergeant."

Sergeant Destroyer said, "Everything is okay, sir."

Captain Apocalypse asked, "What is okay, Sergeant?"

He said, "Ew," and fell on the floor face-first, all that blood soaked in his clothes and his ski mask.

Captain Apocalypse said, "Everybody do a fucking about-face now!" They all did an about-face as Captain Apocalypse took Sergeant Destroyer's ski mask off and saw his left eye was missing.

He said, "Goddammit. Shit! Motherfuckers! Hold on, soldier, hold on. I got you. I got you, soldier. MTs, get here! We got one down!" He then put his ski mask back over his face with all that blood on the floor. Captain Apocalypse continued, "Put Sergeant Destroyer on that plane now! Let's go! Take care, General. We have to go now, sir."

They rushed Sergeant Destroyer on the plane.

General Foster said to his captain, "I am retiring, going back to the United States. You are in charge till someone gets here. Good luck with this post." He then walked out and had a couple of his soldiers drive him home. The general was feeling really bad about Sergeant Night Terror, and now Sergeant Destroyer, and he said, "I don't have what it takes to be in this business anymore. That young soldier came inside of that place to get me out, and I treated him as a criminal and called him a killer and a murderer. Why? Why? Why?"

He just went inside of his house to pack up.

Captain Apocalypse and his team, meanwhile, made it to the United States and immediately rolled Sergeant Destroyer back to his room, again, as the MTs doctored on him and got him stable. They were now monitoring him. Captain Apocalypse came in and stood up there, looking at him, and Sergeant Robert "No Pity" Kristoff, the Destroyer, said, "Don't worry, Captain. I'm okay, sir." He then moved his left eye.

Meanwhile, in the city of Cusco, Captain Apocalypse sent Sergeant Chaos, Sergeant Executioner, Sergeant Redrum, and Sergeant Vicious inside to infiltrate the Shining Path Communist terrorists group that they had to defuse. After they had infiltrated the Communist group that called themselves the Shining Path, Sergeant Chaos, Sergeant Executioner, Sergeant Redrum, and Sergeant Vicious all went in four different directions that evening. The group was supposed to go and attack Government Palace in Lima, Peru. Although Sergeant Chaos, Sergeant Executioner, Sergeant Redrum, and Sergeant Vicious infiltrated that Communist group, they still did not have a clue that each of them belonged to the No-Name Unit.

As they all made it back to the rest of the team at different times, fully dressed back into their original uniform, that was when Captain Apocalypse took another direction and set up all around the

Government Palace, killing all eighty-nine to one hundred of them. They stole one of Cusco City's big truck and placed all those bodies in it, then drove it back to the Sea Stallion, loading it up and carrying it off. As they were flying over the Atlantic Ocean, they pushed the truck off the Sea Stallion with all the dead bodies of those who called themselves the Shining Path.

When they made it home after their four days' attack on the Communist in Peru, Captain Apocalypse made it to his office and saw another envelope in his mail slot. He knew his team was tired and hungry and that they needed some rest, but it was their job to defuse and stop anyone or anything that was a major threat to their country as well to their allied countries. Captain Apocalypse knew that this envelope was very important, and it had to be defused ASAP because thousands of lives were in great danger. It was a group of terrorists in Japan, in the city of Tokyo, who called themselves Aum Shinrikyo, which meant "Doomsday Cult." They had targeted the subway in Tokyo. The authorities in Japan needed a secret special forces team to come over and stop them before it happened.

Captain Apocalypse pushed his intercom button and said, "The following soldiers are to report to the debriefing room ASAP: Sergeant Redrum, Sergeant Viper, Sergeant Death, Sergeant Executioner, Sergeant Vicious, Sergeant Torture, Sergeant Horrific, Sergeant Graveyard, Sergeant Undertaker, Sergeant Wrath, Sergeant Chaos, Sergeant Venomous, Sergeant Grim Reaper, Sergeant Night Terror, and Sergeant Body Snatcher. That's all."

As the new team made it to the debriefing room, Captain Apocalypse was standing up at the table. They all saluted Captain Apocalypse as he said, "At ease, soldiers. Be seated."

They all sat at their assigned seats along with the MTs.

Captain Apocalypse continued, "Team, we have a serious problem here. We got a terrorist group in Japan, in the city of Tokyo, threating to blow up a subway there. They call themselves Aum Shinrikyo, the Doomsday Cult. And they must be stopped now. I know you must be very tired, but it has to be done. Are you ready to take on this mission without the others?"

They all stood up and saluted Captain Apocalypse.

Captain Apocalypse said, "All right, then, team. Let's move out!"

They all went to the tunnel door and went to that new Suzuki 500cc trail bikes, going to the elevator shaft. As they made it to the shaft, they then went down to the C-5 Galaxy.

Sergeant Boogeyman said, "Where to, Captain Apocalypse?"

Captain Apocalypse said, "To Japan, and then we will take the Sea Stallion to Tokyo airport and ride Suzukis into Tokyo's subway."

They flew for well over nineteen hours, making it to Japan and taking the Sea Stallion, looking down with their Suzukis, going to Tokyo's tunnel. As they made it to the tunnel, Captain Apocalypse separated everybody into sections and positioned himself as well. Two hours later, at 0300, the Aum Shinrikyo came in with backpacks on them. The team was watching them as they were walking around with their flashlights, speaking to one another in Japanese. Captain Apocalypse hit his code, and the last group came in. All in the team were killing their targets and taking their backpacks from their dead bodies. After they had killed their whole entire target, they saw a truck speeding away; they knew that one got away. He must've been the one with the switch to set all the bombs off when his disciples refused to answer their radios. They all then jumped on their Suzukis, bringing them out to the beginning of the subway, where they parked their trucks, cars, and vans.

Sergeant Wrath said in his mechanical voice, "Wait! Someone is missing. Head count!"

The following were accounted for: Sergeant Big Badass Wolf, Sergeant Boogeyman, Sergeant Graveyard, Sergeant Chaos, Sergeant Redrum, Sergeant Torture, Sergeant Horrific, Sergeant Undertaker, Sergeant Grim Reaper, Sergeant Night Terror, Sergeant Venomous, Sergeant Executioner, Sergeant Vicious, Sergeant Viper, Sergeant Death, and Sergeant Body Snatcher.

Sergeant Wrath said, "Captain Apocalypse, this is Sergeant Wrath."

There was no answer.

Sergeant Wrath said again, "Captain Apocalypse, this is Sergeant Wrath. Respond!"

Still, there was no answer from Captain Apocalypse.

Sergeant Wrath commanded, "Find the captain, and find him now!"

They all got on their Suzukis, going to Captain Apocalypse's position. As they were getting closer, that was when they saw a body lying across the track, not moving. They pulled up to the body and saw eleven bodies that belonged to the Aum Shinrikyo lying there, dead, while Captain Apocalypse's body had three Japanese swords going all the way through his head. The team picked up his body and laid it in one of the terrorists' vans, along with his demolished Suzuki. They then loaded up their Suzukis and drove away in all those terrorists' trucks and vans and cars, driving them off a cliff where their Sea Stallion was sitting. They refused to pull the swords out of the head of Captain Apocalypse. They all loaded up on the Sea Stallion, flying to the C-5 Galaxy. As they landed the Sea Stallion behind the C-5 Galaxy, they immediately took Captain Apocalypse's body on a gurney to the MTs, who took his pulse and checked his heartbeat. The MTs just dropped their heads and slowly pulled the swords out of his head.

The team knew that he was dead, and so did the MTs.

His chance to still go live was gone when the first sword went into his head. The whole team just stood over him in a salute. When the C-5 Galaxy landed at their base, none of them came out of the Galaxy. Sergeant Boogeyman and Sergeant Big Badass Wolf just stood at the door of the Galaxy.

The old squad came down, walking around the whole entire circle of the new squad, comforting them and easing them off the plane. The MTs took Captain Apocalypse and prepped him for burial.

Three days later, they took Captain Apocalypse's body to a special cemetery in Arlington, Texas, and marked his grave with a special mark; only they knew who was in this grave. As they finished burying Captain Apocalypse, the whole thirty-five of them knew that Captain Apocalypse would jump down their throats for showing some fucking pity, so they just saluted him, walking off, going to their tour bus. Sergeant Big Badass Wolf drove one, and Sergeant Boogeyman the other. Sergeant Boogeyman was driving through the back way to the base behind Sergeant Big Badass Wolf. When Sergeant Big Badass Wolf stopped his bus, Sergeant Boogeyman had to stop his bus. When Sergeant Boogeyman stopped his bus in the pitch-black darkness, Sergeant Wrath jumped out of the bus, going back to his regular unit and collecting all his things.

Five days later, a voice came through the intercom, saying, "I am Lieutenant Obliterate. I am your lieutenant. I heard what happened to our captain, and I am deeply sorry about our brother. I know the new team knows me, as they were once under my command. I am asking you all to report to the debriefing room ASAP."

They all came to the debriefing room, where Lieutenant Obliterate was standing up, and they all saluted him

Lieutenant Obliterate said, "At ease, soldiers." He saluted them too. He the continued, "You all know that we have lost our captain, and we will indeed miss him, especially the team that went into battles with him. We all knew him in our own ways, and we know that he died with honor and is buried with bravery. We will continue to be who he made us to be, and that's some true soldiers.

"But I also would like to make some readjustments while this meeting is going on. The first topic is that I have to remove three soldiers from this crew. These soldiers are on the injured list, and they still can, at some point, perform their duties, but if we really actually need them to go into a war zone with us, they will be very detrimental to us all. This is something that I don't want to do, but I have to do it. I am sorry, Sergeant Destroyer, Sergeant Flood, and Sergeant Rattler. As of now, you three can go to your rooms and pack all your belongings and leave the unit. I know Captain Apocalypse still had faith in you three while he was in charge, but I have to disagree with that.

"Now, does anybody have any disagreement with this decision?"

They all wanted to say something about this shit, because they all knew that the only way out was death, but they knew that Captain Apocalypse explained to them before and after their training to never question their leader of the unit. So the whole team just sat quietly and continued to let him talk. As Sergeant Rattler and Sergeant Destroyer pushed Sergeant Flood out of the debriefing room, their teammates stood up and embraced them with a salute. They were leaving the room to pack their things to leave their unit, which they have called home, where men lived to honor men for eternity.

These soldiers that belonged to the No-Name Unit knew their rules, one of which was not to walk in a line of insubordination to their squad leader and squad.

Lieutenant Obliterate said, "All right, men, back to our meeting. Give me six months with you all and I'll ensure you my loyalty to the crew. Do any of you have any questions?"

There wasn't a question asked, so Lieutenant Obliterate said, "This meeting is over. You can go back to your quarters now, men."

They all got up at the same time, saluting Lieutenant Obliterate, quickly leaving the debriefing room. The whole team went down to Sergeant Flood's, Sergeant Rattler's, and Sergeant Destroyer's rooms, watching them pack. They knew they couldn't show any pity, but who could tell under their stocking cap and ski mask? As they finished packing their stuff, Sergeant Big Badass Wolf and Sergeant Boogeyman picked up some of their things and walked toward the tunnel's door, and the rest of them did the same thing. Sergeant Big Badass Wolf knew that these guys had been in here ever since they were eighteen to twenty years old, and they were now in their midthirties and forties, with no real home to call theirs. He gave them all a card with a message on it that read, "I'm giving them all a condo unit in my apartment complex rent-free for the rest of their lives. I want you to fully furnish it with all their special needs, no questions asked. Signed, Mr. KTU."

They all loaded up on the Sea Stallion, taking them to their new homes. There were three big moving vans waiting for them when the Sea Stallion landed, and they all loaded their trucks up as the people who worked for Mr. KTU were waiting to take them to their place. Sergeant Flood had his personal driver until they could find a way that he could drive himself. They all left and went to the apartment complex, where they saw a personal license plate on three cars that looked just like their colors. The team knew that Captain Apocalypse would be proud of them for protecting their brothers, as they had vowed to do.

As they made it back to the unit and got ready to order themselves a meal, Lieutenant Obliterate said, "A new rule comes into effect right now: no leaving this unit for anything unless I go with you, like I am the grown-up and you are the children. Am I clear?"

They all saluted him, standing at attention. Lieutenant Obliterate said, "I'm going to be rougher than Captain Apocalypse. Do you understand?"

They all just saluted him again as he walked off and turned away, then said, "So where are they living?"

Sergeant Boogeyman said, "We just dropped them off where three trucks were waiting for them, and they just left, sir. We don't know where they went, sir."

As he turned back around and walked off, going to Captain Apocalypse's office, he saw how clean it was, with maps all around the globe inside. He said, "Captain Apocalypse was a fucking mad man with all this shit, and this man called our mission 'death mission.' We—no, I mean, I am going to change that little jinxed motto, because our mission will be just a mission and not a death mission."

As he was in the office, he hit the intercom button and said, "I would like to see the unit medical team as soon as possible in my off."

Nobody knew what this was about, but when they made it to his office, Lieutenant Obliterate said, "Your service will no longer be needed, because the team will go to the hospital like regular soldiers, and if their life is threatened, then we will send them to a place where they will be attended to. I'm sorry, but you three are no longer needed. You're excused."

They did not pack their stuff; the team just saw them go into their rooms, cutting their lights out and hanging their keys on the doors as they were told to walk out of the door so the whole base could see them. The team knew that nobody was allowed to leave out the door as they all formed a line, saluting their medical team as they were leaving. They took them to the elevator shaft and down to the Sea Stallion, where they all loaded up with the medical team, dropping them off out the main hospital. They requested the head of administration to call Da Nang Air Base and speak to a captain who was in charge to receive his staff; this was an order by Captain

Apocalypse and General Foster, a five-star general, as they hired these three on the spot without sending them anywhere.

The rest of them then went back to the Sea Stallion to go back on the base. Lieutenant Obliterate said, "Everybody on the battle field now. Go train until I tell you to stop, and that's an order! Now!"

They all went out to the training course Captain Apocalypse–style times a hundred. The whole entire house was shaking with the sound of tremendous thunder clapping. This went on for, like, twelve or thirteen and a half hours. The lieutenant was afraid to go out there to tell them that it was time to stop and take it in. The soldiers were having a war outside against something that was unseen to the eyes. Then, all of a sudden, the noise of clapping thunder just stopped, though they still could feel the vibration of the war. The generals, majors, and colonels that were not allowed in this unit had come inside of it and went to Lieutenant Obliterate's office.

The general then said, "Lieutenant Obliterate, what in the fuck are you trying to do to these soldiers? We've been hearing this for well over twelve hours now! Why in the hell haven't you stopped them? Let's go now!"

As they all went out back to the training section, there were dust, tear gas smoke, and foglike smoke was badly setting, and when it did, they saw all of them with all their weapons lined up neatly in front of them, in the same order. None of them were off-key as they were in a salute to somebody or something. The generals, majors, and colonels walked past these soldiers and looked at them, their weapons, and how they had demolished this whole entire training ground. It looked like a real war field, where war had taken place in their backyard, but without any casualties to be counted. These ranking officers had heard many noises coming from over there many times before, but not like this one.

The general of the training base, General George T. Staples said, "At ease, soldiers."

All of them were still standing at attention as General Staples continued, "As I said, soldiers, you can at ease now. Captain Apocalypse is no longer with us, so at ease, soldiers."

They were still standing there as General Staples said, "Lieutenant Obliterate, at ease your soldiers so that they can go get themselves some rest."

Lieutenant Obliterate said, "All right, men, take it in."

The soldiers still stood there, just saluting; they were still confusing these generals, colonels, and majors. They were like a statue as a voice in the sky said, echoing, "Enough! Enough! Enough! Enough! Enough! Enough…At ease! At ease! At ease! At ease! At ease!"

As all the soldiers just stood there, and so did all the generals, majors, colonels, and Lieutenant Obliterate, listening to that echo. They all see a shadow figure walking toward them all with authority, like Captain Apocalypse. This shadowy, person-type figure seemed to take his time making it to them. As he finally made it to them, raising his head, looking at the soldiers, he said, "Good job, soldiers. Damn good goddamn job. I feel sorry for the poor bastard whom you fought against."

The other generals, majors, colonels, and Lieutenant Obliterate still didn't know who he was, but as he stopped walking and slowly raised his head, that was when these generals, majors, colonels, and Lieutenant Obliterate noticed that this was a five-star general, General Foster.

General Foster said, "Let's move out!" And they all started running in single file. The five-star general added, "Who's over this outfit here? Report now!"

Lieutenant Obliterate said, "Sir, I am, sir."

General Foster said, "Then why are these soldiers out this late and not getting their goddamn rest? These soldiers will not question your methods, Lieutenant, but I'd be goddamned if you or anybody else will abuse these soldiers. Stop calling them men, because that's one thing that you can never mess with or challenge them for, being a man. They are a team that moves and works together, as a team. Remember, Lieutenant, you have to be a prime example for your soldiers."

The lieutenant general said, "Five-star general Foster, why did you yell out *enough* and *at ease* before making to them?"

General Foster replied, "What? What are you talking about, Lieutenant General?"

The lieutenant general said, "We all heard you yell to these soldiers after General Staples ordered them to at ease, after the order of this lieutenant, Lieutenant Obliterate, went unnoticed by those soldiers. We heard you yell that at them as you came out of nowhere, sir."

General Foster said, standing up there in his five-star general's uniform, "I did not say a word, and I did not hear anybody yell as I was walking in this direction. Now, I'm here to see General Sherman Huckabee."

General Bradford Blackstone said, "General Huckabee has retired, sir. I took over this unit when he left. I am General Bradford Blackstone. How can I be of assistance to you, sir?"

The five-star general said, "Well, he was a very close friend of mine, and since I was passing through, I figured I should pay my respects to him. I guess I just have to visit him at his home."

They all were saluting him as he started walking off, making it to the distance where they saw him appear, and now he disappeared. They were still saluting him when he said out loud, "At ease! At Ease! At Ease! At ease! At ease!" his voice echoing in the distance of the night.

General Blackstone said, "What is this all about? Lieutenant Obliterate, you are under a microscope, and you'll be watched very closely. These soldiers are not a nobody, they are somebody. Do you understand? I put you in this position, and I can take you out of it. Do you understand? You are not Captain Apocalypse, remember that, Lieutenant."

They all left him standing there by himself, going back to the base to their office, watching the general's helicopter fly off into the night. Lieutenant Obliterate was just standing there, knowing that his chance to be a leader like his mentor, Captain Apocalypse, was about to fly away from him until he could prove his style was not like Captain Apocalypse's, only similar to his. His way was not above the ways of the other sergeants in his squad just because he was a lieutenant in the unit that he came from before this unit. Captain

Apocalypse just had him as an overseer of the new recruit group because he was at the boot camp with him as his drill instructor, as did the other soldiers.

Lieutenant Obliterate said to himself, "Captain Apocalypse, you were a captain with your own ways and style of doing things. I am the lieutenant of this unit, and I have to let the authorities know that we have to do things their way and give them authority over this squad. I will not disrespect the ranking superiors or officers on this base. Like it or not, you can turn over in your grave as you wish, but your way is not mine."

He started walking backward, looking at all the damage these soldiers had done to this compound. He knew that removing Sergeant Destroyer, Sergeant Flood, Sergeant Rattler, and the sergeant MTs of their crew was the beginning of this new style of his.

Now, meanwhile, the five-star general Foster was not aware that Lieutenant Obliterate had dismissed those six from his unit, and neither did the other generals, majors, or colonels. Lieutenant Obliterate knew that keeping this to himself was better, as the other soldiers could not tell, although they disapproved of him for doing this unjust thing to their unit.

As he made it to his office and sat back with his face into his paperwork, his phone rang. He just looked and looked at it. The phone had rung four times when he picked it up and answered it in his normal voice, saying, "The No-Name Unit, Lieutenant Obliterate. How can I help you?"

There was just silence on the other end.

Lieutenant Obliterate said again, "This is Lieutenant Obliterate of the No-Name Unit. How can I help you?"

Still no response on the other end.

Then he finally said with anger, "Whoever your ass is playing on this line will be court-martialed. This is not a phone to be taken as you feel. So stop ca—"

The other end hung up on him while he was talking. he said, "Good! Hang up, motherfucker! Stop calling, you piece of shit!" Then he hung up by slamming the receiver down.

It was now April 24, 1981, nine months after Captain Apocalypse's death and the dismissal of Sergeant Flood, Sergeant Rattler, and Sergeant Destroyer, and the sergeant MTs. Lieutenant Obliterate was at his desk, on the phone, talking, when what came down the mail slot was an envelope with big red letters reading "URGENT." He opened the envelope, giving him the first assignment for him and his crew. He pushed the intercom button and said, "To all you soldiers, meet up at the debriefing room now."

Lieutenant Obliterate was so excited to receive his first mission he was there before the team was there to salute him while he walked through that door like they all did Captain Apocalypse. When the soldiers made it there, as they were entering the door, coming into the debriefing room, they all saluted Lieutenant Obliterate as they stood there at their assigned seats.

Lieutenant Obliterate said, "Sit. Have a seat."

They all sat in their seats, in a little confused state of mind, when Lieutenant Obliterate said, "Men, we have a mission to go and destroy a cocaine plantation in the northern part of Colombia. The intel tells us that five hundred tons are about to come in. We need to destroy the plantation while the boys on the water apprehend their cargo ship from coming into the US. Now, Sergeant Boogeyman and Sergeant Big Badass Wolf, you two are going to fly us to Barranquilla in the C-5 Galaxy, and after we land, then we will take the Sea Stallion to Santa Marta. We land the Sea Stallion there and take the Suzukis to Colmilitar . We will hike on foot to the Sierra Nevada de Santa Marta mountain range, where the plantation is located. This jungle is pretty rough, and we shall have this wrapped up within an hour or two once we get to the final spot. Are we ready to go, men?"

All of them just saluted him.

Lieutenant Obliterate said, "I don't understand the answer to that question," speaking to them without his voice detector. "Now, you answer my questions from now on and I will not take too much of this any longer. Do you all understand?"

They all said at the same time with their mechanical voice, "Sir, yes, sir, Lieutenant Obliterate, sir."

Lieutenant Obliterate said, "When we come back from this mission, we will not be eating or wearing these masks and voice detectors any longer. This is the last time that we will meet up like this, because I want to see who got my life in their hands, and I would like to talk to him face-to-face. Do I make myself clear? I am not Captain Apocalypse. I am your lieutenant, Lieutenant Obliterate. Do you all understand?"

They all said in their mechanical voice, "Sir, yes, sir, Lieutenant Obliterate."

Lieutenant Obliterate said, "Good! Now, let's get moving to destroy this cocaine plantation. Move out!"

They got up from their seats and went to pack up all their weapons. They packed up their M25 sniper rifles, mini AR-15, M67 fragmentation grenades, TAC-15 crossbow with scope, ranger bowie knife, and their EyeClops night vision goggles. Some still packed up their old weapons because they loved how they reacted to their touch. They all met up at the tunnel's door and got on their Suzukis, watching Lieutenant Obliterate halfway to the shaft. He did not wait for his crew to escort them, as Captain Apocalypse always did. When they made it to the elevator shaft and were going down it, Sergeant Big Badass Wolf and Sergeant Boogeyman were waiting for them in their saluting stand.

Lieutenant Obliterate said, "Sergeant Big Badass Wolf and Sergeant Boogeyman, you two should be in the cab of this unit and ready to go when we get here, not standing out here, waiting for them to arrive. Now, go get inside. And that's an order!"

They just ignored him until the team loaded up. After they had all made it inside, Sergeant Big Badass Wolf and Sergeant Boogeyman went inside and slowly took off in the Galaxy. They flew for well over twenty-seven hours, making it to Barranquilla in the Galaxy. After landing, they took the Sea Stallion up in the air, going to Santa Marta. They arrived in Santa Marta and landed the Sea Stallion in a secluded area, taking out their Suzuki 500cc trail bikes and riding them for well over two hours to Col Militar. Once they had made it there, they hiked on foot double time through the Colombia jungle, going to Sierra Nevada de Santa Marta mountain range. Lieutenant

Obliterate looked at his watch and said in his normal voice, "It's 1605, and we will wait until 2200 before we go the rest of the five hundred yards to take over that plantation. So set your watches at 0300 as our time to come up out of there and be on our way out of here."

It was getting darker, with all these wild animals still making their little calls. Sergeant Horrific, Sergeant Grim Reaper, Sergeant Night Terror, Sergeant Evil, Sergeant Furious, Sergeant Polarize, and Sergeant Lowlife were standing guard before the attack that was scheduled to start at 2200. As they were standing guard there, their teammates in their circle, they did not see any movement or anyone out and about. Sergeant Horrific said to the circle that it was still, calm, and peaceful.

However, the Colombian soldiers were watching them with their night vision goggles on, then the signal to let their arrows go at the same time was given. Their arrows, dipped into a deadly, paralyzing poison, hit Sergeant Horrific, Sergeant Grim Reaper, and Sergeant Evil in the heart and neck, killing them silently and quickly. The other arrows hit Sergeant Furious, Sergeant Night Terror, Sergeant Polarize, and Sergeant Lowlife in the head. And the arrow of one of the Colombian soldiers went through Sergeant Furious's head, hitting Sergeant Animosity in the neck, making him hit the ground like a big tree. The rest of them jumped up, looking all around and not seeing anything. As Lieutenant Obliterate was about to speak, that was when Sergeant Big Badass Wolf put his left arm around his neck and his right hand over his mouth, saying, "Shhhhhh, the guerillas are out there somewhere. You can't see them, but they can see us."

Lieutenant Obliterate stood there for a second after Sergeant Big Badass Wolf released him. Lieutenant Obliterate said, "Don't you fucking ev—"

They shot him in the head with some type of a powerful gun, blowing Lieutenant Obliterate's forehead off his face, killing him on the spot where he stood.

The No-Name Unit could not see these soldiers as they were not moving a muscle. Sergeant Big Badass Wolf was shot in the jaw by the same bullet that hit Lieutenant Obliterate. The Big Badass

Wolf hit his code for the whole team to know that his time was about to come to an end. As they lay still for well over forty-five minutes, that was when they saw about eleven or thirteen soldiers walking in a circular motion, coming toward them. When they got closer, they stood up and opened fire on them, and that was when the Colombian soldiers opened fire on them. The Colombians sent those soldiers out to make the No-Name Unit give up their position as it worked very well. The No-Name Unit killed those eleven to thirteen soldiers but lost their lives doing it. The Colombians were still not going into that camp because they were not sure that these soldiers were all dead.

The next morning, at about ten o'clock, the Colombian soldiers went into their little camp and saw all these dead soldiers. The captain of the Colombian soldiers said, "Dead people shouldn't have pretty things. Take their shit from them. Where is the transportation? How did they come here? Strip them naked and let the animals have something to eat."

They stayed in their camp as a call came on their captain's radio. He said, "What?"

The called answered, "We found their ride about three to four miles out from where you're at, heading west."

The captain said, "Good, good, good. We'll be there. Now, go find their other means of transportation."

The Colombian soldiers had taken all the clothes off the bodies of the American soldiers from the No-Name Unit. The only soldiers left were Sergeant Rattler, Sergeant Flood, Sergeant Destroyer, and the sergeant MTs. Nobody had a clue that these soldiers were dead. The Colombian soldiers left all these dead bodies laid out like human fertilizer for the ground, as well as food for the animals.

Five hours after the Colombian soldiers had left, Sergeant Body snatcher was lying there as fire ants were biting him, with bullet wounds going through and through his stomach, side, right hand, both upper and lower part of his legs, and left forearm. His eyes were burning to the goggles that he had on that night especially, as the fire ants were biting him, swelling him up. He was crawling on his stomach blindly, crawling on top of Sergeant Redrum's and Sergeant

Undertaker's bodies. He noticed that they were dead, as he couldn't feel any pulse or heartbeat. He used the blood from their dead bodies to wash the fire ants off his face and head. Sergeant Body Snatcher knew that he had to nurse himself back to health if he really wanted to live. He had crawled for two and half to three hours in this jungle, knowing that there had got be some water somewhere close. He was trying to find the water hole that they saw on their way inside. "The water hole can't be that far off," he said to himself. He squinted his eyes, trying to see, and that was when he saw this big-ass snake lying on top of one of the Colombian soldiers. His water canister was lying there, with a strap attached to it. With this dried-up blood on his face, he squinted at the snake. This boa constrictor was smelling human blood on a live body, since he could sense the heat coming from Sergeant Body Snatcher's six-foot-four and 290-pound body. The boa constrictor was crawling toward him as Sergeant Body Snatcher was using his might to break a branch, making a sharp point on it as he breaking it.

When he turned around, he sensed the snake getting closer upon him as he used the same tree that he removed this branch from to prop himself up. His leg was still bleeding but now was movable. When that boa constrictor tried to wrap itself around Sergeant Body Snatcher, that was when Sergeant Body Snatcher started stabbing it time after time after time after time. Stabbing him all the way through his body at least seventy to seventy-five times, killing him, as his body was still propped up against this tree. He looked at this big boa constrictor just lying there and not moving. Fifteen minutes went by, then Sergeant Body Snatcher looked at his legs and slowly moved them from side to side and back and forth. He slowly stood to his feet and fell down again, landing on top of this boa constric-tor, and said, "I see that you wanted to eat me too, but I can't allow that right now. Sorry, Mr. Snake. Maybe next time, in the next life." He crawled over him, going to the dead Colombian soldier that was killed by the snake.

He made it to him and took his water canister and shook it. It had a little less than half in it, so he took four sips and a small drink out of it as he just sat there, getting himself some rest. He rested for forty minutes to an hour. He then started undressing the dead Colombian soldier. He took his shirt and pants and made a wrapper for the lower part of his body and took his socks and underwear as well. This soldier did not have a gun or a knife on him. He knew the snake did not take it. Sergeant Body Snatcher looked around for it as he said to himself, "You piece of shit! Where is your fucking knife or gun? What kind of soldier are you without your tools? I know the snake did not take it, or maybe your teammates sacrificed your cowardly ass to that snake in order for them to pass. What are friends for, huh, soldier?" He just slowly walked off, still trying to find that water hole.

An hour and twenty-two minutes later, Sergeant Body Snatcher found the water hole when he fell to his knees and then lay facedown in it. He jumped into the warm and cool water, washing the blood and dirt off his body.

After being in the water for well over forty-two minutes, give or take a few minutes more, he brought his naked body out of the water and picked up a handful of mud, placing it on each bullet wound, trying to stop the bleeding. As he fixed his wrapper back around his body, he refilled his water bottle and made his way back to his camp, where his teammates were all dead. He got there, acknowledging them as who they were and not who they had been, because to him they were still alive. All their secrets would remain with him, and he would take it to his grave. He stood up slowly, forcing himself to walk around to find something to dig graves for his friends. He walked around for at least four hours and still couldn't find anything, until he saw this cold, dark, empty cave, which was only ten minutes away from their camp, where they were coldly and boldly murdered. He went to start bringing them one at a time, and he was getting very tired when he made it to the twenty-third one. He sat down to get himself some rest, noticing those tree branches already down. He tore some strips of clothes and tied them around those branches, then made a sled out of it. He then took a swig of water and rested for another ten minutes or so and loaded three bodies at a time to the cave. Then he got all of them inside, lined up against the wide dark wall, not knowing if snakes or bears or any wild animals were in there. He just wanted to put them inside a very special place, until he could give them a proper burial. He cleaned up the trail as if anyone had dragged stuff across this ground.

He sat in the middle of the cave ground very quietly, just watching over them with his injured body. Nine hours passed, and he knew he was hungry. He stood up and said, "Team, I'll be back, and I will get all of you back home." He left the cave, making a booby trap catch and kill anybody or anything for trying to come inside that cave. Sergeant Body Snatcher knew back at the fresh spring water, he could find something to eat if he were patient. He just sat there, thinking how he could catch himself at least one fish. He got up and went back to that place where that big boa constrictor was and used his hands to rip that snake open all the way down. He then went through its guts and found a piece of wire almost like a clothes hanger, but a little thinner. He brought some of the snake guts with him. Sergeant Body Snatcher made a pole out of a branch and used fifteen strips of thin cloth, making a line and putting his homemade hook on it, with some snake guts for bait. He threw it into the water and let it sit in there for eight or nine minutes, when something pulled on it.

As he slowly pulled it out of the water, a big fish was holding on to it. He unhooked it, and there was another one in there, and he caught another one. He used his fingernail to very carefully scrape the scales off it, twisting it head off and ripping it open to pull its guts out, washing it and eating it raw. He knew that raw fish could be eaten, but this was his first time eating it. "This raw fish isn't bad," he said to himself. He looked up at the sky and saw that it was getting kind of dark; he needed to relax and let his bullet wounds heal up. Sergeant Body Snatcher knew that he had to find a way home and bring somebody back to get the rest of his teammates.

Now, those Colombian soldiers were wearing their clothes and riding their Suzukis, acting as if they this stuff belonged to them, when their captain said, "Hold down. Quiet! I said shut the fuck up! Yeah, tell General Poques that the threat has been removed as the target. Continue on without any worries. You're welcome. Thank you, sir. We'll be there in two more days, sir, as we are still looking for the other transportation that brought these fucking Americans to our country. All right, sir! Right!"

After he hung up the phone inside of his truck, he said, "We'll stay for a while to find their other means of transportation, because we know that they did not ride these trail bikes over here. Now, go out and find their other means of transportation."

They then left on the No-Name Unit's soldiers' Suzuki trail bikes. The captain was looking at the map and plan, seeing that they were after their cocaine field to destroy it, and he said, "These sons of bitches really thought they were actually going to fuck with our money when everybody in the world comes to us for their supplies. All of them Goody Two-shoes want to stop our business."

He just looked at their dog tags, seeing their names on it, and said in a normal tone of voice, "Sergeant Big Badass Wolf, Sergeant Evil, Sergeant Boogeyman, Sergeant Illusionist, Sergeant Redrum, Sergeant Shadow, Sergeant Hocus Pocus, Sergeant Death, Sergeant Graveyard, Sergeant Vicious, Sergeant Grim Reaper, Sergeant Eliminate, Sergeant Hectic, Sergeant Horrific, Sergeant Consequence, Sergeant Animosity, Sergeant Undertaker, Sergeant Chaos, Sergeant Executioner, Sergeant Polarize, Sergeant Nuclear, Sergeant Fatal, Sergeant Torture, Sergeant Viper, Sergeant Wrath, Sergeant Furious, Sergeant Tornado, Sergeant Maniac, Sergeant Lowlife, Sergeant Venomous, Sergeant Night Terror, and Sergeant Body Snatcher. What the fuck is this? These are no goddamn real names! The fucking Americano uses strange fucking names to come in our country. I guess we are their fucking nightmare with our night terror!" He and some of his other soldiers were wearing their outfits and using their radios for communication. These names were really messing with the captain. He did not know how to come to a conclusion. Looking at his soldiers wearing these guys' clothes and not seeing US, or any other country's name, on these clothes, he said to himself, "Are these the soldiers of the Mafia, or are they terrorists that we haven't heard about. Who are these dudes? How did my general know they were coming? Who gave my general this information?"

His thought was not putting him at ease. Killing all these guys might wake up a sleeping beast, and he just threw all their dog tags on the hood of his truck, putting on the dog tag that said, "Sergeant Night Terror." He said, "Now I am Captain Night Terror," smiling at his comment.

Four hours later, the Colombian captain's soldier came back and said, "Captain, it was dark, and we needed some petrol to finish searching. We rode thirty miles out and came back in a different direction. We'll start back tomorrow."

The captain said, "All right. Get some rest. Here, put this on." He gave this guy Sergeant Evil's dog tag and gave him the rest to pass out to the other soldiers. He still had seven of them in his hand and threw them inside of his truck.

The next day, Sergeant Body Snatcher was feeling a lot better after being shot six or seven times. He didn't know how to start off trying to find his way out of this wild jungle. He ate his raw fish and sipped on his water and went into the cave where the rest of the soldiers were at and sat in the middle of them. He said, "Soldiers, get up. Soldiers, get up! SOLDIERS, GET UP!"

They all just sat there very still.

He said again, "SOLDIERS, I SAID, GET THE FUCK UP NOW! GODDAMMIT!"

That was when Sergeant Body Snatcher's naked body fell forward, his head landing on his knees. Sergeant Body Snatcher jumped up and turned to find out who moved. It was dark in the cave as he felt around and dragged his body to the doorway of the cave, saying, "Are you alive? Are you alive? Are you alive?"

He really didn't know who this soldier was, as they hadn't seen each other's face. Whoever this soldier was, he died with his eyes open. Sergeant Body Snatcher looked at him in the eyes and said, "I really wish I could see what you saw," as he slowly closed his eyes, looking at him as this soldier was in his arm. Sergeant Body Snatcher looked into the wild jungle and said, "I got to get y'all home and finish our mission." He then looked back down at him and saw his eyes staring back up at him. Sergeant Body Snatcher did not know that this soldier was Sergeant Night Terror. Sergeant Body Snatcher said, "Shit, soldier! Goddamn. You have some scary fucking eyes." Shooting chills all over Sergeant Body Snatcher's body. Sergeant

Body Snatcher stood with this soldier still in his arm and picked him up and looked down into his face. That was when he saw that this soldier's eyes had closed. He said, "You were up, huh? I guess I have to be up for us all." He saw all of them in this dark caves. He put this soldier back into his spot and stood in the middle of the cave, saying, "Soldiers! I hear you loud and clear. It will be done. I live to die. I will *die* for this team. I will put you to rest with the best!"

Saluting them all, he said, "Attention!" Then continued, "At ease, soldiers. Now go. Move out!"

He walked out of the cave as he heard a whispering voice echoing, "Body Snatcher, Body Snatcher, Body Snatcher, Body Snatcher, Body Snatcher, Body Snatcher..."

He turned around and saw someone standing there, looking like one of them, dressed up in their uniform. He started off walking, then jogging, and then running in full speed, moving branches and tripping over vines, then got up, still looking at this figure. As he got there, he realized it was a tree. He said, breathing hard, "W-w-what the fuck! Shit!" Still breathing hard, he continued, "Goddamn it! A fucking tree, Body Snatcher. A goddamn tree!"

He just kept walking, going to scout this jungle out, leaving a trace for himself that only he knew where to look. He got his feet wrapped up because the shoes of that Colombian soldier that was killed by that boa constrictor were too small for him, as were his clothes. Three and a half to four weeks have went past. Sergeant Body Snatcher hair have gotten long on his face and head. He was sitting down eating some raw fish as he was just hearing the animals making their noise.

As he was sitting there very quietly, he started hearing what sounded like musical instruments playing. He stood up, throwing his raw fish away, and walked toward the sound. As he got about sixty yards from where this sound was from, he heard someone say, "Hey, Sergeant Boogeyman, watch this," as one of the Suzukis started up. Sergeant Body Snatcher knew that it was getting a little late, and he knew that he was outnumbered, but it wasn't the first time that he had been outnumbered. He knew that their guns had those permanent silencers on them. He saw two of them getting ready to take a swim. Before the second one could get undressed out of his uniform, he said, "I'll be back." He jogged off, going back into their camp.

Sergeant Body Snatcher eased into the other side of the pond and went under the water, swimming toward him without him knowing it. Sergeant Body Snatcher eased out of the water behind him as he turned around and saw Sergeant Body Snatcher, his eyes wide open. He was about to scream for help when Sergeant Body Snatcher shoved a small part of a tree limb inside of his mouth, pulling his neck toward him, forcing the stick down his throat. He swam to the bank with his body and hid it, then went back in the water again. He didn't mess with the gun on the ground, but he did get the ranger bowie knife and went back into water, swimming in circles and going under. The other Colombian soldier came running back, putting his gun and clothes next to his, and start swimming toward him. Sergeant Body Snatcher went under as the Colombian soldier said, "I'll go under too." He went under. This Colombian was under for about twenty-one or twenty-two seconds and came back up, wiping his face, laughing. "I got—"

He did not see him. Sergeant Body Snatcher was tugging at his feet as he said, "Come on, Quarz!"

Sergeant Body Snatcher put his left arm around his neck, choking him, and put his ranger bowie knife inside of his mouth and started turning it, cutting his tongue, teeth, and gum, making him swallow his own tongue, teeth, gum, and blood, killing him, and to make sure that he was dead, he pushed that ranger bowie knife through his temple. He dragged him out of the water and put his body next to his friend. He took three of their guns and two knives off the first two. These guys had extra clips of theirs, and they must've known that these guns had silencers on them.

He saw one taking a shit and two more taking a piss. The one that was taking a shit, he shot him in the neck, killing him instantly, and the two that were taking a piss with their back turned to each other, he shot them in the head three times each, killing them where they stood. As he slowly went around, he heard the voices of four to five men talking, then laughing. He unloaded the AK-47 and M16 into all of them, his AK-47 in his right hand, and his M16 in his left.

He climbed up in the tree, seeing eight guys talking to the one guy standing by the truck.

He was really trying to calculate these guys as they were standing there talking. He knew that he couldn't let any of them get away from him to try to get some help. He only saw about twenty-one of their Suzukis, meaning that thirteen were missing. Sergeant Body Snatcher looked through his sniper scope and said, "What kind of soldiers lay their weapon down eight to ten feet away?" He zoomed in, hitting the captain in the back of his neck, blowing his throat out. One of the other soldiers was hit by the bullet on the forehead, blowing his brain out. The other soldier stood there trying to figure out where the shot came from, just as Sergeant Body Snatcher shot another soldier in the center of his forehead, and another one in the heart. The other three hit the ground with their heads covered by their arm, and Sergeant Body Snatcher shot two of them in the top of their head twice as the third one got up and tried to run. Sergeant Body Snatcher shot him once in the back as he was walking very slowly, and he then shot him in the back of the head, making one flip over and land on his back. He was using his scope to see if there were any movement, but there wasn't any. He climbed out of the tree and went into the camp, shooting each of them again in the head to make sure that these motherfuckers were dead. He said, "This shit wasn't any business of yours, but it is now."

He started undressing the Colombian soldiers, removing their unit clothes off them and stripping their asses buck-fucking-naked, like they did them. Two of these dudes were his size, and he put his whole entire uniform on as he found his EyeClops night vision goggles in the truck as well as his mechanical voice detector. He took two ropes out of the truck and cut them both into pieces long enough to go around their ankles. When he finished, he took another rope out of this two-and-a-half-ton truck, threading it between their naked legs and tying an end on the bumper of the truck, dragging all seventeen inside the wood. He got out of the truck and walked back there, looking at the bodies, and took the dog tags off their necks. He then threw that end of the rope that he untied off the bumper and threw it up in a tree, a little piece, into the woods. He threw that rope on a big solid tree branch and hooked it back up to the truck, then drove it back in same spot as if it had never been moved. He lined the Suzukis in a straight line and placed their guns on them, hoping that when the last eleven came back, they would do the same thing. Their camp was fifteen feet from the rest of the trail bikes. He knew that these guys didn't have any EyeClops on, because all of them were accounted for.

He went into the edge of the wood, not knowing which way they were going to be coming from. He had sat here for almost three hours when he heard the Suzukis coming. He got three AK-47s on his left side, hanging off his shoulders, with one in his left hand, and three M16 hanging off his right shoulder and one in his right hand, all off safety, with double clips in his front pack, ready to go. Five minutes later, the trail bikes pulled up next to the other bikes, and they heard the loud music coming from the area that their friends were at when they left. They took their guns off and the TAC-15 crossbows and laid it across the seat for the next crew to go out. As they got six or seven feet from the bikes and gun, Sergeant Body Snatcher came out of the pitch-black darkness with his EyesClops on, shooting them in the head, leg, back, and shoulders. Killing five of them instantly by blowing chunks of meat out of their necks and the side of their heads. The ones that were shot in the legs, backs, and shoulders were yelling for help. He walked to two of them as one tried to help the other one. He looked at them and shot them both in the head three each with his AK-47. He saw two trying to get back to the trail bikes, and he said, "Not this time, gentlemen," shooting them in the legs again, crippling them, until he got back with them. He said to himself, "I have two somewhere. Now, where can they be?"

He looked everywhere for these last two. He knew they couldn't have gotten too far, because they both were shot with bullets through their backs. He walked over and turned the radio off, and as he was coming back toward the truck, he saw some movement under it. He just kept walking, going to the other side, and stopped. He lay flat on his stomach real fast, looking under the truck, where he saw both of them. One of them said, "Please…please…please. Pleassssss!"

Pff pft pft pft pft pft pft pft pft pft pft pft pft pft.
He killed both of them with the M16. He then stood up, walking toward the two with their legs blown off as he emptied the M16 into both of their heads. He saw all their Suzuki 500cc lined up in a row. He saluted them and said, "I'm not finished yet. Our mission is not over, soldier. I have to complete our mission."

He cut the rope of the truck and put all their uniforms inside, then drove it just three or four feet from the cave. He went inside the cave and picked them up, putting them in the truck. It took him an hour and twenty minutes, give or take a few minutes. He made it back to those Colombian soldiers' camp. He started dressing them in their full uniforms beside their guns. He was afraid to put their dog tags on because he didn't know what belonged to who, but he did know that Sergeant Big Badass Wolf was the biggest and Sergeant Boogeyman was bigger than the rest of them, so these were definitely crowned with theirs. He took a big boulder and wrapped that rope with the bodies tied up with it and used the truck to roll that rock to the cliff on its edge. He then cut a tree down and rolled it to the front of the truck and put one at the bottom of the boulder and the other end against the bumper of the truck. He pushed that big fucking boulder over the dead, and it dragged those twenty dead Colombian soldiers' bodies with it. He then backed the truck up and turned around, going back to his teammates.

He knew that the Sea Stallion was nowhere near Santa Marta as he drove them that little trip and unloaded them inside the Sea Stallion fully dressed with their dog tags. He got back into the truck as it was getting back daylight outside. He hoped that nobody came here looking for these Colombian soldiers. When he pulled up, the trail bikes were still in order. He got out of the truck and started loading up the Suzukis; that was when he heard some movement around in the woods. He lay down on the ground under the truck, looking. He just lay there for three minutes, and that was when he saw a mountain lion and two cubs walking, sniffing the ground. The big one rose up, looking at him, and went into a different direction. He finished loading up the trail bikes and went back to the Sea Stallion as he loaded all of them up, except for his. He took some of that gas out of the truck, filling up his Suzuki, and then drove the truck off a cliff into the ocean as well.

He got on his Suzuki as he saw a Colombian soldier walking at 0800, shooting him five times with his mini AR-15. He picked him up, laying him across the front part of him, taking him to the Sea Stallion. He pulled up in the back and let up the door. He sat that dead Colombian soldier in the copilot seat and braced him in and kept him steady as he hit the switch, starting the Sea Stallion up and studying its paddles. He slowly went into the air and pushed the stick, and it was slowly flying, going to the C-5 Galaxy. He flew back to Barranquilla and landed the helicopter and unloaded his team-mates and their trail bikes, except for his. He went to the cockpit to see if everything was working. After seeing everything working, he left this place and went back in the Sea Stallion, flying very fast, as he had gotten used to the Sea Stallion, going close to the Colombian Army base at Calcutta.

He landed the Sea Stallion and got on his Suzuki, riding it at eight hundred yards, running twenty yards, hiding in an old, beat-up shack until it got very dark out. He saw one tower and plenty of soldiers walking around. As it came to 0230, the tower guy was standing up, looking at him. He shot him in the throat with his M25 sniper rifle, and that tower man was still standing there, but dead as hell. Three soldiers were walking in different directions with dogs, and he sniped the soldier's dog and then him. He killed all six of them as he left out of the shack, going to their general's Killaman attack helicopter. As he made it to it and was about to get in, a soldier put his hand on his soldier and pulled out his big ranger bowie knife, sticking it under his chin, through his mouth, where it came out of the top of his head. He snatched it out and put it back in its holster, climbing up in the Killaman attack helicopter, turning it on. As it started, he then went up in the air. A lot of the Colombian soldiers came out with their guns as Sergeant Body Snatcher used the chopper's guns, killing twelve or thirteen in there steps. He could hear them yelling at the tower to shoot him down, but they did not know that the guy was dead. He was firing directly at them with that Gatling gun in front, and then fired off a couple of missiles.

He flew that chopper at 0315, firing on that cocaine plantation and blowing everything up, leaving a mass hole in the ground. After emptying everything that was in this Killaman attack helicopter, he put on the parachute and took the helicopter over where his Suzuki trail bike was and jumped out of the helicopter. As he hit the ground ten seconds later, the helicopter blew up on that base, blowing up a lot of shit that was on it. He took off the parachute and put it on the Colombian soldiers. He said, "Now you're a dead good guy, soldier." He saluted him and said, "Good job," as he got on his Suzuki, going to the Sea Stallion. Twelve minutes later, he made it to the Sea Stallion, going back to the C-5 Galaxy. It was 0445, and he said on the radio, "This is the Lockheed C-5 Galaxy and crew with the Sea Stallion, calling for some assistance. Mayday, mayday! Come now! Soldiers are in need."

A voice came across. "C-5 Galaxy, we've been looking for you for over nine months. Where are you? Tell us your location. Hit your switch under the copilot dash. That'll tell us where you're at. Do it now."

He hit the switch, and the voice said, "We'll be there in twenty minutes. Your location is on the Barranquilla ground. Are you okay, soldier?"

He said, "I'll be dead by the time you make it here. All my teammates are dead…" *Cough cough cough cough.* "I'm going back to my seat until you get here."

He put the radio down and went back in the back and said, "Sergeant Big Badass Wolf, Sergeant Boogeyman, Sergeant Shadow, Sergeant Evil, Sergeant Lowlife, Sergeant Tornado, Sergeant Illusionist, Sergeant Eliminate, Sergeant Consequence, Sergeant Fatal, Sergeant Furious, Sergeant Hectic, Sergeant Maniac, Sergeant Hocus-Pocus, Sergeant Nuclear, Sergeant Polarize, Sergeant Animosity, Sergeant Redrum, Sergeant Viper, Sergeant Death, Sergeant Executioner, Sergeant Vicious, Sergeant Chaos, Sergeant Torture, Sergeant Horrific, Sergeant Graveyard, Sergeant Undertaker, Sergeant Wrath, Sergeant Venomous, Sergeant Grim Reaper, and Sergeant Night Terror, you are going home now, and we will meet again. I vow that to you. I live to die, and I'll die to live for us all. Later, my brother soldiers." He left out of the cockpit of the plane, getting on his Suzuki with all their guns and ammos going into those trees. He looked at the fire attack helicopters landing by the C-5 Galaxy, going inside and coming back out. Some of them were holding their nose, some of them vomiting, as they could not take the smell of these brave soldiers. The pilots got in the plane, taking off with the C-5 Galaxy, the Sea Stallion, the Suzukis, and his teammates as he was standing straddled in his Suzuki, saluting them, until it was nowhere in sight. He just looked around, trying to figure out which way he was going as of now. He just started up his Suzuki and just rode off as it was turning into day.

The new pilot, Lieutenant Peter "Fly High" Walls, got on the C-5 Galaxy radio and said, "Connect me to the admiral of the fleet at once."

About two minutes had passed when the admiral of the fleet said, "Admiral of the fleet, how can I help you?"

Lieutenant Walls said, "Sir, these soldiers that were on this plane were not your average soldiers, sir."

The admiral said, "What were you stressing out about lieutenant? What do you mean that they were not your average US soldiers?"

Lieutenant Walls said, "Sir, I have their roll chart with names on them; well more like nick name, sir."

The admiral said, "Stop beating around the goddamn bush Lieutenant, what the damn hell were you saying?"

Lieutenant Walls replied, "Well, ah, Admiral, sir, these guys' names are Sergeant Big Badass Wolf, Sergeant Boogeyman, Sergeant Illusionist, Sergeant Evil, Sergeant—"

The admiral cut him off saying, "Stop talking! Stop talking now! You take that goddamn plane to Fort Kobbe in Panama, and I'll call in ahead for you. Set those choppers around that plane and do not allow any Panama soldiers within two hundred yards of that plane. And that's an order!"

The admiral of the fleet got off the radio with Lieutenant Walls and picked up his phone and called the president of the United States, Thomas A. James II. His personal hotline rang three times without a word being said by the president, then the admiral said, "President James, sir, I am Admiral Kenneth Sloan here in the Philippines, and I got word that they found a very special cargo of yours, sir. It's the C-5 Galaxy, sir. With thirty-two fully dressed and dead, sir. They have been dead for a while, sir. I told a lieutenant of one of the fleets to take it to Fort Kobbe in Panama and that no Panama soldiers were allowed two hundred yards of that plane. What do you want to do, sir?"

President James II said, "Admiral, order your lieutenant to fuel up the C-5 Galaxy at the Fort Kobbe Military Base in Panama and fly it to the US at Vanderbilt Air Base in California, and stop over at Wright Patterson Air Base to pick up one of my men in Dayton, Ohio, and bring everybody and everyone and everything here in Washington, DC, at Dulles Airport. I only want two sets of eyes acknowledging these soldiers, and I am one. The other is my special seal. Admiral, that C-5 Galaxy never landed anywhere in those area, am I clear?"

Admiral Sloan said, "Sir, yes, sir," as President James II hung up his phone on the admiral. The C-5 Galaxy took its flight, going to the areas that it was destined to go. As the C-5 Galaxy made it to Wright Patterson Air Force Base in Dayton, Ohio, Lieutenant Walls saw this statuelike figure standing there, wearing the same exact thing that the soldiers in the back of the Galaxy were wearing. That statue-like person did a hand gesture so he could open the door at the back. He walked up on the plane, carrying a very big duffel bag on each shoulder, and hit the switch that went up front to let them know that he was ready. The plane took back off as this soldier was doing something to these dead soldiers. He walked up and down, and he then put his guns in his arms and stood there until the plane landed.

The lieutenant and his copilot saw over three hundred soldiers and high-ranking officers, the FBI, the CIA, and the president of the United States saluting the C-5 Galaxy. As the door came down, eight soldiers took the Sea Stallion off, and they rolled six caskets and spent at least twenty-five to thirty minutes inside, then came out, placing all of them in a hearse each until they got all thirty-one of them off that plane. Their real and true names were written on these caskets so that their family knew who was in what. The president placed a Purple Heart and two more medals on the caskets for their family, with a picture of them in a golden frame. The news media made it a breaking news all around the world, lasting for ten hours.

They took all of them to the Arlington National Cemetery and buried them in one grave, lining them in a single row. People all over the world were watching this happen. Some were happy, some were sad, and some were worried, although they did not know who these soldiers were or what they looked like. The president's man that he sent stood there in silence as a helicopter came and landed. Six got out of it and saluted the statuelike figure of a person and faced those grave sites and walked off, getting into the helicopter.

Before the statuelike figure of a person got in the helicopter, he said out loud, his voice echoing in the quiet, "At ease! At ease! At ease! At ease! At ease! At ease! At ease!" His voice was still echoing as he entered the helicopter, flying off with five more soldiers.

All the people were looking at them as they all were saluting them, going into the air and disappearing in the midst of the pretty blue sky as they started going back to their vehicles. President James II said, "My right hand has been cut off, General. It's no damn good day anymore. We have to take care of ourselves the best way we can and let the world see who we are to our soldiers. The soldiers that live to die and die to live."

CHAPTER 7

Sergeant Body Snatcher took care of his teammate for a year and four months, not knowing that much time had passed him by. He did not know that it was August 7, 1982, when he got his teammate back home, but his vow was kept to them. He was living off the land of the jungle of Colombia and being careful that no Colombian soldier or citizen saw him and reported him. He knew he could not allow even one person to see him.

As night fell, he looked at his watch, with his time set by the Colombian time, and noticed that it was 1825. Sergeant Body Snatcher got on his Suzuki and rode until he came to a little town of Colombia called San Martin. He knew that he needed some gas for his trail bike. After he had sat there, he got off it and started pushing it in the bushes. He put the AK-47 with a double clip in the gun on each shoulder, two mini AR-15s across his chest, two 7mm with their holster, one on the left and the other on his right, and with his garrote string hanging off his left-side pants pocket. He knew he had to get some gas, but these Colombian soldiers that were on the border of Venezuela in this town of San Martin were terrorizing these people. He knew this was not his business to interrupt in these soldiers' affair, but they were beating the men, women, and children and were raping the women and little girls as young as twelve years old.

Sergeant Body Snatcher was just watching them and ignoring them as he was stealing gasoline for his Suzuki. He got this five-gallon plastic jug and filled it with gas from this pump. As he was screwing the cap on the jug, he heard these women and little girls screaming for them to stop. The soldiers were just laughing at them. As Sergeant

Body Snatcher was still kneeling down, he was feeling that he wanted to help these people, and that was when he saw a shadow walking up behind him, saying, "Ah, you! What are you doing out here?"

Sergeant Body Snatcher just stayed there, still kneeling. The soldier had his gun barrel up to his neck and said, "You answer me, or you answer the god of your choice. Now, what are you doing out here?"

Sergeant Body Snatcher slowly pulled out his ranger bowie knife and stood up very fast, snatching the soldier's rifle out of his hand and pushing his bowie knife all the way inside his navel. He then pulled it all the way to his throat, cutting his clothes as his guts were falling out of him. He dragged him by the back of his collar to where his trail bike was hidden. He gassed up his Suzuki and got on it, and he was about to start it up when he heard the voice of a little twelve- or thirteen-year-old girl begging for them not to touch her. He just looked at the dead soldier on the ground and got off his trail bike, putting both of his feet inside this soldier's stomach, which was gutted open, and walked to the sound of the little girl crying. He ease inside of the house, where they had taken this little girl's clothes off. She was in the corner of her room, backed up, scared. Sergeant Body Snatcher turned the lights off, shot the three soldier with his mini AR-15 nine to ten times each, spraying it into the back of their heads and back. The little girl did not know that these three soldiers had been killed. Sergeant Body Snatcher saw the little girl's father was dead, with a bullet in his head.

He heard four or five soldiers in the other room laughing as one of them said, "Damn, how long does it take? Hurry up! My turn next."

Sergeant Body Snatcher was peeping in the door, where he saw a woman with her mouth gagged; her eyes had a blindfold, with her wrist tied to the bedpost. He eased his AK-47 off his left shoulder and put the barrel of it in the crack of the door, killing the four men that were sitting in the chairs, waiting for their turn. Blood and brain matter were everywhere as the soldier that was on top of this lady got up and said, "Now it's your turn, Ezekiel. Be a man and make her scream." As he turned around, he saw all four of them dead. "What the fuck is this! Who is in here?"

Sergeant Body Snatcher opened the door really slowly as this soldier tried to find his gun under all their clothes. Sergeant Body Snatcher pulled out his 9mm and shot him in both legs and both shoulders and walked over there to him, looking at the lady to make sure that she was still alive. He knelt down on his right knee and raised up the soldier's head, letting him see him, but never his face, as the Colombian soldier said in pain, "Who are you?"

He eased to his left ear while putting the barrel of his 9mm inside this Colombian soldier's mouth and said, "The Body Snatcher," shooting him six times in the mouth, then pulled his gun out of his mouth. He took their bodies out and carried them to an old shack where his trail bike was at. After he reloaded his 9mm and AK-47, he went back into town and went into a bar, and as soon as the light went out, the stripper started dancing. Sergeant Body Snatcher went through killing all the Colombian soldiers in there as well as the bartender. The scared lady that was forced to strip was crying, and Sergeant Body Snatcher knew that she was doing this against her will. He shot the light over the table that she was on, and that was when the glass fell on her and the sparks from the light.

He walked up there and tied her up and gagged her. As the music was still playing, eight more Colombian soldiers came through the door, and he emptied both of his AK-47s into them in the dark. He saw one still moving; he then took out his 99mm, shooting him two times in the forehead. After killing the nineteen in this bar, he walked back out of the door and saw where two more soldiers were standing guard at this little place that was a headquarters. He shot them five times each on their stomach as he was walking past them, going up the steps. He shot them twice more in their heads. Sergeant Body Snatcher put an AK-47 in his left and right hand, with two more on each shoulder, and three mini AR-15 across his chest. He then went into this little office, firing at all in this dark office.

A Colombian soldier asked, "What is this? What's going on? Somebody say something!"

It was getting quieter and quieter in his office as Sergeant Body Snatcher saw them running and yelling, trying to get out of the darkness. Sergeant Body Snatcher killed all of them beside the ones that they got in their little cells. He saw these three Colombian soldier guards standing up against the wall as he climbed up on the bars and put his garrote string around his neck. He pulled it so hard his head just fell off, then he put his bowie knife in the second one's head and twisted it three times. He went to the third one and put the bowie knife in the right side of his temple, bringing it across and out of both of his eyes. He looked at the guys in the cells and saw that they were wearing uniforms, and he fired his mini AR-15 at them, killing them all.

He went out of the office and looked at his watch, seeing that it was 0249. He took all those bodies in that office. He took their citizen band radio and antenna out of this office and put it in their captain's armored car with two bodies of those Colombian soldiers. He put all his weapons and ammos in the truck. He body trap that office with all of those soldiers inside of it. Claymores, smoke grenades, tear gas, and cs gas, along with M67 fragmentation grenades, were wired all over the place. Whoever tried to remove it could remove the not-so-threatening ones until they tried to move at least thirteen bodies, the telephone, and the cabinets where all their important papers were in. He left out of the office slowly and closed the door very gently. He got their cars, trucks, and vans and parked them in order as their guns were neatly in their hands, as if they were alive, sitting and lying down. Blood, brain matter, and guts were everywhere as some size 14 boot prints were going everywhere inside of this office. Those bloody boot prints were all on the desks, tables, walls, and ceiling. Sergeant Body Snatcher looked at his watch, and he noticed that it was now 0430 and the break of dawn was coming.

He got in that armored truck with all his stuff and two of those dead Colombian soldiers driving off slowly, going forward toward Venezuela, in get-out-of-Colombia territory. He pulled the armored truck and his stuff over inside a jungle area that was not too far from Puerto La Cruz, Venezuela, to go to Valencia Army Base. He sat there and watched them count their little soldiers.

Now, back at the small town of San Martin, the people of the town woke up not seeing any soldiers walking or driving around and threatening them. They were very confused. They saw all their cars, trucks, and vans out there parked nicely and neatly. All of them saw where ropes and chains were going around the doors of the office.

The little thirteen-year-old girl went inside of her mama's room, seeing her still tied on the bed, and she said, "Mama, Mama, Mama, are you alive?"

She saw that her mother was breathing as she untied her and took the thing off her mouth and eyes, fixing her hair. She got up and put a bedsheet around her and covered her mother up. She went into the bathroom and drew up some bathwater and then went back into her mother's bedroom and helped her out of the bed and into the bathroom, into the tub. As she was bathing her mother, her mother whispered, "Aguinalda, are you okay? Did they hurt you, baby?"

Aguinalda said, "No, no, Mama. They didn't get a chance to touch me."

Her mother said, "It's going to be okay. It's going to be okay."

As they were talking, three more ladies came running in the house, yelling, "Maria! Maria! Maria! Answer me! Maria, Aguinalda, where are you?"

Aguinalda said, "We're in here! We're in the bathroom!"

As Della, Sonia, and Guilla made it to the bathroom, they saw Aguinalda bathing her mother. Sonia said, "Maria, Maria, are you okay?"

Maria just nodded as her little daughter was still washing her off. Della said, "Tell her, Sonia. Tell her!" She was whispering.

Aguinalda asked, "Tell her what, Ms. Della?"

Guilla said, "About those goddamn soldiers."

Maria asked, "What about them? The only thing that I want to hear about those bastard is that all those raping bastards are dead."

Sonia said, "Maria, they are."

Maria said, "They are what, Sonia? They are what?"

Della said, "Dead. Dead, Maria."

Guilla added, "All of them are dead. Every last one of them is dead, Maria!"

Maria asked, "How do you know that they are dead. How do you know?"

Sonia said, "You haven't seen your living room, have you? Take a look at your bedroom. You really haven't seen it, have you?"

Maria said, "They killed my husband for trying to protect us. They killed him in cold blood and raped us! They raped us!"

Aguinalda said, "Mama, they didn't get a chance to do anything to me. I heard them laughing at me when I balled up in the corner, and I just stayed there, wondering why they didn't touch me. They stopped laughing at me. I fell asleep and woke up still balled up, and I came into the front room and saw Miguel dead, and I came into your room. Mama, my room, the front room, and your room are full of blood, guts, and brains everywhere, Mama. I mean *everywhere*!"

Della said, "You haven't seen our homes, and the scariest part about this is that the soldiers' station is literally on lockdown. You really need to come out to see this, Maria. Our husbands took Miguel out for you. Come on out. It'll make you feel better. Come on."

Maria slowly stood her naked body out of the tub and stepped out as they all helped Aquinalda dry her off and help her into her panties and bra. She put her gown and robe on, and then her slippers, as she came out of the bathroom, walking really slowly for having been abused almost six hours. She saw all this blood, guts, and brain matter all over her bedroom, front room, and Aguinalda's bedroom. They helped her outside as she didn't see any Colombian soldier anywhere. She had been in this little town of San Martin for twenty-eight years, and this was the first time that she had ever seen this in this town.

As they walked to the soldiers' station, they saw blood and brains on the steps, and one other big spot with blood and guts. They did not hear any gunshots being fired out in this town. Sonia said, "My son said that he saw some of these soldiers floating in the air, but they were bent over something tall that he couldn't see."

Maria said, "Your son is seven or eight, and he watches too many cartoons, Sonia."

Maria's daughter, Aguinalda, said, "Mama, I barely peeked to see who was going, but something was carrying them out of my room, and I really got scared of them. Mama, it was el Soldado Invisible."

Maria said, "There's no such thing as an Invisible Soldier, Aguinalda."

Guilla said, "Maria, you can't really say that or believe that there is no such a thing as an Invisible Soldier. Ask yourself, How else could this have happened? Who killed over eighty-five to ninety soldiers in five to seven hours without making a sound or being seen? How was it possible?"

Maria said, "I don't know. I just don't know."

As she was walking off, going back to her home, she said, "Thank you, el Soldado Invisible. Thank you."

Her friends knew that Maria was very thankful to that Invisible Soldier.

Now it was getting dark outside as Sergeant Body Snatcher looked at his watch. He saw that it was 1850, and he knew that he was about 420 yards from Valencia Amy Base, as he got his eyes locked in on that Russian MI-24 helicopter. He waited and waited until it was 0115. Then he took off running in half-full speed, with his guns ready to go. He went under this airplane as he took his M25 sniper rifle, shooting those two towers' gunmen, the three guards/patrolmen walking about, the four that were sitting up, drinking whatever was in that bottle, and made one bullet kill two that were coming behind each other out of the doorway. Killing the two guys that were sitting in their jeeps. He knew that he got to terrorize this base because he had to pick up some stuff that was at his little camp. He eased his way around the base, placing three to four Claymores and M67 fragmentation grenades on those other helicopters and airplanes and under a couple of those dead soldiers' bodies. He went to the Russian MI-24 helicopter, started it up, and got about five to seven feet off ground, and that was when thirteen to twenty soldiers came running out, shooting at him.

He fired off two missiles and let the Gatling gun go, killing them all as he started sending missiles inside of that compound, blowing it up just as those soldiers were diving to the ground for cover as he was flying off, and that was when a lot of the helicopters and planes and other Claymores and those M67 hand grenades blew up in the distance. He landed the Russian MI-24, loading up his weapon and Suzuki trail bike, leaving the armored truck with those two dead Colombian soldiers in it. He then flew off in that Russian helicopter. The soldiers ran down there, making it too late, and saw the Colombian soldier in it dead. They got inside the truck and drove it back to their base, and about thirty of them were sent to the town of San Martin in Colombia and pulled up in front of the soldiers' station as the citizens of that town went into their homes. The captain and lieutenant as well as those other soldiers went in, while nine of them were by the cars, trucks, and vans of these Colombian soldiers. As Captain Rodriguez and his soldiers went in, they saw all these soldier look like there was alive but were really dead. The last soldier allowed the door to close and lock as Captain Rodriguez said, "Find the key and find it now!"

As they started moving the bodies and slamming them forward, the lieutenant saw a line holding one soldier up. He said, "Hey, Captain, check this sh——"

Boommmmmmmmm! Boommmmmmmm! Boommmmmmmm! Boommmmmmmmm! Boommmmmmmmm!

The outside soldiers tried to get in the cars, vans, and trucks, and as soon as they tried to open the doors…

Boommmmmmmmm! Boommmmmmmmmmm! Boommmmmmmmm!

After all this damage done to these soldiers, not one of those citizens was injured. Their homes and properties were still sitting there with the other stuff all in their yards, on their automobiles, and on their porches and the top of their houses. All of them came out of their homes, looking at the soldiers' station and their automobiles blown to smithereens. Della, Sonia, Guilla, and Maria said at the same time, "El Soldado Invisible. The Invisible Soldier."

Later, they all started cleaning up the mess in their little town, admiring the work of whoever did this for them. Aguinalda walked back and saw a piece of paper that had *USA* on it. She just cupped it into her little hand and carried it to the kitchen and was burning it when her mother asked, "Aguinalda, what are you doing?"

She said, "Nothing, just lighting the stove." She was just protecting el Soldado Invisible, she thought, a little smile on her face as she said to herself, "Your secret is safe with me, el Soldado Invisible."

Meanwhile, as Sergeant Body Snatcher was flying this Russian MI-24 helicopter, going to Libya, he saw the paper back at the soldiers' station in San Martin that United States soldiers were going to Libya to stop the weapons of mass destruction. The Colombian soldiers never gotten the chance to spread the word out to the Libyan authority as they were going to try to blackmail the Libyan for some weapons of mass destruction. Sergeant Body Snatcher left from Puerto La Cruz, Venezuela, in the Russian MI-24 helicopter that he took from the Valencia Army Base. As he flew for six or eight hours, he knew that he needed some fuel to make it to Libya. He made it to Cape Verde, flying over that little base, where he saw where he could fuel up. He flew past, looking at his watch and seeing that it was 2235 as he went around, finding a nice spot to land for about three hours. He then took a little nap, and his watch alarm woke him up. He got out of the helicopter and walked for about twenty minutes, excising his legs. He checked his clips and shot a round out of each gun to make sure that they were ready to go. He got back into the helicopter and started it up and flew really low, landing it at 0143 on the refueling base as two Cape Verde soldiers came over to his helicopter.

One said, "What do you want here? Who are you? You can't land here."

Sergeant Body Snatcher didn't say a word as he pulled out his 9mm's out of his left- and right-side shoulder holsters, shooting both of them in their hearts three times each. He pulled the fuel nozzle up and put it in the MI-24's fuel tank, cutting the fuel on and filling up his tank. He noticed that three more Cape Verde soldiers were walking toward his chopper. He holstered his 9mm's and put his two mini AR-15 in each hand, walking toward them, shooting their heads and chest, killing them. As he walked past them, he noticed the eyes of one of them was still open. He shot them each again in the head as he kept walking. He walked to the office of this fueling station and shot eight of them. One was behind the counter, calling for help, and he shot him five times with his mini AR-15, removing his face. After he took their little citizen band radio and gas-operated generator, he loaded it on the MI-24 and then took the fuel's nozzle out of his helicopter. He then let the fuel continue to pump out as he got into his helicopter and got at least thirty to forty feet off the ground as the other soldiers made their way to the fueling station. Sergeant Body Snatcher flew about two or three minutes off, and that was when he turned back around high in the air, watching them run for safety and shoot at him. He just flipped the lever to his ear stick and sent two missiles and about two rounds of his Gatling gun into the fueling station, blowing the whole entire place up to smithereens, not leaving a single person or thing standing.

He turned his helicopter back around and dropped a missile bomb to that place as he went past, making a big-ass mushroom cloud of fire and smoke. Sergeant Body Snatcher knew that his time was short as he got to make it to Libya before those American soldiers. He did not want to see any one of them lose their lives to these murdering sons of bitches.

He flew for ten or eleven hours, making it in the country of Tunisia and landing his helicopter in the Jebil National Park. He sat there, looking over the papers that he found when he was in the little town of San Martin in Colombia, realizing that somebody in Libya wanted revenge on the United States and its soldiers. He noticed that there were plenty of black lines on most of all these papers, but he didn't know what these black lines were covering or who the black lines were covering, but someone or something was being covered up. "But I'd be goddamned if I allow these soldiers to die for it," Sergeant Body Snatcher said to himself.

After six hours of resting, he got out of the MI-24 and took his Suzuki trail bike out and rode around. He found two Tunisia soldiers walking around, and he pulled up between them as they were looking at the way he was dressed, which confused them.

They did not know who was under all these clothing and all of the guns and ranger bowie knives on his side. One of the soldiers pulled his gun on him and said, "Put your hands up!"

He put his hands up.

The soldier then said, "Get off. Get off on the motorbike, now!"

Sergeant Body Snatcher saw that they were a little scared. He eased off his Suzuki, letting it hit the pavement, and that soldier said to the other soldier, "Take his guns off him."

The soldier was slowly trying to take the AK-47 off his back, but he couldn't. He then tried to take the M16 off of his back, but he couldn't. The soldier with the gun on Sergeant Body Snatcher said, "Try these up in the front."

As he tried to take one of his mini AR-15s off his chest, Sergeant Body Snatcher brought his hands down real fast, using his left hand to push the soldier's right shoulder and his right hand to push this soldier's left shoulder, as well as using his right hand to pull this soldier's body to protect him. Then he put his left arm around the Tunisia soldier's neck and shot the soldier with the gun on him with his 9mm in the center of his head two times and in the heart once. He said, "You're dead," in the ear of that soldier, shooting him in the back five times. He grabbed ahold of both of them by their collars and dragged them from that area and covered their bodies up.

He went back and got on his Suzuki, riding it around, and saw this big Tunisia soldier just an inch or two smaller and shorter than him coming out of some sort of restaurant. He eased his Suzuki behind him and got off the Suzuki trail bike, walking within reaching distance behind him, and said in his mechanical voice, "Excuse me, soldier. Can you tell me how to get to the Tunisia Medenine Army Base?"

That soldier kept walking, thinking somebody was playing games with him by the way his voice was sounding. Sergeant Body Snatcher said again, touching him on the shoulder to get his attention, "Excuse me, soldier, can you please tell me how to get to Tunisia Medenine Army Base?"

The Tunisia soldier turned around very fast, replying with his sentence cut short, "Look, man, I'm not for any goddamn bullsh—"

That was when he saw this dark-dressed figure standing there. As he tried to swing on Body Snatcher, that was when Sergeant Body Snatcher pulled his ranger bowie knife out, making the soldier cut himself for trying to hit him. Sergeant Body Snatcher looked at him as he was looking at Sergeant Body Snatcher. That Tunisia soldier was backing up with his hand half-cut off. Sergeant Body Snatcher put his bowie knife back into his knife holster and then took his 9mm out and shot him in both of his feet. As that Tunisia soldier fell to the ground and was about to yell for help, Sergeant Body Snatcher ran to where he was headed and placed his left knee on the soldier's throat and his 9mm in his mouth and down his throat. That soldier tried to talk, saying, "Hmm, hmmmm mmmm, hmm, hmmmm. Hmm, mmmm." *Cough cough cough.* "Urggh, urggh, urggh." Vomit was coming out of his nose and mouth. Sergeant Body Snatcher pulled his 9mm out of the soldier's vomiting mouth and said in his mechanical voice, "T-t-t-the...the base. The base..." *Cough cough cough.* "I will tell you."

Sergeant Body Snatcher put the 9mm's barrel inside of his left eye socket as he was trying to scream. Sergeant Body Snatcher then put the bottom palm of his right hand inside of the soldier's mouth and pulled the trigger of his 9mm two times, killing him. Sergeant Body Snatcher took this soldier's clothes off and put it on himself, throwing the dead soldier's body in a dumpster. He got back on his black Suzuki, going back to the Jebil National Park and changing into the Tunisia soldier's uniform. He took the soldier's backpack and put twenty-five M67 fragmentation grenades in it with six Claymores and rode off, going to the Medenine Army Base. When he pulled up, he counted at least four hundred Tunisian soldiers, and each one had two guns to protect the base. He was walking around, wiring those M67 fragmentation grenades and those Claymores in their position. He then got on his Suzuki and was about to start it up; that was when a lieutenant said, "Where did you get that from? That's nice. Can it fly like a bird?"

Sergeant Body Snatcher started and revved up his motor as the lieutenant said, "Shit! That motherfucker is quiet!" He took off on the Suzuki, with the back wheel screeching, the front wheel all the way up in the air. He then disappeared into the night. He made it back to the Jebil National Park and put the Suzuki back in it, and he put ten C-5 gas canisters, ten smoke grenades, and ten tear gas cans on a string and had the pins already halfway out to release the chemicals inside. He got in the Russian MI-24 helicopter and went up in the air as he flew over back to Medenine Army Base. He landed it to the soldier to fill it up. The soldier was just admiring the Russian MI-24. He noticed that he had fired off three to four missiles as the soldier reloaded everything that the helicopter had lost. It appeared that this ground soldier was one of theirs, but in reality, he belonged to the United States. When he finished, he said to Sergeant Body Snatcher, "Hey, you have to sign this." That was when Sergeant Body Snatcher had changed his clothes into his original uniform. The soldier outside of his door said, "Hey! What are you d—"

Sergeant Body Snatcher snatched his head inside the helicopter, pinning it in his lap and sticking his basic knife in his right ear, twisting it three times. He then pushed his dead body out of the door and stepped out of the helicopter with those canisters, throwing them all over the base, the blades from his helicopter helping him to spread the smoke and CS gas all around the base. He walked in this stuff, killing these soldiers. He made it inside and threw four tear gas canisters and seven CS gas canisters along with fifteen land mines on the floor. When he came back to the door, some of the soldiers were waiting for him, as they knew they couldn't get to his helicopter without blowing up theirs.

He was going up to the second floor when he saw his general, Khaled Saor; his captain, Tareq Al Aziz; and his sergeant, Fatima Al Sissi, just standing there, looking at him walk toward them. As he got eight feet close to them, General Saor said, "Look, whoever you are, you won't be ab—"

That was when Sergeant Body Snatcher pulled the two AK-47s from behind his shoulder, shooting and killing the two males, while the female was hit but still living. She just held a bloody piece of paper in her hand. He looked at it and saw money transferred for the amount of five hundred million dollars to somebody's name with blood on it. He said to the female sergeant in his mechanical voice, "Who is this general that this is going to?"

She just looked at him, still bleeding from the shoulder, stomach, arm, and both legs. She just looked at him as he said, "Wrong answer," shooting her in the chest seven times as he put a Claymore with them although they were dead. He went to the window and saw two gunmen in the towers, just waiting for him as he pulled his M25 sniper rifle out from his back, shooting and killing the two tower gunmen, as the soldiers did not know. He went to the area where it was heavy with smoke, and he just came right out the door with his AK-47 in his right hand and an M16 in his left hand. With the silencers on them, it was very quiet as he killed those soldiers. The M16 was emptied, and he pulled his second M16 out from behind him as he continued firing on those Tunisian soldiers. His AK-47's top clip was emptied as he flipped it over and continued shooting as the soldiers yelled, "Where is he! I can't see him! Can anybody see him?"

Some were dying from the CS gas.

He made it to his helicopter with the tail in the air, spinning the helicopter around in circles, killing soldiers and blowing up the Medenine Army Base. As the building was falling on top of the Claymores that he placed inside and outside, it went up like falling of dominos.

He left the Medenine Army Base in Tunisia, heading toward Libya. The Medenine Army Base could not call for help, and neither could they call Libya to tell them that some soldier was coming to wreck the country like he did them. But they did not know that he had destroyed two Army bases before he came to them. He did a sneak surprise on all of them beforehand. At least the Colombian soldiers should've known that their fucking asses were going to be hit for killing a team of soldiers with the help of somebody of great authority. He just flew in the Russian MI-24 helicopter that he took from Valencia Army Base and used their own equipment to destroy them. As he flew for well over nine and a half hours, daylight was coming up on him. He saw Libya as he flew in distance, coming toward it. Thirty minutes later, he made it to the landing zone that he had picked. He flew around it two or three times, with his finger on the firing switch of his MI-24. Everything was clear to land when he landed at Al Hamamah.

He got out of the helicopter and put a mini AR-15 in each hand, walking around to see if anyone was walking around. He saw that everything was at a standstill. After all this flying and battle to get here, he knew that he had to get himself some rest. So he set his watch alarm to wake him up at 0145. He sat back in the darkest spot that he could find, keeping an eye on everything in the distance, and he could see if someone was coming.

Now at 1537, he was awakened by the sound of a vehicle approaching his area. He fixed his eyes and put his binoculars on and saw this Libyan soldier's vehicles still coming toward his spot. He picked up his M25 sniper rifle and followed it with his scope and saw that there were two of them inside this vehicle. He noticed that one of them was a lady soldier that was with this male soldier. As they pulled fifteen to eighteen feet past his helicopter, they stopped and backed up and parked the truck. Both of them got out and looked around, seeing where the blades of the helicopter had knocked a few branches out in a path in this area. These soldiers must regularly patrol this area to have noticed that something wasn't right. The Libyan soldier was looking around, then slowly started walking toward the area that he put the helicopter at.

Both of them pulled their pistols out and continued walking as Sergeant Body Snatcher said, "I need some information from one of you. So which one will be more than happy to speak to me? Eeny, meeny, miney, mo, catch a tiger by his toe. If he holla, let him go! Eeny, meeny, miney, mo…"

Pft pft pft.

He killed the female soldier, shooting her three times in the heart. The male soldier did not know that she was dead until he looked back and saw that she was three feet behind him, lying down on the ground. He was running to her to see if she just fell or what. When he made it to her and knelt down beside her and saw blood coming out of her chest, he jumped up, looking all around, not knowing who shot and killed her. His gun was still in his hand as he slowly walked toward his truck. He was trying to get to his truck to call for some help, and as he got about seven feet, Sergeant Body Snatcher shot him in both of his leg, in his kneecaps. Sergeant Body Snatcher walked to him as he was crawling on his stomach, still trying to get to his truck. Sergeant Body Snatcher stepped in front of him with his M25 sniper rifle, putting the barrel on his forehead, and said in his mechanical voice, "I'll let you die a happy man if you tell me what I need to know, and if you don't, I'll find somebody that will tell me and I'll still let you die as a happy man. So tell me, will you answer my question?"

This Libyan soldier knew that this guy wasn't bullshitting with him. He knew that he was staring death in the eyes, but he could only see himself in the reflection of Sergeant Body Snatcher's night vision goggles. He said while in pain, "Don't kill me, please, mister, don't kill me!"

Sergeant Body Snatcher said in his mechanical voice, "How many soldiers are in Omar Al-Mukhtar University?"

He said, "Three…three…three hundred and ninety-five to four hundred and ten. Please, mister, please don't kill me, mister!"

Sergeant Body Snatcher shot him in both of his elbows, both of his hands, and both of his ankles. The Libyan soldier said, "A-a-are… are you going to kill me?"

Sergeant Body Snatcher replied, "No, I won't kill you," as he knelt down, looking into his eyes, letting this soldier see his face and eyes as the Libyan soldier screamed, "You're…you're…you're… you're…you are…"

Sergeant Body Snatcher stood up, walking off, going to his helicopter, as the Libyan soldier continued, "I'm dying and I'm not happy. You said that I am going to die a happy man."

Sergeant Body Snatcher turned around and knelt down in front of him, saying, "You want to die a happy man? Okay. Your wish is my every command."

Sergeant Body Snatcher opened the Libyan soldier's truck door open and ripped it apart so that he couldn't start it up or call for any help or even blow the horn. After wrecking that truck inside and out, he went to get the female soldier and undressed her, naked, throwing her clothes on the floorboard of the truck, her panties on the dashboard, and let her bra hang out of the passenger-side window. He spread her dead body's legs, with her head up against the passenger door. He then started undressing the Libyan soldier, and that soldier said, "W-w-w-what…what are you doing, mister? What are you doing? She's dead. Don't do this, please!"

Sergeant Body Snatcher picked up his naked body and laid him down gently between her dead legs. As he fixed him in there on top of her, he said, "You want to die a happy man? So now you can die a happy man." He shot him in the back of the head three times as he closed the driver's-side door, hanging his pants and shirt outside the driver's-side window. He then removed his footprints going back to his spot, to his helicopter, waiting for his time. He took his Suzuki trail bike out of the MI-24 along with the garrote string, twenty Claymores, twenty-five M67 fragmentation grenades, TAC-15 crossbow, twenty-one smoke grenades, fifteen tear gas canisters, and twenty-three CS gas canisters. He tied his duffel bag with all these arsenal inside of it. He started up his Suzuki and rode up to that truck, looking at the two dead Libyan soldier, and said, "You two got off lightly, trust me," as he rode off, going into the Al Bayda City, to Omar Al-Mukhtar University on Alo Seth Road, where this lady Mrs. Shad Al Alum was working to help with these weapons of mass destruction.

As he was riding, he saw a stoker. He stopped and broke into it and took five spools of three-pound test line. He found a nice, safe, dark condemned building, hiding himself and his Suzuki inside it. He then left out with the fishing spools, the smoke grenades, along with some M67 fragmentation grenades, tear gas, and CS gas, as they were threaded and lined up one after the other. He circled it around the building that he was in. He knew he had a fight on his hand, but being an outnumbered soldier was something that did not bother him, because he didn't have to worry about losing a fellow brother soldier but himself. People could at least say that this one mother-fucker raised pure hell with this fucking country.

He put Claymores underneath the seats of the Libyan soldiers' vehicles and their motorcycles. After placing the line of arsenal around the building and booby-trapping their vehicles and motorcycles, he then went into that condemned building and to the floor that he was on and saw Libyan soldiers on four buildings getting ready to watch the main building, where Mrs. Shot Al Alum was at, fixing their country some weapons of mass destruction. As he was watching them set themselves up a command post to watch, he pulled out his M25 sniper rifle and his TAC-15 crossbow. He counted three on the first building, two on the second building, five on the third building where the building that Mrs. Shot Al Alum was in, three on the fourth building. He looked at his watch and saw that it was 0210, and he said to himself in his mechanical voice, "Now it's time to go to work. I live to die. I die to live. I'll die for my brother soldiers!"

He zoomed in on the first soldier on the building, shooting one of the first soldiers in the head, the second soldier in the heart, the third soldier in the leg and then in the head, the fourth one in the stomach, as the fifth one finally saw him as he ran to help him, and that was when Sergeant Body Snatcher shot him in his head, and the fourth one in his body two more times, killing him. He then turned his attention to the first building with the three on the building. There was one in each corner, not paying any attention to each other as he killed the first one, shooting him in his neck, the second one in his temple, and the third one in his heart.

The second building was close to him, so he got his TAC-15 crossbow and killed the first one by shooting him in his heart and head with an arrow as the second soldier raised his walkie-talkie to call. That was when Sergeant Body Snatcher shot him in his mouth with an arrow as he was still trying to get that walkie-talkie up to his mouth to call for help. Sergeant Body Snatcher said in his mechanical voice, "Okay, motherfucking tough guy, here! Eat another one!" He shot him again in his mouth, but that son of a bitch was still standing as he said, "Okay. You got me, tough guy. Try this one, then." He said this in his mechanical voice and shot him in the mouth for the third time and went backward a few inches, pinned up to a wall as his hand fell to his side, letting him know that he was dead.

He then turned his M25 sniper rifle to the fourth building, seeing those four soldiers on each corner staring out at the street as he took two in their temple, one in the neck, and the fourth one in his shoulder, turning around and then making a clear shot in his head. He put his rifle and crossbow back into the big duffel bag with three AK-47s on his right shoulder and one in his right hand, three

M16 on his left shoulder and one in his left hand, three mini AR-15s across his chest, his two 9mm on the left and the right, with his garrote string hanging off his bowie knife on his left side. His bowie knife on the right side had five M67 fragmentation grenades hanging from it. He came out of the building and stood up in the doorway of that condemned building, looking out into the street, and said in his mechanical voice, "Let's die with bravery and honor, soldier," as he popped five of his. Two of the canisters were tear gas, and three were the CS gas. As those five were going off into the air, he then popped five smoke grenades. As the Libyan soldiers came running out of the building, seeing all this smoke going up in the air, they looked for the person who was responsible for it; that was when Sergeant Body Snatcher saw the buildings that they were in.

He raised his AK-47 and shot the lamp pole holding this street and building power surge and shot it eight times, blowing it up as the wires fell to the ground, electrocuting five of the Libyan soldiers. They could not see him as they were gagging, choking, and dying from the CS gas. The smoke was not allowing them to see their bodies dying. He was just walking in the middle as his AK-47 and M16 were killing them as fast as they come. He flipped both clips and continuing firing on all of them as he was killing these soldiers. He made it to the building where Mrs. Shot Al Alum was in, as the Libyan soldiers could not see him but he could see them, shooting them all with his M16.

The only thing Sergeant Body Snatcher heard were the sounds of a bunch of Libyan soldiers yelling for help and "What's going on?" The Libyan soldiers thought it was some Goody Two-shoes trying to make a stand against them for trying to make a stand against other countries, especially the United States soldiers, for being the way that they were toward other countries. After killing all those Libyan soldiers, he went to the basement, where they were waiting for him to come. He popped three CS gas and two tear gas canisters, throwing them down the hallway. As it filled with smoke, choking those soldiers and killing them. As they tried to gag for air, he went into the room and saw this lady standing there, and he just looked at her and said in his mechanical voice, "I'm sorry, but this must be done," and he shot her four times in the chest and picked up all the necessary papers of Mrs. Shot Al Alum's chemical work for the weapons of mass destruction. As he was looking at those two closed doors, he took his last five Claymores and gently turned it upside down, popped his last two CS gas canisters, and threw his last tear gas canister. As it filled with smoke, he heard them coughing and gagging for air.

He put all those papers in his canister bag and headed out the side door, going back to his post and getting on his Suzuki, riding off, going on the main street, where the Libyan soldiers were shooting at him as he was riding very low, going to his chopper. He looked at his watch and saw that it was 0422 and knew he had to make it halfway from this country. The Libyan soldiers jumped in their trucks, cars, vans, and motorcycles, chasing him for well over twenty-eight to thirty miles out of the city and back to Al-Hammah, where he rode into those wooded area, and as soon as the soldiers saw one of their trucks already there, the leader of the truck jumped out of the passenger side, and *boommmmmmm*, the Claymores went off. The soldiers in the other vehicles tried to jump out of theirs too. *Boommmmm! Boommmmmmmm! Bommmmmmmm! Boommmmmmmm! Boommmmmmmm! Boommmmmmm!* None of the Libyan soldiers knew that they were blowing their own selves up when they got out of their vehicles.

Sergeant Body Snatcher took his MI-24 up in the air flying and killed the rest of those soldiers, the flying to UAE. He landed his MI-24 and wrote in oil from the helicopter, replying in code: "No TRK. I'm USA. SLDR.

He got back into his helicopter and flew off, going to some place to set up a command post for himself.

Three days went by, and the US Army was traveling down this road, going to the UAE Al Dhafra Army Base. As they were driving, Captain Shaun Timblim saw a backpack on the side of the road, and he said to the driver, "Lance Corporal, pull over."

The lance corporal pulled over the truck. Captain Timblin got out of the truck and said, "Rest of you soldiers stay in the tanks and trucks."

He walked up to the thing and saw that it was a backpack with a United States brand on it, along with a note that read, "No TRK. I'm USA. SLDR." Captain Timblin had slowly moved his left hand to the backpack and note when the lance corporal said, "Captain, you better not do that, sir. It might be a trick, sir."

Captain Timblim said, "Shut the fuck up, Lance Corporal. Shut up!"

He slowly picked up the backpack and took the note off it, then said, "This note was written in oil."

The lance corporal said, "What? What did you say, sir?"

Captain Timblim said, "This is a backpack that belongs to some special ops soldiers, and this note was written in motor oil."

He opened the backpack and saw all those papers indicating people in three different countries were out to kill any and all United States soldiers. He went to the last page, which read, "Job done, sldrs. Go home."

Captain Timblim said, "What the fuck is this? Who wrote this fucking note?"

The lance corporal asked, "What? What does that talk about, sir?"

The captain jumped back up in the convoy and said, "Let's go," as he was looking at the papers. They then made it to the UAE Al Dhafra Army Base. The captain and his team loaded up on their helicopters and landed in the same area that Sergeant Body Snatcher was at and saw all those dead Libyan soldiers and their blown-up vehicles. Captain Timblim said to his pilot, "Take us down."

The pilot said, "Sir, there are only dead bodies down there, sir. Looks like this is three to four days old, sir."

The captain replied, "I don't give a shit, soldier. Now, take us down, soldier. Do it now!"

The pilot said, "Yes, sir, Captain," as he landed the helicopter and got out, looking all around.

He went to the truck that was not blown up, but the dash had all its wires ripped out, the motor wires ripped and cut, and the two dead bodies of a naked female and male soldiers were in there, as if they were having sex. The lance corporal said, "Well, hell, Captain, at least this soldier died a happy man!"

Captain Timblim said, "Well, Lance Corporal, I'd rather live as a sad man than die a happy man, then."

As they loaded back up in their helicopters, flying away from the scene, they flew to the mark that they were going to hit as their mission. They saw bodies everywhere. They saw bodies on the rooftops of four buildings and in the doorways. The streets and the buildings of the university in Al Bayda City on Aloseth Road was still smoking as they put on their gas masks. Captain Timblim said, "Take us down."

They all landed their helicopters and walked around, going into the main building, where their mission was located, and found dead bodies after dead bodies. Bullet holes where everywhere, as if it were Swiss cheese.

Captain Timblim said, "These soldiers came here to do one thing, and that was to seek and destroy whoever was in their path. These soldiers helped us out, although they should have followed protocol, by doing this shit. These fuckers are a terrorist's nightmare! And I do believe, sooner or later, we might have problems out of the sons of bitches who created this goddamn fucking chaos. Look at this shit. Look at it! You can't tell which one is the worst one of all these fucking scenes! All I can say is, if we have to go against these goddamn people, we better have our shit in order, because if we go against them with some bullshit, then we all are dead, dead, dead! Let's go and report it back to the base."

They all left out of the building, going to the helicopter, when the lance corporal said, "Captain. Captain Timblim, where are the other people, sir? There is not one person out here, and it is daylight, sir."

Captain Timblim said, "Lance Corporal, your guess is as good as mine, soldier. Let's go."

They all loaded up and flew off from Libya, looking at those dead bodies and bullet holes all in the vehicles that were still there as one of them went *boommmmmmmmmm*! Captain Timblim said, "Fuck! Shit! What the fuck is that?"

One of the American soldiers said, "A Libyan soldier's vehicle just blew up, sir."

Captain Timblim said, "Who are these fucking soldiers?"

They continued flying, going to report that their mission had been done by some other special ops forces. As they made it to the UAE Al Dhafra Army Base, the captain ran inside and got on the phone to his headquarter and said, "General Blackstone, please."

The receptionist said, "Please hold, sir," as she connected him to General Blackstone.

General Blackstone said, "This is General Blackstone. How can I help you?"

Captain Timblim replied, "Sir, this is Captain Timblim with some good news and some bad news, sir. Which one would you like to hear first?"

General Blackstone said, "Give me the bad news, Captain."

Captain Timblim replied, "General Blackstone, sir, we were on our way to do our mission and we came to this backpack on the outskirts that we took, and it had a note on it that read on that outside, 'No TRK. I'm USA. SIDR.' And the inside said, 'Job done, soldiers. Go home.' That was written in motor oil, sir. We thought it was a joke. We flew out to our landing zone in Al-Hammah, and all we saw were dead soldiers everywhere, and their vehicles were blown to smithereens, except for one, as a couple of Libyan soldiers got caught in the middle and died while having sex in the vehicle. After we left there, sir, we then went into Omar Al-Mukhtar University in Al Bayda City on Aloseth Road, and there it was a war zone inside and outside that university. Sir, there were over three hundred dead Libyan soldiers, and the target that we were after was dead. Mrs. Shat Al Alum is dead, sir!

"Now, for the good news. We got the papers along with some more papers from a place in Colombia about a cocaine plantation being destroyed, and some papers also were talking about killing US soldiers when we come into their country. There are papers after papers speaking about some…hold on, General Blackstone, sir."

Captain Timblim was off the phone for eight to ten minutes, then he said, "General Blackstone, sir, I just got word over another line that a small Army base in Puerto La Cruz in Venezuela had been taken over by soldiers who took a Russian MI-24 helicopter fully loaded with arsenal, killing over six hundred soldiers, sir. These soldiers were fucking shi—hold on again, sir."

Captain Timblim was off for thirteen minutes this time and then said, "Sir, you won't believe this, sir."

General Blackstone asked, "What, Captain?"

Captain Timblim said, "These same goddamn soldiers landed that same helicopter, the Mi-24, in Cape Verde and hid that chopper in the Jebil National Park in Tunisia and, later that night, went to the Medenine Army Base and refueled that chopper, killing over two to three hundred of their soldiers, sir. What the hell is going on?"

General Blackstone said, "I don't know, Captain, but I do kn—"

He was cut off his sentence by Captain Timblim, who said, "Sorry for cutting your sentence short, sir, but you really need to hear this, sir."

General Blackstone said, "Hear what, Captain Timblim?"

He said, "It's a small town in Colombia that is called San Martin, reporting that ninety to a hundred Colombian soldiers were killed by a person, one man that they call el Soldado Invisible."

General Blackstone said, "What the fuck does that mean, Captain Timblim? What the hell is el Soldado Invisible? Please tell me!"

Captain Timblim said, "Well, General Blackstone, sir, that *el Soldado Invisible* means *the Invisible Soldier*, sir. The people of that town knew that it was only one person who did this, because there were no vehicles or helicopters involved. Sir, what do you want me to do?"

General Blackstone said, "What can you do? Everything is over, Captain. You and the boys come on home."

Captain Timblim said, "Yes, sir, General," as they both hung up their phone.

Captain Timblim then said, "All right, soldiers, load up and let's go!"

They all loaded up on their helicopters, going their way back to the USA.

Now General Blackstone was just sitting there, pondering who in the hell was this soldier or soldiers doing this, as he knew one soldier couldn't kill that many people and live to tell about it. General Blackstone stood up and walked to his window and saw the old abandoned building that they called the No-Name Unit. He said to himself, "Captain Apocalypse, you and your soldiers are dead. What is one of these soldiers doing out there, avenging your death as well as your soldiers' death? Who in the fuck are these fucking soldiers?" He knocked all his shit off his desk as his secretary and a sergeant ran into his office, and the sergeant said, "General Blackstone, is everything okay?"

The general did not hear him, and he said very bluntly, "General Blackstone, is everything okay, sir?"

They both picked up his things off the floor as the general said, "Huh? Yeah! Yeah! Yeah. Yeah, everything is okay. Just leave that stuff alone. I'll clean it. You can leave."

As they were still squatting down, General Blackstone said out loud, "I told you I got it! Now leave! Leave!"

They stood up fast, saluting him, then going out of the door. General Blackstone was just staring out of the window at the No-Name Unit, like he was seeing a ghost. He said to himself, "There's no fucking goddamn way that one motherfucking soldier can kill that many soldiers and is not dead, unless he is immortal. And there isn't such thing a person being immortal, besides people on TV in Hollywood. Who are these soldiers?"

As he was about to turn away from the window, that was when he saw a ghost himself. He saw a six-foot-three figure standing there, looking up toward his window, looking directly at him. Chills shot all over his body. He stared at him as this figure was staring back and didn't move a muscle. The general blinked his eyes as it got watery for staring at it for well over four minutes, his heart beating fast. His blink just lasted for a split second, a tenth of a second, and that figure was gone; it just left inside of his watery, blinked eyes. He started looking all over the base area to see if he could see that image, but it couldn't be found anywhere. The general was shaken scared as he knew that this figure looked like Captain Apocalypse. He didn't know what to say or do.

General Blackstone pushed the intercom button and asked, "Is that sergeant still out there?"

The secretary said, "Yes, sir, General."

He said, "Send him in, please."

The sergeant came through the door while saluting, saying, "Yes, sir, General Blackstone, sir."

General Blackstone said, "Sergeant, Sergeant Van Stamp, take some soldiers down there to the place known as the No-Name Unit and clean it out and destroy everything that is in it. Do you understand my order? Here is a note to pass to anybody who has a problem with it. Take care of it first thing tomorrow morning. Do you understand?"

Sergeant Van Stamp said, "Yes, sir, General Blackstone, sir. Do you have a key for us to use to get in, sir?"

General Blackstone said, "Yeah. Take this key and return it back to me when your team has finished, Sergeant."

Sergeant Van Stamp took the key and left the building and went to choose twenty-five soldiers. He said, "Tomorrow at 0600, I want all of you to meet me down at the No-Name Unit, and we're going to clean everything out and destroy it. Now, get some rest, and I'll see you in the morning."

They went back to what they were doing as General Blackstone was still staring out that window with those chills. And it wasn't coming from the window; this chill was a cold, death chill. He knelt down, cleaning his floor up and putting his things back on the desk in fear.

The next morning, Sergeant Van Stamp and his team of soldiers went down to the building called the No-Name Unit and saw all these Restricted signs. One of the privates said, "We're not supposed to be here, are we, sir?"

Sergeant Van Stamp said, "Look, Private, we were told by a general to do this, and we are going to do this, understand?"

The private replied, "Yes, sir, Sergeant."

They all went in and found the light switch and turned the lights on. The whole entire place was empty. This unit looked like no one had been in there for well over twenty years. A bunch of spiderwebs was everywhere, and dust was so thick you could stick your pinky finger in it. The boot prints in there were theirs when they walked all the way through this unit. The sergeant and his team did not find even one single thing to carry out and destroy.

Sergeant Van Stamp said, "Okay. I have seen enough. Let's go, soldiers." They then left, going in different directions, just as Sergeant Van Stamp took the key back to General Blackstone.

He said, "General, sir, that place is empty. Not one single thing is in there to be carried out and destroyed. Maybe somebody else cleared that out for them once they left."

General Blackstone said, "What do you mean, Sergeant? That place can't be empty. You sure that you went to that unit?"

Sergeant Van Stamp said, "Sir, we went inside of that unit and gave it a walk-through, sir. It looks like nobody's been in that unit for well over twenty years, sir."

General Blackstone said, "Sergeant, these soldiers died over three and a half to four years ago, and nobody—and I do mean *nobody*—has gone to that unit and cleared it out. So don't tell me that that fucking place is empty! Have a fucking seat!" He then picked up his phone and said, "Captain Manske, go down to the No-Name Unit and report to me what that place looks like. Break the fucking door down if you have to. Do it now!"

General Blackstone slammed the receiver down and stood there looking at Sergeant Van Stamp, as he just stood there. He then walked to the window, watching for Captain Manske to walk to that unit. General Blackstone was just staring out of his window when he saw this six-foot-three figure standing there, looking at him, saluting with the wrong hand. Captain Manske walked right past him, going through the fence to the No-Name Unit. This figure was staring him down until the phone rang, breaking General Blackstone off his trance, and the six-foot-three figure was gone once again. General Blackstone picked up his receiver and said, "General Blackstone. What! What the fuck you mean empty? What! That place has not been abandoned for twenty fucking years! What the fuck are you saying, Captain Manske? Yeah, get out of the place." He slowly sat down in his chair and said to himself, "How can that be? Those soldiers are dead. All of them. Who could've taken that shit outta that unit? When did they take it out? What is this shit?"

Sergeant Van Stamp said, "Sir...sir...sir, General Blackstone, sir."

General Blackstone said, "Oh. You are excused. You leave now. Thank you, Sergeant."

Sergeant Van Stamp got up, saluting General Blackstone, then walked on out of the door. General Blackstone was very puzzled with this bullshit because he knew that this unit had only been out of commission for three to four years. And who was this six-foot-three figure that kept staring at him out of his window?

He picked up the phone and said, "Captain Manske, please. This is General Blackstone calling."

Captain Manske replied, "General Blackstone, this is Captain Manske. How may I help you, sir?"

General Blackstone said, "Captain, before you went through that gate, did you see a man standing six foot three and weighing about 280 pounds, dressed in all black? You did not. You sure that you didn't? Well, I thought that you passed by somebody I once knew a while back. Thank you, Captain." As he hung the receiver, he just contemplated on this figure.

He knew that he saw this figure, but how come Captain Manske couldn't see it? He just sat there and stared at the wall and got up, went to the window, and looked at that unit. And he looked and looked until he snatched his keys off the desk and walked out of his door, saying to his secretary, "If anybody calls for me, please tell them that I am in the unit that is called the No-Name Unit." He then walked out of the door, going to the No-Name Unit.

When he made it there, he saw where Captain Manske had busted the door open. He walked around and saw everything was missing, like the soldiers had reported to him. He could not understand this, even if he had seen it himself. This unit was so deserted, as if it had not been lived in for well over twenty years. As he walked deeper and deeper into this unit, he saw this six-foot-three figure again, and he said, "Who are you? What are you? Are you my conscience? I am General Blackstone, and you are on my base. I run this outfit! Now, who are you, before I have you arrested?"

The six-foot-three figure said in a mechanical voice, "You know who I am, General Blackstone."

General Blackstone started laughing and said, "Captain Apocalypse. Captain Apocalypse, you are in some trouble for deserting your post and allowing your soldiers to die. Now, come on, I'm taking you in."

The six-foot-three figure was just standing still, and not one part of his body moved. General Blackstone said, "Captain Apocalypse, are you coming, or do I have to come and get you myself? Now, bring your ass here. And that's an order!"

That six-foot-three figure said in his mechanical voice, "You don't want me to come with you, because it'll be the other way around, General Blackstone. So do you really want me to come to you?"

General Blackstone said, "You don't scare me, and you are disobeying my order. You are being insubordinate to your superior officer. Now, come on!"

That six-foot-three walked toward General Blackstone, and as he got about seven feet from him, that was when General Blackstone's blood started rushing, and fear had come over him. As he was trying to back up and run, he fell to the floor. He was watching this six-foot-three figure just two steps from him, and he said to that six-foot-three figure, "Please! Please! You can't do this to me! I am a general. Stop it. Leave me alone. Get away from me. Stop! Stop! Stop! Somebody help me! Somebody. Somebody! Help me. Hellllllllllp! Meeeeeeeeeeeee!"

CHAPTER 8

Two weeks passed by and no one on the base knew where General Blackstone was. They called and called and called his office personally as they had his personal and private numbers. His secretary did not hear his office phone ringing, and she thought that was kind of odd. She just sat at her desk and placed calls through to General Blackstone when they called his regular phone line. She hadn't seen General Blackstone in two weeks. The last time she heard from and saw him was when he told her that he was going to the No-Name Unit, and that was at about 1722, and nobody on this base had heard from him. General Blackstone hadn't shown up to work in two weeks. Where could he be? people started wondering.

General Blackstone's secretary, Cindy, was sitting at her desk, answering all of General Blackstone's calls and taking his messages, when a three-star general, Warren Stensil, called General Blackstone's office. His secretary, Cindy, said, "General Blackstone's office. This is Cindy. How may I help you?"

General Stensil said, "Yes, I'm General Stensil. I am looking for General Blackstone. Will you please connect me?"

She said, "Sir, I have plenty of messages here for General Blackstone, but he hasn't been in his office for two weeks now."

General Stensil said, "Two weeks? He's been out of his office for two weeks and none of you heard from him?"

She said, "Sir, yes, sir."

He said, "Put me on hold and call his private number for me. Do you have his number?"

She said, "His private number, sir? I did not know that he had one, sir."

General Stensil said, "Sweetheart, all generals have private numbers. I take it that you didn't have any knowledge of that, then? So I want you to put me on hold and dial (636)-504-9949 and tell him that I need to speak to him ASAP."

She put him on hold and dialed (636)-504-4949, and a computer came on and said, "We're sorry. The number you have dialed is no longer in service. Please hang up and try your number again."

Cindy hung up the phone and dialed the number again, and it said, "We're sorry. The number you have dialed is no longer in service. Please hang up and try your number again."

Cindy clicked back over to General Stensil and said, "Sir, you sure the number is (636)-504-4949, sir?"

General Stensil said, "Sure, I'm sure. Why?"

She said, "Well, sir, it's a computer that said the number is no longer in service. I hung up and tried it again, and it repeated the same thing to me, sir. His number has been disconnected, sir."

General Stensil said, "Do you have any way of getting inside of his office?"

She said, "No, sir, I do not, sir. Can I ask you why, sir?"

He said, "He might be on the floor, dead, especially if you haven't seen him in two weeks. Just sit tight. I'll send someone to his office. And don't be alarmed, okay?"

She said, "Okay," as they both hung up their phones.

Twenty-two minutes later, Colonel Terry Bingerham and Captain Manske came up to General Blackstone's office with a whole lot of keys. It took them almost forty minutes to try 170 keys, and none of them worked. Colonel Bingerham went into the hallway and took a fire ax off the wall and brought it back into the room and said to Captain Manske, "Knock this fucker off its hinges!"

Captain Manske hit the door where the doorknob was, knocking the doorknob off on the outside as well as the inside. He said, "Excuse me, Cindy. Do you have a flashlight in here?"

She said, "Yes," and then went inside of her left-side desk drawer and pulled it out then gave it to him. Captain Manske knelt down and shone the light through the doorknob hole, and he saw the office was empty. I mean *empty* empty, with not one single thing in it. He said, "You got to be shitting me! You got to be shitting me! Colonel Bingerham, sir, that office is empty! There is nothing in it, sir."

Colonel Bingerham asked, "What are you talking about, Captain?"

Captain Manske said, "Sir, there is not one single thing in this office," as he was standing up and kicking the door in the rest of the way and turning the lights on. They both were looking at an empty room, with dust everywhere. Cindy came to the doorway of General Blackstone's office and said after looking around, "Where is his desk? Where are his blinds for his window? The trash can is gone, too, sir!"

Colonel Bingerham said, "What is this? What is this? I won't believe that General Blackstone has gone AWOL. He has to be a missing person!"

Colonel Bingerham went to the secretary's desk and took her phone and unplugged it out of the wall and carried it to General Blackstone's office and plugged it up. He dialed (636)-504-9949, and it said, "We're sorry, the number you have dialed is no longer in service. Please hang up and try your number again. We're sorry, the number you have dialed is no longer in service. Please hang up and try your number again. We're sorry, the number you have dialed is no longer in service. Please hang up and try your number again. We're sorry, the num—"

Colonel Bingerham just hung the phone up and said, "Where could he be?"

That was when Cindy said, "The last thing he said to me was that he was going to the No-Name Unit, but he never came back."

Captain Manske said, "Yeah, he called me to go down there and look the place over, and I did. The place was so dirty and dusty it looked like no one had been in there over twenty years, sir."

Colonel Bingerham said, "You two talking about Captain Apocalypse's unit?"

They both said at the same time, "Yes, sir."

Colonel Bingerham said, "Captain Apocalypse and his new and old teams had been dead for some time now. Captain Apocalypse and his new recruits went to Tokyo and stopped a terrorist from blowing up the Tokyo subway. Somebody put three old Japanese swords in his head, and only his head. Now, about two and a half to three years after that, his whole entire team was mass-murdered in Colombia when they were sent there to destroy a cocaine plantation. The mission was completed, and just a year or so after, those soldiers and then some were destroyed by a team of soldiers. There is something to that as well, but we don't believe it."

Captain Manske said, "What is that, sir?"

He said, "Well, it's just a story that was given to our intel here in the States."

Captain Manske said, "Please, sir, tell me what you are saying, sir."

Colonel Bingerham said, "Captain, Captain Manske. You won't believe me, but I'm going to tell you anyway." He was shaking as if his life were in great danger.

Captain Manske said, "What is it, sir. You're shaking real bad, sir. Are you okay, sir?"

He said, "Yes. Yes, I'm okay. Well, Captain Manske, for your information, Captain Apocalypse and his soldiers were very special. The only person that could give them an order was one person, and that was the president of the United States. These soldiers that Captain Apocalypse called team were the only persons that could give them an order. He made every last one of them a sergeant. You did not ever see their faces. Their own teammates had never seen one another's faces, heard their normal voice, as they talked through a voice detector that made their voice sound mechanical. You, any other high-ranking officers, or even I couldn't go to that unit that Captain Apocalypse called the No-Name Unit. Don't ask us what those soldiers' names were, or Captain Apocalypse's name. All we know is that once upon a time, they were a part of this outfit, but all that has done a disappearing act. No paper trace for any of those soldiers. Now, since I've told you this much, Captain Manske, hold on to your hat. You see, somebody or something in this town of San Marta in Colombia killed over a hundred Colombian soldiers by himself, or itself. Those people praise him, or it, right to this very day. They call him or it el Soldado Invisible."

Captain Manske asked, "Excuse me, sir, but what is *el Soldado Invisible*?"

Colonel Bingerham said, "*El Soldado Invisible* is Spanish for *the Invisible Soldier*. I know, I know, I know that there isn't such a thing as this invisible person, but, Captain Manske, we sent a team of soldiers and doctors to Colombia, and believe me, it is true, not the part about somebody or someone being invisible, but the terrorizing of those soldiers for terrorizing those people. We don't know who or what he is, but he is on our side, as they were planning to kill any United States soldiers that entered into their country after they had killed Captain Apocalypse's team and the person that he left in charge, by the name of Lieutenant Obliterate."

Captain Manske said, "Whoa! Whoa! Whoa! Colonel, sir, what are you saying? Those aren't names, sir."

Colonel Bingerham said, "You really don't know too much do you Captain Manske. Those soldiers had names that they represented to the fullest as they specialize in their names. These soldiers names was "Sergeant Lowlife, Sergeant Rattler, Sergeant Shadow, Sergeant Flood, Sergeant Illusionist, Sergeant Consequence, Sergeant Evil, Sergeant Eliminate, Sergeant Fatal, Sergeant Furious, Sergeant Destroyer, Sergeant Hectic, Sergeant Hocus Pocus, Sergeant Maniac, Sergeant Nuclear, Sergeant Polarize, Sergeant Animosity, Sergeant Boogeyman, Sergeant Big Badass Wolf, Sergeant Tornado, Sergeant Redrum, Sergeant Viper, Sergeant Death, Sergeant Executioner, Sergeant Vicious, Sergeant Torture, Sergeant Horrific, Sergeant Graveyard, Sergeant Undertaker, Sergeant Wrath, Sergeant Chaos, Sergeant Venomous, Sergeant Grim Reaper, Sergeant Night Terror, and Sergeant Body Snatcher. I know that I didn't say the name of Lieutenant Obliterate. You see, Lieutenant Obliterate was Sergeant Wrath, because he took over for Captain Apocalypse. You said, Captain Manske, that you went to that unit. Well, you probably didn't get a chance to see their training ground out back of their unit. It looked like a grand canyon for this base. They trained with live ammo one full day for fifteen hours nonstop, until they ran out of ammo. When we went out there to order for them to stop, they were standing there at attention, with their arsenal lying neatly in front of them. The fucking ground was still vibrating, with the sound of their ammunition still echoing in that cold night air. That was the same night that I met the five-star general, and they recognized him before they recognized us. I think sometime later, they were all killed in Colombia."

Captain Manske said, "Colonel Bingerham, sir, General Blackstone called me back and asked me if I had seen a person outside the fence of the No-Name Unit that stood six foot three and weighed at about 280 pounds, which I hadn't. I did not see a person standing on that sidewalk, sir. But he did say that it was staring up at him while he was looking out the window at me going through that fence. Maybe it was his conscience bothering him, sir."

Colonel Bingerham said, "Well, his conscience has kidnapped him, then, Captain Manske," as they all walked out of General Blackstone's office, going to their own station, wondering where General Blackstone was. Colonel Bingerham knew that he had to satisfy his curiosity, so he walked to the closest barracks and ordered the whole entire barracks to follow him. They all went to the No-Name Unit, where one of the soldiers said, "Colonel, this place is restricted, ain't it, sir?"

Colonel Bingerham said, "Not anymore, soldier," as they continued.

As they made it to the door, the whole entire place was empty. No boot or shoe prints were on the floor in this building. The dust and dirt were so thick that you could measure it.

Colonel Bingerham said, "Split up in twos and search for any disturbance indicating someone was here."

They searched this place for well over five and a half hours. They looked everywhere in this unit, and still there was no sign of General Blackstone. As they were about to go to the training post of the No-Name Unit, that was when Captain Manske came in and saw Colonel Bingerham and his soldiers searching for the general, since this was the last place he came to before he went missing. Colonel Bingerham said, "Come on, Captain Manske, let me show you what

I was telling you back in General Blackstone's office about these soldiers' training ground. You will be impressed and scared at the same time."

Colonel Bingerham ordered the other soldiers to go back to their barracks as he and Captain Manske walked down that long tunnel and got on the elevator shaft, going to the training ground. When they got ready to step out of that elevator shaft, a pile of dirt was in front of them, and they were looking all over that training ground when Captain Manske said, "What happened here? You mean to tell me that this was part of a training? This was a training course that these soldiers were doing to have this place looking like this, sir? Whom were they training to go launch an attack against, sir?"

Colonel Bingerham said, "I think that they train to attack themselves. These soldiers put fear in the devil himself. Satan and his demons wouldn't dare challenge these soldiers. I truly believe that they ran Satan and his follows out of hell. These soldiers would ride with death, Captain, and they will walk right in the middle of a battle of hell and come out to tell about it, until their last mission, where something went so very wrong."

Captain Manske asked, "What? What went wrong, sir?"

"They all died, Captain Manske, they all died," said Colonel Bingerham. He then continued, "Doesn't it feel as if you're being watched?"

Captain Manske said, "Yes, sir. It doesn't feel too comfortable on this compound. It feels as if we're violating an order from higher up. It's creepy, sir."

Colonel Bingerham said, "I told you, didn't I, Captain? Let's go."

They left the training ground with cold chills running all over them. Now, Sergeant Body Snatcher flew to Muscat, Somalia, and found a place to land and set up himself a command post. He used all those things that he took from that small Army base. The gas-operated generator turned on as he was listening in on call after call of the United States news, just waiting so that he could make a run. He knew that he couldn't sit in one place too long with a big, huge Russian Mi-24 helicopter. He knew that those other countries were still chasing him well, at least, looking for a person in a Russian Mi-24 helicopter. Sergeant Body Snatcher was just waiting patiently for his next move before leaving Somalia. He was looking at his main map of all these countries where he located most of the US soldiers were sent to to try to conquer terrorism, which were mostly on small countries, requested by their authorities.

Sergeant Body Snatcher was still thinking about his team and wishing they were there with him, although all of them taught one another their own style, and he mixed their styles with his. He didn't know that four countries were calling him many soldiers and an invisible soldier. He also didn't know that his own country was calling him a terrorist, and many as well as having an immortal life for killing all those soldiers and getting to live behind each action. He just stared into the open of the small hills of this desert in Somalia.

It was now eight months later, April 11, 1983, and the United States was still looking for General Bradford Blackstone as he still had not appeared or made a call to say that he was all right. Sergeant Van Stamp was called to Colonel Bingerham's office to tell his story of when he saw General Blackstone last.

As he made it to Colonel Bingerham's office, he was met at the door by Captain Manske, who saluted three-star general Stensil, Colonel Bingerham, Captain Manske, and Lieutenant Phillip. General Stensil said, "Have a seat, Sergeant...uh...uh...uh... Sergeant Van Stamp. We called you in so you can tell us what you and General Blackstone talked about the night that he sent you to the No-Name Unit. He's been missing for well over eight months, and we have to find our general. So will you please tell us what your account of that night is?"

Sergeant Van Stamp said, "Well, Colonel Bingerham, what I know is probably the same thing that Captain Manske knows. General Blackstone ordered me to sit down and called Captain Manske for the same reason that he called me, and that was to get some men and go to the No-Name Unit and take everything out and destroy it. When we went in, we turned on the lights and we didn't see anything in it. I reported it back to him and told him, and he got very pissed off and called Captain Manske. He called back about twenty-five to thirty minutes later and reported the same thing to him that I did. He hung up the phone and eased into his chair as if he saw a ghost from his past, some captain by the name of Captain Apocalypse. He said it couldn't be him because they all were dead, and I asked him what he said. He just told me that I could go. I'm telling you, General, that place did not look like anyone had been in there over twenty years."

Colonel Bingerham said, "See, General, we all have the same story to tell you, sir. What else can we do?"

The three-star general asked, "Is this Captain Apocalypse dead or alive?"

The colonel said, "Dead, sir!"

General said, "Where was he buried? At Arlington National Cemetery?"

The colonel said, "With his soldiers, sir. I helped buried all of them, and the president himself was there right with the CIA and the FBI. Yeah, it was a strange thing that happened while we were there, sir." He paused a bit. "There was a person standing out there, wearing all black, watching us bury all those soldiers that the admiral of Fleet 71, lieutenant, and sergeant brought in on the Galaxy C5. A person that the president called his right hand. Now, as he stood there after he got off one of our chopper, another chopper came, landing right next to him, and five of them came out of that chopper. Those five turned into six as all of them saluted those dead soldiers. Then he yelled out loudly, 'At ease!' his voice still echoing in the distance. The most bone-chilling thing, though, was, when he turned around and followed behind those five, who dressed just like him, in black, his voice was still echoing, even when he got in that chopper and flew off, sir. Now, that person was a person that would have put death to shame as he stood there in all his six foot three and weighed about 280 pounds. The ones that were with him were almost that size as well, sir."

The three-star general said, "Where are these guys now?"

There was no answer from anyone in the room. Three-star general Stensil asked again, "Who were the soldiers? I said!"

Colonel Bingerham said, "Sir, nobody ever saw their faces or knew of their names. They were a part of this base once upon a time, but their names, social security number, date of birth, nationality, fingerprints and handprints, and whatever we can use to find them have been removed, as if they were never even born, sir. Their parents were never in contact with them, and if you do show them any pictures, they couldn't tell you anything because their identity was withheld from one another. Sir, they really actually don't exist, sir."

General Stensil said, "We find them, then we find General Blackstone, so get off your asses and find this goddamn general! And I do mean *now*! This meeting is over, like, yesterday. Why are you all sitting here? Up! And! Out!"

They all got up and left the room wondering how they could find this general. They didn't know if those unknown people had him or not, but it was something to look at and put out on the wire worldwide. They didn't know that they had just put a hit out on Sergeant Body Snatcher, as he was hearing it on his radio. He knew he now had to change his style in a way that nobody could ever see him again. He knew how to camouflage himself like a chameleon. His duty of a soldier just got more and more complicated. He said, "The world was my battleground. The soldiers were my life. The innocent were my blood. The stars were my eyes. The moon was my energy. God was my heart. My soul was my death. As my words were honorable and true."

He just stared into the ground, waiting for dark to come up on him. Sergeant Body Snatcher just drifted away in the midst of the desert by himself, listening to his radio about the wars all over the world.

Now, it was three days later, back in the US, and General Stensil was still on that boot camp, where he went to General Blackstone's office, where he looked out of the window at the No-Name Unit. He kept looking at it, thinking that somebody was going to come to it at 0100, but no one ever did. He just kept staring. As he was about to nod off, he caught himself and said, "What the hell! I'll go down there myself."

He left out of the office of General Blackstone and went inside of those gates. As he saw the Restricted sign, he said in a normal tone, "Restricted my ass!" and a cold chill came across his body. A little fear came across his fifty-three-year-old body. He just kept walking and made it to the door. He said, "Come on, Tracy, get a grip on yourself." He walked through that door, feeling around, until he found that light switch and turned the lights on and saluted the inside of this unit. He said, "All right, soldiers. At ease and as you were."

He just smiled, walking all over this unit. He then went to the tunnel, where it gotten even spookier as hell. He said, "Calm down, Tracy. Shit, you better get a fucking grip before you have a fucking heart attack!"

He made it to the elevator shaft and went to the ground level. As he got off the elevator, he saw the training ground wrecked so fucking badly, as if this base went through World War IV without any bodies. He said, "Did these soldiers have a battle with the devil? Because if they didn't, they sure in the hell terrorized his home! These soldiers were who we want and who we made, but who betrayed them?"

He just felt all the pain of this ground of war as he was staring into the sky. General Stensil said out loud, his voice echoing, "Attention! Attention! Attention! Attention!"

He stood straight up and saluted as he heard a voice in the wind echoing, saying, "At ease! At ease! At ease! At ease! At ease! At ease!"

Now he knew which way it came from or who said it when cold chills went over his body, and his crying voice said, "Captain! Captain! Captain! Captain! Captain! Apocalypse! Apocalypse! Apocalypse! Apocalypse! Apocalypse! Apocalypse! Apocalypse!"

As there was no answer.

Two minutes passed by as the three-star general Stensil said again, his voice echoing over the night sky, "Apocalypse! Apocalypse! Apocalypse! Apocalypse! Apocalypse! Apocalypse!"

Another two minutes went by as General Stensil just started walking off, going back inside. He was just looking around this dirty and filthy unit and said as he looked at the wall, turning the lights out, "I'm going to have to get somebody over here to clean this place up."

Now, when he held his head up, he saw something that looked like an image of a person standing there in a salute. Saluting him. He squinted his eyes, trying to see in the dark as he slowly eased his hand to the light switch, cutting the lights on very fast; the image was gone when the lights came on. He knew that he didn't blink or turn his head so that it would be gone, but he knew that darkness can play tricks to the eyes. General Stensil just turned the light back off, and the image wasn't there as he said in his normal voice, "At ease, soldiers, at ease." He then walked out of the door. Now it really was a wonder if somebody had betrayed these soldiers or they were really dead? Who could really tell us about these soldiers, as they did not know who these or those soldiers actually were on this base, because nobody could tell besides the person who made them. And the question was, Who made them?

Now it was November 16, 1986, three years and seven months later. Sergeant Body Snatcher knew it was time for him to go as he had sat here in Muscat, Somalia, long enough. He turned his radio up and heard the United States warning Pakistan about the nuclear weapons that they were making. Sergeant Body Snatcher said, "Right on cue. I got it, President. Your soldiers will not have to die coming over here to correct a wrong."

As he was standing up to finish putting his things in the helicopter, that was when he heard on his citizen band radio that the Red Cross plane had dropped off some food for the Somalia people who were starving, but the Somalia soldiers were taking it from those hungry people. Sergeant Body Snatcher got all his things loaded up as he started up his helicopter, going up in the air and flying about forty feet off the ground. He saw where these soldiers were trying to make it to this drop. There were four trucks and eight jeeps full of Somalia soldiers with guns and bazookas. He flew over them real fast as they started shooting at him; he turned back around, firing five missiles back-to-back, blowing up their trucks and jeep, and he turned back around with his Gatling gun, firing off an easy five hundred rounds. He landed the helicopter and went over there to kill the last three that were moving. He used his bowie knife and a piece of the parachute and tied it to the parking bars of the helicopter and dragged those two big crates across the sand and gave it to the Somalian people in their village. He then used the wind of his helicopter to remove the trail away from their village.

As he was about to head out to Pakistan, that was when he saw three more trucks, seven or eight jeeps, and two motorcycles heading toward the first little wreckage. Sergeant Body Snatcher got in good distance of them, where they couldn't hear or see him. He then shot three missiles, flipping over all the little cars that they had on their convoy, and after blowing up their little convoy, he shot up the rest of them with his Gatling gun. He knew that this second group didn't get a chance to call for any help, so he just flew on out to Pakistan.

Sergeant Body Snatcher flew away from Muscat, Somalia, going to Karachi, Pakistan. He was looking at beautiful ocean and sea, daydreaming of how it could be not being a soldier, but that was the only thing that he had actually known for well over three and a half or so years in the service. He was only seventeen when he came into the service in 1972, and now it was 1986. He had no children and had never been married, as he dedicated himself to his teammates and country. It was not like they did not go out into the world back at the base and go out and have sex with a woman of their choice; they just didn't start a relationship with a woman and have children because the missions that they went on never guaranteed them a return back home. Every serviceman or servicewoman that put themselves into dangerous missions was not promised that they'd live through it or lose any part of their body. That was why Captain Apocalypse fed his soldiers and himself their last meal as if they were in a prison on death row, waiting to be executed for a crime. They all knew that their only crime was loving the country and the people in it. That was why Sergeant Body Snatcher never stopped doing what he was trained to do as a soldier.

He flew for well over ten and a half hours, making it to Karachi, Pakistan, where he saw five Pakistani soldiers trying their best to cover this guy to get him to safety. He killed all of them. One was still living when Sergeant Body Snatcher said with a demanding mechanical voice, "Is this person Abdul Qadeer Khan?"

The dying Pakistani soldier said, "No, no, it's not him. They're on the way to get him, General Pervez Musharraf, Lieutenant Zulifa, Captain Bashir, and Captain Abdus. They went to the basement to come out around the back and get picked up by them."

Sergeant Body Snatcher knew that this soldier was dying, so he just walked off, going through the building. He went all over the building, not finding him. He saw the helicopter with other Pakistani soldiers getting out of it with gas mask on, setting up their posts, waiting for him. He picked up his big duffel bag and ran outside of the basement door, where he saw five people running to a helicopter. He killed three Pakistani soldiers, turned the corner in front of him with his AK-47 and M16 as he made it up the stairs, and ran to where his Suzuki was parked. He got his TAC-15 crossbow and took a bundle string and cut it three times, tying four M67 fragmentation grenades on the end of an arrow, pulling their pins and shooting it on the outside of the helicopter and watching it blow up in midair with all of them on it. He watched all those other Pakistani soldiers looking for cover to keep from being hit with the falling debris as Sergeant Body Snatcher started throwing his M67 fragmentation grenades in their area, blowing them up as he got on his Suzuki, going back to his camp, where his Mi-24 was at. He took his Suzuki down the street with eight or nine Claymores in his duffel bag, throwing them in the direction that he was heading, on the side.

When the Claymores flipped and bounced, that was when they blew up. When one of the Pakistani soldiers tried to pick one up to throw back at him, that was when he got blew up to smithereens. As he was riding, going to a shorter direction, he saw some Pakistani soldiers with a roadblock waiting for him. He went off to the side and laid his Suzuki down and ran in full speed, making his way behind them, killing the four soldiers at the back of the trucks, their roadblock. He went to the left side, killing those five, and got on top of the truck and opened fire with two AK-47s, one in each hand, killing all thirteen of them and shooting their tires out and throwing M67 fragmentation grenades, blowing them up. He could hear the warning siren going off in the midst to let their country know that they were being attacked by their enemies.

He let his Suzuki run as if he were racing with someone. His Suzuki was so quiet the people didn't know that it was him until he went past them, when they then started shooting at him. Men, women, and children were trying to kill him as he reached inside of his duffel bag, putting out M67 fragmentation grenades, throwing them, and as he passed them, he rode very low on his Suzuki, going at 130 miles per hour, leaving one of those CS gas canister every fifteen seconds as the wind was now pushing that CS gas ahead of him.

As he made it past the house where he took those clothes from, the lady and her husband came out, shooting at him. He made it to his helicopter as the warning sirens were still blaring. He was where he landed his Mi-24 helicopter, hiding it in those mountains. Sergeant Body Snatcher knew that he had to find his way to Hyderabad, Pakistan, to the Old Campus Colony, where this nuclear scientist Abdul Qadeer Khan was designing those nukes. Sergeant Body Snatcher didn't know the location, but he would soon find out. He looked up at the scorching-hot sky, waiting for the evening to become night, and said to himself, "Well, team, we're at it again. Walk with me and battle with me. We don't want all brothers of arms to die in the hands of these fucking Pakistani." He got his binoculars and looked around and saw some Pakistani clothes hanging up, drying; he eased himself down to the shack that was called their home and took the clothes from the clothesline. After taking those wraps, turbans, and clothes back to his camp and letting it finish drying in that scorching heat, he had to eat a little something before heading out.

Now, when he finished eating, he got up, the daylight still shining on him. He got dressed up like a Pakistani, putting two of his 9mm guns under his wrap for his chest, and two AK-47s on his back, one on each shoulder. He then got on his Suzuki trail bike, riding off the desert sand, going to Hyderabad, Pakistan. Before making it to Hyderabad, he saw a soldier walking. As he pulled over, that soldier got on the back of his Suzuki with his back against his back. He rode to a place that was deserted and raised up his Suzuki on its back wheel, throwing that Pakistani soldier off. Sergeant Body Snatcher turned his trail bike back around and placed it over this Pakistani's neck and said, "Where is the Old Campus Colony?"

The Pakistani soldier just looked at him, smiling.

Sergeant Body Snatcher took his 9mm out from his left side and said the second time in his mechanical voice, "I know that you think this is a game or a joke that is being played on you, but I bullshit you not, soldier. This is more than real, more than you'll ever know. So I ask you again, soldier, where is the Old Campus Colony?"

The Pakistani soldier stopped smiling but just looked at him with a frown on his face, his eyes squinting, as if death didn't frighten him.

Sergeant Body Snatcher said, "I understand. What's understood shall not ever need to be explained. You'll talk before you'll die, that much I do know, soldier."

Sergeant Body Snatcher put his Suzuki in first gear, riding across the Pakistani's neck and face, just as the Pakistani soldier was lying there in pain. Sergeant Body Snatcher got off his Suzuki and walked three feet back to him and stood up over him, saying, "You still can't talk, huh? Okay, let's try this on for size."

He knelt down, taking the Pakistani soldier's gun off his back and tying his mouth up so that he couldn't yell out for help. Sergeant Body Snatcher pulled out his other 9mm and, standing over this Pakistani soldier with both of his 9mm's in his hand, shot the Pakistani soldier in both of his shoulders. He said, "Where is the Old Campus Colony?"

The Pakistani soldier was muttering under that wrap covering his mouth. Sergeant Body Snatcher put both of his 9mm's up and pulled out his two ranger bowie knives, asking, "Soldier, where is the Old Campus Colony?"

The Pakistani soldier was muttering loudly as Sergeant Body Snatcher knelt down and put both of his ranger bowie knives in each of the Pakistani soldier's kneecaps. He then stood over him, looking down at him, just as the Pakistani soldier was still trying to talk but only muttering his words. Sergeant Body Snatcher stepped on the top part of both his ranger bowie knives as they were sticking inside of this Pakistani's kneecaps, pushing them all the way through his knees as the Pakistani soldier was crying. So Sergeant Body Snatcher took the wrap from around his mouth and said, "Soldier, where is the Old Campus Colony?"

The Pakistani soldier said, "It's…it's…it's…it's on Thandi Sarak Highway. It is on Thandi Sarak Highway!"

Sergeant Body Snatcher looked at him while kneeling down and took those bowie knives out of his kneecaps. The soldier said, "Please don't! It hurts bad, mister. I can't take the pain! Please have mercy. Please!"

Sergeant Body Snatcher said, standing up, "Okay. I show you some mercy." He pulled out his 9mm before that Pakistani soldier could speak and shot him three times in the head, killing him instantly. He said, "Pain is gone now, soldier," taking his bowie knives out of his bloody kneecaps. He picked up the dead Pakistani soldier's body and put it in a condemned building. As he came out still dressed like a Pakistani soldier, that was when a Pakistani police came behind the condemned building and saw him going to his Suzuki. The passenger got out of the police car and said, "Soldier, I need to see some type of identification."

Sergeant Body Snatcher just stood there, looking at him.

The second officer got out of the car and said, "What's the problem here, partner?"

His partner said, "This soldier refuses to give me his identification, Sergeant."

The sergeant said, "You're refusing this officer your identity, soldier? I strongly suggest to you that this officer will now show you any pity here, soldier. I will assist him in battering your ass. Now give him your identification. Now!" They both then pulled their clubs up and walked slowly toward him.

Sergeant Body Snatcher untied his wrap off his body, and that was when the Pakistani police saw his gun as he pulled them out, shooting them both in the chest. They both fell to the ground, trying to get their breath, as Sergeant Body Snatcher picked them up one at a time and sat them back in the car and shot both in the head, killing them. He was about to leave and went back into the condemned building and got that dead Pakistani soldier. He put those cuffs on him and put him and his gun in the car with the two dead Pakistani police officers. He got on his Suzuki and rode off, going around the city, looking for the Old Campus Colony. After riding for forty-five minutes to an hour, he found the Old Campus Colony. He was just looking at all the Pakistani soldiers patrolling this place. He rode another hour and found the Pakistani Army base. The Qasimabad Army Base.

He had to hit this place right after he did this mission. Sergeant Body Snatcher turned his Suzuki around, going back to his little camp, and took off the Pakistani soldier's clothes as he got back into his original outfit. He got his duffel bag and packed up twenty-eight Claymores, thirty-five CS gas canisters, twenty tear gas cans, twenty-five smoke grenades, and forty M67 fragmentation grenades. He put three AK-47s on his left shoulder and three M16 on his right shoulder, three mini AR-15 across his chest, his M25 sniper rifle, and his TAC-15 crossbow on the handlebar of his Suzuki. He noticed that it was getting dark at 1744, and he stood up at attention, saluting his teammates, and said, "This is what we live and die for, so I will die before any more will die."

He got on his Suzuki and started it up, going back to Hyderabad, where the Old Campus Colony stood on Thandi Sarak Highway, to stop nuclear scientist Abdul Qadeer Khan from finishing making those nukes. After thirty-three minutes of riding his Suzuki carefully for others not to see him, he finally made it to Hyderabad, Pakistan, making his command post a hundred yards from the Old Campus Colony. He parked his Suzuki behind a big dumpster and stacked a lot of garbage on it, going into that broken-down old building that looked like a library. He went to the roof, and five Pakistani soldiers were on two buildings, as the rest of them were on the ground, walking with dogs. He zoomed on the three soldiers, first killing them with heart, head, and neck shots, and the other two, he shot in the head. He took his M25 sniper rifle and TAC-15 crossbow back down the stairs and behind the dumpster. As he was about to turn around, that was when two Pakistani, a man and a woman, saw him as he was saying, "Shhhhhhhhhh." They both started talking and whispering and still looking at him.

Sergeant Body Snatcher didn't know that he or somebody dressed like him had been broadcast worldwide as the lady pulled out a whistle and were about to blow it, that was when Sergeant Body Snatcher shot them both with his mini AR-15 in the stomach and chest killing them. He threw the man first in the dumpster and when he picked up the woman, her purse fell down as stuff came out. As he threw her in the dumpster and she was about to put her purse in there, that was when he saw that poster of him or one of his teammate with a two billion dollar wanted out on him, dead or alive. He just folded it up and put it inside of neck of his stocking cap and ski mask. He ran in half full speed and carefully not too make any noise with his duffel bags full of arsenal and his guns from making clatter sound as he made it to the main building that he needed to throw the canisters off of before he attack these Pakistani soldiers. He looked at his watch after being up on the roof for two hours and saw that the whole little were traffic have died down as he said to himself, "It's time for you all to die with or without me."

He popped the first three canisters of tear gas, throwing them in front of vehicles and in the middle of their little street. He knew that they couldn't see him, as they were choking off the tear gas. That was when he popped four of the CS gas canisters, throwing them in four different directions. He heard them yelling and choking at the same time, and that was when he popped ten smoke grenades, throwing them to make it even worse to see him. Sergeant Body Snatcher left from the top of that building, picking up his AK-47 and putting it in his left, where his other three were on, on his left shoulder, and picked up his M16, putting it in his right hand, where his other three were on his right shoulder. His AK-47, M16, and mini AR-15 all had double clips to them, but his 9mm was only one clip, with other clips ready to go. His silencers on these guns didn't give up his position. As the tear gas, the CS gas, and smoke grenades had the area so fucking smoky, the Pakistani soldiers were dying, while some were trying their best to run as Sergeant Body Snatcher was killing them. He was shooting them in the back, the back of their head and neck, in their stomach, chest, and head. He emptied both clips as he flipped them upside down and started back shooting. He then walked down the street, dragging his big duffel bag as he was putting down Claymores under the passenger and driver's side of the vehicles.

He put his empty clips inside of the duffel bag, then pulled out eight M67 fragmentation grenades, throwing them inside of a building, blowing it up, killing the nine Pakistani soldiers that he saw trying to see him. He went into the building still dragging his duffel bag, very carefully looking for Abdul Qadeer Khan. Sergeant Body Snatcher loaded up his Suzuki, guns, duffel bags with his arsenal, his TAC-15 crossbow, and got into his Mi-24 and started it up, going up into the air. After being in the air for four seconds, he let the Gatling gun go on the lady and her husband, blowing up their house. As he flew off, going to the Qasimabad Army Base, Sergeant Body Snatcher saw five Pakistani helicopters coming his way, and he started firing missiles at them, firing into the houses below and the buildings, blowing them up and the people. He flew past a nuclear power plant and dropped twenty-five Claymores and thirty CS gas canisters along with twenty M67 fragmentation grenades inside of the nuclear plant's smoke pipe, blowing it up and all the power to it, sending that CS gas all over the air.

He made it to the Pakistani Qasimabad Army Base, blowing up their base, planes, helicopters, tanks, trucks, and jeeps. As the break of dawn was coming up on him, the warning sirens were still sounding out his threats; he then flew to his safety, going to the mountains in Kuwait.

After flying for well over twelve hours, he made it to Kuwait and landed his Mi-24 helicopter in a closed-in mountain. He sat there for three minutes, as he now knew that he had a bullet in his right shoulder, a bullet hole in his right leg, and one on his right side. He took off his clothes and started nursing his shoulder, leg, and side. His bulletproof vest didn't stop three bullets—well, at least two of them. He really didn't feel as if his life were leaving him, as he was just tired. He finished doctoring on himself and forced himself to eat a little meal and set his watch to wake him up at 1745 so that he could nurse on himself again. He sat up for another fifteen minutes and fell asleep inside his well-hidden Mi-24 Russian helicopter.

Now, eight days later, back in the United States, a breaking news from the world was broadcasting a small war in Hyderabad, Pakistan, where four hundred Pakistani soldiers and over two hundred Pakistani citizens were lying out dead on the street and in the houses and buildings as well as a blown-up nuclear plant. The Pakistani president didn't know who did this, but he was blaming the United States for destroying their nuclear plant and their Army base.

The news reporter said, "I am Kendrick Thompson, reporting for STF News. I spoke with a couple of witnesses who said that it wasn't an army of soldiers that did this. They stated that this was an act of one person, but they could not see him doing it. They call him the Invisible Soldier.

"This is what they had to say."

The lady Raioni said, "He…he could not be killed. He was immortal. He was invisible as the bullet went through him. I…I…I couldn't see him. I couldn't see him!"

Kendrick took the mic from her and said, "Shaun, the cameraman, show the world what this place looks like." They were still wearing gas mask. Shaun was pointing his camera at all those dead bodies as Kendrick said, "I was told that General Musharraf, Captains Bashir and Abdus, and Lieutenant Zulifar, along with chemist Abdul Qadeer Khan were blown up in their helicopter. The United Nations had these five people on their top list to remove as they were threatening to shoot off the nukes. The United Nations doesn't have to worry any longer, as their threats have been eliminated. Thanks to the soldier, or soldiers, that stopped the nuclear threats."

The three-star general Stensil got on his phone and called Colonel Bingerham, Captain Manske, Lieutenant Janson Friendly, and Sergeant Van Stamp and said, "Colonel Bingerham, you call Captain Manske, Lieutenant Friendly, and Sergeant Van Stamp. I want all of you to meet me in my office in ten minutes, and thirty seconds are already gone." They both hung up the their phones.

Six minutes into the nine and half minutes the three-star general gave them to meet him in his office, they were already there.

They came in saluting him as the general said, "At ease. Have a seat. Now, look, soldiers, I don't know who we have out there doing all our bidding overseas with the terrorists and these countries making their nuclear weapons of mass destruction. We need to eliminate this person because those other countries truly believe that we are acting out against them. It was very bad when children were trying to kill him just like the adults in those countries. I have a tape to show to you, and look at the work of the person that a Pakistani citizen called the Invisible Soldier."

General Stensil put the taped news in the box as Colonel Bingerham, Captain Manske, Lieutenant Friendly, and Sergeant Van Stamp watched the tape for well over forty minutes. General Stensil said, "This guy has to be one of Captain Apocalypse's soldiers, don't you think? I can't believe that an ordinary soldier or soldiers can get away from battling like this against those terrorists of that country. Those people kill their people and ours without losing any sleep over it."

Colonel Bingerham said, "Then what do you want us to do, General Stensil? What is on your mind, sir? Because if this soldier or soldiers have put out a lit fuse, then who are we to punish him for a well-done job, sir?"

General Stensil replied, "I don't want to punish him for what he has done, but I am very sure that he can find General Blackstone. You do remember General Blackstone? He has been missing now for well over three years and counting. We haven't received a phone call, a note, or a demand. Now, I thought I heard a voice the night of the third week of General Blackstone's being missing. I was saluting just to be saluting, and that was when I heard an echoing voice saying, 'At ease,' to me."

Captain Manske said, "You sure that you heard that, sir?"

General Stensil said, "I don't know, Captain. I really don't know. We just need to find that person who is responsible for these personal wars and find General Blackstone."

Captain Manske asked, "How would we do that, sir? How? Please give us an idea of what we should do, sir."

General Stensil said, "I'll come up with something for you all to do in order to fix this broken situation that has us pulling at all our heads. I know that we have our work cut out for us trying to catch this soldier or those servicemen or vigilantes. Now go and find our vigilante or vigilantes so that we can ease the whole world's minds."

They all got up and left out of General Stensil's office, going back to their own office, trying to figure out how to catch this soldier or these soldiers. They were really confused with how they could stop this soldier or these soldiers when an army couldn't stop him or them. They even called him or them invisible.

Now at Sergeant Flood's, Sergeant Rattler's, and Sergeant Destroyer's condominiums and apartments, they were saluting their television set, knowing in their blood that this soldier really had got to be one of them, but who was it? As they all were in their apartments four days after that news had been broadcast, a note came under their bedroom door while they slept. It read, "It's time for us to finally meet. Meet me at the Grand National Park in the middle room and knock on the door in your code. After reading this note, please destroy it ASAP."

They all woke up the next morning seeing the envelope on their bedroom floor with big letters written on it that said, "For Your Eyes Only." They opened up their letter and read it. Sergeant Destroyer's letter said to pick up Sergeant Flood and Sergeant Rattler in full dress uniform. Sergeant Flood and Sergeant Rattler knew that Sergeant Destroyer was coming to pick them up at 0100. Now it was 2350, and Sergeant Destroyer pulled up in front of Sergeant Flood's and Sergeant Rattler's apartment as they both came out by themselves. Sergeant Destroyer knew that Sergeant Flood was paralyzed from the waist down, but how in the hell was he walking on his own? It was with two crutches, but still walking. They made it to his car, where they both got in and didn't speak a word as they knew that it had been over eight to nine years since they saw one another.

They drove for about three hours and a half, going to another state out from theirs, where they found the Grand National Park and stared at the middle door for ten minutes. They got out of the car when it was 0200, then knocked their code on the door. The door opened as the six-foot-three and 280-pound soldier was sitting there between two more soldiers. The third one closed the door behind them. The three chairs that were at the long table across from those four soldiers were across from Sergeant Flood, Sergeant Rattler, and Sergeant Body Snatcher, and they sat down, staring at him. As they saluted him, he saluted them back.

He said, "At ease, soldier. Job well done, Sergeant Destroyer! Have a seat. Job well done, Sergeant Rattler, have a seat. Job well done, Sergeant Flood. Have a seat. MTs, well done. Have a seat. It's seven of us here, and only six of us will survive this year. I want you to know that I...that I...that I..." *Cough cough cough cough, cough cough.* "I...I ...I...am..." *Cough cough cough cough.* "I..." *Cough cough cough cough.* "I...I...am..." *Cough cough cough cough, cough cough.*

CHAPTER 9

Sergeant Flood, Sergeant Rattler, and Sergeant Destroyer came out of the shelter, going toward the jet-black mobile home and looking it over to make sure it was theirs. Sergeant Destroyer climbed up on the side step and saw three envelopes with their names on it. He said, "This is ours," and stepped back down and opened the side door, where a ramp automatically came out. They all went into it as the ramp automatically came back in. Sergeant Flood and Sergeant Rattler went to their seats as Sergeant Destroyer went to the driver's seat and drove off with thoughts on his mind about the meeting they had just had. He knew that those four people were part of the No-Name Unit, but who actually were they? Because he knew that Captain Apocalypse was dead. Sergeant Destroyer thought to himself, Who was this person that gave him the order to bring this soldier home?

Sergeant Destroyer drove their mobile to Milwaukee, Wisconsin, as a pass-through going to Minneapolis, Minnesota. As he was driving, they pulled over to refill their fuel. Sergeant Destroyer put a black headscarf on his head, with dark black sunglasses on, making it hide his identity, as people were in the parking lot, looking at him in fear, as Sergeant Rattler was filling up the fuel tank. Sergeant Destroyer went in to pay for their fuel; people were just looking at him in fear, as if they had seen a statewide, nationwide, and a worldwide broadcast picture of a person that was dressed just like them. The people were so afraid that the store manager and a couple more people called the Milwaukee Police Department for the reward on Sergeant Flood and Sergeant Destroyer, as they did not see Sergeant Flood inside of the mobile home, monitoring the whole outside as well as the people in the store. Sergeant Flood and Sergeant Destroyer was outside, talking between themselves as their codes were clicked by Sergeant Flood, letting them know that people at the store and out in the parking lot had called the police on them.

Sergeant Destroyer and Sergeant Rattler looked around at the people in the store and the people in the parking lot, seeing fear all over their faces. Sergeant Rattler went to the side door and opened it up. Sergeant Flood came out of the mobile home and stood at the doorway of their RV mobile home as Sergeant Destroyer and Sergeant Rattler stood up at each end. Four minutes later, thirteen police cars, five petite wagon, a SWAT team, news media, and about six plain detectives' cars pulled up and surrounded them as they just stood there like a statue. The sheriff of Milwaukee County, Ken Noblesome, called their tag in the back at the dispatch and said, "This is Sheriff Noblesome. Please run this tag, 001-The35."

The dispatcher said, "Yes, sir. Please hold."

Seven minutes went by before the dispatcher said, "Sheriff Noblesome, sir, the RV mobile home is not to be touched or questioned. I repeat, do not approach and do not speak to them. I was told that that is an order."

Sheriff Noblesome said, "Okay, we had an all-look-wide lookout on these people, so tell me, who gave you this order to order me and my men not to bring these sons of bitches in? They're wanted men as armed and dangerous."

The dispatcher said, "Sheriff, the one that they're looking for is over in Kuwait somewhere."

The sheriff said, "I don't give a shit if they're in Bomb Fuck, Egypt, goddammit! I'm going to bring them in."

As the sheriff and dispatcher were talking, all the lights and power went down in downtown Milwaukee, at the Federal National Bank on Wisconsin and Warburen, across from North Western, which was being held up by fifteen robbers with thirty-four hostages. The sheriff and the other officers, along with the Milwaukee County SWAT, heard over the police scanner of shots fired.

The sheriff said to the dispatcher, "Are you positive about these men that I have in my sight? This is a government vehicle?"

The dispatcher said, "Sheriff, the vehicle is not to be pulled over, and those men are not to be questioned under any circumstance."

The sheriff got on his radio and on his intercom and said, "All officers, get in your vehicles and leave the premise. This situation is a none of our authority and jurisdiction. You men in the RV mobile home continue on to your destination, I'm Sheriff Noblesome, and my men and I apologize for our ignorance. All right, Officers, load up and follow me."

Sheriff Noblesome got into his car and sped off as his officers followed him, with their lights and sirens blaring out loud. The bystanders were staring at Sergeant Destroyer, Sergeant Flood, and Sergeant Rattler as they got into their RV mobile home. Sergeant Destroyer had started up the RV when he noticed two old men standing there, dressed very poorly, with scraggy beards, saluting them. Sergeant Destroyer just stared at them for about two minutes, then he got out of his driver's seat and went to the back of the RV. The bystanders were still staring at the RV as the door came open and the camp came back out as all three of them came back out of the RV and walked toward those two men that were still standing in their saluting stance. The bystanders were standing there very quiet, as if they were afraid of Sergeant Destroyer, Sergeant Flood, and Sergeant Rattler. They were going to approach until they walked past them, going to the two poorly dressed bums standing next to a big dumpster, looking very proud of them for being who they were and what they were to their country. Sergeant Destroyer, Sergeant Rattler, and Sergeant Flood stood directly in front of them at attention, and Sergeant Flood and Sergeant Rattler took off their military coats, ski masks, gloves, and special night vision glasses and put them on the two men. Sergeant Destroyer went into his coat pocket and pulled out four of his military pins and pinned them on the two men, who were still standing in a salute at them. Sergeant Destroyer went into his pants pocket and pulled out all his cash and three credit cards, as did Sergeant Flood and Sergeant Rattler, and gave all of it to these two men. The two men were still saluting them as a cab pulled up to pick up a passenger; that was when Sergeant Rattler whispered to the cabdriver in his mechanical voice, "Take those two men to the Hilton Hotel on Sixth Wisconsin. Here's 1,500 dollars. Take them in these and be sure that they get the golden card treatment. These men were soldiers and gave their loyalty to their country. Please take care of my brothers."

Sergeant Rattler stood up and saluted the cabdriver and walked back in formation with Sergeant Destroyer and Sergeant Flood as they escorted the two men to the cab. Sergeant Flood opened the passenger-side door as Sergeant Flood, Sergeant Rattler, and Sergeant Destroyer stood up at attention and saluted as the two men saluted them as well as they were getting in the cab. Sergeant Destroyer closed the cab door, and as they stood there, one of the men said, "At ease, soldiers. As you were." Sergeant Flood, Sergeant Rattler, and Sergeant Destroyer put their hands down as the cab drove off with the two men.

All the bystanders were standing there in shock and couldn't believe what they had just witnessed before their very eyes. Sergeant Rattler, Sergeant Destroyer, and Sergeant Flood walked back to their RV and went inside and drove off as the bystanders were still staring at them as they left. As Sergeant Destroyer was driving their RV down to go get on the expressway, they saw all those police cars lined up, at least sixty cars, vans, SWAT team vans, and trucks. They saw five news helicopters in the air, reporters and cameras and their vehicles all packed in, reporting this live as it unfolded. Sergeant Destroyer drove four blocks away from the whole scenery and parked their RV but left the engine on. He went to the back and said to Sergeant Rattler, "You drive around for about an hour and ten minutes, and that'll give me enough time to help the sheriff and those hostages out. We don't want anyone to get killed in this standoff."

Sergeant Destroyer was about to say something, and that was when he heard this lady screaming into the news camera and microphone, saying, "Please don't kill my son! Will somebody please do something?"

The news reporter placed her name on the screen, and that was when Sergeant Rattler said, "I know her. I know that lady. Mrs.

Alicia. I went to school with her eldest son, Wayne. His baby brother, Kayron, always tried to hang with us when I came to his mom's house. They were people that treated me like I was part of them. We need to get him out of that place!"

Alicia was still crying live on television, on the news, then she said, "That's my baby. He's the baby. Please, somebody! Why aren't the police doing anything? He might be dead, for all we know!" She tried to run through the crowd of reporters and police, crying for Kayron's safety; that was when the police grabbed her, holding her.

Sergeant Rattler said, "Sergeant Destroyer, go get my little brother out of there for her, please." Sergeant Destroyer didn't say a word.

Sergeant Rattler said, "Sergeant Destroyer, please, man, get my little brother out of there." His mechanical voice was sounding as if he was in tears.

Sergeant Rattler said, "Sergeant Destro—"

That was when Sergeant Flood said, "You better go get in the driver's seat and drive around, because Sergeant Destroyer has been gone for well over four or five minutes. He heard you the first time, Sergeant Rattler."

Sergeant Rattler said, "Mrs. Alicia, Kayron is coming home to you, Mama. Sergeant Destroyer is bringing him to you. Don't cry. Don't cry."

He knew that she couldn't hear him, but he could hear her, see her, and feel her pain. He got up and saluted Sergeant Flood as Sergeant Flood said, "At ease, Sergeant."

Sergeant Rattler went to the driver's seat and started driving around, as Sergeant Destroyer instructed for him to do. Now, Sergeant Destroyer knew that all the power was cut off to the bank, and he set his watch for an hour and ten minutes. He knew that most of the people around this area wouldn't be looking at him, as the attention was on this chaos that was going on. Sergeant Destroyer saw four SWAT members tearing off the back door. As the door was about to fall off, that was when Sergeant Destroyer shot all four of them in the back of their shoulder with a small dose of DMT (dimethyltrypt-amine), which the military called devil's breath. A good dose would have them out for at least twenty-four hours, as if they were dead, but he shot them with a dose so small they would awaken in three to four hours or less. He took their zip ties, come-along, handcuff, and radio and set them up very comfortably, with their gins in hand, inside the doorway and placed the door back up as if it never were broken. He went into the basement and found the main wire for the emergency lights and cut it, making it pitch-black inside the building.

Sergeant Destroyer knew that he was outnumbered, but that wasn't the thing that bothered him. The thing that did bother him was that he didn't want these people holding these hostage to start shooting. He made it to the floor where the bank robbers and hostages were at and counted the gunmen. Two were at the door, five were on the floor, holding their guns on the hostages, two were standing on the counter, and three were at the vault, taking the money. The three in the vault were using a cigarette lighter to get the money. The first guy took the first money bag and carried it off as Sergeant Destroyer put his left arm around the first robber's neck and choked him out, putting him to sleep, then placed the other two in the buttock, knocking them out with a small dose of DMT—the devil's breath. He placed the zip ties on their ankles and wrist. He saw the five gunmen on the floor at least ten to thirteen feet apart from one another. He eased up behind the first and stuck a needle of DMT into his neck while holding his mouth and gently laid him down. The second and the third ones were kneeling down with their guns on the floor, knowing that the hostage could not see them, but he could. He stood up in front of them, and they did not know that he was there, just as he stuck those two in the back of the neck at the same time.

Sergeant Destroyer was looking at the other six, who were still off a distance from one another. The two on the counter and the other in front of the hostages. With the silencer on his dart gun, he probably could get all of them, but the two gunmen on the floor and the two on the counter could hide very fast, so he eased behind one of the other floor gunmen and stuck a needle in his back and laid him down very gently.

The fifth floor gunman whispered, "A Yellowboy—what are you going to do with all your money? I have a bitch that I need to take care of. What about you?"

Sergeant Destroyer removed his mechanical voice detector and said, "What? I can't hear you. Come closer."

Shawn said, "Man, how can I come closer when I can't see a motherfucking thing?"

Sergeant Destroyer said, "Shit, I can see your fucking ass."

Shavon said, "Then you bring your fucking ass to me, because I can't see a goddamn thing!"

Sergeant Destroyer said, "All right, I'm on my way." He slowly walked to Shavon, then said, "Can you see me now."

Shavon said, "Fuck, now, I told you I can't see shit!"

Sergeant Destroyer got right up in his face in the pitch-black darkness and said as his body was touching Shavon's body, "Can you feel me now?" Before Shavon could assist him, he stuck a needle in Shavon's neck with the devil's breath and laid him down gently on the floor.

He looked up and saw the two counter gunmen at the bank teller drawer, feeling for money and putting it in their pockets. He shot both of them with the devil's breath packed in his dart gun. The last gunmen at the door or the hostages did not know that these were the only two left. The news helicopters shone a light at them as they closed the curtains to not be seen, and that was when Sergeant Destroyer tiptoed, running up to them in the dark and shooting them both in the chest with the devil's breath. He put the zip ties on all these robbers and laid them in a fashion, with their guns above their heads. He walked around until he saw Mrs. Alicia's son Kayron, just as he put a zip tie on his ankles and wrist and gagged his mouth so that he would not talk or make a sound. He threw Kayron on his shoulders and walked back to the area where the emergency light wires were at and twisted them back up, making the emergency lights come back on. Kayron saw this six-foot-four and 265-pound person in all black guarding over him as he was trying to talk but couldn't, as his mouth was gagged.

Sergeant Destroyer said, "Don't be afraid, Kayron. Your mother, Alicia, sent us to get you out. We heard her cry, we saw her cry, and we felt her cry. You're safe now." He bent down and picked him up and put him back on his shoulders.

He made it back to his original parking place as Sergeant Rattler was pulling up, clicking his code and Sergeant Destroyer's code on his radio. He laid Kayron down on the street as the RV stopped right beside them. The door opened up and a ramp came out. That was when Sergeant Rattler came out with his ranger buck knife, kneeling down, cutting Kayron's zip ties off his ankles and wrist. He said, "Tell Mrs. Alicia that I said thanks for everything that she taught us boys as children. Tell your big brother, Wayne, that I said I'll see him soon too, okay? Now, get up, little Kayron, and let us take you to your mom, before she hurts somebody over her baby."

Kayron got up with a smile on his face as they all got in the RV and drove a block from the bank. Kayron was about to step out of the RV when he turned around and Sergeant Destroyer said, "You don't need to know who we are, and you don't need to thank us."

Kayron just turned back around, and Sergeant Rattler stood up and said, "Permission, please. Please, just once, never again."

Sergeant Destroyer and Sergeant Flood looked at each other for about forty or forty-three seconds and turned their back, clicking their radios, giving them the go-ahead with this one.

Sergeant Rattler walked to Kayron as he removed his ski mask, stocking cap, and voice detector and said, "Shhhhhhhhhhhhhh, no one needs to know," as he then put everything back on his face. Kayron stepped out of the RV and walked toward the crowd very shocked because he knew this person who was with the man who rescued him. He knew that he couldn't tell his mother or his big brother, Wayne.

Sergeant Flood picked up the RV mobile phone and called the Milwaukee County Sheriff's dispatcher and said in his mechanical voice, "These are Sergeant Flood, Sergeant Destroyer, and Sergeant Rattler. We were the ones your sheriff wanted to arrest in the earlier part of the day. We have defused your bank robbers, and hostages have taken over. There are four of your officers at the back door of the bank. They're not dead men, they were just shot with a drug called DMT, dimethyltryptamine, which we named the devil's breath. The devil's breath will wear off in three hours. The robbers are zip-tied, and your sheriff and his team can go in and get them without an incident or injury to them or the hostage. Remember, they are not dead men, and let the sheriff know that the drug's name is dimethyltryptamine and that it only makes another person think that they are dead, but they're not, okay?"

The dispatcher said, "Okay, sir." The dispatcher then said, "Sheriff Noblesome? Sheriff Noblesome, the RV that you questioned earlier today just called and reported that you can go in and get the suspects and hostages. The suspects are not dead, sir, and the four officers at the back door of the bank also are still alive. They were shot up with a drug called dimethyltryptamine, or DMT, better known as devil's breath."

Sheriff Noblesome said, "Bullshit! Those robbers and hostage are still up and accurate. Now, get off the radio!"

Sergeant Flood overheard their conversation and said, "I'm Sergeant Flood, Sheriff Noblesome. One of the hostages has been release and is going to this mother, who has been crying for him, and he should have found her as we speak."

The sheriff saw the crowd of news reporters surrounding Mrs. Alicia and Kayron as he and his officers ran into the bank and had the lights turned on. They saw the hostages still lying on the floor with their heads covered, and the robbers were lying on their stomach with zip ties on their ankles and wrists and their guns lying neatly in order with them above their heads. The sheriff reached down and felt their pulse and their jugulars, and he didn't feel a pulse from either man. He said, "These men are dead. Get the coroners and let them know that we have twelve dead."

One officer said on his radio, "Sheriff, we have four officers down. They're dead, sir."

Sheriff Noblesome said, "Correction, tell the coroner that we have sixteen dead. Put an APB on that military vehicle for sixteen counts of first-degree homicide and thirty-two counts of first-degree reckless injury."

Lieutenant Skolke said, "Sheriff, where is the blood from these men? We didn't hear any shots or any scuffle of any sort. How did they kill these men in pitch-blackness without having been seen?"

The sheriff said, "Lieutenant Skolke, get the tape and take it to the mobile van and have them look at it and that we saw what went down here tonight."

As the coroners came in the bank with the gurneys and picked up the first robber, and as soon as they strapped him down, the robber opened up his eyes and said, "Ahhhhhhhhhhhhhh!" The second, the third, and all the robbers screamed out loud, "Ahhhhhhhh!"

The sheriff was very shocked and afraid as the coroner was on the floor, backing up, looking at all of them coming back from the dead. The robbers didn't know what had happened to them, as they all knew that they were robbing the bank, and now they were zip-tied from hand to feet. The four officers that were at the back door came to the sheriff and said, "Sheriff Noblesome, sir, I don't know what happened, but whatever happened happened because we all knew that we wouldn't be able to take any of them alive, and maybe we wouldn't have lost a few hostages out of this takeover. Whoever these people were knew what needed to be done to come out without killing a suspect."

Lieutenant Skolke said, "Sheriff, this was an act of one man as he took a hostage out on his shoulders. We couldn't see him at all on the camera. Sir, the man was carrying this hostage, but the camera couldn't pick him up, as if…as if…"

Sheriff Noblesome said, "As if he were what, Lieutenant? As if he were what?"

Lieutenant Skolke said, "As if he were invisible, sir. All you can see is, somebody or something was carrying this hostage on its shoulder. You really need to see it, sir."

Sheriff Noblesome went out to the mobile van and, looking at the tape, saw it for himself. He said, "What the fuck is this? What? Is this a fucking trick? You mean to tell me that this was done by one person or one thing that we can't see? Please tell me that this is a goddamn camera trick."

The officer that showed the tape said, "Sir, we said the same thing. We tried everything that our equipment has, but this is it, sir. That person or thing went and did exactly what his heart told him to do. He brought that grieving mother's youngest son out of that bank and gave him to her as the doctor did when he was born. I'm sorry, Sheriff, but what or who did this needs to be honored, sir."

Sheriff Noblesome picked up the radio and said, "Cancel the APB at once. To the ones responsible for the capture of these bank robbers and the release of the hostages, my administrative force, the hostages, and the state of Wisconsin thank you. We all thank you. If you can hear me, thank you."

After the sheriff put down the radio, about two minutes later, a voice said, "You're welcome, sir. We were just doing our sworn duties as soldiers for our country and the innocent citizens. We were doing what was supposed to be done, Sheriff, and you are very much welcome, sir. Out."

As the radio went silent, the sheriff said, "These soldiers are good. Damn good, if you ask me. I'm glad that we didn't go against those guys earlier. Now, let's wrap this up and lock these sons of bitches up! They want to rob my bank? Not on my watch." He then walked out of the mobile van, going to his car, and drove off.

It was now August 16, 1990. Sergeant Body Snatcher was still in Kuwait's mountain, hiding out from international authorities. He knew that they were looking for him and the Russian Mi-24 helicopter. Sergeant Body Snatcher was not afraid as he knew if he were back in the United States, the special team that he belonged to could've easily requested for him to come and do the thing that he was doing on his own free will. He really wanted to know why the United States was against him for neutralizing what they knew was a threat to their country. Their servicemen and servicewomen and their allies. Sergeant Body Snatcher knew that the war he was in was not an average war. The war that he was battling was an inner battle the he was in when his teammates died by the hand of the Colombians. As he was sitting there, just putting his thoughts together, that was when he heard the United States on the world news on his radio warning Saddam Hussein to stop making chemical weapons to threaten the United States and its allies. Saddam Hussein said negative to the United States warning and continued to make his chemical weapons.

Sergeant Body Snatcher knew that he had to come up with a plan to destroy those weapons, but he also had to get rid of this Russian Mi-24 chopper as well. As he was about to start up his chopper to go to Baghdad to stop Saddam Hussein from making those chemical weapons after the United States had warned him, that was when he overheard the dictator Saddam Hussein give an order over the radio for his men to go and invade Kuwait and kill the royal family in the Dasman Palace. Jaber Al-Ahmad Al Jabal Al Sobeltt, the king of Kuwait, did not know of this threat on him and his family and their little military by Saddam Hussein. Sergeant Body Snatcher knew that he had to rescue that family first and then destroy Saddam Hussein's plans of making those chemical weapons. Sergeant Body Snatcher turned his helicopter back off and took his Suzuki out of it along with all his ammos in three duffel bags and most of his AK-475, mini AR-15, M16, and M25 sniper rifles that he could carry with him on his Suzuki.

After packing everything up, he took some fuel out of the helicopter and two hundred feet of rope in it to let it soak until he got ready to leave. He didn't want to leave while it was still daylight, because he could move better when night fell, although he knew that the Ali Al Salem Air Base would see his little bomb's fire from their base. He didn't want to kill any of Kuwait's soldiers as they hadn't done anything wrong, but he would assist them against the Iraqi soldiers.

So three and a half hours passed by as Sergeant Body Snatcher stood up and said, "All right. It's time to get this shit over with and protect the innocent and destroy the wicked."

He put his hand inside the bucket and start pulling out the ropes soaked in fuel and tied it to the fender of his Suzuki. He then poured the fuel out of the bucket all inside the helicopter and poked small holes in the helicopter's tank. He made a torch from his firepit and got on his Suzuki and slowly rode away from it. He rode until the rope was tighter, as it would not stretch any further. He untied it from his fender and put the torch to it, and the flame on the rope put just a little light in the dark desert. Sergeant Body Snatcher saluted the Russian Mi-24 helicopter and said, "Good job, soldier. Now, rest in peace." Then he rode off on his Suzuki. Sergeant Body Snatcher rode for about twelve minutes on his Suzuki; that was when he heard the Russian Mi-24 helicopter blow up, lighting up the desert. The sirens of the Kuwait Army Air Base at Ali Al Salem went off as their soldiers loaded up, going in a different direction toward the explosion. Sergeant Body Snatcher pulled his Suzuki on the Ali Al Air Base and slowly rode around and saw this M1117 Guardian assault vehicle with a .50-caliber machine guns that could carry twelve people.

As he was about to load all his equipment and Suzuki inside of this M1117. Three Kuwaiti soldiers were walking directly toward his assault vehicle. He knew that they wanted it, but so did he. So he went around on the other side and came up behind them. They only had pistols and their helmets on. He shot all three of them in their legs, crippling them as he walked over them and tied them up and gagged their mouths. He finished loading up the M1117 with his equipment and got inside of it and drove off, going to the Dasman Palace to remove the king and his family from their palace. The Kuwaiti soldiers had the back, front, and both side entrances heavily guarded. So Sergeant Body Snatcher parked his M1117 assault vehicle twenty yards from the darkest entrance on the left side and ran fast, going to the side of the palace. He saw seven soldiers on the ground and three standing on top of the watcher's post. He took out his chloroform knockout gas and threw it to the crowd of seven Kuwaiti soldiers and the three standing on the lookout post, knocking all ten of them out. He made it inside and went to the king's room and chloroformed Jaber Al-Ahmad Al Jabar Al Sabett and his wife. He took the king out first. Six minutes later, he took Jaber Al-Ahmad Al Jabar Al Sabett's wife out, and six minutes later, he took the two children out.

He came back six minutes later, throwing chloroform gases all over the palace, in every room and all over the palace premises, knocking out every Kuwaiti soldier, making it look as if they were dead. Twenty-five minutes later, after doing all this, he got back into the M1117, looking at the royal family sleeping very peacefully. He started the M1117 up and drove them out of Kuwait, going to Saudi

Arabia, to safety. He knew that he was at least three hours to Saudi Arabia from Kuwait. As he was leaving Kuwait with the royal family, he saw that the Kuwaiti soldiers were battling with the Iraqi soldiers. So he rode in with the M1117 Guardian assault vehicle, using its .50-caliber machine gun, killing the ground troops of the Iraqi. He blew up their trucks and tanks with his arsenal. He got out of the M1117 with his duffel bag full of CS gas, M67 fragmentation grenade, and Claymores, killing the Iraqi soldiers.

After all the Iraqi ground troops retreated, leaving the Kuwaiti soldiers alone, he saw the Kuwaiti soldiers chase them. Sergeant Body Snatcher got back into the M1117, driving back to Kuwait International Airport, and drove his M1117 assault vehicles to the Kuwait Airways cargo and took driving up in the back of a Sikorsky MH53 Pave Low attack helicopter. The royal family was still steeping from the chloroform. He got out of the M1117 and closed it up as the .50-caliber machine gun was still smoking and smelling of gunpowder. Sergeant Body Snatcher got in the seat of the Sikorsky MH53 and started it up, and as soon as he was about to take it up in the air, the Kuwaiti soldiers came running toward him, firing shots at him, and the bullets were bouncing off it. Sergeant Body Snatcher just slowly went on up into the air without firing any shots at them.

The Kuwaiti soldiers just stopped and watched him flying off in their chopper in a different direction of the Iraqi soldiers. The Kuwaiti soldiers knew that this person couldn't have been an enemy, because he didn't fire at them or kill them, because they knew that he could have with no problem. Sergeant Body Snatcher just flew off into the midnight sky, going to King Khalid Military City in Saudi Arabia. The first job that he needed to do was done, and that was to protect the royal family from Saddam Hussein and his regime; now, he had to go back and complete mission number 2, and that was to destroy all of Saddam Hussein's chemical weapons of mass destruction. He knew that Saddam Hussein was planning on using his chemical weapons on the United States and its allies, meaning, that he wanted to murder his servicemen and servicewomen who were trying to stop him and his regime. He knew that Saddam Hussein's own people were afraid of him and his authority.

Sergeant Body Snatcher flew for well over three hours, seeing the King Khalid Military City, and stopped his helicopter over Dharan Military Base about a hundred yards. He landed the chopper, leaving its blades rotating for a quick getaway after dropping the royal family off. He backed the M1117 out of the Sikorsky MH53 and drove it eight yards from the base, taking the family out of it and covering them up still rolled up in their bedcover on the ground and pouring a circle of gasoline all around them, giving the Dharan Military Base a signal to come out to see what was out there. After lighting the gas on fire as it circled the royal family, he got back into his M1117 and sped off, going back to his chopper. He made it to his chopper and drove the M1117 inside of it and closed the chopper's cargo door. Then he took the chopper up into the air as the Dharan military was making their way to the royal family. He flew over them and just hovered over them until the family was sitting up and looking puzzled. When he saw that all four of them were okay, he just flew on ahead, going in the same direction that he came from. He was thinking that Saddam Hussein didn't know that his plan to kidnap the royal family with his invasion had been defused. He knew that Saddam Hussein was so pissed off at the person who was responsible for saving the emir of Kuwait. Sergeant Body Snatcher said, "Saddam Hussein, you think that you're pissing mad now? Just wait until I spoil your whole entire plan of your weapons of mass destruction."

He flew for well over four and a half to five hours, making it to Baghdad, Iraq, as he blew up Saddam Hussein's armored tanks, cars, trucks, planes, and helicopters without killing any of his soldiers, as he had already killed over seven hundred of them for trying to invade Kuwait for trying to kidnap or kill the royal family. The Baghdad siren was blaring out loud as Sergeant Body Snatcher was still flying to Saddam Hussein's chemical plant, with soldiers trying to hit him with their ground missiles. He shot a massive bomb at them, blowing it up millions of pieces. He zoomed in on a tower, killing the Gatling gunmen and the twenty to twenty-eight Iraqi ground soldiers and blowing up their vehicles. He landed the Sikorsky MH53 after clearing himself a path and put four AK-47s on his shoulders and four mini AR-15s across his chest, with eight Claymores and twenty-two

M67 fragmentation grenades in his duffel along with ten tear gas canisters.

He killed the seven Iraqi soldiers at the entrance and four more and made it to the door of the main building. He shot seven Iraqi soldiers in the chest and face with his AK-47, blowing their faces, brains, and chests out. He popped two tear gas canisters and threw them down the hallway as the Iraqi soldiers coughed and gagged for air, giving up their position. Sergeant Body Snatcher killed the three of them. He saw the surge electric box and shot it, knocking out the lights inside as it was very dark. The Iraqi soldiers were running into one another and bumping on the walls as Sergeant Body Snatcher was shooting them in the head, chest, back, neck, and stomach, killing them and stepping over their bodies. He came up to this big steel door with at least five big keys to open it. He put three Claymores on against it and pulled out his bigger, larger bowie knife out and cut the head of one of the Iraqi soldiers off and threw it up against the Claymores, then aimed his AK-47 and started shooting the Iraqi soldier's head until it came off, one of the Claymores blowing up the rest of them, knocking down the steel door and half the wall. He threw the last two tear gas canisters inside as he went in shooting and killing the thirteen to twenty soldiers inside as well as the chemist who was making these chemical weapons. He shot up all the machines as he pulled five pins of his M67 fragmentation grenade very fast and gently put them back into the duffel bag with the last eight Claymores and threw it and took off running in full speed.

As he made it halfway down the hallway, the bag went off, blowing up all the different areas of the building. The building was blowing up just as fast as he was running. He saw nine Iraqi soldiers running his way with flashlights as he had his AK-47, knocking them down, clearing his path. He made it to the door as other Iraqi soldiers were trying to get to him, but the building was still going up, making a lot of smoke, choking them as he was killing them, making it to his helicopter. As he was about to get in his helicopter, a shot hit him in the back and he hit the ground. He tried to get up, and that was when another hit him twice more in the back. The four Iraqi soldiers did not know that Sergeant Body Snatcher was wearing two M1951 bulletproof armor on in the front of him as well as the back of him. He lay there still on his back, with his fingers on both of his AK-47 in each hand. The Iraqi soldiers walked up on him and were about to spit on him when he shot all of them in their nuts, in their stomach, under their chin, and on their forehead and jumped up, still shooting them just in their face, blowing it completely off. He took all his guns off, throwing them inside the helicopter as he got inside and closed the door.

He took the helicopter up in the air and shot three missiles into the falling building, destroying its entirety without a beam standing. He flew off, killing twenty-five to thirty more Iraqi soldiers as he went on out of Iraq, going over the desert, heading toward the Konus Turkey Mountain Region, because he knew that his welcome had been worn out in Kuwait and Iraq. He had to find a place to hide at because the countries were still looking for him to kill him. He flew his Sikorsky MH53 Pave Low attack helicopter on the border so he could hide it in the Konus Canyon near Iraq. He found the Konus Canyon and landed his helicopter in it and turned it off. He took off his M1951 armored bulletproof vest and saluted it and said, "Good job, soldiers. Damn good-ass job."

He just sat back, staring at the sun coming up as the break of dawn was turning into daylight.

Now, back in the United States, the military forces received information from the United States president, the commander in chief, Anthony S. Finly. President Finly said on his phone, "Call for my whole military forces to meet me in the Oval Office right now. And I do mean right now!"

As they all came to the table and sat down, President Finly said, "What the hell is going on here with your team, Admirals and Generals? Goddammit, we have a one-man army out there, wiping out everything that we were about to attack. I had Saddam Hussein forty-eight hours to stop it or suffer the consequences, but this person didn't give him seven hours before destroying Saddam Hussein's plans, buildings, chemistry lab, and at least seven to eight hundred of his soldiers. Don't get me wrong. I am very much proud of what he's done, but he needs to understand that we have orders around him. Does any of you know who this person interfering with my order is?"

Admiral John R. Benson said, "Sir, long ago, we had a team of soldiers that was called the No-Name Unit, and the only person that could give them an order was the president and a captain by the name of Captain Apocalypse. Captain Apocalypse and his team were the meanest ones that you could run up against. I never had the pleasure of meeting them, but there's plenty of our military forces who have heard of them and of their works."

President Finly said, "Then where is this Captain Apocalypse and his 'fairy' soldiers at now?"

Five-star general Foster said, "They all are in the Arlington National Cemetery, sir."

President Finly said, "You mean they are dead, General Foster?"

General Foster replied, "Yes, sir. They were ambushed in the Colombian jungle by Columbian soldiers years ago, sir."

As General Foster was trying to finish his sentence, Vice Admiral Ken Blake said, "Sir, somebody finished the mission that they were sent to do and killed over four hundred soldiers and stole a Russian Mi-24 helicopter from an Army base there, and the citizens of a town in Colombia, in San Martin, call this soldier el Soldado Invisible."

President Finly asked, "What in the hell does that mean, Vice Admiral?"

The vice admiral said, "That means the Invisible Soldier, sir. Everybody that he went up against all reported that they never once saw him or even got a look at him. He laid out so much destruction against the ones we were after, but the bystanders were so afraid of the noise and destruction that they went for cover, and when they came out, they did not see any of our men or vehicles with those who were lying in the streets, gutters, ditches, sidewalks, buildings, in and out of windows, and places that we could never imagine. There were dead bodies, sir. They only saw just a helicopter leaving."

President Finly said, "I don't give a rat's ass what you do, Generals and Admirals. You men get this soldier and bring him to me so I can meet him. Do you all understand? I want this damn terrorist, and I want him now. Get out! I said *get out!*"

They all got up and had started walking out of the door when General Foster turned around and said, "Sir, if he is one of our men, he is trained to be your right hand that protects your left hand. This office was the one that elected and approved them, as no other military authority can give them an order. Once you give them an order, they do not think twice of doing it. You have to be honored to have them remove your obstacle, sir, without any question. The same order you gave Sheriff Noblesome in Milwaukee, Wisconsin, to shy away from three of his friends. That is, if he is one of their teammates." He turned back around and walked out of the door, leaving the president in the office alone.

As General Foster made it to his office and sat at his desk, he just stared at the wall and could not believe that his commander in chief felt this way about the soldiers that every president before him had approved and applauded, those soldiers who had put their lives before themselves to protect this country and this country's allies. General Foster pulled his desk drawer open and pulled out this small walkie-talkie and clicked it two times, clicked it three times, and clicked again two times, then put it back into his desk. Before his desk could close, he heard four clicks, two clicks, and three clicks. He just sat there with a smile on his face, with his secretary saying, "General Foster, sir, line 1. General Foster, sir, you're wanted on line 1. General Foster? You're wanted on line 1, sir.

"Ha ha ha ha ha ha ha ha ha ha ha ha ha ha ha ha ha ha ha ha ha ha ha ha ha ha ha ha ha."

Now, President Finly was in his office, staring out the White House window, just looking into the light-blue sky, thinking about what he said about that soldier who was actually removing all his obstacles. He looked down at both of his hands and flipped them over and over, saying as he was flipping them, "Don't ever let the right hand know what the left hand is doing. One hand washes the other one. But on the other hand, I extend my hand to all my supporters. I salute you. I solemnly swear. Damn, you mean to tell me that I have more power in our lives than you can ever imagine? When I said to the wife, kids, family, members, voters, and allies, I put my life in other people's hands, and now I want you to put yours in mine, and you'll see that you'll be in good hands when you vote for me. Shit, I got that soldier's life in the palm of my hand. I don't know if he is one of our soldiers or not, but I have to hear him out. I don't want to destroy a life or a family's life for el Soldado Invisible—I mean, Invisible Soldier—for defusing a live time bomb of hard-core terrorists."

He picked up his hotline and dialed five-star general Foster and admiral of the fleet John Benson and the three that were under them back to his office. Fifteen to twenty minutes went by when they all made it back to President Finly's meeting room and sat down at the long table. President Finly just stood there, looking at them, and then said, "I had to sit back and put my thoughts together about this Invisible Soldier. I am the commander in chief, and I want all my soldiers to come back home to their families. That was an oath that I took for the people of this country. Let's be sure that he is one of ours or just someone that loves to make trouble and leave their place, just as we love to do. Now, what are these soldiers names that we have buried in the Arlington National Cemetery?"

Everybody looked at General Foster as he said, "Here are their names, sir. But before you read them to the rest of this board members, I have to warn you that you all will be in a shock and chills, because these soldiers were what it says they were, sir."

President Finly said, "General, just give their names and let me be the judge of how I feel."

General Foster said, "Okay. I have given you a fair warning, sir. Here you go."

President Finly took ahold of the file and opened it up and looked at the names. He said, "What the hell is this, General? Is this a goddamn joke? Now, give these soldiers' names."

General Foster said, "Sir, what you see were their names. I can't explain to you why these things were considered as names, but they were accepted in our database, as you can see."

President Finly said, "Then what are their names, their real government names before these names?"

General Foster said, "When I met them face-to-face and talked with them, their captain, Captain Apocalypse, never revealed their names, but we know their title was the No-Name Unit, so that is self-explanatory to reach and all, sir."

President Finly said, "You mean to tell me that Captain Apocalypse, Sergeant Flood, Sergeant Rattler, Sergeant Destroyer, Sergeant Shadow, Sergeant Lowlife, Sergeant Tornado, Sergeant Illusionist, Sergeant Consequence, Sergeant Evil, Sergeant Eliminate, Sergeant Fatal, Sergeant Fury, Sergeant Polarize, Sergeant Animosity, Sergeant Boogeyman, Sergeant Big Badass Wolf, Sergeant Redrum, Sergeant Viper, Sergeant Death, Sergeant Executioner, Sergeant Vicious, Sergeant Torture, Sergeant Horrific, Sergeant Graveyard, Sergeant Undertaker, Sergeant Wrath, Sergeant Chaos, Sergeant Venomous, Sergeant Grim Reaper, Sergeant Night Terror, and Sergeant Body Snatcher…"

The whole board was quiet, staring up at the president as President Finly's face was stuck, as if he had seen a ghost. He was in a trance, as well as the board members.

General Foster was just looking around the table, at all of them and at the president. The room was so quiet you could hear a bug crawling on the four-inch-thick carpet. General Foster stood up and went over to where President Finly was standing and eased the folder out of his hands. President Finly stared into General Foster's eyes as General Foster said, "Yes, sir. I know, sir. These soldiers were what you feel, and those facing was in me, as I have seen them and heard their names. Those soldiers ate their last meal before they went on their death missions. They removed death before we sent the soldiers in to remove the only regime that you ordered us to do. I don't know who that soldier was who was eating, as he was one of those we sent, but he had to live off all the ones who died in Captain Apocalypse's squad. Let me tell you this, sir, and the rest of you members as well. When I received my five stars after they rescued me from the North Vietnamese soldiers and the prison that they called Hanoi Hilton, or the Hoa Ho Prison, they sent one soldier they called Sergeant Night Terror in to infiltrate as a North Vietnamese soldier, and he took me and a dead US soldier out there, and by himself, he killed over two hundred North Vietnamese soldiers, and the rest of them were on the outside, waiting for us to come out. Now, it gets better. They saved my son and his wife earlier that year. Now, this gets even better. I went to their training base, and it sounded like it was thundering, lightning striking, as the whole entire ground was vibrating, and while I was walking through all the dust and noise, I swear I heard a voice echoing, saying, 'Enough! At ease!' Everything got quiet, but the sounds of gunfire were still echoing in the night. They trained for fourteen to fifteen hours nonstop was what I learned. When I made it to the soldiers that were training, that was when I saw generals, colonel, and majors along with Lieutenant Obliterate standing in front of those soldiers that you just read off this paper. They were standing there at attention, and their weapons were lined up very neatly in order as they were, sir. As I was leaving, I heard that voice echoing again, 'As you were,' as they all started running toward their unit. Here is another kicker: their base was the only base that got a grand canyon on it. You know, some say that their unit is haunted by those soldiers, sir."

President Finly asked, "General Foster, do you believe that this soldier can be brought home if he is one of ours?"

General Foster replied, "No. I don't believe that he can be brought home, sir."

President Finly said, "Why do you believe that, General?"

General Foster said, "Sir, we don't know who he is, sir."

President Finly said, "What do you mean, General Foster?"

General Foster said, "Here's the other side of them, sir. We don't know what they look like, what their nationality is, what their voices sound like, and to be frank with you, sir, their own teammates don't know what one another looks like or sounds like. The only person that did know was Captain Apocalypse, and we don't know how Captain Apocalypse looked like or sounded like too. One of us can be one of them and we will never know. All I knew, sir, is that you can be Captain Apocalypse, sir. I am very serious, sir. We do not have a single clue of who these soldiers are and what they look and sound like, but we do know one thing for sure, sir."

President Finly asked, "What's that, General Foster?"

General Foster said, "That they didn't mind dying for you and this country, sir."

All of them just sat there in silence as General Foster went back to his seat and sat back, staring all over the room again. President Finly went to his seat and sat down and stared at General Foster for five or six minutes as General Foster stared back at him. The whole table was looking at both of them when the president said to General Foster in a whispered respectful command, "General, bring him home. Bring our boy home." He then stared into the general's eyes as General Foster just nodded.

CHAPTER 10

It was now February 24, 1991, six months later. Sergeant Body Snatcher was still hiding in Konus Canyon in Konus, Turkey, from the authorities that were trying to kill him. As he was eating his little meal from the campfire, he heard a broadcast coming across his scanner that there was a cult compound in Konus Canyon and that they were armed and dangerous. The radio personnel said, "The Pezinkuk Compound is responsible for thirty-one deaths, eighty-five kidnappings, and two hundred and seventy-five torture cases, but they all were dismissed due to lack of witnesses and evidence. A witness saw a group of people from the Pezinkuk Compound throwing a pregnant woman and her three-year-old daughter out of their thirteen '85 Ford van with racing stripes on it. So if anyone has ever seen this van, please do not approach. Just call it in and report it."

Sergeant Body Snatcher knew that he was already here in the spot that they were talking about. He got his high-powered binoculars and started looking around with its night vision, but he couldn't see a thing, only trees and big rocks. He lay for days, stretching out his back, too. He just sat back down and said to himself, "That compound must be on the other side of the mountain region. I'll check it out later, after I eat something and get myself some rest."

Sergeant Body Snatcher knew that this compound was heavily armed, but who actually cared? How would he be able to tell who was actually the cult group and the innocent one that was taken? He just sat back, pondering his thoughts very hard, because he knew that these dangerous people would kill them sooner or later.

Now, back in the United States, President Finly asked admiral of the fleet John Benson, "Did you set the trap for this soldier?"

General Foster said, "Trap. What trap, sir?"

President Finly said, "The trap for this goddamn invisible soldier. This son of a bitch has been a thorn in my side long enough, and this boy must be brought in to answer to the charges of all those murders and for violating a treaty on other countries for something that was not ordered by me or any military authorities."

General Foster said, "Sir, you can't do that, sir. Please reconsider it. Please, sir, reconsider it."

President Finly said, "I did. That's why they will give that chance or die—his choice. I got a phone call two days ago from Ali Al Salem Air Base in Kuwait that they have tracked down their Sikorsky MH53 Pave Low attack helicopter and their M1117 Guardian assault vehicle with a .50-caliber machine gun. They tracked the location in Konus, Turkey, near Iraq, in the mountain region. This soldier has been hiding under our noses on the border in the Konus Canyon. We'll have him dead or alive in three days. I want him alive, though, because he probably can give us some information on the whereabouts of General Bradford Blackstone, as he has disappeared for some time now without a trace. Yeah, yeah, yeah. I know he wasn't in this country or even on that base when General Blackstone came up missing. We can deal with him to get him back for the return of General Blackstone."

General Foster said, "Mr. President, what are you assuming, sir?"

President Finly just dropped his head and said, "Somebody knew what happened, and I want them prosecuted for their action."

Sergeant Flood, Sergeant Rattler, and Sergeant Destroyer had made it back to the town where their base was located and waited until it was pitch-black outside. Sergeant Rattler and Sergeant Destroyer put Sergeant Flood on a sleigh and strapped him down, holding on tightly as they ran in full speed, pulling him across all those downed trees and bumpy hills for twelve minutes. They jogged for seventeen and a half minutes and stopped for four minutes, catching their breaths, and started back running in full speed for twenty-three minutes, making it to their old unit as they knelt down and unstrapped Sergeant Flood and helped him up. They were still looking at their old unit as they stood up at attention while they heard an echoing voice saying in the distance, "At ease! At ease! At ease! At ease! At ease! At ease! At ease! Bring him home! Bring him home! Bring him home! Bring him home! Bring him home! Bring him home!"

They loaded up their old Sea Stallion helicopter onto the Lockheed C-5 Galaxy airplane, and they saw all these weapons on the plane waiting for them. They thought it would be worth it to read the instructions: "These guns are not the ones that'll kill your own men that are hunting your brother in Konus, Turkey. He took one of their choppers from Kuwait and another military vehicle. It got a tracer on it, and they found his location on the border between Iraq and Konus Canyon. They want him back, dead or alive, and I want him back alive. Don't kill or injure those American soldiers that are going after him, just disarm them. Nothing more, nothing less."

The guns that they had were stun guns that would render them helpless if they had to use it. So Sergeant Destroyer ripped them up and burned them as he and Sergeant Rattler went to the cockpit of the plane and started it up, looking at how the ground was torn up by their other teammates. Sergeant Destroyer and Sergeant Rattler took the plane off the ground, and they could not believe that this thing still could run. It was so good that the base never knew in all those years that they had ever come and gone from this base; that was just how quiet this C-5 Galaxy was. As they made it in the air, going to Konus, Turkey, to rescue their brother, they did not know that a special ops team was already half a day ahead of them.

As all the teams were in the air to go bring Sergeant Body Snatcher home, dead or alive, Sergeant Body Snatcher did not know that the helicopter and assault vehicles had trackers on them, and he didn't know that the president had sent some special ops team to come and get him, dead or alive. And he also didn't know that his team was coming to get him, to bring him home.

The president and his board members did not know that the No-Name Unit teammates were coming to bring him home. He went on the other side of the mountain and put his night vision binoculars on his face as he looked for a good one eight to ten minutes. He saw that compound that he heard about as he was looking for some movement, but there, it'd be turning daybreak, and he could then see everything. Right at that moment, he couldn't see a soul at all, not one person standing guard. So he got three AK-47s and put them on his back, four mini AR-15s that he put across his chest, ten tear gas canisters, and his garrote string, placing it on the handle of his ranger bowie knife on his left side. As he got on his Suzuki and started it up, he rode quietly through the woods, heading toward that compound to rescue the people that were kidnapped, which he heard about on the radio. Sergeant Body Snatcher rode his Suzuki for about five minutes and was at least two hundred yards from the Pezinkuk Cult compound. He stopped his Suzuki and turned it off, then eased off it and grabbed his duffel. He looked at his watch, knowing that it was about to turn light outside, as the sun was coming up and shining bright.

He slowly walked through the woods and made it at least sixty-five to seventy yards, getting closer to the compound. As he was making it to the edge of the trees, he heard a helicopter flying up above. He looked up, trying to see what type of helicopter it was, as he ducked and hid under a bush, the helicopter going and disappearing over the other mountain. He still didn't see any movement in the compound. As he was easing through the woods, still going to the compound, he saw two people standing behind a tree, and he slowly eased up behind them and came from the right side of the tree, shooting them, but he was very shocked. He was looking down at them when he noticed that they were not real, just dummies. He got down very fast as he knew that these cult members were very serious on this compound. Sergeant Body Snatcher was looking through his binoculars at the other part of this compound and through the woods, seeing the curtain in one of the houses moving. He knelt down, very still, for thirty seconds, looking at that window as he was still not out of the woods yet. He saw the van reported about in the news that was used in kidnapping those people, and that the owner and the rest of the Pezinkuk Cult Compound members had killed and tortured people.

Sergeant Body Snatcher knew that he had to sneak into this compound. As he was about to stand up, that was when he heard an airplane coming from behind him in the sky, but he couldn't see it from the trees, and the sun was blocking his view, beaming in his eyes. He said to himself, "I know the night is my protector, but it is my enemy as it can show me to reach and all, but I am a soldier who lives and dies for the innocent, and my oath is to be a soldier for the country that believes in freedom and liberty. Thank God for America!" He saluted the beautiful blue sky. Sergeant Body Snatcher stood up and was still looking at that window, hearing that airplane still flying in the distance. He took out three of his tear gas canister and six of his smoke grenades as he still thought about the two dummies that they had put up against the tree. As he was making it to the edge of the woods to make it twenty-five yards from the compound, he looked at all the vehicles just sitting there and still did not see one single person, so he now felt that by killing these two dummies, the leader and his followers must have them wired up to let them know somebody was on their land.

So he put his duffel bag on the ground and pulled four smoke grenade pins at the same time and started throwing them all over the compound, smoking it up. He pulled his tear gas canisters' pins and threw them one at a time. As this place was cloudy so bad, he ran and jumped the small wooden fence, making it to the first house, and stood outside of its side door for four seconds as he eased the door open, going inside in the kitchen area. He saw this woman standing up at the stove, reaching up to the cabinet, trying to get something out of it. He said in his whispered mechanical voice, "Ma'am, how many are here with you?"

She just stood there and didn't move.

He asked again, "Ma'am, how many are in here with you?"

The lady just stood there as Sergeant Body Snatcher tiptoed up behind her and touched her right shoulder, asking again, "Ma'am, how many—"

The lady fell on the floor, falling into pieces; that was when he noticed the she was not real. He checked what she was reaching for, but it was empty, then he picked up all of it and checked it, throwing it on the floor. He said to himself, "A decayed house," as he went through a small portion of the house and saw these male mannequins and some baby mannequins. He looked out the window, at the house where he saw the curtains moving, and edged to it. He went in the back door and saw another woman dressed just like the mannequin at the first house, doing the same exact thing. He walked up behind her and pulled the wig off, and she was reaching for the same exact thing. He went into the front part of that house and saw the same male and baby mannequins in the exact same spot of the ones in the first house. He now knew that this was a set up, but from who? He slowly eased back toward the back door of the house as he looked out of the door, looking around.

The smoke grenades and tear gas were still filling the compound. He was about to come out when he saw two soldiers climbing up in a tree. He put his high-powered binoculars on and zoomed in and saw them and the tags on their clothes, and that was when he noticed that they were United States special ops forces. He knew that he couldn't kill or injure them, as they were going to capture him or kill him, so he decided, death before he dishonored Captain Apocalypse's order, and that was to not allow oneself to be captured by anyone. He saw three more special ops forces members spreading out, and he just watched them. As he watched these five still trying to get themselves situated, he ran out and closed the door behind him and made it back to the first house, leaving the back door open and going through the first door, making it back to his duffel bag, just as one of the special ops was at it. Sergeant Body Snatcher was walking slowly up behind him and stood up there.

The special ops soldier said, "I found his arsenal bag, sir. He has some old but cool toys in it. What do you want to do with?"

Sergeant Body Snatcher said in his mechanical voice, "Pick it up and give it to him."

The special ops soldier turned around and saw this six-foot-five and 280-pound person staring down at him. As he tried to pull his gun, Sergeant Body Snatcher pulled his side-holster 9mm out on him so fast and pushed it well up to his left eye. The special ops soldier just shook his head and let go of his gun, putting both hands in the air.

Sergeant Body Snatcher said, "I am one of you and I am not one of you. I am sorry that I have to do this to you." He then hit him in the chin, knocking him out and tying him up with his own little rope that he was carrying. He picked up the special ops soldier and sat him up in the truck that was next to his duffel bag and took that soldier's radio. And that was when Sergeant Body Snatcher also noticed that one of the soldier's pistols had twelve or fifteen dart type of weapon that was possibly a tranquilizer, so he took it off him too. He looked into his duffel bag and saw the last four tear gas canisters and ten smoke grenades. He picked it up, going around in a different direction, making it around to the trees that the special ops soldiers had climbed from and popped a tear gas canister right under them.

One of the special ops soldiers said, "Terry, this tear gas never made it way over here. Are you okay over there?"

Terry said, "Shit no! This fucking shit is strong! I have to get down. I don't see that motherfucker anyway from all this goddamn tear gas smoke. I'm going down to the ground, Kevin. I'll meet you in the ground."

Kevin said, "Give me a couple of minutes and I'll watch over you, okay?"

As Terry made it to the ground, Sergeant Body Snatcher pushed him very hard to the tree and snatched his head mic off and threw him to the ground and tied him up and gagged his mouth. Kevin said as he was coming down the tree "I don't see how anybody can saw or even breath in this fucking ski," that was when Sergeant Body Snatcher put his left arm around Kevin's neck cutting his wind of circulation off putting him to sleep and tying him up and gagging his mouth and removing his head mic. Sergeant Body Snatcher knew that three more went in the direction from the ones in the trees, so he slowly walked through the woods as he heard two or three people coughing. He eased up behind them and shot them all in their asses with the tranquilizer gun, knocking them out as he tied them up. As he continued to walk slowly and gently through the woods, he saw two more soldiers standing there with rags over their faces, trying to stop taking in the tear gas as he eased up behind them. He then shot them with the tranquilizer gun and knocked them out and tied them up, removing their head mic. These special ops forces were trying to position themselves to capture or kill Sergeant Body Snatcher, but Sergeant Body Snatcher had foiled their plans. He now saw four of them going to the house that he went to, with the back door left open.

He ran back to it in full speed and made it. As the last one was about to go in, he snatched him up and put his right arm around his neck, putting him to sleep, and removed his head mic. He went in and shot all three of them in the back of the neck with the tranquilizer gun and tied them up and gagged their mouth. He went back outside and tied up the first soldier that he put to sleep and tied and gagged him. Sergeant Body Snatcher was walking back to the duffel bag as the tear gas was still heavy in the air, and he heard coughing coming from behind the van that he heard about on the radio. He eased to the other side as he saw four soldiers sharing a gas mask. He shot them on their shoulders, knocking them out and tying them up, then removed their head mic from them. All sixteen special ops forces members were out and tied up. Thirteen minutes later, Sergeant Body Snatcher had finished lining the sixteen special ops soldiers in a row, with their weapons on them, and that was when a voice said on the head mic that he took from the very first soldier, "Are all the team members ready to go? Is the suspect still in the house?"

There was no response from any of the special ops team.

The voice said, "I repeat. Is the team in position? Is the suspect still in the house? Answer!"

Still, there was no answer to his command.

As he was about to repeat what he said, Sergeant Body Snatcher said, "Your men are in their positions. They are waiting for you. They are not dead, they're just out from their tranquilizer."

Sergeant Body Snatcher was about to tell him who he was when he heard and saw a helicopter with rangers jumping out of it. He saw at least fifteen so far, and others were still coming out as the voice on the head mic was saying, "Move out! Move out! Move out! Air strike! Air strike!"

Now, Sergeant Body Snatcher knew as stood there that the soldiers that just came out of the helicopter would start shooting at him and the air strike would light this whole compound up, killing their own men for trying to kill him. So he waited just as he saw all the rangers come out of that helicopter. He then ran in full speed with his duffel bag in a different direction from his Suzuki, making it 350 yards away from his Suzuki. As he stood there three seconds later, he heard the voice of one of the rangers say, "There he is, out on the east side of the compound, in all black. He's mixed up in the tear gas smoke!"

Another ranger saw him and said, "Got 'em!" and another ranger said, "I see 'em!" The captain said, "Kill 'em!" and they all started shooting at him. Sergeant Body Snatcher knew he couldn't fire back at these soldiers. He was running in full speed. He then got hit in his left shoulder, and he was still running in full speed. Sergeant Body Snatcher hid behind a shack as he heard one of the rangers say, "He went behind the shack!" They then started shooting the shack. Sergeant Body Snatcher jumped up after taking a minute and a half of rest and started back running in full speed, just as he heard the airplane coming a second after he made it to the woods. He was still running in full speed when he heard a ranger say, "He's in the woods! He's running like a pack of antelope! You won't believe this shit. Captain Manske, this motherfucker is running through trees!"

Captain Manske said, "What the hell are you talking about, Ranger? Just shoot the son of a bitch and end it!"

The ranger said, "I would if I could, sir, but this son of a bitch is running so goddamn fast my scope can't keep up with him, and when I think these trees are going to make him slow down so that I can get a shot, the trees allow this motherfucker to run through them, or this fucking boy is a damn ghost! I can't get a beam on this man!"

Sergeant Body Snatcher saw his Suzuki and the airplane was firing shots at him, and so he detoured in a different direction as the bullets from the airplane ripped his Suzuki apart. He just looked at it, knowing that he was about seven to eight hundred yards from his original place. He just stood there, resting for a minutes, because he knew that the airplane shooters didn't know about his Suzuki, which they had torn up. He just knelt down, looking all around the woods, hearing the rangers getting into their positions behind him. He stood up after resting for five or six minutes, then he heard a ranger say, "Chopper 1 has found his chopper."

Captain Manske said, "Don't leave it, because he is trying to get to it, so set your men up there and wait for him. And that's an order!"

The ranger said, "Roger that, sir."

Sergeant Body Snatcher put his high-powered binoculars on and looked around and zoomed in. He saw a nice spot to hide at up on a small mountain that looked like a cave behind the bushes lounging over it. So he took off, running in full speed, when he heard a ranger say, "I see him but can't get a shot due to the fucking trees getting in my way. He's running ahead of us about three hundred yards, and this boy is turning into a blaze. And he's gone now, sir!"

Captain Manske said, "Stand down and stand back. Air strike, go up and hit everything in the three within a six-hundred-yard radius, and I do mean light that fucking place up. Knock every god-damn thing down!"

Sergeant Body Snatcher heard the air strike coming. As he threw his duffel bag down and took off running in full speed, the air strike dropped napalm bomb on his wannabe-invisible ass.

The air strike said, "Roger that, sir," as they flew and dropped the napalm bomb. As it hit the ground, hellfire spread out all over the area, and the rangers on the ground could feel the heat from it four hundred yards away. The air strike said, "Captain Manske, sir, the bomb has cleared your path, sir, but I do warn you not to go in it yet because the heat still can cook you, sir. There's nothing standing, not even a tree, sir. What- or whoever you are looking for or are after is no more, sir. Out!"

Captain Manske said, "Roger that, air strike."

Captain Manske said to the rangers, "Go out and find the bodies of the special ops team, and let's take them back home to their family. That murdering bastard got sent to hell with open arms."

Sergeant Phillips replied, "Captain Manske, we have all sixteen special ops team members right here in front of us, alive and well, sir. The only things hurting on them are their pride, their asses, and their heads from the tranquilizer that he used on them. Sir, he knew that we were trying to kill him, so he took us away from them because they would've died in the crossfire, sir. Whoever this guy is that we have been sent to kill has to be some special forces way more advanced than we can ever imagine in our lives. We should've tried to connect with him, sir."

Captain Manske said, "You mean to tell me that every last one of them is alive? Then tell me why they didn't answer me when I called them for their position?"

Sergeant Phillips said, "Their head mics were off right next to them, still fully dressed with their firearms, but tied up and gagged. They were still out a little, until we put the smelling salt to them. Now, ask them to report."

Captain Manske said, "I'll be there in five minutes. Start searching for him and see if we can find any proof that we got him."

Sergeant Phillips said, "Roger that, sir." Sergeant Phillips then ordered, "All right, spread out and look for any signs of our target."

The special ops team and the rangers got all their stuff together as they walked ten feet apart from one another, looking for any type of sign of Sergeant Body Snatcher. They had walked for well over two and half to three hours when one of the rangers said, "Ranger 3 to Sergeant Phillips, I have something, sir, on your left, about sixty yards from you."

Captain Manske and several other special ops and rangers ran over there and saw Sergeant Body Snatcher's Suzuki trail bike under a lot of dirt as they dug it out and looked at it. One of the rangers said, "What the fuck is this, Captain Manske? Who are we after? This guy had been one of us, don't you think?"

Captain Manske said, "I don't know, Ranger, I don't know. I am following orders just like you. I really can't say no when an order is given, and you are under my order, so don't question orders, Ranger, as I'll report you. Are we clear, Ranger?"

The ranger just nodded and stood there in silence.

As they were still walking, a special ops team member saw a dog tag on the ground, but this dog tag was nothing like he had ever seen. He bent down and picked it up and cleaned it off with water from his canteen and wiped it off. He saw the words that read, "Sergeant Body Snatcher," on one side and the number that he couldn't make out, but it had "US Marines" on it. The special ops member said, "Hey, Captain, you really need to see this, sir."

Captain Manske said, "See what?"

As he jogged over there to him, the rest of the search party went with him to the captain. Captain Manske asked, "See what, soldier? What's so important?"

The special ops member said, "This, sir. This is a US Marine dog tag, sir. You should read what's on the other side, sir."

Captain Manske said, "That dog tag can be from any soldier that belongs to this country, as they do hide out in it for training."

The special ops member said, "Not this one, sir. Will you please look at it, sir?"

Captain Manske took the dog tag and turned it to the other side, and it read, "Sergeant Body Snatcher." Captain Manske then said, "Fuck! Fuck! Fuck! Fuck!"

Sergeant Phillips asked, "What? What's wrong, Captain? Captain Manske, what's wrong?"

Captain Manske held his head up and looked all around at the destruction, knowing that no one could ever survive the fire from the napalm blast. Captain Manske said, "He was one of us, Sergeant. He was one of us. We set him up to be murdered by our hands. This soldiers was the last one from his team that was called the No-Name Unit. This was his name, Sergeant. His name was Sergeant Body Snatcher. He kept a lot of you, them, and me from walking into the hands of the enemies and dying in the process. We just killed the last of the most hard-core soldiers that ever lived."

They all stood up in a circle, saying a prayer for him.

Little did they know, Sergeant Body Snatcher was standing up in the cave that he saw about ten minutes before that plane came with that napalm bomb and dropped it. He felt the heat from it as he just barely got away from it. He was standing in the door of the cave that was covered by a whole lot of bushes, like a waterfall coming off a cliff. His binoculars were zoomed in on all of them, and he saw their faces were sad. That was when Sergeant Body Snatcher said up in a salute, "I'm sorry to let you think that I am dead, but it has to be done. I can't let you take me back. Now, go home, soldiers, and be with your family."

Two special ops and two rangers picked up his burnt-up Suzuki and carried it with them as Sergeant Body Snatcher said, "Good job, soldiers. Damn good goddamn job."

He sat down and took his shirt off and saw this bullet hole in his shoulder, and he knew that he had to live with it in his shoulder for the rest of his life. As he sat there and heard the helicopter and airplane leaving, he looked in his high-powered binoculars and saw that it was them leaving. Sergeant Body Snatcher looked at his watch and saw that it was gone. He didn't have any way of telling what time it was, so he just lay back on the cold ground in his cave and went to sleep.

As Captain Manske, the special ops team, and the rangers made it back to the United States and landed the plane and helicopter on the landing strip, the generals, colonels, and majors came out to meet them. Three-star general Stensil approached Captain Manske and asked, "What news do you have for me, Captain?"

Captain Manske looked into General Stensil's eyes and said, "Sir, we killed one of our own boys, sir."

General Stensil said, "You didn't kill him. The terrorists that you were after were the ones that killed him. So don't let it worry you, son, because whenever we search that son of a bitch, you believe we're going to bury his ass, Captain."

Captain Manske took the dog tag out of his pocket and said, "Read the engravement on it, sir."

As General Stensil was receiving the dog tag from Captain Manske, the five-star general Stensil walked up as they all saluted him. General Foster said, "At ease. What is going on?"

General Stensil said, "We lost a man for trying to catch that criminal that disobeyed orders and took it upon himself to act as if he were the authority."

Captain Manske said, "General Stensil, please read the engravement on the dog tag."

General Stensil flipped the dog tag over and saw Sergeant Body Snatcher's name on it as he looked all around at the special ops team and the rangers with sadness on their face. One from the special ops team said, "Permission to speak, sir."

General Stensil replied, "Permission granted, soldier."

The special ops member said, "Sir, that soldier could've killed us all, but he just disarmed every last one of us. He had to be somebody from a team way in advance than us, sir. I mean he knew moves that this whole would die to learn and will die doing it. He took danger from was when he knew that we tried to gun him down. Sir that soldier knew how to disappear like he was a ghost. I saw why they called him the Invisible Soldier. I knew for a fact that I had him in my site and that man out ran my site and look like the trees was protecting him from us. I swear, this man ran through trees, sir, and if he didn't run through the trees, then the trees moved for him and blocked us from killing him. I believe that Sergeant Body Snatcher was never a harm to us but to the ones that was trying to harm us and our country."

General Stensil said, "Then how do you know that he is dead, then, soldier if you didn't shoot him?"

The special ops said, "Because we dropped a napalm bomb on him, two of them, sir. What you have in your hand is his Suzuki trail bike, the only thing that barely survived that blast, sir."

Five-star general Foster said, "Give me that dog tag, Stensil. You kill your heart of any war that you may be asked to partake in and we will lose a lot of men because of this, Stensil. You had your orders, but your orders are alive and, if he put up a fight, then dead. Your order was just to kill, and you didn't know on what or whose side he is on. But it is self-explanatory that he is on our side. You better be honored that his teammates are already dead, because they would've brought you up on charges to the president. Now, salute your superior officer."

General Stensil saluted the five-star general. As General Foster started walking off, he made it to the door of the building and opened the door. He said out loud, with his voice echoing, "At ease! At ease! At ease! At ease! At ease! At ease!"

The special ops team and the rangers were saluting. General Stensil said, "At ease, soldiers. You're excused."

They all left, going to their two helicopters to leave the base. Captain Manske said, "Sir, it was just a mistake, sir. What happened happened, and we can't change that, sir. We just have to live and learn, that's all, sir."

General Stensil looked up and said, "We still have to find General Blackstone, Captain. He's been missing now for at least six or seven years, or maybe he's just hiding out under the AWOL. I don't really actually know, Captain. I was just trying to find him. You're excused too, Captain."

Captain Manske saluted him and walked off, going to his building, feeling bad for what he had done to Sergeant Body Snatcher.

The next day, as Sergeant Body Snatcher woke up in pain from his gunshot wound to his shoulder, he sat up and said without his voice detector, "Shit, I need a cup of coffee."

He stood up still with his night vision EyeClops on to see if he could see if any wild animals had sneaked in while he was sleeping. As he looked around, he saw a person just standing there, dressed just like him, with his arms crossed, standing six foot seven and weighing about 262 pounds. Sergeant Body Snatcher asked, "Who are you?"

The six-foot-seven and 262-pound man said, "I am you and you are me. I'm here to take you home, Sergeant Body Snatcher."

Sergeant Body Snatcher said, "Who are you? Are you here to kill me too, whoever you are? Who are you, if you are me and I am you?"

He said, "I am Sergeant Destroyer. I am here to bring you home. My order is from Captain Apocalypse, Sergeant Body Snatcher. He told me that you did very good, soldier, and he is proud of you and your work. He also told me to tell you that he has something very important to show you and only you can make the call. So are you ready to come home?"

Sergeant Body Snatcher said, "How can I trust that you are really Sergeant Destroyer? My trust in people is long gone, Sergeant Destroyer—that is, if you are really Sergeant Destroyer."

Sergeant Destroyer said, "All right, Sergeant Body Snatcher, I'm going to break the rules, and so are you, and we both will keep this secret and carry it to our graves. Take your face equipment off and identify yourself."

They both took their ski masks and stocking cap off, and Sergeant Body Snatcher said, "You're—"

Pffff.

Sergeant Destroyer shot him with a dart gun with some dimethyltryptamine (DMI), the stuff that was shot for devil's breath. It would fake death for twenty-four hours. Sergeant Destroyer walked over there and pulled Sergeant Body Snatcher's stocking cap and ski mask back over his face and pulled his back down. He then picked him up and carried him for 375 yards to the Sea Stallion. Sergeant Destroyer said to Sergeant Rattler and Sergeant Flood, "Sergeant Body Snatcher got a bullet in his right shoulder. Take it out before he bleeds to death. He's not gonna feel a thing because the devil's breath has seen to that for you."

As they made it to the C-5 Galaxy and rolled the Sea Stallion inside, they headed off to the United States. They flew for well over seventeen hours, making it back to their old airstrip behind their unit. Sergeant Destroyer looked at his watch and said, "Let's get Sergeant Body Snatcher inside and comfortable, so the MTs can complete his surgery."

They rolled the gurney onto the elevator shaft and went up to the top and put him on the little four-wheeler as Sergeant Rattler and Sergeant Flood got on a four-wheeler, going to the tunnel door. They took the gurney up the short stairs and rolled him to medical service, where Captain Apocalypse and the three MTs were at. Sergeant Destroyer saw Captain Apocalypse sitting in his seat with his head down. He said, "Captain Apocalypse, Sergeant Body Snatcher is home, sir."

Captain Apocalypse just sat there and didn't move. Sergeant Destroyer raised up Captain Apocalypse's head and said, "Captain Apocalypse, Sergeant Body Snatcher is back home, sir."

Captain Apocalypse's words were slurred from his mouth when he said, "G-g-g-good job, soldier. My time is upon me. Help me up so I can see him for myself."

Sergeant Destroyer helped Captain Apocalypse up and stood him over Sergeant Body Snatcher. Captain Apocalypse said, "About-face, soldier."

Sergeant Destroyer turned his back, and Captain Apocalypse said, "Sergeant Body Snatcher, welcome home. Now all my team is back home. I'll fight it until I show you the truth, soldier, so please hurry up and wake up. I...I...I t-t-tri—"

He hit the floor very hard.

The MTs came running over there and said, "Put him on the gurney next to Sergeant Body Snatcher."

Sergeant Destroyer picked up Captain Apocalypse and laid him down on the gurney and said to the MTs, "What's wrong with him, MTs?"

The main MT said, "Captain Apocalypse is eighty-four years old. His last mission was to infiltrate in the White House to find Sergeant Body Snatcher after you had brought General Blackstone here and deserted this unit. He fought to find out who set up the team when they got ambushed, and he did. And he also found the last mole of their corruption. He wouldn't tell us until you made it back to the US with Sergeant Body Snatcher."

Sergeant Destroyer just stood over him and said, "Sergeant Ibdam, Captain Ibdam, my captain, Captain Apocalypse, raise your left eyebrow if you can hear me."

Sergeant Destroyer took his ski mask and stocking cap off as he took Captain Apocalypse's ski mask and stocking cap off. Captain Apocalypse raised his left eyebrow, as did Sergeant Destroyer, better known as Sergeant No Pity. Captain Apocalypse just smiled and said, "I know. I know. Remember, no pity, soldier." He then closed his eyes and went to sleep, breathing very heavily.

The seventh hour came as Sergeant Body Snatcher woke up and saw Sergeant Destroyer, Sergeant Rattler, Sergeant Flood, and the three MTs standing around him and another soldier lying on the gurney. He asked, "Where am I? Where am I?"

Sergeant Flood said, "You're back at home. The No-Name Unit."

Sergeant Destroyer said in a whispered voice, "Sir, Captain Apocalypse, sir, Sergeant Body Snatcher has awakened, sir."

Captain Apocalypse said, "H-h-h-help me up to my feet."

As the three MTs and Sergeant Destroyer helped Captain Apocalypse to his feet, Captain Apocalypse said to Sergeant Body Snatcher, "Soldier, get up and follow me."

Sergeant Body Snatcher got off his gurney with the help of Sergeant Rattler, and they went into their debriefing room, where General Bradford Blackstone was sitting in come-along handcuffs around his wrist and ankles. Captain Apocalypse said, "Here is your traitor, Sergeant Body Snatcher, and he had one more accomplice that worked with him. There are the papers and tape of everything that he did against this country and what he did for you, so you call the judgment of whatever you desire."

Sergeant Body Snatcher said, "NO-A-RET, EGAP-NO-PSE ROF-NOIT-UEE-XE."

Captain Apocalypse said, "By whom shall it be carried out?"

Sergeant Body Snatcher said, "By the United States of America."

Captain Apocalypse said out loud, his voice echoing through the whole place, "No-Name Unit, done! Done! Done! Done! Done! Done! Done! Done! Done! Done!"

Captain Apocalypse collapsed forward toward the table and onto it, then said, "Five-star general Foster, did you hear that, sir? Now you can bury me with the rest of the team."

Captain Apocalypse died at the age of eighty-four. They put Captain Apocalypse in the Sea Stallion helicopter, leaving General Blackstone in the unit with all the information about him and his accomplice.

They flew up in the air and let the helicopter hover around their unit until everybody on the base saw them. All the generals, colonels, majors, captains, lieutenants, sergeants, and soldiers, as well as other staff, came out and looked. As they flew off, all the ranking officials, led by five-star general Foster, went into the No-Name Unit fence and then into the unit. They saw how nice it was in here, just as they had heard in stories that this place was empty without anything. But it was not true, because everything was in its rightful place.

General Blackstone said out loud, "I'm back here! I'm back here!"

As they all ran back in the No-Name Unit briefing room, they saw General Blackstone, well-dressed, well-fed, and well-groomed, sitting in the chair, with a confession tape going and papers showing that he and three-star general Warren Stensil betrayed the No-Name Unit. General Blackstone said, "It's a lie. It's a lie! I did not betray any soldier. Captain Apocalypse forced me to say this. He would not feed me or give me water, so I told him what he wanted to hear, so he could let me go. It's a lie! Stop looking at me like that. Stop it! Stop it! I'm a goddamn general, goddammit!"

Five-star general Foster said, "MPs, place three-star general Warren Stensil under arrest and General Bradford Blackstone under arrest for treason and espionage right now. And that's an order."

The MPs said, "Yes, sir. Three-star general Warren Stensil and General Bradford Blackstone, you both are under arrest under the authority of the United States of America for treason and espionage. You have the right to remain silent. What you say will be held against you in the court of law. You have the right to have your own attorney, and if you can't afford one, one will be appointed for you. Do you understand your rights that I have read to you?"

They both just nodded, and the MPs put some come-along handcuffs on each of them and walked them out.

General Foster was still looking around this unit, seeing the setup that these soldiers had. General Foster knew that Captain Apocalypse was a very intelligent man, but he did not know just how intelligent he was. Just looking at his debriefing room told General Foster that the No-Name Unit was more advanced than any other special forces team he had ever encountered.

General Foster said, "Captain Apocalypse could've been a god-damn general or worked in the intelligence agency if he wanted to, because this place was set up to find anything and everything under-neath the earth and on top of the earth! Captain Apocalypse and the No-Name Unit, I salute you all, sir, and I'll never allow you all to go down in vain."

As he just stood there, still saluting, he heard an echoing voice say, "At ease! At ease! At ease! At ease! At ease! At ease..." It was fading away in the distance to his ears. He turned around and saw one of the MPs standing there.

The MP saluted him and said, "You ready, General, sir?"

General Foster said, "Did you hear that, Sergeant?"

The MP said, "Hear what, General?"

General Foster said, "That voice saying *at ease*."

The MP said, "No, sir, General, I didn't hear, sir. You know, I was told years ago that this place is haunted by the soldiers who ran this unit."

General Foster said, "Well, we know there's no such thing as a ghost, don't we, Sergeant?"

The MP said, "Yes, sir, General Foster."

General Foster took his salute down as they were walking out of the debriefing room, when the other MP said on the radio, "Sergeant Quinn, come in. This is Corporal Spencer. We have an ugly situation around the back of the unit."

MP Sergeant Quinn said, "What is the situation, Corporal Spencer?"

Corporal Spencer said, "The helicopter that we saw leaving about twelve minutes ago before we went into this unit...well, the helicopter is back, empty and cold to the touch, with dust and spi-derwebs all in it, sir."

MP Sergeant Quinn said, "Then there must been two helicop-ters around back and they took their pick."

Corporal Spencer said, "Sir, it was only one chopper and one plane back here, sir, and I know that as I was told by General Stensil to keep an eye on this whole entire compound, sir."

General Foster and the MP Sergeant Quinn just looked at each other in silence.

Now, Sergeant Destroyer, Sergeant Flood, Sergeant Rattler, Sergeant Body Snatcher, and the three MTs had Captain Apocalypse embalmed and redressed and gave him an honorable burial at his grave site at the Arlington National Cemetery. They all saluted their teammates, and Sergeant Destroyer, Sergeant Rattler, Sergeant Flood, Sergeant Body Snatcher, and the MTs all saluted with sadness when Sergeant Destroyer said out loud, his voice echoing all through the cemetery, "No pity! No pity! No pity! No pity! No pity! No pity! No pity! No pity! No pity! No pity! No pity! No pity! No pity!"

CONCLUSION

Now, do you see why I call this soldier, or soldiers, the Invisible Soldier? I know that I was under that hellfire of bullets from all those shooters and wasn't shot, not even grazed. How they missed him is way beyond or above me. Some of those soldiers died, but not all of them. Nobody knows where the remaining ones are in this world this very day. People are reporting how some of their own countries' terrorists have been caught without dying beside the ones that protected them. But their leaders and their leaders' head guys were captured and placed into a prison for the rest of their lives. The information that I have come up with is what I have told you, and as a general, I stake my reputation on it, because I know that it is very much true. One of these days, you'll be in a situation where you feel maybe your death sentence and your faith of hope have left your power of thinking, and when you least expect it, you're alive and well back at your family, like me. The best part of your rescue will be that you will never know who saved you from the hand of death. It's scary to know, but it's scarier to be in a death position, to know that you are about to die.

I am a general that started off as a regular soldier at the age of seventeen, and I have been in many rainy nights, cold nights, stormy nights, wintery nights, and hot nights, where you wonder, When will this shit end? But my answer never came to me on any of those nights; hell, not even in those days, because the days were way worse than the nights, when the enemies could see you a lot better.

And you have probably met Captain Apocalypse, Sergeant Destroyer, Sergeant Rattler, Sergeant Flood, Sergeant Lowlife,

Sergeant Big Badass Wolf, Sergeant Chaos, Sergeant Boogeyman, Sergeant Hocus-Pocus, Sergeant Fatal, Sergeant Illusionist, Sergeant Tornado, Sergeant Maniac, Sergeant Animosity, Sergeant Hectic, Sergeant Furious, Sergeant Nuclear, Sergeant Polarize, Sergeant Eliminate, Sergeant Evil, Sergeant Redrum, Sergeant Shadow, Sergeant Consequence, Sergeant Viper, Sergeant Undertaker, Sergeant Wrath, Sergeant Venomous, Sergeant Body Snatcher, Sergeant Grim Reaper, and Sergeant Night Terror—those were the names of the soldiers that came from a unit that was called the No-Name Unit. If you are still standing, sitting, talking, or eating with one of them, then please do consider it as an honor, because if only things happen while you're there with them, then he will be gone like Superman or the Invisible Man. Hell, they might be reading up on what I have written in this story to you, as I know that they should be honored for protecting you, me, and this country from all the bad people that are trying to erase us as if we were lead from a pencil.

I smile for them, because their smiling days were over when they joined Captain Apocalypse's team. Their faces were only shown to one another when a special occasion called for it to happen, but they had to take their looks to their graves. Captain Apocalypse gave his protégé permission to see his left eyebrow get raised, as that was their only code between them. Sergeant Destroyer, who was still Sergeant No Pity, was personally trained by Captain Apocalypse, and that was why Captain Apocalypse always called on him to get his men and brothers as well as himself out of death's way. Sergeant No Pity, Sergeant No Pity! Well, Sergeant No Pity! He had to have a protégé under him, or maybe it was he who saved me through that hellfire of bullets. Shit, I don't know who it was, but I am alive and telling you about this story because of him. You can believe me or disbelieve me; either way, it did happen, and I know it happened because, as I said, I am alive, telling it to you.

So as I sit here at my desk and with the data and research that I have found, I, General Benson "Shotgun" Thorpe III, am saluting all the soldiers who fought for this country, who are fighting to this day for this country, who are protecting this country, who are dying for this country, who was injured to protect this country, who long ago have died for this country, and now who have died for this country, my true salute is to you all who have done, who are doing, and who will do something for this country.

The End

I, General Benson "Shotgun" Thorpe III,
give thanks
to all the soldiers,
for all their bravery,
all their honor,
and all their lives.
And to all their families.

ABOUT THE AUTHOR

Bernard Wells is a very dedicated person who believes in the truth of life as well as the person who lives it. He writes because of the enjoyment it brings to himself, and maybe to others, too.

CPSIA information can be obtained
at www.ICGtesting.com
Printed in the USA
LVHW030444301121
704812LV00001B/60